RANDOM
HOUSE

LARGE
PRINT

ALSO BY ALEX BERENSON

The Wolves
Twelve Days
The Counterfeit Agent
The Night Ranger
The Shadow Patrol
The Secret Soldier
The Midnight House
The Silent Man
The Ghost War
The Faithful Spy
The Number (nonfiction)

THE
PRISONER

A JOHN WELLS NOVEL

ALEX BERENSON

RANDOM HOUSE
LARGE PRINT

Copyright © 2017 by Alex Berenson

Penguin supports copyright. Copyright fuels creativity, encourages diverse voices, promotes free speech, and creates a vibrant culture. Thank you for buying an authorized edition of this book and for complying with copyright laws by not reproducing, scanning, or distributing any part of it in any form without permission. You are supporting writers and allowing Penguin to continue to publish books for every reader.

All rights reserved.
Published in the United States of America by Random House Large Print in association with G. P. Putnam's Sons, an imprint of Penguin Random House LLC, New York.

COVER DESIGN BY ERIC FUENTECILLA
COVER ART © SHOKULTD / SUTTERSTOCK

The Library of Congress has established a Cataloging-in-Publication record for this title.

ISBN: 978-1-5247-5624-6

www.randomhouse.com/largeprint

FIRST LARGE PRINT EDITION

Printed in the United States of America

10 9 8 7 6 5 4 3 2 1

This Large Print edition published in accord with the standards of the N.A.V.H.

For PEN America, and all the writers
around the world jailed for their words

Everyone had done well out of the war except for those who had fought in it.

—Kate Atkinson, A God in Ruins

PROLOGUE

HARRAN, TURKEY

THE HORSES KNEW.

They shied and stumbled as the Syrian smuggler named Mahmoud led them out of the battered trailer. Four brown geldings, wide-eyed and frightened. Resigned to trouble ahead. Kareem Batta wasn't sure how, but they knew.

The tallest of the four, a handsome youngster with a white blaze on the left side of his head, was more skittish than the others. As his hooves touched the crumbly Anatolian soil, he swished his tail, pushed up the ramp. But Mahmoud jerked his reins and muttered at him. After a moment, he quit the protest.

The beasts feared the men around them even more than the trip they were about to take. They were gentle animals. Batta didn't like using them this way. But he had no choice.

They were the best way over the border into Syria, the only realistic way to avoid the Islamic State's jihadis. Those modern-day trolls watched the roads from every angle, with checkpoints and rolling patrols and even drones. They needed no excuse but their black flags to snatch unlucky travelers.

Batta circled the geldings, examining them like a trainer at a yearling auction. He was hardly an expert. He'd grown up in a two-bedroom apartment in Detroit. But he'd ridden enough in the last five years to spot trouble. These four looked strong. They breathed easily despite the early afternoon heat. Their backs were straight, their eyes bright. Not like other nags smugglers had foisted on him. Batta had learned to check the hard way, after a mount dropped under him on a rocky trail in the Anti-Lebanon Range, two hundred miles and a dozen front lines southwest. He had left the four-legged corpse behind and staggered out of Syria on a broken foot.

"Think I bring losers?" Mahmoud said in English. "When my brother and I go, too?" He was a skinny twenty-something who wore black jeans and motorcycle boots. His brother, Ajmad, was even skinnier, and even younger, with a wispy mustache and smooth cheeks. They had taken Batta to Syria twice before, first to meet a Kurdish commander, an easy run, then a riskier mission to scout a warehouse where hostages were supposedly being held. The warehouse had turned out to be an ammunition depot, but the brothers brought Batta back to Turkey with his head attached. A win. A tie, anyway.

Batta still didn't entirely trust Mahmoud. But Batta didn't entirely trust anyone over here except his brothers-in-arms from the Central Intelligence Agency's Special Operations Group, or SOG. Even the Turkish intelligence service played both sides. The **Islamic State of Iraq and Syria**, the **Free Syrian Army**, the **Martyrs of Syria Brigades**, the **Soldiers of Islam**, the **People's Protection Unit**, and a hundred others . . . In Syria and Kurdistan, outsiders couldn't tell the players **with** a program. Sometimes even the combatants were confused. Batta had seen a firefight sputter out after the commanders realized that their bosses had agreed to a cease-fire the week before. A cosmic joke, even if the guy who'd been shot in the head wasn't laughing.

Mahmoud pulled out a bag of sugar cubes, gave two to each gelding. "A little scared, but they'll be fine once we move."

"They're not bad," Batta said in Arabic. Though he'd been born in Michigan, he was fluent, thanks to his parents, immigrants from Jordan. "I've seen worse, anyway." He ran his hand over the tall gelding's flank. **Sorry, buddy. If it makes you feel any better, I'm nervous, too.** "What's his name?"

"Baraq. Why, you want to buy him?"

"Only if he can grow wings." In the Quran, Baraq was the name of the steed who had flown Muhammad to Heaven.

"Money-back guarantee."

On that note . . . Batta handed Mahmoud a backpack, cheap blue nylon with a faded Mickey Mouse logo.

"M-I-C-K-E-Y . . ." Mahmoud unzipped it, thumbed the stacks inside. "This is one hundred," he said in English. "We said three-fifty." Three hundred fifty thousand dollars. A fair price for two days' work, considering the risk of beheading by the friendly folks south of the border.

The man they were bringing out was worth more than that to Batta's bosses at Langley. Batta knew him as **Abu Ibrahim**, an Islamic State bureaucrat who had helped the CIA track the group's oil-smuggling routes. He now promised information about its secret bank accounts in the United Arab Emirates, if the agency could just get him out alive.

"Three hundred fifty," Mahmoud repeated, with the slight sulk that came so naturally in Arabic. "**Wahid, ithnan, thalatha . . .**" One, two, three . . .

"When I come back." They both knew the terms, and they both knew Batta wouldn't stiff Mahmoud. The agency would never have another safe trip over the border.

"If you don't?"

Exactly. "I thought you planned to bring me home."

"**Insh'allah.** But things happen."

"In that case, send an after-action report, explaining the lessons learned, with a self-addressed, stamped envelope and request payment within sixty days."

Batta saw that Mahmoud didn't get the joke, but the smuggler smiled anyway. "All right, Kareem. I trust you." He called to Ajmad, and together the brothers trotted to the Mitsubishi pickup pulling the trailer. A burly man in his fifties stepped from the truck and hugged them both.

"If they don't come back, I'll kill you," the man yelled to Batta.

If they don't come back, you won't have to worry. I'll be dead already. Batta just waved.

Mahmoud tossed the knapsack into the truck.

The man stepped in, gunned the engine, pulled out with the trailer rattling behind him. Then the brothers were alone with Batta and his partner, Bill Girol.

Girol had joined the agency after nine years in the Marine infantry, mostly in Recon. He and Batta made a strange pair. Batta was huge, six-seven and two-forty, with fence-post arms, curly hair, and a beard that had faded from brown to reddish blond in the Turkish sun. Girol had prematurely gray hair and calm brown eyes. He was five-six and easy to underestimate. He weighed one-fifty, benched three-fifty, and seemed to need no sleep at all. After four years around Syria, he spoke decent Arabic, too. But he would never pass for a local, and he preferred to let Batta do the talking. Even back at the CIA base in Gaziantep, Girol kept quiet. Batta had once made the mistake of asking him about his Navy Cross, which ranked second only to the Medal of Honor as an award for military valor.

For bravery in the course of my divorce, Girol said. **Any more questions, genius?** From then on, he always called Batta **genius.** Batta called him **Mighty,** as in **Mouse.** Batta figured they'd each take a bullet for the other. He hoped not to find out.

"Ready?" Mahmoud said.

"Let's go over it once more." A final run-through never hurt.

Mahmoud pulled a battered map from his jeans, unfolded it against Baraq's flank like a cowboy, then changed his mind and laid it on the ground as Girol and Batta squatted on either side. "Okay, we're here, yes. Harran." He pointed to a spot north of the border.

Harran was ancient enough to have earned a mention in Genesis for playing home to Abraham in his pre-Isaac days. As far as Batta could tell, the village hadn't changed much since. It lay about twenty kilometers north of Akçakale, a dusty Turkish town so close to the border that the crossing split it in half, like El Paso and Ciudad Juárez. The Syrian side was called Tal Abad. Kurdish militias had recently retaken it from the Islamic State.

This region was something of an afterthought in the Syrian conflict. The serious fighting took place to the west, as the Islamic State battled Bashar al-Assad's army and other militias for control of big cities like Homs. But despite its relative unimportance, Tal Abad was the border crossing closest to Raqqa, the capital of the Islamic State. Abu Ibrahim lived there.

The Islamic State could almost certainly have

retaken Tal Abad from the Kurds by shifting a couple of thousand jihadis from the front lines. But its commanders had chosen not to try. They were almost inviting an attack on Raqqa. They seemed to believe the city's defenses were impenetrable. Or maybe they didn't want to move fighters from the battles to the west. Whatever their logic, Batta wasn't arguing. By backing off the border, the Islamic State had made this mission possible.

Mahmoud moved his finger to the border, left of the Akçakale–Tal Abad crossing.

"Nine kilometers west of Tal Abad, a new cut in the wire." To defend itself against the Islamic State, Turkey had moved thousands of soldiers into Anatolia. But the border stretched almost a thousand kilometers. Monitoring it all was impossible. In the eastern half of the country, strings of razor wire were all that separated the two countries. "Big enough to ride through. Some Kurds put it there. Maybe three weeks ago. Daesh, they don't know."

Arabic-speaking enemies of the Islamic State called it Daesh. The nickname denied the group's Muslim legitimacy by stripping the word **Islamic** from it. Jihadis hated the name and had been known to cut the tongue out of anyone they caught saying it.

"You sure they don't know?"

"The Kurds control down to Ain Issa now. Daesh sticks to the crossing." In other words, Islamic State spies still watched the vehicles that passed through Tal Abad, probably putting every license plate into a database. But by giving up the border, they had lost their chance to patrol the fence. "We cross after dark, ride to Ain Issa, seventy-five kilometers from here." Ain Issa was a speck of a town northwest of Raqqa. The Kurds had taken it from the Islamic State a few weeks after winning Tal Abad. It was friendly territory. "Rest tomorrow, a warehouse my friend owns, make sure the horses are fine, nobody bothers us."

"Then tomorrow night—"

Mahmoud stroked a finger across the map, following the east–west road, the M4. "Everything down here is Daesh, Daesh, Daesh." He spoke the forbidden name with the relish of a child cursing. "All around Raqqa, checkpoints. What we do, tomorrow, after sunset, we ride south. Different dirt paths we can take, quiet, only farmers, they won't bother us. They don't like Daesh either, they want everyone to leave them alone. We get close to the river"—the Euphrates. "Good cover there, palm groves and canals. Close to fifty kilometers."

He hooked his finger to the right, along the river. "Now, I told you two weeks ago, Daesh knows this way. Of course. It's Raqqa, they know every way in. But a friend of mine went through last week with cigarettes, he didn't see anyone. Most of the time they don't guard it. No cars come, only horses, so it doesn't bother them much. Anyway, they like cigarettes, too. We have twenty cartons in case we run across them." As a cover story and also for bribes.

"And if they won't take the cigarettes?"

"They're men, they take bribes."

Batta shook his head. They both knew plenty of Islamic State jihadis were true believers and couldn't be bribed.

"Let me handle it," Mahmoud said. "I know these men. If I see a problem, real problem, I say, Everyone likes Marlboro. In English, so this one"—Mahmoud nodded at Girol—"understands. That means we get out, no matter what."

"Everyone likes Marlboro."

"**Nam.** But, **Insh'allah,** they watch somewhere else tomorrow night."

Insh'allah, Insh'allah, Insh'allah—God willing. Like God paid any attention to this ugly little war. Like its endless barbarity and cruelty wouldn't have made Him sick in the unlikely event He noticed it. **Insh'allah.** Batta heard the phrase a hundred times a week, a tic of language he couldn't escape. He hated it more each time. Truly, he had grown to hate everything about this place. He stayed because he hated the Islamic State most of all. The week before, an aid worker had told him about three girls who'd clawed out their own eyes after months of being passed among the jihadis. Girls, not women. Thirteen, twelve, and eleven. They had all decided to blind themselves rather than endure more rapes. **I thought, They'll kill me now,** the oldest girl had told the aid worker. **They'll have to. Even they won't want a girl with holes in her face.** Instead, the jihadis had dumped her at a border crossing, literally thrown her off the back of a pickup truck. **It's better now, though. This way, I can't look at myself.**

"Remember, the cigarettes are last," Mahmoud said. "If they stop us, first they want to see our cards"—identity cards. Batta's claimed he was from Lebanon, and Girol's from Bosnia, a way to explain his less-than-perfect Arabic. "They ask us to pray, we pray." Mahmoud looked at Girol. "You can pray?"

"**Nam**"—Yes.

"Show me. The **Fatiha**"—the Quran's first surah, or verse—"and another."

Girol turned south to face Mecca. "**Bismillah al-Rahman al-Rahim al-hamdu lillahi rabbil'alamin—**"

"Enough," Mahmoud said. "They don't really care, once they hear a few words, they just want to make sure you're Sunni." The two sects prayed in slightly different ways. The most obvious difference was that the Shia kept their hands by their sides while the Sunni held them together at the waist.

"Good," Girol said. "I only know one more verse."

"A prayer to be named later," Batta said. He wished Girol had practiced more. But even if Girol memorized the Quran cover to cover, their cover identities would withstand only brief questioning. They would depend on Mahmoud's quick tongue, a well-timed bribe, and the laziness of whoever spotted them. Not great odds. If they were detained for a longer interrogation, they would have no chance at all.

Batta already knew he would die before letting that happen.

IN GAZIANTEP a month before, Batta's SOG commander—an ex–Delta op named Oden Durette—had sounded almost embarrassed to be pitching this op. No one had ever tried an exfil from Raqqa.

"I'm asking you and Bill because you're the best. You say no, that's it."

"Dude can't get to the border on his own? He needs a taxi?"

"Guys like him have to have permission to leave the city and he's afraid to ask. I don't know for sure, but my impression, he was working for the Syrian oil company when our friends came to town. He's Sunni and good at the job, so they left him to do it, but they don't really trust him. And he doesn't have the stones to break for it without us holding his hand."

"He's worth the trouble?"

Batta meant, do we trust him? It was possible the Islamic State already knew about Abu Ibrahim and was dangling him to lure them into Syria. In that case, the mission was simple suicide.

"An 8-C. I wouldn't have asked otherwise."

The CIA scored its agents on many different

scales. The simplest and most important was called the **10-A**. The number measured the value of the information the source had provided, from **1** to **10**, **10** being best. The letter measured the agency's confidence that he was genuine and not secretly controlled by another country's intelligence service, from **A** to **G**, **A** being **Most confident**. In practice, **10**s were reserved for presidents, **9**s for ministers and generals. **A**s and **B**s were similarly tough to find. **8-C** meant that the agency believed "the source had provided important information at serious personal risk and was probably uncompromised."

"He's given us good stuff about pipelines, their smuggling routes. Stuff that's actionable, cost them money. We don't think they would have put him out as a dangle, especially since they couldn't know we'd come over the border."

Durette had a broad, flat face and pale blue eyes that pressed gently yet remorselessly. He had lost a foot to a mine in Afghanistan. He never ordered any of his men into missions. He always asked, and he never downplayed the risks. Yet everyone always said yes.

"I'll see what Mahmoud says," Batta said.

Mahmoud had said three hundred fifty thousand. More than double the price of the warehouse job. Still, the number gave Batta a certain confidence. If the Syrian thought the job was impossible, he would have thrown out a ridiculous figure, a million or more.

Three hundred fifty meant he wanted to try.

Now, in Harran, Batta was feeling more than the usual pre-mission jitters. Raqqa wasn't a red zone, it was a black hole. Even if Abu Ibrahim hadn't been doubled and Mahmoud didn't plan to sell Batta and Girol to the Orange Jumpsuit Film Co., they didn't know the place well enough to judge the on-the-ground risks. Did they face a ten percent chance of hitting a checkpoint? Fifty? Ninety?

Batta forced the fear from his mind. He had survived five years of this stupid war. He'd survive the next forty-eight hours. Before he knew it, he and Girol would be back in Gaziantep, having a drink. Or ten. A few days after that, the murderers in Raqqa would be wondering where their bank accounts had gone. Easy.

"So, through the canals, we find your friend here. Midnight." Mahmoud pointed to a spot on the map, just off a dirt road that dead-ended in a tiny village northwest of Raqqa. "If he's there."

"He's smart, he'll have no problem finding

it." In truth, Batta had no idea of Abu Ibrahim's sense of direction. Batta had never met the man, didn't even know his real name. Safer for everyone.

"He's waiting, we pick him up, switch horses."

"Switch horses?"

"Five of us, four horses. Did you want him to walk?"

Batta felt more than a little foolish. Despite all the preplanning, he hadn't considered the issue.

"Ajmad comes with me, the two of us together weigh less than you," Mahmoud said. "He rides Ajmad's. He can ride?"

"Yes." Something else Batta didn't know. But even if Abu Ibrahim had the world's worst case of hippophobia, he would get over it tomorrow night, given the alternative.

"Back the way we came. We have a crescent moon, not too much light, not too little. We do it all between sunset and sunrise, we get back to Ain Issa, we're safe."

Maybe even if they couldn't get all the way back. Batta hadn't told Mahmoud, and wouldn't, but he had a couple of aces tucked away. Tomorrow night, the agency would put a helicopter on standby just north of the border. The Islamic State had captured radar systems and anti-aircraft missiles from the Syrian Air Force and moved them to Raqqa, so the copter couldn't risk landing inside the city. But Durette had promised he would try an emergency exfiltration even twenty-five kilometers outside Raqqa, if Batta asked.

Better still, they would have a pair of guardian angels, two Reaper drones overhead. The drones would carry full payloads, four Hellfire missiles each, and operate under the agency's loosest rules of engagement. The lawyers at Langley called it **non-identification/one-call launch**. In plain English, if the Reaper pilots spotted armed men closing on Batta's team, they could fire without knowing exactly who their targets were. They wouldn't even need to speak to Batta or Girol. They did have to call, but if the men on the ground didn't answer, the pilots could assume that they were in trouble and fire.

The rules made sense. No other Americans, soldier or civilian, were in the area. The risk of friendly fire was nil. The area was farmland, so the risk of civilian casualties was low, too. The one advantage of operating alone in hostile territory was the chance for massive air support.

The pilots had also promised to give advance warning of jihadis in their way. Batta wasn't counting on the help. Distinguishing a check-point from farmers hanging out would be al-most impossible. And if they ran across a checkpoint, the drones wouldn't be much use. The Hellfires had a kill radius of a hundred feet. They would vaporize Batta and his guys just as efficiently as the jihadis around them.

But if the mission was a trap and the Islamic State's soldiers had set an ambush, the Reapers would give Batta's team at least a chance to es-cape.

"So to Ain Issa with our new friend," Batta said. "Then home sweet home."

"And you pay. Three hundred fifty minus one, that's two hundred fifty. Thousand."

"Nothing would make me happier."

"Then we agree." Mahmoud tapped Baraq. "Lucky you, you get to ride this one. You'll break the others."

THEY FOLLOWED Mahmoud south through miles of pistachio groves. The trees looked like bushes on sticks, twenty feet high, with nuts that hung heavy in clusters. They were ugly, and didn't offer much shade, and Batta didn't mind when they thinned out.

Mahmoud had made sure they had plenty of water for the horses. Otherwise, they were traveling light. In his pack, Batta carried only a spare phone, a bedroll, a Makarov, a GPS handheld, a cheap map and binoculars, and a basic first-aid kit—all plausible enough. Girol had the same gear, plus a beat-up short-stock AK.

Though Batta did have one other piece of equipment, one that the CIA had hardly used in fifty years. The scientists at Langley called it an L-pill. Despite the name, it was not a pill at all but a pea-sized plastic ampule covered in rubber. The ampule held a concentrated solution of potassium cyanide. Biting through the rubber and plastic released the cyanide. Unconsciousness from oxygen deprivation occurred in seconds, death in minutes.

During the 1950s, operatives had carried the ampules in their mouths as false teeth. As the Cold War settled down, they fell out of favor. Now they were back, at least around here. To eliminate the risk of accidental poisoning, surgeons attached the ampules behind the ear with skin-colored tape. They were invisible, except for the closest of inspections, but easy to reach and tug off.

Without the cyanide, Batta wasn't sure he would have gone ahead with this mission. Dying was bad enough. He couldn't imagine spending his final moments on camera as a masked idiot behind him made an inane speech. Then the final shot, his head laid atop his body, eyes wide in disbelief. Death **and** dishonor in one neat package.

Batta knew Girol carried a pill, too. Of course they'd never discussed it. He imagined what the Marine would say if Batta asked: **Yeah, genius, I got the Hershey-covered version—if it goes tits up, I want chocolate to be the last thing I remember. Delicious. What about you? Hummus, right? One thing all you sand crabs have in common, you all love hummus.**

No. Girol would never give a speech that long.

After the pistachios, they passed an olive grove, these trees more pleasing, thick-trunked and wavy-branched and reaching for the sky. Van Gogh had painted them, Batta remembered. Crazy Vinny van Gogh, who'd cut off his ear. But crazy as he might have been, van Gogh wasn't the one riding into Syria.

They tracked south and east as the afternoon wore on. For a while, they could glimpse the two-lane road that stretched north from Akçakale, but it was mostly empty. Only smugglers, jihadis, and refugees traveled here now. Even so, Batta found himself almost enjoying the ride. Baraq was a fine horse, with a long, easy stride.

The sun dipped in the sky. They left the last cultivated fields behind and rode on a track that Batta could barely distinguish from the dusty plains. Batta didn't need a map or a sign to know they were nearing the border. Instead of sheep, goats wandered the fields, poking sullenly at the dirt. Then the goats disappeared, too. Piles of trash appeared at random, burial mounds for zombies. Even before the war, no one had wanted to live near Syria.

The trail dipped. Mahmoud raised a hand, and they stopped and followed him down from their mounts. The sun was setting, the sky above turning a somber blue. An easterly breeze quickened and cooled the air. Mahmoud poured a jug of water into a metal bowl and offered it to his horse. Batta poured his own bowl for Baraq. The horse ducked his head and lapped gratefully, though his eyes stayed wary. Or maybe Batta was projecting.

He pulled on his jacket against the cold night to come, finished watering his horse, and saddled up. The sky was nearly dark, and Batta knew the stars overhead would be momentous out here, with so little light pollution. Satellites and constellations were already jostling for place.

Ahead, twin lines of razor wire created a dirt

no-man's-land not even ten meters wide. No signs marked the end of Turkey or the beginning of Syria. No floodlights or guard posts. Just the wire, unspooling east and west, held by wooden posts. Metal stitches, only they divided the world instead of pulling it together.

The smugglers had chosen the perfect place for their crossing. To the east the lights of Akçakale glowed faintly, but Batta saw no houses or lights south of the border, and the nearest Turkish settlement was at least three kilometers north.

Batta couldn't see a break in the fence, but Mahmoud led them toward a post marked by a trash heap topped with a tire. As they closed on it, Batta saw that the smugglers had hidden their work by attaching the cut wires to handles attached to a fence post. A helicopter survey wouldn't catch it.

"Hold on." Batta reached for his phone. It looked like an ordinary Samsung Galaxy but could run on both mobile and satellite networks. It didn't have full worldwide coverage, but it could reach the satellites the Defense Department kept in fixed low-earth orbit over Syria and Iraq. The satellite antenna was hidden inside the phone, so it was safe to carry even here. But connecting to the satellite network

old. Beside him, Girol came off his own ride, a short but well-muscled horse who for some reason was named World, in English.

"All right, genius?" Girol seemed fine, adding to Batta's embarrassment.

"Guess it pays to be a shrimp on these rides."

But Girol wasn't listening anymore. He had tipped his head to the side like a dog hearing a coyote's howl. Soon Batta caught the sound, too, the rumble of an engine to the south. Batta remounted and urged Baraq up an incline on the left side of the wash, to the east. At the top, he saw it. The vehicle was three or four miles away, its headlights white specks in the night, bouncing over the black soil like a ship riding a gentle sea.

At this distance Batta couldn't tell what it was, much less if it had military insignia or flags. But its lights seemed high off the ground, like a pickup on big tires, or possibly a five-ton truck. Or maybe it had spotlights mounted on the roof. It bounced hard, coming as fast as the soft earth would allow, forty or fifty miles an hour.

Batta turned, rode back down. The others had remounted. "A truck. Maybe a pickup."

"Just one?" Mahmoud said.

"I think. Be here in four, five minutes."

"We split up. You and I, down the middle. You"—he nodded to Girol—"and my brother get out of sight, you follow him there." He pointed to a low hill on the right side of the wash, to the west, maybe a half kilometer down.

Batta saw what Mahmoud wanted to do. The hill wasn't much, but if Girol and Ajmad could reach it, they would be behind the truck and whoever was in it.

Ajmad looked doubtful.

"West thirty seconds, south thirty seconds, back. **Go**, brother."

Ajmad kicked his horse into a gallop. Girol gave Batta a thumbs-up and a big sarcastic grin and followed. Marines—the best.

Mahmoud slapped his horse and trotted off. Batta shoved his Makarov into the back of his jeans, urged Baraq to follow. For three minutes, Batta couldn't see the truck. But he could hear its engine rumbling toward them. Then it crested a low rise and he saw it, close now. It had a spotlight mounted on the roof, and its front headlights were parallelograms, a shape that marked it as a Toyota Hilux. Jihadis loved Hiluxes. It was using its high beams, and those combined with the spotlight mounted on the roof to create a wall of white. Batta shielded his eyes and forced himself to keep Baraq trotting.

The good news was that the lights were focused in a tight cone. The men inside the truck would have little chance to see outside it. Girol and Ajmad should have a chance to set up.

The Hilux was a hundred meters away, fifty, twenty. Mahmoud and Batta rode out of the streambed and waved it past. Instead, it stopped. A man standing in the pickup bed swung its spotlight on them.

Baraq was tense beneath Batta's legs, taking mincing sideways steps to relieve his anxiety. Four men stood in back of the Hilux, all carrying AKs. The driver and a single passenger sat in front. Batta fought the spotlight to look at the men. They wore civilian clothes and were clean-shaven, no beards. They didn't obviously belong to the Islamic State. But they weren't Kurds either. As a rule, Kurdish men had medium brown skin, jutting noses, strong chins. These six had the sandy skin and narrow eyes of desert Arabs.

Smugglers or jihadis.

They raised their rifles. The man in the passenger seat stepped out onto the dry wash. He was short and squat. "Raise your hands."

Mahmoud lifted his arms. Batta followed. "Down. Now."

Batta's eyes adjusted enough for him to see a

cylindrical tube attached to the truck's body behind the driver's door. It was a foot long, three inches in diameter. A flag holder.

Only one group stuck flags on pickup trucks around here. Black flags with the Muslim creed, the **shahada**, in white Arabic script across the top, and the words **Muhammad is the messenger of Allah** in a circle in the center.

The Black Standard, the emblem of the Islamic State.

Batta couldn't wait for Mahmoud to see the flag holder. They had no time. If they dismounted, they were as good as dead.

Batta whistled and kicked Baraq hard, spurring the horse to the right. The men in the bed of the truck swung their AKs on Batta and fired into the night. But the horse was moving wildly, an impossible target. Then Girol and Ajmad opened up with their own AKs from the hillside. The jihadis went down like puppets whose strings had been cut, three into the pickup's bed, the fourth over the side, like he wanted a head start on burying himself.

The driver accelerated forward, but Mahmoud opened up with his Makarov, popping holes in the windshield. The truck stuttered to a halt as the driver slumped over the steering wheel. The fat man looked around. He'd very obviously made the mistake of leaving his pistol in the pickup. He ran for it, but Mahmoud galloped at him, bowling him over a step from the door. He tried to stand, but Mahmoud stilled him with three rounds.

Batta and Baraq were a hundred meters away by then. The horse thrashed like a mustang, trying to throw Batta and break for Turkey. Batta leaned low into his neck and hung on. Finally, Baraq calmed, and Batta nudged him to the pickup. Mahmoud rooted in the truck as his brother and Girol watched.

"Daesh?" Ajmad said.

"Nam."

"Maybe not." Mahmoud came out of the truck with a black, hard-sided suitcase. He unlatched the locks and flipped the case open. Hundreds of pill bottles of all sizes were stuffed inside. Mahmoud opened one, poured tiny white pills onto his palm.

"Captagon."

Captagon sounded like it belonged in a sci-fi novel. But it was real, a type of amphetamine popular in the 1970s before the United States outlawed it as overly addictive. It continued to be used in the Middle East. Militias in Syria produced it in underground labs. Despite its supposedly anti-drug stance, the Islamic State profited from the trade.

"Smugglers." Mahmoud sounded irritated. "We didn't need to shoot them."

"Maybe." Batta led him and the others around the pickup to the flag holder attached on the driver's side. "You said they didn't know about that cut."

"If they were looking for us, they would have had ten trucks. Not one."

Or maybe the Islamic State wouldn't have risked sending ten trucks into Kurdish territory. Maybe it would have sent one, with guys who could have passed as smugglers. Or **were** smugglers. But of course if the jihadis had somehow learned the CIA was sending a team into Raqqa, why intercept them here? Why not wait?

Mahmoud was right. This encounter had been coincidence. Probably. Maybe. Batta wondered if they should search the pickup, check for identification or phones, but he wanted to move before they bumped into anyone else.

"You want to go back, Kareem?" Mahmoud's voice had an edge, like Batta was a coward even for considering the possibility.

Dumb question. Of course he wanted to go

back. He looked at Girol. "How are you on ammo?"

"No worries." Girol nodded at the bodies in the truck bed. "They can spare theirs."

"What do you think?"

Girol shrugged. He didn't answer those questions.

Batta looked at Mahmoud, knew that, right or wrong, he couldn't back down in the face of the smuggler's certainty. "We'll talk about it in Ain Issa." Knowing they wouldn't, that he'd made his choice.

They left the truck and the bodies and mounted up and rode south, every stride of their horses bringing them closer to the black hole.

PART
ONE

1

JOHN WELLS had never expected to fall in love again.

She was the most beautiful girl he could imagine: tall, brown-eyed, a dimple in her chin and a ballerina's legs.

Her name was Emmie.

She was two.

WELLS HAD ENDED his last mission with a shattered wrist and an itch to go to ground in western Montana, a town called Hamilton. Where the plains met the mountains. Where he'd grown up. He'd barely seen it in twenty-five years. His parents were dead. His friends from high school had moved to Missoula or Seattle. But Wells didn't miss the people. He missed the narrow trails off the logging roads, the streams that pooled beneath granite ledges, the firs that cooled the valleys even on summer's hottest days. He'd grown up in those mountains, hunted deer with his father. Learned to track and kill.

Learned to kill, and put the lessons to good use. For twenty years, Wells had lived in the shadow world, as an operative and then a free-lancer for the CIA. **Messy** would be the best word to describe his career, **blood-splatter messy**. But like the United States itself, he had survived his mistakes. He was tall and broad-shouldered, with brown eyes that seemed warmer than they were and a tight, quiet mouth.

On his first day in Hamilton, he bought a two-room cabin in the Sawtooths, twenty miles from town, no electricity or running water, a mile off the nearest dirt road. A hunting shack. But a stream ran through the property and it was summer. Wells would worry about winter when winter came.

The best thing about the place was that he couldn't get cell service. No phone, no Internet, no way for anyone to touch him. He passed the summer hiking, fishing, remembering how to survive in the woods. Born Christian, Wells had converted to Islam more than fifteen years before, as he lived with al-Qaeda jihadis in the Hindu Kush. His belief had ebbed and flowed over the years. Now it was waning again. God seemed everywhere in these mountains, prayer almost irrelevant. Wells felt an animism overtaking him, a mystic belief in the goodness of nature, that would last only until the first snow. His old friends in Afghanistan would have called him an apostate and cut off his head. But they would have cut off his head for a hundred reasons.

Every couple of weeks, he drove into Hamilton to pick up supplies, check emails, call his son, Evan. He was in a camping store on one of those trips, looking for a sleeping bag warm enough to last the fall, when his phone buzzed.

A 603 code. New Hampshire. Which could only mean Anne, his ex. They'd lived together in a farmhouse in the woods outside North Conway, a hundred forty miles north of Boston. She was a cop turned detective for the state police. She was smart and tough, and understood that Wells carried his secrets in a vault that even he couldn't open. Almost a year before, Wells had proposed. Anne turned him down. He loved the field more than any woman, she said. He tried to argue, but he knew she was right. They had spoken only once since.

Seeing her number surprised him. The excitement he felt surprised him more. He couldn't imagine her telling him she'd changed her mind. She was the opposite of fickle. The idea that she'd call for a casual chat was even more far-fetched. Had his world somehow touched hers? Had someone found her, threatened her?

Maybe the answer was simpler. She was getting married, wanted him to know.

"Anne?"

"John."

"This is a surprise." He didn't know what to say next. He wanted to apologize for not calling her, but he feared he would sound self-justifying and lame. **I wanted to give you space.** "How are you?" The most banal of questions.

"I'm fine." She seemed uncertain. Unusual for her. She'd never had trouble telling him what she thought.

"Is Tonka okay?" he finally said. Their dog. Anne had custody.

She laughed. "Tonka's indestructible . . . John, we need to talk."

"Sure."

"In person. You in D.C.?"

"Montana. What's wrong, Anne?"

Behind her, Wells heard the high, plaintive squeal that couldn't be confused with any other sound. An infant's wail. And he knew.

THE NEXT DAY, at the farmhouse in North Conway, she told him she was sure she'd conceived their final time together. "I remember," he said. The night after she turned down his proposal. They'd both known it might be the last hurrah. They'd been aggressive, almost desperate. She had closed her eyes at the end and squeezed his biceps so tightly, the marks hadn't faded for days.

"Yeah. Pretty good."

"Just pretty good?"

"You want a medal? I guess you got one."

Anne told him she had never even considered an abortion. She wanted children, and she had watched too many of her friends struggle to get pregnant to give this one up, even if she had to raise the baby alone.

"There's a new OB group in Conway, bunch of doctors, I figured it was closer and I'd need regular visits. I'm barely in the door, say I'm pregnant, the first thing the tech says, **Is this baby desired? Like, You like this sweater or should I put it back on the shelf? . . . This baby desired?** Is that really the relevant question? This baby's a baby. I guess some women say no. I went back to Dr. Gordon."

"Can I hold her?" Wells said. Emmie was barely a month old, round-faced and chubby-fingered and pushing out her tongue like a third lip, streaks of brown hair plastered to her head. After the briefest hesitation, Anne handed her over. Wells was shocked how insubstantial she seemed in his hands, how in need of protection. She blinked at him and shook her arms wildly.

"She likes you."

"You say that to everyone."

"Yes."

"She's perfect."

"In case you're wondering, there's a hundred percent chance she's yours."

"I wasn't wondering." Wells had known immediately. From the cast of Emmie's eyes, the faint tint of her skin, the ease he felt with her.

"I wasn't going to tell you, John. But when she got here, I realized I had to. For her, not for you. She deserves to know you . . . This has nothing to do with us getting back together, by the way."

"I know."

Anne didn't say anything. Wells realized she'd wanted him to disagree, he shouldn't have dismissed the prospect so quickly. The baby whimpered and pushed her head against his chest.

"She wants milk," Anne said.

Wells handed her back. Anne lifted her shirt, no modesty in front of him, maybe her way of reminding him of what they had once been.

"I can help."

"I don't need your help."

"If you'll let me. I have money, Anne." Far more than he needed.

"What, you rob a bank?"

"I told the President to give me ten million dollars and he did." A story that sounded like a lie but wasn't. "I gave half to the shelter where we got Tonka."

"**That's** where that came from. Should have known."

They were at the scratched wooden table in the farmhouse's kitchen, the autumn sun streaming through the window, casting long shadows. Fall in New Hampshire was tricky. Sunny days seemed almost gentle, but the nights came on fast, with teeth.

"I'll get a place here. Whatever you want."

"Until the phone rings. Some mission where only John Wells can save the world. I'm amazed the sun rises every day without you to cart it around."

"I learned my lesson with Evan." Wells had missed his son's childhood and adolescence. He had worked to rebuild the relationship, but he knew that Evan would never see him as a real father.

"Just don't make any promises you can't keep."

He'd learned that lesson, too.

He rented a furnished apartment a few miles away, a charmless one-bedroom condo near the North Conway outlet malls. He had to admit that the first couple of weeks were a chore, not much for him to do but change diapers and watch Emmie breast-feed. But Anne went back to the staties when Emmie was three months old, and Wells had the chance to take care of his daughter. A stay-at-home dad. He heard her first word—which was neither **Dada** or **Mama** but **dog.** Saw her take her first step. She transfixed him. He had been a professional liar and killer for so long that he had forgotten he could be anything else. But Emmie knew nothing about him except that he picked her up and read to her and tossed her in the air. He loved her long eyelashes, the way she wiped her nose on Tonka's fur, her giggles when he held her upside down. He loved everything about her.

Meanwhile, the world he'd left behind, the world of secrets and lies, spun on. Wells watched in horror and amusement as his old boss Vinny Duto won the presidency going away. Duto was the former CIA director, a man who'd saved Wells's life more than once. But Wells neither liked nor trusted Duto. If the man had any principles other than a Nixonian love of power, Wells couldn't find them. On Election Night, Wells watched Duto's victory speech with bleary eyes, wondering how Duto had fooled the country.

Or maybe he hadn't. He hadn't tried to hide his edges. He was a throwback. Like Nixon or Johnson or even Truman, he promised tough leadership for an unforgiving world. During the final presidential debate, Rachel Maddow asked Duto if he had overseen "extralegal activities" at the CIA.

"Yes."

"You admit breaking the law, Senator?" Duto had become a senator from Pennsylvania after leaving the agency.

"I just did."

"More than once."

"More times than I can count."

"You were involved with rendition—"

"Wiretapping, assassinations, all of it."

"Shouldn't that disqualify you for the White House?"

"The choices I made, I'd make them again tomorrow. I did what I did to keep America safe. America and Americans. My conscience is clear."

"You have no doubts."

"If I did, I'd never share them with you. I don't much care what you think, Rachel. You can't understand that, too bad. I'll take my chances with the people out there."

I don't much care what you think, Rachel sealed Duto's victory. He went from one point down to five points ahead and never looked back. Now he had the power he'd always wanted. Wells wondered what he'd do with it.

A few days later, Wells's phone buzzed. The code was 703 this time. Virginia. Wells was out on a walk with Emmie and Anne. He hated to take calls while he was with them, but he supposed he could make an exception for the President-elect.

"Vinny." They hadn't spoken since Wells went to Montana.

"I won't ask if you voted for me. Respect the secrecy of the ballot."

Duto sounded high to Wells. High on victory.

"No way."

"I want to invite you down for January"—

the Inauguration. "My personal guest. Couldn't have done it without you."

Have to rub my face in your coronation. "I'm trying to atone for that."

Duto went silent. "You change your mind, I'm here," he finally said. "Maybe a tour of the West Wing—"

"Good luck, Vinny."

Wells hung up. He had barely tucked away his phone when it buzzed again. Another Virginia number. Ellis Shafer, Wells's old boss at the agency. They had fallen out near the end of Wells's last mission. But Wells still trusted Shafer more than anyone else, with the possible exception of Anne. Shafer was clever always, wise sometimes. His sharp tongue had infuriated decades of agency executives.

"How's Emmie?"

"Awesome. Is it a coincidence that you're calling me five minutes after Vinny?"

"Our little boy, all growed up and president now. I'm so proud of him."

"Let me guess. He invited you to the Inaugural. And you're going."

"Maybe I am. It'll be **fun**, John. You remember what fun is?"

"You want to hang out with a bunch of rich guys in tuxedos."

"It doesn't mean you have to be secretary of commerce. It's a once-in-four-years party and we'll be VIPs. Up close with Jennifer Lawrence."

"Jennifer Lawrence isn't interested, Ellis. She sees enough slobbering old men in her day job."

"Ask your girlfriend—"

"She's not my girlfriend."

"Your baby mama. Whatever. Bring Emmie, tell her Grandpa Ellis wants to meet her."

"Grandpa what?"

Anne looked at Wells, silently giving him the **Pay attention to your kid, who do you think you are, being on the phone?** stink eye.

"Gotta go, Ellis. Tell Jennifer Lawrence I said hi."

Wells wanted to ask Anne what she thought. But he feared she would agree with Shafer, tell him that his silent protest made no difference, that—Inaugural tickets or not—he would jump if Duto called with a mission. So he didn't.

TWO MONTHS LATER, they sat in the living room, fire roaring, snow cascading, Emmie napping, a picture-postcard New Hampshire January. They watched Duto swear to defend the nation and give a grim yet resolute Inaugural Address: **We will not shirk our challenges.**

That's not my way. It's not the American way. Together, we will face them. Overcome them. We will lead the world, because our leadership makes the world a safer and better place. Thank you. God bless you. And God bless America.

"How does it feel to have the President on speed dial?"

"Anyone even have speed dial anymore?"

She laughed. "You've been good up here. You're a better dad than I thought you'd be."

"That's pretty much the definition of a back-handed compliment."

"But I know it won't last. And I want to tell you, it's okay. When the call comes—"

"No one's calling. If they do, I'm not answering."

She leaned close, hugged him. "Shush. I want this little girl to have a brother." She touched her hands to his face, kissed him hard and deep. And led him to the bed that they had once shared.

A YEAR PASSED, and part of another, and nothing changed. Anne got pregnant, but she miscarried. The world seemed to have forgotten Wells.

Then it remembered.

Even now, Anne sent him back to his apartment every night. She said seeing him in the house in the morning would confuse Emmie. Wells didn't think Emmie was the one who'd be confused, but he didn't argue. So he was alone when his phone buzzed him from a nerveless sleep. A mysterious number, led by a country code he didn't recognize. An unknown country, a 2 a.m. call.

Wells knew picking up would lead him down the rabbit hole.

"This is John."

"John Wells?" The voice carried the slurred consonants and long vowels of Eastern Europe. "Oleg Kirkov. From Bulgaria. Remember me?"

"How could I forget?" Though Wells didn't remember Kirkov sounding quite so movie villain–ish. Kirkov ran the Bulgarian intelligence service. At least he had three years ago, when he helped Wells escape a tough spot by picking him up on the Black Sea coast. Inevitably, Duto had arranged the favor. "How's Bulgaria?"

"So rich that soon Greeks come to us instead of the other way around."

"You say so."

"Joke. Greeks too lazy to emigrate. They starve first." An Eastern European chuckle rippled out of the handset. "But you are wondering why I call you at this hour. We must talk,

John. And this is not a joke. It's very serious." Suddenly Kirkov's accent was almost gone. "In person. Face-to-face."

Don't tell me you had my baby, too. "I haven't been in the game for a while."

Kirkov laughed, a laugh that said **Guys like you never quit.**

"Call Virginia."

"When I tell you, you see why I can't." A pause. "I do this as favor, I promise. To you and your friends."

If Kirkov said he had something, he did. Had the Bulgarians discovered a nuclear terror plot? A Kremlin plan to invade Eastern Europe? Why not go right to the agency, then? Or maybe Kirkov's men had stumbled across an attack directed at Wells personally. Wells had given the Russian intelligence service a sharp poke on his last mission. The Russians had long memories and didn't like losing. But they reserved their most poisonous venom for one another.

Whatever it was, Wells couldn't say no. "Face-to-face. In Sofia?"

"I don't make you come to Bulgaria this time of year." Now that Wells had agreed, Kirkov's accent was creeping back. "We meet halfway. London. Lunch at the Dorchester. One p.m. tomorrow. Very civilized."

"You're not the one taking the red-eye."

"You remember what I look like?"

"Without you, I'd still be doing laps in the Black Sea, Oleg. I remember."

Wells hung up, reached for the light on the bedside table. The bed was queen-sized, too small for him; the condo, water-stained and low-ceilinged, overlooking a Target parking lot. The traffic never stopped. Even at this hour he heard tractor-trailers unloading. For a year, Wells had promised himself he'd buy a house near Anne's. He'd never looked. He'd told himself that he was waiting for Anne to ask him to move in.

Maybe he'd been waiting for this call.

Yet now that it had come, he felt unready. Age, maybe. Wells was closer to forty-five than forty now and all the push-ups and sit-ups and running in the world couldn't save him from losing a little muscle every month or keep his reflexes from slowing. Only fractionally, but he was only too aware that fractions meant life and death in his business.

But not just age. He didn't want to leave Emmie. For toddlers and dogs, absence was absolute. She wouldn't understand why he'd left or when he'd be back. He'd miss her, too, the toothy grin she offered when she was about to misbehave, the way she scrambled up the slide at the tot park, yelling, **Look, Daddy! I not scared**.

Or maybe he feared the opposite. That as soon as he met Kirkov, he would forget his daughter, that the last two years would prove to be nothing but a pleasant dream.

SIX HOURS LATER, he let himself in the farmhouse's back door, found Anne in the kitchen, spooning yogurt into Emmie's mouth. He didn't usually show up on weekday mornings, but she didn't seem surprised.

"When do you leave?"

Wells found himself with nothing to say.

"You think I don't know that face?" She reached down for another spoonful. "Don't worry about me. Worry about your daughter. What you're going to tell her."

But the more he explained, the louder Emmie cried, a two-year-old's depthless anguish, until her chest shook and the house echoed with her grief and Tonka whimpered, until Anne shook her head and pointed at the door and Wells raised his hands in surrender and backed away.

LONDON WAS raw, gray and wet. Wells hadn't slept on the plane. Instead of an umbrella and mackintosh, he wore a cowboy hat against the rain. Effective, even if the doormen eyed him disdainfully. He shook the water off the brim, stepped past the Bentleys and into the polished marble lobby. The hotel epitomized what the English capital had become in the twenty-first century, a city that gladly accepted Russian oligarchs, Saudi princes, anyone and everyone. Everyone except its own natives, who no longer could afford to live here. The cheapest rooms at the Dorchester ran a thousand dollars a night. Suites overlooking Hyde Park started at five thousand.

Wells found Kirkov by the concierge desk.

"A walk in the rain?"

Amen. Wells wasn't in the mood to spend a hundred bucks for lunch. Kirkov unfurled an umbrella and led Wells into Hyde Park, nearly empty today, the rain chasing away joggers and nannies. They found a bench, sat side by side.

"You know we still have a prison."

Wells needed a moment to understand. "A rendition site." After September 11, the CIA had worked with American allies to open secret prisons for suspected terrorists. But over the years, pressure from human-rights groups had caused the host countries to close the prisons. The agency moved some captives to the American base at Guantánamo Bay and sent others home. These days, the United States preferred to assassinate rather than capture suspected terrorists anyway. "I thought they were all gone."

"Technically speaking, we closed the old one, but three years ago we opened another. An annex, we call it. Inside a prison called the Castle, where we keep our own criminals, too."

"In Sofia?"

"The mountains. The foreigners are present for holding and transit. The lawyers tell me if we do it that way, it's legal. Don't ask me why."

Kirkov stopped. He seemed to expect congratulations.

"Of course we only get one or two a month now," he said after a few seconds. "Al-Qaeda from Yemen. Islamic State from Syria, Libya, Iraq. Mostly, Islamic State."

"How many in all?"

"Twenty-eight. We were up to thirty-three a few months ago, but the lawyers said if we went over thirty-five, it would be a problem. We have to tell the EU more. So we warn the agency and they take some. Always, we find the things the laws don't know about."

As if not just the lawyers but the **laws** themselves were hunters Kirkov needed to evade. The paradox of trying to run a secret prison, a place that existed at the edge of legality, in a European country. Even before Kirkov came to the heart of the story, Wells saw why he was in no rush to send an official report to the agency.

"Lot of work for twenty-eight prisoners."

"The agency helps us, too," Kirkov said almost primly.

Wells thought of a song from an animated kids show called **Daniel Tiger** that Emmie had just started watching: **Friends help each other, yes they do, it's true**. No doubt the CIA was expressing its friendship in its preferred form, suitcases of fresh hundred-dollar bills. Wells decided not to ask how much the United States paid Bulgaria every year for the prisoners at the Castle, if Kirkov kept any for himself. "And all twenty-eight are under CIA control, not the military?"

"Yes. They send me file on everyone, not long, page or two. Some the CIA catch, some the Deltas. Either way, our deal is with Langley, they notify us, they deliver and take them away."

"Anyone senior?"

"Two. Both Islamic State. One came six months ago, the other three months. Hani, he's on the Shura Council"—the group of men who oversaw the Islamic State. "In charge of the religious police, someone fooled him into going to

Turkey and handed him over. I have his real name, but he calls himself Hani and that's what we call him. Latif al-Jelloun, the other one, was a commander in Homs. I don't know how your people caught him or where. We kept them mostly separate from the others."

"Kept?"

"Your people moved Latif again two weeks ago. I think to Morocco, where he's from. Planned transfer, nothing to do with this."

"So he's gone."

"He's gone, but we have Hani. And you'll hear on the tape, Hani's the important one."

"You ever interrogate them?"

"We don't question anyone, we don't know what to ask, and, technically, they're not our prisoners."

"The agency does."

"Another rule the lawyers made is the Americans can only talk to each prisoner for two days a month. Stupid rule. With most of them, it doesn't matter, but with the important ones we need to change it."

Of course if the agency wanted more quality time with those men, it could keep them in its own custody. But no one wanted to bring more detainees to Guantánamo, which had become a worldwide embarrassment.

"Another stupid rule, we let them pray together on Fridays. Half one week, half the next."

"Nice of you."

"But one thing we do that isn't so stupid, we have microphones in the prayer room. The annex isn't new but the prayer room is, we built it for this. Your people gave us money."

"The lawyers are okay with taping prayers?"

"It's a prison, we can watch and listen wherever we like. No expectation of privacy, even in the bathroom. Of course we don't tell them that when they come. So we make these tapes. Nothing on tape anymore, all digital, but we call them tapes still."

"You send the files to Langley?"

"We haven't."

"Because of the lawyers?"

Kirkov seemed embarrassed. "No one asked. Besides, only two, three guards speak Arabic, and the last time they checked, a few months ago, the tapes are all praying."

In other words, both the agency and the Bulgarians had more or less forgotten the files existed. The problem wasn't a new one. Conversations were expensive and time-consuming to translate, and ubiquitous surveillance meant that innumerable calls and face-to-face conversations were recorded every month. The National Security Agency had spent a billion dollars on software to translate Arabic and Pashtun, and flag suspicious phrases for priority review by human translators. But as anyone who had recently called an airline 800 number knew, voice recognition software had a ways to go. So unheard recordings piled up on hard drives in data centers in Utah and Maryland and the Australian desert.

"But last month, one of our men, a senior guard, he speaks Arabic, getting divorced, his wife kicked him out. He moved into an empty office at the prison. Nothing to do at night, so he decided to listen."

"Instead of drink?"

"Lucky us."

Kirkov pulled an iPhone from his pocket. "You speak Arabic."

Wells nodded.

"Seven weeks ago, the first time that Hani and Latif were together." Kirkov opened a file, gave Wells the phone. "The first one who speaks is Latif, then Hani. You can listen to all of it, you can come to Sofia and listen to all the files we have, but he tells me this is the one that matters."

Wells clicked on the file. He heard prayers in the background and then two men murmuring.

————

THEY told *me* this is Bulgaria. Is that true?

Yes.

Where is that?

Hani laughed. His voice was assured, his Arabic more graceful than Latif's. Probably from the Gulf. Their voices took Wells out of bare-branched Hyde Park and into a white-walled room filled with men bowing toward Mecca.

Near Turkey.

But it's the Americans who have us.

Better them than Assad. Hani laughed again. Already Wells didn't like him.

Does anyone know we're here?

The Red Crescent, you mean? I haven't seen anyone.

Do you think they'll bring us to Guantánamo?

I don't think so. It doesn't matter.

It does to me. My family doesn't know what happened to me. No one knows.

They'll find out.

How?

They will.

What if they think I'm a traitor? That I defected. Maybe they make martyrs of my sons.

Don't worry, Latif.

The ones who vanish—

Listen. A snap in Hani's voice. Wells didn't need an Islamic State org chart to hear that Hani outranked Latif. **I'm telling you, they know where we are. And what happened to us.**

How?

Someone tells them.

Someone here? Latif said. **A guard?**

Silence, the silence of someone who feared he'd said too much. **Don't worry about it,** Hani finally said.

Another pause.

So it's true? About the gay. I didn't believe it. Wells paused the playback to consider what he'd heard. In this case **gay** probably had nothing to do with sexuality. Arabs used the term as slang for **informant** or **spy.** The usage had sprung from the Mossad's success in forcing homosexual Palestinians to spy for Israel or be outed. Now, all over the Middle East, moles were routinely called gays.

Latif's words implied that someone with access to the CIA's worldwide database of its secret prisoners was helping the Islamic State. Of course that person wasn't necessarily inside the agency. The CIA disclosed some information to the Red Cross. But the word **gay** implied a mole, not just a third-party source.

Wells returned to the playback.

Let's say that it is.

He'll know about me?

A laugh from the other man, Hani. **He knows everything. When you were taken, where you are, if they move you. But let me ask you, my friend, what did you hear? Because no one should know. Only a few of us on the Council. And even we don't know everything.**

I didn't hear, not really, Latif said. **But in the spring I told Abu Yusuf**—the commander of all Islamic State's fighters in Syria—**I thought the Americans might send their own men to strike us. He said that the Americans didn't trust the Shia enough to do that. Then he said if the Americans made a big attack, we would know before their soldiers did. Not just Homs, anywhere in the caliphate**—the Islamic State's word for its territory. **I asked him how and he told me don't worry about it.**

That's all, Latif? Nothing more?

Nothing. I swear in Allah's name. I never told anyone. The way he said it made me feel I shouldn't. I wondered for a few days and then I forgot it, I had battles to fight. But

when you spoke of someone who knew where all of us are held, I remembered.

A relieved sigh.

I'll forget everything we spoke of today, Hani.

Yes. Let's pray.

PRAY THEY DID, until Wells turned off the playback and came back to London and Kirkov. The soft Arabic voices vanished, leaving him with the drizzle tapping off his cowboy hat, that ridiculous but useful accessory.

The first question, always: Is the other side setting up one of your officers, faking and trapping? A successful dissimulation operation could drive a spy agency to madness chasing its own nonexistent moles. But for this conversation to be part of that game, Hani and Latif would have to know that they would have a chance to meet, even though they were captured months apart in different countries. They would have to know that they would wind up in the same prison and have a chance to talk in a taped prayer room.

"You're sure they hadn't spoken before?"

"This is real, John. Even the old KGB, the masters, they couldn't have set this up."

The conversation sounded real to Wells, too.

He understood why Latif was worried about what might happen to his family if the Islamic State believed he had defected. The jihadis were known to drag spies behind trucks until their bodies snapped apart. To reassure Latif, and possibly to put him in his place, Hani had said too much. Then Latif had realized something that both men wished he hadn't.

Next question: If the men were telling the truth, how senior was the mole inside Langley? That question was easier to answer. He was someone who knew about the covert ops the CIA and Pentagon ran inside Syria. Someone who could dive into the agency's detainee program without raising questions. Wells would check with Shafer, but he suspected only a handful of officers in the agency had those clearances. The director himself. The deputy director of operations. The assistant deputy director for counterterrorism. Also, the agency had created a desk dedicated to fighting the Islamic State. Whoever ran that would have full access.

Those four. Maybe others. But not many.

"Someone senior." Kirkov seemed to read Wells's mind.

"If it's real."

"You know it's real."

"Someone on the seventh floor"—where the agency's top executives worked—"an American, betraying the United States to the Islamic State."

"Don't act so surprised." Kirkov smiled. "It's what they thought about you and al-Qaeda."

Wells took off his hat, tilted back his head, let the rain wash his face. More than a decade before, Wells had come back to the United States from Pakistan and found the agency didn't trust him or his conversion to Islam. It had kept him under house arrest. Even Shafer had doubted him. Only his handler back then, Jennifer Exley, had believed. **Exley.** His handler, and his lover, too. He rarely let himself think about her anymore. About what they'd been. She was part of the past, and Emmie seemed to have sealed her there. Hard to imagine a past or a future with a woman you hadn't seen in almost a decade when you were raising a daughter with another.

Even so, her name burned his heart.

Kirkov misunderstood his silence. "John Wells the traitor. Isn't that what they thought?"

"They were wrong."

An answer, true but incomplete. Wells had been loyal, yes, but he'd also been deeply alienated after all those years in the Kush. Part of him had hated his fellow Americans for their wastefulness, their inability to understand their luck. Wells had never gone over, but he'd stood at the edge of the cliff, looked at the ruins below.

"Tell me it's impossible," Kirkov said.

Wells stared into the blank gray sky and tried to remember his daughter's voice. Instead, he heard Hani, a man he'd never seen, in a secret prison two thousand miles from here, murmuring, **Someone tells them . . .**

"Nothing's impossible."

2

NEAR RAQQA, SYRIA

WHEN they reached Ain Issa, Batta found that their hidey-hole for the night was not a warehouse but an abandoned stable, its stalls empty, its concrete walls pocked with bullet holes. Batta was too tired to ask. He threw down his bedroll and slept as hard as he ever had.

He woke to find Mahmoud and the others drinking coffee. Just like old-time cowboys only they were sitting on beach chairs instead of hay bales and Ajmad was playing a video game on his phone. Batta's ankle burned like he'd barbecued it.

"Might start calling you Sleeping Beauty instead of genius," Girol said.

"Time is it?"

Girol ignored the question until Batta looked at his watch for the answer: 9:16.

"Nah, stick with genius."

"Cigarette?" Mahmoud said.

Batta hadn't smoked since college, but this morning seemed like a good time to start. He lit up, and took the last beach chair. It was neon green, with a tropical theme, palm trees and coconuts. Nice. He rolled down his sock, found a blister on his ankle the size of an oyster shell but not as pretty. He would cover it in moleskin and hope for the best.

"How do we feel about last night? It was good for you, was it good for me? Anyone?"

Mahmoud sucked on his cigarette. Ajmad jabbed at his phone.

"Going to Raqqa," Girol mumbled. "Right?"

"Unless Durette calls it off." But Batta knew Durette wouldn't call it off. He would leave the choice to them, and they'd made their choice.

Girol closed his eyes: **Then let's not worry about it.**

They spent the morning watering and feeding the horses. No one bothered them. Batta figured the stable's owners were refugees, over the border in Turkey. At noon, he powered up the satellite phone for a call to the Special Operations Group base in Gaziantep. The sat was probably an unnecessary precaution. The Islamic State wasn't running real-time surveillance on mobile networks—not yet. But better safe than headless.

Durette picked up right away, and Batta heard the series of beeps and hisses that meant the encryption was working.

"Sir."

"So far, so good?"

"Ran into a pickup with six red team last night. All gone now." Batta sketched out the skirmish.

"I hate coincidences," Durette said. "Maybe we should bring you back."

"You'd have four angry men down here." A lie. Mahmoud and Ajmad just wanted their money, Batta would be happy someone else had decided for him, and Girol didn't get angry.

"No one's bothered you today?"

"Not a soul."

"Give me the coordinates. I want to see it myself. Call you back."

"I'll text them." Batta hung up, sent Durette the location.

Thirty-five minutes later, his phone buzzed.

"Still there," Durette said, without preamble. "The truck and the bodies, too. I think it was bad luck. Anything else, they would have fetched the bodies already. But you want to turn around, I get it."

"What about Abu Ibrahim?" Batta felt safe using the cover name on this encrypted network.

"Just emailed his final go."

"Our eyes in the sky?" The drones.

"As promised."

"Then we'll leave at sunset. Back here by dawn."

"We'll be watching. **Insh'allah**, my friend."

"Not you, too."

"Good luck, then."

THE AFTERNOON passed interminably. Girol broke apart his AK, cleaned it, oiled it, rebuilt it. Then he blindfolded himself and repeated the exercise. Batta did the same with his Makarov, mainly to prove he could. Mahmoud and Batta squabbled about whether Mahmoud could call his girlfriend. Mahmoud agreed to wait until they returned from Raqqa. Batta dressed the blister on his ankle and stretched his legs and back every way he could imagine. But the night didn't come.

The horses were jittery, too. Batta offered Baraq a sugar cube and nearly lost a finger.

"He doesn't like you because you're so fat," Mahmoud said.

Fear and impatience ground together. Batta couldn't remember feeling so uncertain about a mission. Paradoxically, he wanted nothing more than to start. The sooner he started, the sooner he finished.

Finally, the sun dipped low and a dusky orange tinted the sky. Batta powered up the sat phone. No messages. So they were cleared for takeoff. From here on, he would leave the phone on so that the drone pilots could call them with warnings. To make sure the drones didn't target them accidentally, Batta's GPS handheld secretly doubled as a transmitter. He could use it to send a radio signal marking them as friendly. But any jihadis with wide-spectrum receivers in the vicinity could track the signal, too. They might not know what it meant, but they would know their side wasn't sending it. So Batta was leaving the transmitter off. As long as he and the others were mounted, the pilots should have no problems recognizing them. They had to be the only group of four men on horses within fifty miles.

They saddled up. As the sky turned black they heard the sunset Muslim call to prayer, the **Maghreb**, whispering to them from the south. As if the jihadis wanted to remind them where they were going. Mahmoud leaned over his horse, spat in the dust. Batta had never seen a Muslim respond that way to a prayer call.

Mahmoud must have caught the surprise on Batta's face. "Daesh, they've ruined it. Every word. Let them pray until Allah sets them all on fire."

They came to a rutted two-lane road whose edges crumbled into the featureless desert. To the west, taillights chased the last glimmers of sun. To the east, the road was empty.

"M4," Mahmoud said.

The front line.

"Look both ways," Batta said, and followed Mahmoud across.

Ain Issa's glow faded. Only the moon and the stars lit their way. The night was silent except for the breathing of their horses. This land had no irrigated crops, not even much trash, only knee-high green bushes scattered at random. The soil was dry and sandy, an ugly red-orange under the moonlight. Say what you wanted about the Islamic State, it wasn't a real estate play.

Unlike their route the night before, this path seemed to be exclusively for horses. Batta saw occasional piles of manure, no tire tracks.

No one spoke for two hours, until Mahmoud

raised his hand to indicate a stop. "Fifteen minutes for the horses." Baraq had worked up a lather. Batta wiped his flanks, gave him as much water as he could drink. The GPS showed that they had ridden twenty-one kilometers. Another thirty to go, three hours of riding, plus stops. They were aiming to reach the pickup spot a few minutes before midnight. They had a narrow window, a half hour at most. Every minute raised the risk that a random patrol would spot them.

Batta pulled the sat phone, found a single text from ten minutes before. **C. C** for **Clear.** The drones, their secret protectors, circling in the darkness. "Good night for this," he said, just to hear his voice.

They rode. "Careful here," Mahmoud said after about half an hour. They came over a rise and Batta saw they'd reached cultivated land, straight-edged fields split by narrow dirt roads. Beyond the fields, maybe two kilometers south, a few dozen lights glowed. The village was bigger than it seemed. This part of Syria no longer had a working electrical grid at night. Only buildings that had their own generators could stay lit. Probably a few hundred houses and a couple of larger structures. The wind carried the sound of humming generator engines.

"This way." Mahmoud led them to an irrigation channel, twenty feet wide and ten deep. He tied a handkerchief over his mouth, urged his horse down an eroded dirt wall.

Batta followed—and too late realized that the channel carried runoff, not freshwater. It was nearly dry, no risk of drowning, but the stench of animal waste stung his nose. The leftover fertilizer coated his tongue with a foul chemical taste. Worse, their passage stirred up clouds of flies. The horses flicked their tails wildly. Batta forced himself to hold the reins instead of swatting. Mahmoud hadn't mentioned they'd be riding through what was essentially an open sewer. No wonder he'd been so confident that they wouldn't hit checkpoints. Batta leaned close to his horse and tried not to think how long they'd be down here.

Ahead, Mahmoud kicked his horse into a fast trot. Batta urged Baraq to follow. They passed under a narrow concrete bridge. Baraq didn't like the enclosed space, the sudden darkness. He stopped abruptly. "Come on, boy." Batta felt the horse quivering under him. He feared Baraq might rear up, smash both their heads against the concrete. He squeezed Baraq's flanks until the horse stepped tentatively forward and they escaped.

"Next time, gallop him through," Mahmoud said. "When they run, they're not scared."

Next time? Batta would have no chance to control the horse if Baraq panicked at full speed. But as they neared the next bridge, Batta decided to trust the smuggler. He kicked Baraq into a gallop and the horse surged through.

Finally, Mahmoud led them out of the canal into an empty field. They had bypassed the village entirely. Its lights were a kilometer to the north. Fly bites covered Batta's face. He'd have to ask the SOG doctor in Gaziantep what diseases flies transmitted. And get shots.

They walked until the smell of effluent faded. Mahmoud raised his hand and hopped down.

"You should have told us that was coming," Batta said.

"Want to ride through town, Kareem?"

"We could have wrapped our faces."

"I warn you now. Another one in three kilometers."

Great. Batta pulled his phone, found he'd received another **C** for **Clear** text while they were in the sewer. At least the route seemed to be worth the trouble.

"Come on, let's give them water."

For the next two hours, the ride was uneventful, no checkpoints or Captagon smugglers. As they approached the Euphrates, the land once again turned green, fed by irrigation canals that stretched north from the muddy river. They came across clusters of farmhouses and another village, but Mahmoud found ways around all the settlements. For nearly twenty minutes, they followed another sewage channel, this one still damp with runoff, even more fetid than the first. Batta tried not to breathe.

They emerged only a few kilometers northwest of Raqqa. Here, the Euphrates kept the desert at bay. All the land around them was cultivated, and for the first time they couldn't avoid traveling close to roads and houses. Mahmoud led them east through palm groves on a path that seemed meant as a foot trail, the gap between the trees barely wide enough for the horses. Cars sped along a road a few hundred meters to the south. They passed close enough to farmhouses to see the glow of televisions flickering inside. Even with the map and the satellite overheads, Batta hadn't realized how claustrophobic this route would become. He felt as if they were working deeper into a cave with their flashlights fading. But Mahmoud led them without hesitation.

The groves to the south thinned. Through the open patches Batta saw the lights of a city in the distance. Raqqa. The killers in charge of the Islamic State made sure their capital had electricity. The difference between a centrally powered grid and individual generators was obvious.

They rode another five minutes before Mahmoud turned them off the path and into the grove. It was 11:47 p.m. They had left Ain Issa six hours before. They were less than a kilometer from the meeting site, but Batta couldn't imagine how they could ride in without being seen. The groves ended just ahead, leaving open fields between them and the pickup spot.

Mahmoud dismounted.

"We tie the horses and walk. Through the grove and then there." He pointed at an elevated path for tractors and carts. It dead-ended at the one-lane dirt farm road where they would meet Abu Ibrahim.

"You and your brother wait here," Batta said. "We'll get him, bring him back." The presence of two men would be less strange than four, if anyone saw them.

Mahmoud nodded. Batta checked his phone, found another C for **Clear** only nine minutes before. He decided to call Gaziantep, make sure the pilots knew they'd be dismounted. Durette picked up after one ring.

"You see us?"

"In the grove."

"Bill and I are walking the rest of the way. The brothers will stay with the horses. So, two on foot."

"I'll tell the pilots. Everything looks good. Normal traffic, fields are empty, no unusual movement in that **ville** to the north."

"And you don't see our guy yet."

Durette paused. "They're telling me they picked up a guy on a bike near the Equestrian Hotel." The building was on the northwest edge of Raqqa, two kilometers away. "Could be him."

"GTG."

"TTYL." The operators had adopted the habit of using texting slang at these moments, a backhanded way to defuse tension. **How much danger can we be in if we sound like teenage girls?**

BATTA STUFFED his pistol in his waistband and led Girol along the edge of the elevated dirt track. It didn't offer much cover. The road to the south was about a kilometer away, but anyone who looked hard would see them. Worse, generators pounded in the village to the northeast, and the farmhouses there had more lights than Batta had expected.

Batta saw a man bicycling in the distance. **Abu Ibrahim.** He wore a backpack and rode cautiously over the rutted road. He gripped the handlebars rigidly, the tension in his arms and shoulders visible even from there. Good. A man who was about to flee the Islamic State shouldn't look relaxed.

The sat phone buzzed. A single word: **Down.**

"Down." Batta threw himself onto the dirt. Seconds later, he heard what the drones had seen. A pickup truck rolled out from the village to the northeast. Not a Hilux, a rusted two-door Mitsubishi. Two men inside, none in the back. It bounced down the track that connected the village and main road. Batta and Girol were five hundred meters away, clumps in the dirt. Batta didn't think the guys in the truck had seen them. He watched as the truck approached Abu Ibrahim, who pulled his bike out of the way. The men in the pickup had a short conversation with him, and then the truck rolled past.

"Not good," Girol muttered. Batta agreed. The timing was odd.

Batta thumbed out a text: **Anything else?**

"Abort?" he said over his shoulder to Girol.

"Not sure what that even means, at this point."

Batta had never wanted to cut and run worse

in his life. His pulse was a snare drum in his skull. But Girol was right. They were fifty kilometers from safety, five hundred meters from their man. If the jihadis knew they were coming, they would face an epic dragnet. If not, they needed to finish this mission.

Anyway, they still had their eyes in the sky.

You are clear.

Batta stayed down for another minute in case the pilots had anything more to tell him. He hoped his courage would come back. It didn't, but he stood anyway.

Abu Ibrahim had reached the meeting point. He stood leaning over his bike's handlebars. Batta and Girol walked toward him. When he saw them, his back arched like lightning had hit him. He nodded vigorously but didn't move.

Batta stopped walking. No reason to go farther. They would just have to retrace their steps to the grove. He waved Abu Ibrahim over with both hands. The Syrian seemed weirdly standoffish, but eventually he dropped the bike and cut across the field toward them, kicking up dust as he went. He was short and chubby and wearing only a short-sleeved shirt and jeans despite the cool night air. Batta pitied whichever horse Mahmoud chose for him.

Batta no longer liked Abu Ibrahim's body

language. Fear was reasonable, under the circumstances, but the guy seemed terrified. Maybe the guys in the truck had spooked him. Batta pulled his Makarov, held it by his side. No reason to give this man much rope.

Finally, the Syrian reached the narrow track where Batta and Girol stood. "Stop," Batta said. Up close, Abu Ibrahim looked even worse. His shirt was wet with sweat and his eyes were fireworks in his face. He wore the backpack cinched too tight over his shoulders, like he was a geeky kid on the first day of school.

"Mighty," Batta muttered in English. "Back up." He wanted to create some space, give Girol a firing angle.

As Girol backed away, Batta stepped toward the Syrian. "Abu Ibrahim?"

"Yes. You are CIA, yes?"

Suddenly Batta realized what bothered him more than the guy's abject terror or even the way he'd just called Batta out. The **backpack.** Abu Ibrahim knew the agency would resettle him with everything he needed. He knew he wasn't supposed to draw any attention as he made his way out here. So why the backpack?

"What's in your backpack?" For a moment, Batta flashed to those stupid credit card ads— **What's in your wallet?**—and he wished more than anything that he was on his couch watching the Packers stomp his Lions again. Even before he'd finished the thought, he felt the sat phone buzzing in his pocket. He raised his pistol. "Take it off."

"I can't—"

Too late, Batta knew. He squeezed the Makarov's trigger—

Whatever was in the backpack detonated and tore Abu Ibrahim into a thousand pieces. The blast wave caught Batta and flipped him end over end as easily as a craps player tossing dice. He landed on his back, semiconscious, in darkness so total that for a moment he wondered if he was dead already.

He blinked, blinked again, but the darkness didn't go. He reached for his face, but when he tried to trace his eye sockets, nausea clenched his stomach. The blast must have shredded his eyes with dirt. The thought should have panicked him, but he felt strangely calm.

He realized, calmly, that he was in shock.

AKs rattled in the distance, and one close by. Girol. Then **Whoosh** overhead, a distant explosion, another. The drones and their Hellfires, Batta imagined.

The crack of a big gun, a heavy rifle. A man thumped down beside him.

"Pricks have a Dragunov," Girol said in his ear. A Russian sniper rifle. "Lucky for us, he can't shoot."

"I'm blind. Get out, Mighty."

"Sure. My magic carpet." Girol laughed, hard and bitter. Batta couldn't help himself. If they had to die, he was glad they would do it together.

The Dragunov cracked again, though this time it seemed to come from another direction.

"Pricks have **two** Dragunovs," Girol said. "Ain't sporting. Second guy can aim a little, too."

Two more big thumps from the Hellfires and a single scream carried to them in the night.

"Yeah, that'll smart," Girol said.

"Guess they knew we were coming."

"This one was no good from the start and it's my fault for not saying so. The tough guy who never talks. Buncha—"

Both Dragunovs cracked almost at once. Girol sucked in his breath, groaned quietly.

"You hit, Mighty?"

Two more Hellfires thumped down. "Looks like they smoked a pickup." Girol's voice was a whisper. "Nice."

They were fine as long as they had air support. But the drones had fired six of their eight missiles. And once they were out . . .

"Any ideas, genius?"

Batta had no ideas, just a question. Who'd set them up? Mahmoud? Abu Ibrahim? Had the man he'd seen even **been** Abu Ibrahim? He'd die without answers. That uncertainty seemed as bitter as death itself.

"Gimme the AK, go for the horses," Batta said. The horses. He wondered what would happen to them. Past his control now, like everything else.

"Wouldn't get ten feet. Besides, I never said anything, because I didn't know if you'd understand, but I always had feelings for you."

Batta didn't know what to say. Girol was the last guy on earth he would have imagined making this confession—

A whispery laugh.

"Don't tell me you believed me. Genius to the end."

Batta reached behind his ear and, after a moment of panic, found the pill exactly where it was supposed to be. He tugged at the adhesive, peeled it off.

"Mighty."

"Do what you gotta do. I'll see you on the flip side, Kareem."

The first time in years that Girol had used his real name. Before the fear could paralyze him, Batta popped the pill in his mouth, crunched it between his teeth. A foul-tasting liquid trickled down his throat, burning as it went. Too soon it landed in his stomach and every cell in his body screamed at once, an agony that rose and rose, he couldn't **breathe**, what had he done to himself, worse than he could have imagined, he was starving for oxygen, where was the blackness now, the mercy, he tried to beg but he couldn't speak, where was it, where—

3

LANGLEY, VIRGINIA

THE CIA was a gossipy place, not surprising given that its denizens had given themselves the job of knowing the world's secrets. Almost everyone at Langley had heard of Ellis Shafer, the scrawny oldster with the curly white hair whose pants never fit. The **hall reports**—agency-speak for **rumors**—said that Shafer had played a role in the sudden resignation of the prior director, a Marine general.

But the stories about Shafer went in every direction. In the directorate of intelligence, most analysts thought Shafer was Vinny Duto's personal spy at Langley. The officers in the directorate of operations had a more perverse view, that Shafer couldn't stand Duto and refused to retire simply to spite him.

On the seventh floor of the Original Headquarters Building, the director and his deputies had more information but only slightly more insight. They knew that Duto had used Shafer and Wells for missions where the agency needed not just plausible but complete deniability. But the details remained a mystery. Nor did anyone know why Duto had chosen Shafer and Wells, who both had reputations for being difficult, for those missions. Or what they had received in return.

Not power—not in the conventional sense anyway. Wells didn't even have an office at Langley. The CIA kept him on its payroll as a **Senior Field Operations Trainer**, a title that existed only for him. Once a year, he held a question-and-answer session with new case officers at the Farm. Aside from that, he was a wraith. Shafer had an even more ridiculous title, **Director of Quality Assurance**. These days, he had a third-floor office, where his neighbors were accountants and auditors who might as well have worked for the Department of Agriculture.

The best guess on seven was that Duto had used Shafer and Wells on missions that advanced his personal interests. Shafer and Wells played along in return for favors of their own.

Over the years, the three had learned so many of one another's secrets that they were inextricably tied together.

SHAFER WANTED to dismiss that view as unfair, too simplistic. But he knew it held more than a little truth. Duto had repeatedly outplayed him and Wells, using them in ways they didn't recognize until too late. Other times, they had outplayed themselves, putting themselves in situations where they had to beg for Duto's help. Duto always did help. But he inevitably collected on his chits. Sometimes right away. Sometimes later, after Wells and Shafer let themselves believe he'd forgotten.

For longer than he should have, Shafer had believed that the truth always won. Shafer was an atheist. Truth was as close to a god as he had. Hard, inalienable facts. **Don't tell me you weren't speeding, I have you on the gun at eighty-one.** The CIA pretended to agree. Etched into a wall of its main lobby was a quote from the New Testament, John 8:32—**And ye shall know the truth and the truth shall make you free.**

A masterpiece of cynicism. The men and women at Langley knew better than anyone the limits of truth. They prayed to other gods.

They spent their lives keeping mental ledgers of favors asked and granted, secrets hidden and exposed. No one kept more careful accounting than Duto.

Duto was on Shafer's mind more and more. He had realized a couple of years back that he grudgingly respected Duto. Shafer wasn't physically fearful. The idea of dying hardly bothered him, though he knew to his core that there was nothing on the other side. How could you fear nothing? How could you fear sleep? He wasn't self-doubting either. He wore his intellect as armor. But more than anything, Shafer was a **critic**. He second-guessed everyone and everything, including his own motives. He considered himself a professional outsider. But he knew his attitude could be viewed as misanthropy, an unwillingness to lower himself into the trenches where everyone else lived.

In his old age, Shafer had grown to see that the world needed men like Duto. Men who grabbed what they wanted. Who weren't afraid to build skyscrapers and cut patients open. If they lost one or two along the way, so be it. And unlike a lot of those guys, Duto was no chicken hawk. He had risked his life to help Wells during their last operation.

Yet Shafer would never trust Duto, much less

like him. Duto was a boss, not a leader. Leaders
risked their own power for the people they had
sworn to serve. Bosses made deals with other
bosses to protect their own interests. Shafer
didn't hate Duto. But at times he hated himself
for helping Duto rise to the most powerful office in the world.

After Duto won the election, Shafer thought
about retiring. Nearly everyone his age—fine,
drop the **nearly**—everyone his age had left the
agency. Even his old buddy Lucy Joyner. But
Shafer was in a unique position. No one could
make him quit. And he couldn't pull the trigger. He told himself he had seen too many guys
leave and six months later drop from heart attacks. He told himself he and his wife liked
northern Virginia. If he quit, they'd have to
move somewhere he wasn't reminded every day
of the job.

The real answer was that he would never tire
of reading the classified traffic, the NSA's intercepts, the cables—still called that, though they
were sent via fiber-optic networks now—from a
hundred different stations. The world's hidden
comedy, as seen through the unblinking eyes of
the United States government. The truth. He
couldn't own it, but he could rent it. No one
had better access than he did. Not even the di-

rector. The director couldn't call a desk officer who handled Tibet and ask about the Dalai Lama's second cousin. Shafer could. Shafer **had**. In part, to prove that he could. The seventh floor let him, the price for keeping him occupied. After a while, people stopped asking why he was asking and just answered his questions. He might be the agency's weird old uncle. But he was a weird old uncle that case officers and analysts ignored at their peril.

So Shafer stayed. The ultimate minister without portfolio. He was in a state of suspended animation. But he knew something would happen sooner or later. It always did.

THE CRITIC-STAMPED traffic started flowing just past 4 p.m. The Islamic State had trapped two SOG operatives near Raqqa. The agency had drones overhead, giving it a real-time view. The SOG commander in Turkey asked the Near East desk head, who was watching from the Langley drone ops center, for permission to send a rescue helicopter.

The desk head kicked the question to the deputy director of operations. Then Shafer knew the operatives were in real trouble. The drone feed must show such overwhelming enemy force that the desk head knew he couldn't risk the copter. He wanted cover to reject the request. Shafer wished he could see the feed at his desk, but even the director had to go to the ops center to see live drone footage.

Shafer was debating whether watching the footage would be voyeuristic, exactly the kind of concern that Duto never had, when another round of cables came through. The operatives were dead. The drones had fired their last Hellfires to vaporize their bodies so that the jihadis couldn't mutilate them. The DDO was calling an emergency meeting at 6:30 in his conference room.

Shafer wasn't invited. He called the DDO's admin, said he'd be there.

FOR LONG STRETCHES of the CIA's checkered history, the deputy director of operations had held more power than the agency's director, his nominal boss. The DCI—or DCIA, as he was now properly known—served at the pleasure of the President. Duto had lasted almost a decade, but the average director survived only three or four years.

Most directors were outsiders who came in with plans to reform the agency, or at least change it. The ones who pushed too hard learned quickly why the CIA, especially the directorate of operations, had earned its reputation for impenetrability. Wise directors forged bonds with their deputies, who were agency lifers.

But weak directors—ones who overreached, or couldn't handle their deputies, or simply had the bad luck to try for changes the agency didn't like—floundered. Only rarely did a director face open rebellion. The dysfunction was more subtle. He didn't receive the information he needed to make good decisions in time. He wasn't given every operational alternative. Case officers followed his orders to the letter rather than the spirit. Ultimately, he was embarrassed before the President and Congress. Sometimes he even faced public humiliation, though the agency played that card less often these days because of the government-wide crackdown on leaking.

A long list of DCIAs and presidents had learned beating Langley at its own game was impossible.

But Duto was in a uniquely strong position. Both internally and externally, he was viewed as the best director in the agency's history. He had led the CIA to success on its most important post–September 11 missions. It had prevented major terrorist attacks on the United States, decimated al-Qaeda, helped kill Osama bin Laden.

Meanwhile, Duto had taken control of the entire intelligence community. He beat back challenges to the agency's primacy on secret operations from the Pentagon. A decade after the mess of rendition, the CIA had more money and power than ever. Since ascending to the White House, Duto had given the agency even more responsibility. He might have moved across the Potomac, but he still had a hammerlock on Langley. Infighting hadn't disappeared, but it had dropped notably. The DCIA, DDO, and section chiefs all played for the same team. Team Duto.

So as Shafer walked into the DDO's conference room for the postmortem, he didn't feel the rancor he had expected. Grim faces all around, of course. But the principals at the table weren't trying to stare one another down. The attitude seemed to be **Let's fix this.**

Of course no one had said a word yet.

The room itself was windowless and utilitarian, gray-painted walls and bare wooden floors. Theoretically, the lack of ornamentation made planting bugs more difficult. No picture frames to hide transmitters. In reality, the seventh floor faced little risk of compromise. These corridors were as heavily guarded as any in the world. Getting inside the White House was easier.

Most other offices up here had wood paneling and shelves filled with junk. This room's lack of ornamentation signaled its seriousness. Successful missions were discussed in the DCIA's conference room. Failures went here.

A space awaited at the table. Instead, Shafer took a seat against the wall, with the aides. "Ellis," the DCIA said, without enthusiasm. He was a twenty-year veteran of the agency named Peter Ludlow. He had helped Shafer and Wells on their previous mission. Shafer knew he'd done so only at Duto's insistence.

Ludlow had cool blue eyes and lank hair he wore parted low on the right. He'd come up through the agency's stations in Beijing and Hong Kong and spoke flawless Cantonese and Mandarin. He had the low-key charm of a good college professor. But he came off as thoughtful rather than tough, and he had been only peripherally involved in the fight against terror that had been the agency's focus since September 11. Conventional wisdom held that Duto had chosen a relatively weak leader as director so that he could rule unchallenged. For once, Shafer agreed with the conventional wisdom.

Four other men and two women sat at the table, but at this meeting only three mattered, all men: Reg Pushkin, the DDO; Vernon

Green, the assistant deputy director for counterterrorism; and Walter Crompond, the head
of the special unit the agency had created to
fight the Islamic State, which was called
Gamma Station.

Pushkin was a big, beefy guy who had the
antiterror experience Ludlow lacked. Under
normal circumstances, he would have eaten
Ludlow alive. But Shafer figured Pushkin had
decided to check his ambition and wait for Duto
to reward him, maybe as the National Security
Advisor.

Green was the highest-ranking black officer
in the agency's history. He had joined at thirty-
five from the Deltas, where he'd been a major,
and risen quickly to the top of the Special Operations Group. He had no experience in conventional espionage. His rise testified to the
agency's focus on counterterror, as well as its
desire to diversify. Green was now almost fifty.
He might have a hard time becoming director,
considering his lack of experience outside special operations. But if Duto wanted to make
history by appointing the first African-American director, Green would be the guy. He was
lean and dark-skinned, with deep-brown eyes.

Crompond's relatively junior title hid his importance. He had been the number two in

counterterror until a couple of years before, when he moved to Gamma Station. Crompond had a calm, unlined face that made him seen too young for the responsibility he shouldered. He'd gone to Princeton, an unusual pedigree these days. By all accounts he was a hard worker, smart, and devoted to the job.

Pushkin tapped on the table to start the meeting.

"A quick recap. Twenty-three fifty local time, two SOG operatives and two locals arrived at an exfil site outside Raqqa. They crossed on horse from Turkey yesterday afternoon, slept near a Kurdish-controlled village, rode the rest of the way today. Kareem Batta and William Girol. Maybe our best guys in Turkey."

If Shafer hadn't already known they were dead, the praise would have told him.

"The night before, they ran into a pickup truck with six smugglers. They handled the situation, all six red team KIA. After consulting with the SOG chief in Turkey this afternoon, Batta chose to move forward with the mission."

"We don't know if that incident was related to what happened tonight, correct?" Ludlow said.

"Yes, Director." If the interruption bothered Pushkin, he hid his impatience. "We had two drones overwatching them tonight. As they reached the site, the drones spotted a truck. It passed and their exfil arrived shortly thereafter on a bicycle. I'll let you see for yourself what happened next. It's less than five minutes."

Pushkin clicked on the screen and an aerial feed came up. In CIA jargon, it was **processed** rather than **time-of-event**, or live. Thus, it could be viewed outside the drone room. The new drones had high-definition 4K cameras, and the night had been clear. Even from four hundred feet up, the video was good enough to distinguish faces.

Which didn't make what followed any easier to watch. Especially near the end, when Batta put his hand to his mouth, spasmed, and went limp, his lips pulled back from his teeth in an unnatural grin. "We've offered L-pills to everyone who operates inside IS territory since 2014," Pushkin said. Girol took the other way out, putting a pistol between his lips and pulling the trigger.

When the video finally ended, the room was silent. Losing your own guys was terrible. Losing them on a mission that someone had betrayed and doomed was worse. Two more stars on the lobby wall, the stars that stood for the deaths of CIA officers. There'd be a ceremony.

Someone would make a speech about courage and valor. Batta and Girol would still be dead.

"No question the bad guys knew," Pushkin said. "The sniper nests were dug in so deep they didn't give the drones a heat sig. And they had at least fifty guys in the compound at the end of that road. They weren't taking chances."

Green leaned in. "Who was the exfil? And how did we find him?"

"Nazir al-Habbaya," Crompond said. "Senior guy in their oil finance department. And he found us. As you know, we have no American assets on the ground there. We handle everything electronically via local contacts."

"Not an ideal situation," Ludlow said.

These flat statements were high on Shafer's list of pet peeves. Why did people in charge sum up what everyone already knew? **Four aces beats three threes. Taxis are hard to find in the rain.** They must have all gone to the same management seminar.

"Eighteen months ago, Nazir offered to pass us information about IS oil-smuggling routes. We were wary, but everything he gave us was gold. I would say we viewed him as our top asset inside IS. Hard to say no when he asked for an exfil."

"We sure he's the guy we just saw?" Shafer asked.

"Good question. The guy on the video matches the photo we have, but we never actually met him," Crompond said. "We've pulled the wire for our connect. So far, nothing from him either."

Meaning that the Islamic State might have killed the middleman, too. The icing on the cow pie cake.

"Obviously, Daesh may have discovered Nazir, made him ask for an exfil," Crompond said. "Could also be the smugglers who brought our guys in. Two Syrian brothers. During the firefight, the drones were focused on Batta and Girol. When we looked again, the horses were there, but the brothers were gone. They may have gone to ground in those groves to the west."

"Or sold our guys to IS for a million bucks," Pushkin said.

"We worked with them before, paid them well, and their family has lost men to IS."

"What about the MIT?" Ludlow said.

The letters referred not to the university but to the Turkish intelligence service, the Milli 'Istihbarat Tes,kilati. Just as the Pakistani intelligence agency helped the Taliban, the MIT aided the Islamic State. Twenty million Kurds lived in Turkey, Iraq, and Iran. They hoped to carve out their own nation. Turkey saw a breakaway Kurdistan as a greater threat than the Islamic State. But the Kurds were a staunch American ally. Turkey didn't want to oppose the United States openly. So the MIT played both sides, letting the United States attack the Islamic State from bases in Turkey while passing it money and intelligence.

"What about them?" Crompond said. "We told them we had something going this week, nothing specific. But they know where the SOG base is. I mean, it was a training site for their cops, they **gave** it to us. If they wanted to play dirty, they could have tipped IS when our guys headed out. But it's one thing for Turkey to tell IS, **Postpone that meeting you have tomorrow if you don't want it bombed**. Getting our guys killed, that's different. And one more thing. It's like IS wanted us to know they had advance warning. They could have made a more subtle move, picked up Batta and Girol at a checkpoint. This is broadcasting. You have a leak."

"We've had other close calls, too," Pushkin said. "That thing by Homs. And the one in Aleppo."

Shafer would have to look up the thing by Homs. And the one in Aleppo. They'd snuck by him. Probably he'd been catching up on Ukraine or China or the Kashmir. The downside of being a one-man band. He had a long night ahead.

"We need to look at the MIT," Ludlow said. "And I'm gonna warn DoD about telling the Turks too much. And suspend any deep ops in Syria."

"What Daesh wants," Crompond said. "When we're finally making progress."

"That what you'd call today? I'm not sending guys to get hunted down for sport."

Shafer could read Crompond's mind: **Ludlow's done his recruiting at embassy parties, doesn't know real fieldwork has risks.**

"Director—" Crompond caught himself before he went too far. Reg Green kept a studiously neutral expression.

"Right," Pushkin said. "As of now, no overnights in Syria. Walter, the commander over there, Durette, I want him on a flight back here tomorrow."

Reasonable moves. Though they'd missed one possibility, Shafer thought. The most important. He waited for someone to mention it. No one did.

"Shouldn't we consider one other potential pool of suspects?" Shafer said. "Us."

They all looked at Shafer as if he'd let out a world-record fart. Even now, past seventy, he loved provoking that reaction.

"**Us**, as in this room?" Ludlow said. "A blue badge"—the color worn by CIA employees—"passing information to the Islamic State. For money, Ellis?"

"Could be." Though money was rarely the only driver. The counterintelligence acronym MICE stood for money, ideology, compromise—or blackmail—and ego. The four main reasons that people betrayed their countries. "When we find him, we'll ask."

"You can't think an American would help them," Crompond said.

"Aldrich Ames." Ames had betrayed the agency to the Soviet Union, causing the deaths of dozens of Russian agents.

"Daesh makes the USSR look like Santa's workshop."

"Those ten million peasants Stalin starved might disagree. Listen, I'm just saying smart detectives look at opportunity first, motive second. And if we look at who had the best opportunity to betray these ops, it's not the MIT and it's not smugglers. It's us."

"You want to chase this, be my guest." What Ludlow really meant was **I can't stop you**, as Shafer knew. "Do me a favor and find some actual evidence before you embarrass anyone." Ludlow stood. "Excuse me for not indulging this, but I need to call the families."

He walked out. The others followed, until only Shafer and Green were left. Shafer couldn't escape the feeling that Green had taken his time so they would be the last two in the room.

"Never learned that trick, Major."

"What's that?"

"Keeping your own counsel."

Green didn't answer, proving Shafer's point.

"What do you think of my theory?"

"I think you're right, guessing at motive is a dangerous business. You can know everything about a man but what goes on in his head."

Green winked. And walked out, leaving Shafer alone, wondering what he'd meant.

4

ALEXANDRIA, VIRGINIA

HE looked in the mirror. The traitor looked back.
Traitor.
He'd say it. Why not? What exactly was he betraying? A country whose people could not have misunderstood themselves more. They imagined they were hardy, God-fearing pioneers. In truth, they were so desperate to self-medicate that, with five percent of the world's population, they used three-quarters of the prescription opiates. They excused every poisonous choice by bleating about the nobility of their motives. They pretended to want peace but went to war more than any other nation.

In the last fifty years, how many countries had the United States attacked? The man who called himself Wayne could hardly remember them all: Vietnam, Cambodia, Panama, Serbia,

Afghanistan, Iraq . . . That didn't count the meddling in Latin America . . . The drones that killed at random over Pakistan . . . The idiocy of the endless war on drugs that had made Mexico a graveyard . . .

The United States spread pain all over the world and expected love in return.

The place he worked lay at the center of the madness. The bull's-eye, the beating heart. The secret chamber in the center of the pyramid where the priests claimed they found the answer to every mystery. No one noticed that they always offered the same solution. Buy off anyone who was for sale. Kill the rest. Do it all on no-bid contracts, the better to fleece the tax-paying sheep. God bless America.

Once, he might have gone to **The Washington Post** or **The New York Times**, told them the truth. How the agency wasted billions. How it held innocent detainees in Guantánamo because the White House was too embarrassed to free them. How its drone pilots didn't even pretend to know their targets. But going public would make no difference. Even if he sent the raw files to Wikileaks or The Intercept so the world could see for itself, nothing would happen. The agency never held itself accountable. Congress and the White House feared it too much to try. Even the idiot psychologists who'd crafted the torture program after September 11 remained untouched. Forget criminal charges. They hadn't had to pay back a penny of the eighty million dollars—yes, **eighty million dollars**—they'd received.

Besides, the White House and Justice Department treated whistle-blowers like traitors these days. If they caught him leaking, he'd spend his life in jail. Why not go all the way?

HIS NAME wasn't Wayne, of course. He called himself that in homage to a man whose legend came from a lifetime of two-hour lies. A man who pretended to be a soldier but had claimed a shoulder injury to duck out of World War II. A man who at the height of the horror of Vietnam made a movie defending that war. **The Green Berets.** The film famously ended with a scene of Wayne walking hand in hand down a beach with an orphaned Vietnamese boy—as the sun set in the east.

John Wayne, the ultimate American hero.

The traitor was almost embarrassed when he remembered his enthusiasm after September 11. He'd volunteered to be in the first wave of officers going to Afghanistan. Even then he'd had some idea of the sorry history of Americans abroad. His father's brother had died in Vietnam, an ambush near Da Nang, three months into his tour.

But this time was different. This time, **they** attacked **us**. They needed to pay.

He never did catch Osama bin Laden. Instead, he wound up in Iraq. The first tour, in the fall of '03, the operatives all pretended to be badasses. They rattled around in convoys of white SUVs with antennas sticking off the roofs. Might as well have had cia painted on the sides. For security, they had Blackwater guards carrying souped-up subbies and automatic shotguns. The private military bros did love their gear.

No matter, the country hadn't blown apart yet. They screamed down to Najaf to meet with the Shia militias, went to talk to the sheikhs in Ramadi. Everyone told them that they were sitting on a cauldron. Saddam had been a nasty dictator. But he'd kept the streets safe. Now the Iraqi Army was gone. The police didn't leave their buildings. Ordinary people lined up for hours for basic supplies. Week by week, political and criminal violence was rising, the country inching toward chaos. The Shia saw the power vacuum as a sign that the United States wanted them to settle scores with Saddam's

Sunni Ba'athists. But the Sunni didn't plan to roll over and die. They were organizing their own militias and terror groups.

All that fall, Wayne went back to the Green Zone and filed reports. His bosses rewrote them to erase ninety percent of the truth. The idiots at the Coalition Provisional Authority, the White House appointees who supposedly ran the country, ignored what was left.

BACK IN IRAQ in '05, he found that everything the sheikhs had predicted had come to pass. The country was a walking, talking slaughterhouse. The agency's senior officers were cutting their losses. They worried about the optics back home if their operatives were strung up from light posts. Wayne barely left the Green Zone, except to travel to a few streets in central Baghdad where Shia leaders had fortified compounds. He grew to hate those men, Ahmed Chalabi most of all. Chalabi had helped cook the invasion, expecting the United States would put him in power. Now he was too afraid of being assassinated to leave his concrete walls.

But the United States enabled Chalabi. The agency, the State Department, and the military all pretended to take him seriously. Wayne sat in endless meetings where Chalabi promised to

improve governance and **reach across sectarian lines** and **rebuild democratic institutions.** Everyone knew all he wanted was to grab the Oil Ministry. Meanwhile, car bombs went off in Baghdad twenty or thirty times a week. Sunni and Shia killed one another in an endless cycle, dumping corpses in the Tigris. Gangs kidnapped children walking to school. Ordinary Iraqis blamed the United States for the chaos and joined the jihadis who had come to Iraq to kill American soldiers.

Wayne couldn't understand why no one told the truth, told Chalabi, **Everything you tell us is a lie. Every change you suggest makes matters worse. President? You're lucky we don't arrest you. Go to Teheran, where you belong.** Only later did he realize the pressure the White House had put on the agency to stick with Chalabi. Even after two years of chaos, the President and his men couldn't admit the truth. They let thousands of Americans and tens of thousands of Iraqis die instead.

HE CAME BACK for his final tour two years later, the spring of 2007. The reality on the ground had become so terrible that the United States had only two choices, leave in defeat or double down by sending enough soldiers to bring order to Baghdad. It doubled down. The shift became known as "the surge."

When historians told the story of the Iraq war, they called the surge a triumph. But Wayne saw its ugliness up close. The CIA played its own part, funneling cash to Sunni tribes and Shia militias, trying to stop them from killing one another—and focus on killing foreign jihadis instead. Paying for murder, more or less.

He was a few weeks into the tour when he met Jane.

Even now, he couldn't say for sure how real the feeling had been, whether it would have survived the trip home. War heightened all the senses, and what was love if not the inflammation of taste and touch and sight?

But it had felt real, more mad and real than anything else in his life. She was a black-haired Irish girl, painfully thin, the skin tight over her jaw, like she'd stepped out of a Depression photograph. A journalist. He first saw her at a Green Zone press briefing. On slow days he'd developed the bad habit of sneaking into the last row to watch the public affairs officers spin. The worst lies came not from the military but from State, which had the wretched job of pretending the Iraqis were working toward a real government.

She sat near the back, too, a row or two in front of him. She took notes but never asked questions. Soon he realized he was watching her more than the people at the podium, watching her reactions to their most outrageous lies. Her face never changed, but she sat up straighter, arched her shoulders, lifted her long, skinny neck. He fell for her neck first.

Finding her in the database was easy enough. Jane O'Connor, a reporter for **The Washington Post**.

He started finding excuses to come to the briefings every day. Then she disappeared. For two weeks, she didn't show up. He pretended to himself he wasn't disappointed until the day she came back.

That afternoon, she sat next to him. She smelled of sweat and coffee. Her hands shook a little.

"Mr. Back Row. Or do you have a name?"

He shrugged.

"Oh, come on. I can't figure out why you're here. You're not a reporter."

"Nope."

"Yet you put yourself through this nonsense. Sit back here scowling like a guy who just stepped in dogshit. In brand-new heels."

"I only wear heels to the prom."

She lifted her identification badge. "Unlike you, I have a name. Jane O'Connor. **Washington Post.**"

"Nice to meet you, Jane."

"Give me something."

"I could tell you, but I'd have to kill you." He knew he'd already said too much. Knew and didn't care.

She took his hand, held it a beat, finally let it go. "What exactly are you doing here, then? Information operations?"

"I just like to know how the war is going."

She hid her mouth behind her hand and turned to him and grinned, her smile wide and beautiful.

They sat for a while listening to the Air Force colonel who had the job of relaying casualty reports. Three dead in western Baghdad from indirect fire, one at Camp Victory of non-combat-related injuries, a phrase that could mean anything from suicide to heart attack to a traffic accident. The military kept casualty information as vague as possible. Obscuring the details made the deaths less likely to be reported in-depth back home.

"I hate this war," she said under her breath.

He barely stopped himself from agreeing.

She looked at him, her black eyes demanding an answer: **Which side are you on?**

"Talk to me."

"Why on earth would I do that?"

"You're sitting here waiting for someone to ask."

"All journalists read minds, or just you?"

She gathered her stuff, stood to leave.

"Wait." He took her notebook, scribbled his name and number. "If you have questions, specific questions, I'll try to answer." He didn't know if he'd made the offer because she was beautiful—though she wasn't beautiful, not exactly—or because she'd challenged him so directly. He only knew that he couldn't disappoint her.

They didn't see each other much. The **Post** had a fortified house near the Green Zone where its reporters lived and worked. She split her time between street reporting, military embeds, and the Zone. But they could hardly hang out in the Zone; inquiring minds would notice. Meeting outside was even more impossible. So they fell in love like teenagers with overbearing parents, over the phone and email.

He crossed the line first, alone in his office, working late, just a week after they spoke for the first time. A careful instant message. **It** must be hard for your boyfriend, knowing you're here, worrying about you every minute and every hour . . . Heck, I worry about you and I hardly even know you.

Maybe you know me better than you think.

All at once, he wanted to hear her voice. It was nearly midnight. He had no excuse. But he couldn't help himself. So he pulled out his private phone—no sense in letting the agency know about this call—and did.

Within days, they dropped any pretense of a normal source–reporter relationship. She confessed how she had to take Valium before every embed, how she feared she'd panic if they came under fire and get or the soldiers around her killed. He told her that he wished he could ride with her, that being stuck inside the Green Zone made him feel cowardly and a liar. They talked every night, and when they ran out of words, he listened to her breathe.

"What are you thinking?"

"Wishing you were here with me. Lying with me."

"Tell me."

"Tell you what?"

"You know what."

Nothing, and he feared he'd pushed too far. Then: "My bureau chief sleeps next door."

"I don't care. I want to hear you. Please."

And she did. So he heard her whispered or-gasm before he'd ever kissed her. When he hung up, he told himself it wasn't an affair, not really. But he knew he was lying. The rule was simple: Can you tell your wife? Would she be okay if she knew?

Yeah, not so much.

He spent the next month trying to find a way for them to meet. He'd long since stopped wor-rying she was using him for information. She discouraged him from telling her anything clas-sified. I don't want you to think that's what this is about, she said.

You're not a very good reporter.

And finally, at the beginning of June, the agency's deputy director of operations flew from Virginia to Camp Victory for a one-day flash briefing. Wayne claimed a case of dining hall flu and stayed in his trailer, knowing he'd be alone for once. No one would want to miss the chance for face time with the DDO.

He feared they'd be disappointed, their bod-ies wouldn't match the tales they'd told. But he was wrong. The afternoon turned out as close to perfect as he could have imagined. Somehow, they managed both the trembling expectation of first-time lovers and the intimacy of a couple that had been together for years. When she left, he didn't feel guilty. Instead, for the first time he opened his email and tried to figure out how to break the news to his wife.

TWO DAYS LATER, a fine Thursday, one hundred five degrees at 11 a.m., Wayne flew to a Shia militia camp south of Baghdad. He was delivering a paper bag that held one hundred fifty thousand dollars to a sad-eyed Shia militia commander named Bassim. Bassim's men had handed a dozen Egyptian jihadis to the agency the week before. Twelve thousand five hundred per foreign fighter was the going rate. Considering the damage that a single suicide bomber could cause, the agency was getting a bargain.

A couple hundred feet from the tattered fencing that marked the camp's boundary, he saw a field full of what looked like oversized matches.

Hold on, come around, he told the pilot.

From a hundred feet up, he saw the rows of corpses. The men's arms were tied behind their backs. They'd been shot in the back of the head, neat and clean. That morning, maybe, since Wayne didn't see much bloating. Two men walked up and down the rows, nudging bodies to make sure no one was moving. They wore scarves over their mouths and black gloves despite the heat and stepped as casually as old men out for a morning constitutional. Wayne counted eight rows, twelve to fifteen men each. A hundred men, give or take.

Seen enough? The pilot turned the helicopter away without waiting for an answer.

Bassim ran the camp from a trailer that had once belonged to the State Department and still had Washington Redskins bumper stickers on its walls. After some awkward small talk, Wayne handed over the paper bag. Bassim made a show of not counting it before stuffing it under his desk. "Next time, I want to give you a tour, show you my men. Good soldiers."

"I'm sure they're excellent." **Especially at shooting unarmed prisoners.** "Before I leave"— Wayne decided he had to ask—"the bodies in that field north of camp . . . ?"

Wayne expected Bassim would deny knowing anything about the field, deny the bodies were dead, deny they existed at all. Three tours had taught Wayne that Iraqis happily told the most outrageous lies imaginable.

Bassim simply nodded. "We killed them. This morning." He pointed a finger pistol at Wayne, pretended to squeeze the trigger three times. "Three I did myself."

"Them?"

"A village ten km northeast, forty houses. All one tribe, cousins."

"Sunni."

Bassim blinked at the stupidity of the question. **Of course Sunni.** "They make trouble for a long time, bombs on the Karbala road. It's our land all around them. We warned them since February, told them to leave. Finally, we took care of it."

"They were soldiers?"

Another blink. Another question too stupid to answer. Wayne wondered what Bassim planned to do with the bodies. In this heat, they would be a health hazard in hours. He decided he didn't want to know.

One question left, and this one he did have to ask. "What about the wives, the children?"

"They go to Fallujah, where they belong."

In other words, Bassim had made a landgrab. He was trying to make the district purely Shia. Before the American invasion, Baghdad and the villages around it had held mixed Sunni-Shia populations. Now the Shia majority was pushing the Sunni west and north. Ultimately, the Shia were preparing for a possible split of Iraq. The Sunni hated the idea because their lands lacked oil. But the Shia had the numbers. The United States could hardly complain. Even with

the surge, it barely had enough soldiers to re-
store order to Baghdad. It needed militias like
Bassim's.

"Want to see them?" Bassim said now. Forcing the issue, showing Wayne he knew the score.

"You pick up anybody else we might want,
you let us know."

"The same price?"

"Sure."

"The skinny ones, too?"

**Funny man. Please don't tell me you've been
starving prisoners.** "Even the skinny ones." The
CIA was paying a mass murderer. **He** was paying a mass murderer. What did that make him?
To distract himself from the question, he asked
another. "Do you think it's working?"

"What's that?"

"The surge."

"Oh yes."

As soon as he stepped off the helicopter in
Baghdad, he called Jane. He didn't care whether
telling her what he'd seen would ruin his career,
or even land him in prison. Let her have the
story. Let the world have it.

She didn't answer. Weird. She always answered. She wasn't at the briefing either, though
she'd told him the night before she planned

to go, after a morning embed in Sadr City. He called her again. Still nothing.

He heard that night. She'd been on her way to the embed when her driver happened across a half-dozen Humvees on a routine patrol. The unit was part of the Second Brigade, Third Infantry Division, which had rotated in only a few days before. Fresh and scared and trigger-happy.

Jane's driver had panicked, refused to yield, tried to speed by. So the patrol's commander insisted. Maybe. More likely, the kid on the .50-cal. hadn't given him the chance.

Two seconds and thirty rounds later, Jane and the driver were dead.

"What she gets for trying to cover this damn war," the deputy chief of station said.

Wayne felt every cell in his body fissure. Then he was back together. Like he'd been teleported to the end of the universe and sent back a moment later. The same person, but no more.

Worst of all, no one at the station noticed. He'd kept his secret well. Too well. He could barely acknowledge her death, much less mourn it. He made one change, only one. He deleted the half-finished email to his wife. All the guilt he hadn't felt before swept him now, remorse for cheating and for Jane's death both.

He knew that it would destroy him if he tried to face it, so he didn't. He refused to think about Jane, what they were, what they could have been. He spent the last five months of his tour raising his hand for every possible mission, the more dangerous, the better. He was trying to die, so of course he survived.

BACK HOME, he read all the books he should have read before, especially histories of the Vietnam war like **A Bright Shining Lie**. For the rest of his life he would refuse to give himself the solace of honest sorrow, or even to acknowledge what he'd lost. Instead, he drowned himself in a concrete wave of cynicism.

EVERY COUNTRY made mistakes, of course. But Vietnam was worse than a mistake. The United States had nearly destroyed another nation for no other reason than Lyndon Johnson's ego. For no other reason than that it could. A generation later, the war looked even worse. When it ended, Vietnam was in ruins. Now the Vietnamese had a peaceful society, a fast-growing economy. Amazingly enough, even in the north, ordinary Vietnamese expressed few hard feelings toward the United States. If the circumstances were reversed, Wayne doubted Americans would be so forgiving.

The Iraq invasion was even more unforgivable. At least the war in Vietnam was part of a global conflict between the United States and the Soviet Union. America had attacked Iraq even though no one seriously believed that Saddam Hussein had anything to do with September 11. Hussein's preferred religion was pan-Arab nationalism, not Islam. In fact, the invasion had distracted the United States from its real enemy, al-Qaeda.

Worst of all, the United States didn't need to guess at the dangers of occupying a country whose people spoke a different language and practiced a different religion. It had already been through Vietnam. Wayne began to wonder if the guys who handed out ink-stained pamphlets on the street were the only people telling the truth. Maybe Blackwater and Halliburton really were pulling the strings. Because who else benefited from these endless wars?

He thought about walking away from the agency. He could have gotten another job. But it would have been with a corporate profiteer. They were the ones who hired guys like him. Anyway, despite everything, he entertained the illusion that maybe a new president would force Langley into a new way of doing business. Maybe he could help change it from the inside, honor the memories he wouldn't let himself have.

But Obama or Bush, Guantánamo stayed open. The National Security Agency kept up its illegal spying. Obama left Iraq but ramped up in Afghanistan, a move that might have made sense in 2003 but had no chance in 2009. Everyone at Langley knew Hamid Karzai was even more corrupt than the politicians in Baghdad. Everyone knew Afghanistan, a country whose tribal leaders regularly accepted **children** as payment for debts, was as unfixable as a society could be. Once again, the beneficiaries were the contractors who kept the Afghan war machine humming. And the trauma surgeons, the ones who could practice sewing up soldiers who lost their legs and arms.

The final straw came for Wayne in 2012 and 2013. Iraq went back down the tubes and Syria spiraled out of control. Bush was too busy invading Iraq to fix Afghanistan when he had a chance. Then Obama focused on Afghanistan while Syria and Iraq burned. Wayne didn't know whether to laugh or cry. When it came to America's wars, history didn't just repeat. It looped without end, a Möbius strip. Only the faces of the dead changed.

He knew exactly when he first thought of betraying the United States. In 2014, the Seahawks and Broncos played Super Bowl 48—XLVIII, in the idiotic Roman numerals that the National Football League prefers—in New Jersey. For weeks, the radio hosts talked about how tough the fans would have to be to survive a February snowstorm.

Meanwhile, Wayne was reading the cables and seeing the photos from Syria. Assad's helicopters dropped bombs on schools as the United States did nothing. A new group called the Islamic State sold women and girls into slavery. A country was dying, and people here were talking about the **courage** to watch a football game. Jane would have laughed.

Wayne couldn't tell anyone how he felt. Every morning, he felt a little more alone. His parents were gone. His father had died thirty years before of an alcohol-rotted liver. His mother had died of lung cancer in 2000. Wayne remembered her happily puffing on Virginia Slims. Mass-marketed death, another great American tradition. His wife . . . his wife was a good woman. An elementary school teacher. A loving mother. Pretty to boot. Celebrity gossip magazines were her biggest vice. **Is Jennifer Aniston finally pregnant?** (Even Wayne knew the answer to that one: No!) He'd chosen to marry someone who wasn't in his world, someone who would make him leave the darkness at the office. Too late, he realized he could no more leave the darkness at the office than keep the sun from setting. What would he tell her? **Honey, I want to burn it down. All of it. By the way, what's for dinner?** He should have divorced her after that third tour in Iraq, but Jane's death had somehow stopped him and now he couldn't. The prison might be all his own, but it had trapped him nonetheless.

He tried a couple of times to see if his friends at the agency shared his feelings. Always carefully, always over drinks that for him were more water than whiskey. They mostly complained that the ops rules were too strict, that the White House and Pentagon weren't doing enough.

"Maybe we're mistaking what we can do for what we **should** do."

"You want those throat slitters to win?" his best friend said. "Obviously, the invasion was a mistake, but there's no instant replay. We are where we are."

"Okay, but where are we going to be in five years?"

"Five years? You want me to guess five years ahead? IS barely existed five years ago."

"Exactly."

"Whoever's on deck can't be as bad as these guys. Take care of them, deal with the next problem next."

He stopped trying to talk to his friends.

Who, then? A shrink? He couldn't imagine unveiling his secrets to a little man in a sweater-vest and glasses. A pastor? His faith, never strong, had died as he watched Shia and Sunni butcher one another. He hoped for humanity's sake that God didn't exist, because if He did, most of the world was stuck on the downbound train.

He thought about killing himself, a single shot, quick and clean. But suicide was the coward's answer. Besides, he loved his kids. He loved his wife, too, though keeping his anger from her sometimes made him feel like he was having another affair, hiding his most important thoughts from the person meant to be his soul mate. Could he love **hate**? Could he cheat on his wife with it?

I can't do it anymore, he told himself every day as he walked through the lobby at Langley. Yet he did. Despite his torment, he rose, became a star. His success amazed him, until he understood that hate drove it. Hate stripped away his illusions, gave him the strength to ignore the petty jealousies that sucked energy from other officers. Hate made him relentless and focused, a comic-book power he wouldn't have believed if he hadn't lived it.

"I'm so excited for you," his wife said when he told her about his newest job. She was, too. She reveled in his promotions, and not because they meant more Beltway prestige. She wanted him to succeed. Not for the first time, he wondered what she would do if he told her the truth of how he felt.

But he couldn't. He wanted her to have her illusions. His sins shouldn't blemish her.

So HE decided to **act**. Betray his country. Give aid and comfort to the Islamic State. The choice wasn't as irrational as it seemed at first. Despite what the politicians said, the jihadis were hardly an existential threat to the United States. They had no air force, no nuclear weapons. They were noisy and nasty, but Vladimir Putin was more dangerous.

At the same time, the jihadis posed a very real threat to his fellow agency operatives. The Russians and Chinese weren't in the business of killing CIA officers. They would use what

Wayne gave them against their own people, bureaucrats who had let themselves be recruited as American spies. Wayne wanted the punishment he delivered to fall on the CIA itself. On the United States. The Islamic State would be happy to oblige.

Plus, as horribly as the Islamic State behaved, it had sprung up in response to the real threats the Sunni faced. In Iraq, the Shia majority had suspended its war of revenge against the Sunni only until the United States left. Ultimately, they had given the local tribes no choice but to rely on foreign jihadis for help. In Syria, the Sunni faced an equally deadly opponent in Bashar al-Assad.

All this brutality ultimately flowed out of the American invasion of Iraq. The United States was to blame.

So what was the solution? Of course the warmongers wanted yet another invasion. But what if the United States backed off, for once? Let the Islamic State **alone**? Maybe the jihadis would settle into a Taliban-type regime, brutal to outsiders but tolerated by the people they ruled.

Everyone at the agency would call him a fool if he dared to mention that prospect. They would remind him the Talibs had let bin Laden plan September 11 from Afghan soil. They would say the West had no choice but to eradicate the regime. But Wayne thought it was time—past time—for a different strategy.

The more Wayne considered the plan, the more it made sense. It would punish the right people—his fellow officers—for the right reasons. Further, his job gave him unlimited access to both CIA and Pentagon operations in Syria and Iraq. Best of all, no one would suspect him. The agency would never believe that a senior officer would betray it to the jihadis.

HE QUICKLY realized the flip side of being above suspicion: the Islamic State wouldn't believe him either. He faced the practical problem of how to pass information. The Islamic State didn't have intelligence officers in Washington. It recruited almost entirely online. Wayne could hardly set up a Twitter account with the handle @ciaforjihad.

He needed someone who quietly supported the jihadis and would work as a go-between. He focused on the dozen or so lawyers and imams who popped up whenever the United States charged Muslims with supporting the Islamic State. One, a prominent local imam, lived in Virginia. Wayne checked to make sure the

FBI wasn't actively monitoring the man. Then he called. He introduced himself as Wayne Smith, kept his pitch vague. "I work for the federal government on issues of interest."

"Issues of interest?"

"Better to explain face-to-face."

The imam agreed to meet at his mosque.

Wayne arrived to find the man walking on a treadmill in his office, watching a DVD of a sermon given at a giant mosque. Tens of thousands of men prostrated themselves in unison. The imam stepped off the treadmill as the video continued to play.

"Do you know Arabic?" He was in his fifties, a handsome brown-skinned man, with deep-brown eyes and a round belly that the treadmill hadn't touched.

"A little." Wayne had picked up basic phrases in Iraq, but nothing more. "Not this."

"He's speaking of the necessity for brotherhood."

"Why I'm here."

"Let me wash my face. I'll be back in a minute."

One minute became five, and then fifteen, as the video continued to play. Wayne wondered if the imam was watching him on a hidden camera, waiting to see if he would be stupid enough to rifle through the office. Hardcovers in Arabic and English filled two walls of shelves. The imam seemed particularly interested in nineteenth-century European history.

He returned a half hour later, freshly showered and wearing a suit. "I was going to let you wait all day, but I need my office back. I fear you've wasted your time, Mr. Smith." His English was precise and cultured.

"You don't even know what I want."

"Let me guess. You're with the FBI. You seek my cooperation in the fight against terror." He put a sarcastic emphasis on **seek** and **cooperation**. "Please, go now."

"You misunderstand."

"I don't think I do. Would you do this to a rabbi? A loyalty oath."

Loyalty oath. Oh, the irony. Wayne realized he was going to have to reveal more than he wanted, and sooner. "My name isn't Wayne Smith. And I've come because I can help you. Not the other way around."

The imam folded his arms over his chest, stared at Wayne. "I'm afraid I am confused."

"For a man in your position, a true believer, these meetings must be frustrating."

"Belief in Allah isn't a crime."

"We always ask. Never tell."

"You want to change that?"

Wayne gave him a single, grave nod, knowing they'd reached the crux. If the imam didn't have the connections Wayne needed or if he was too nervous to move ahead, fearing a sting, he would throw Wayne out now. Instead, the imam went silent again, looking at cards Wayne couldn't see. **In the tank**, as poker players said. And Wayne knew he had a chance.

A minute passed. More. Behind the imam, the prayer service went on and on.

"What would you like in return?"

Wayne shook his head.

"Nothing. I see. A generous man. Shall I ask your reasons?"

"They're my own."

"You are a believer."

Another shake.

"What would I do with this information?"

"Whatever you like."

The imam pursed his lips like he was tasting an exotic new food for the first time and couldn't decide whether he liked it. **Sweetbreads? Tell me again what those are?**

"What's your real name, Mr. Smith? Who do you work for?"

"For now, better for both of us if you don't know. It's what I have for you that matters—"

The imam's face tightened.

"This is the clumsiest sting operation the FBI has ever tried on me. And it's tried a few. Whoever you are, I don't believe you have what you say. Why would I believe you? You won't even tell me your name. You say the information is what matters? Fine. Now go. **Now.** Before I call the police."

The rejection was so humiliating that Wayne felt the imam had actually slapped him. He forced himself to his feet and pushed his way out.

ONLY IN the parking lot did Wayne see what the imam had done. He had played his hand perfectly. He hadn't explicitly encouraged Wayne in any way. He hadn't done anything obvious like patting Wayne down for a wire. He had protected himself. But he'd given the green light, nonetheless, with those final words. **You say the information is what matters? Fine.**

Maybe.

Or maybe Wayne was deluding himself. Maybe he was about to take the insane risk of handing over Top Secret/Sensitive Compartmentalized Information to someone who had said he didn't want it. Who wouldn't know what to do with it. Or worse, who would take it straight to the FBI. No matter that the imam didn't know his name. The mosque had surveillance cameras all over.

For two weeks, he mentally replayed the conversation. He wished he could talk to the imam again, but the man would kick him to the door even faster this time. He'd had his chance.

In the end, more because of the way the imam had looked at him than anything he'd said, Wayne jumped.

He mailed the mosque a thumb drive that held a single document: a spreadsheet with the names of four Islamic State commanders on the CIA drone kill list. More important, everything the agency knew about them. Their aliases, their addresses, their cars, the mobile phone numbers and email addresses the NSA had linked to them. He had chosen information too valuable for anyone to risk giving up in a sting. And the men who eventually received it would know it was real and accurate.

The days that followed were the longest of his life. He'd given the imam no way to reach him. He had nothing to do but wait. Each night he wondered whether he would wake to a pre-dawn knock on his front door, a dozen FBI agents standing outside. He hid his tension from his wife, except in bed, where he couldn't contain himself. Have you been taking something? she said to him. You haven't been like this in a long time. Since before the kids.

You don't like it?

Can't you tell I do? I'm surprised, that's all. It's like you're a new man.

The FBI never knocked. And eleven days after he posted that envelope, the NSA reported that four IS commanders had vanished, their phones and email addresses gone dark. Eureka. What Wayne felt more than anything was not triumph but relief, relief that he had finally given his hate an outlet.

WAYNE LET another week pass before he called the imam. "It's Wayne Smith."

"Mr. Smith. If you're still seeking spiritual guidance, mornings are best."

"Seven tomorrow, then?" The idea of having this meeting on his way to Langley thrilled him.

"As you wish."

Wayne wondered if the imam would move the meeting to a basement or a park, a place that would make surveillance more difficult. Instead, they met once again in the office. The imam seemed to have decided to pretend nothing unusual was happening. "Nice to see you again. Coffee?" He nodded at the Dunkin' Donuts Box O' Joe on his desk.

Couldn't even save me a donut, fat man. Wayne poured himself a cup.

"To give you spiritual advice, I need your name, your real name. And your job."

Wayne knew he'd passed the point of no return when he mailed the drive, but revealing himself made the betrayal fresh. The words stuck in his throat until he forced them out in an asthmatic wheeze.

The imam regarded him almost kindly. "A very senior position. That must be stressful for you."

Now that he'd exposed himself, Wayne wanted to cut to the point. He made himself remember that the imam was deliberately blowing smoke, protecting himself. No one could prove he'd ever received the thumb drive, much less passed on its information. He would avoid specifics as long as he could.

"At times. I was hoping you could help me, give me questions to answer."

"I can do that. I think we should meet regularly."

"Because of the sensitivities of meeting someone like you, I may need my bosses to know." Wayne finding the elliptical rhythm now. "They'll be happy to have us talk." Indeed, the agency would be thrilled he was cultivating this man, who might know of American supporters of the Islamic State.

"Your business."

"Yes, but I'll need a cover story, and you'll need to know what it is, in case anyone asks."

"Will someone ask?"

"I don't think so, but better to be ready. It'll be something simple, like we were both at a restaurant and I took your coat by accident and we started talking. I'll figure it out."

"Good." The imam stood. "Shall we meet next month? I need some time to think about the kind of guidance to offer a man like you." **I'll find out what the boys in Raqqa want to ask.**

"Next month is fine. Give me your cell number, too."

"Is that wise?"

"For emergencies only."

The imam scribbled his number on a card. "See you soon."

So THE MAN who called himself Wayne became a traitor. Over time, his conversations with the imam became more straightforward, though neither man ever precisely acknowledged the truth.

Wayne worried the Islamic State would burn him by making him give up too much too quickly. But the IS intelligence officers had come out of Saddam's **mukhabarat**. They were pros. They recognized his value and let him deliver what he could.

They did have some quirks. They rarely asked questions about strategy. Either they didn't think he could answer those or they weren't interested. They were more focused on tactics, raids, and drone overflights, and of course on traitors within their own ranks. Wayne dutifully answered their questions. Strange to think that being a spy could be as numbing as running one.

As the months passed, a hollowness overtook him. He didn't question the morality of his choice, not even after the Islamic State's atrocities mounted, after it drowned prisoners in cages or encouraged ten-year-olds to shoot them in the head. Not even after its jihadis killed French twenty-somethings listening to music in Paris. Terrorism was always the weapon of the weak against the strong. Let the West taste some of the death that it rained all over the world.

But he hadn't realized how terrible a burden the secrecy would be. Everyone in the agency had secrets, of course. But they were shared. He had no one. Not even someone to run him. The imam wasn't a case officer in any traditional sense, merely a conduit to people Wayne had never seen. He understood better now why the agency promised its spies sign money even if they said they didn't want it. Anything to bind them to something larger. He had people all around him, yet he felt as lonely as an old drinker whom no one ever saw, living in an apartment crammed with boxes of moth-eaten clothes.

Yet he knew he couldn't go back. A confession would bring him no mercy, only a Supermax cell for the rest of his life. Fleeing to his new masters would result in an even more certain death, though at least he wouldn't have to wait as long. In sending that thumb drive, he had launched himself into space. He would float free until the void took him with its cold or the sun burned him alive.

On he went. After a while, he stopped worrying anyone would catch him. Even as major operations floundered, the agency never questioned whether it might have a mole. It lacked the imagination, Wayne decided.

UNTIL NOW. Ellis Shafer had figured out what everyone else had missed. No way would Shafer catch him, not for a while. Too many people knew about the ops that went wrong.

But Shafer's words made Wayne see what he'd known for months. The game was almost over. He couldn't live this way much longer. Plus, though he hated to admit it, his plan had failed. He had gotten frontline operatives killed. But he hadn't touched the people he most wanted to hurt—the people around him, the desk heads and managers and seventh-floor executives at Langley. The high priests.

Before time ran out, he needed to rip off their robes and make them pay.

5

WELLS booked a flight to Dulles as soon as Kirkov left him in Hyde Park. Didn't tell Shafer he was coming. They were overdue anyway. The last couple of years, Wells had seen Shafer only on his way down to the Farm. Shafer habitually dragged Wells to Shirley's, the run-down Northeast D.C. bar where they had planned their last mission. Wells refused to talk business, so they traded stories about their families and complained about their favorite baseball teams—the Nationals for Shafer, the Red Sox for Wells—like a couple of codgers. The bartender never remembered them. **Shirley's: Where nobody knows your name.**

Shafer had offered to come to North Conway more than once. Wells always said no. Maybe he wanted to keep the agency and his life with Emmie apart. Maybe he wanted to punish Shafer for what Shafer had said at the end of their last mission. Maybe he'd been unfair.

HE LANDED after dark, cabbed to Shafer's house. The D.C. suburbs were middle-class no more. Constant federal expansion, and the lobbying and lawyering that came with it, had made them rich. The houses in Shafer's neighborhood had grown like the government that served their owners. BMWs and Lexuses filled the driveways. Shafer had an old Crown Vic sedan, rusted brown with a cracked rear window. If he kept it much longer, the neighbors would sue him for hurting property values.

The house's lights were on, but the Ford wasn't in the driveway. On the porch, Wells hesitated. If the car wasn't here, Shafer wasn't either. Then the door swung open to reveal Shafer's wife. Rachel was a tall, heavy woman in her late sixties, with soft brown eyes and a round face. For years, she had looked ready for grandchildren. Still didn't have any.

She opened her arms, hugged him close. She wore a young woman's perfume, light and lemony. She led him to the kitchen, put on the kettle. The house spoke of lives lived with purpose and care: the bookshelves filled with well-thumbed hardcovers, the black baby grand piano, the family photos from a dozen countries, the kitchen table rubbed smooth as marble by ten thousand dinners. The Shafers had lived in this house since Ellis's last foreign posting. They'd been married almost forty years.

"Sorry the place is such a mess." The place was anything but. "Ellis told me he'd be late tonight. Didn't mention you."

"He didn't know."

Rachel raised her eyebrows. **Trouble ahead?** "Planning on staying over, John?" From someone else, the words might have been an accusation. From her, they were merely a question. "I'll make up the pullout downstairs."

"What a great mother you must be."

"The kettle boils, you know what to do." She opened the door to the basement.

"How do you do it?" Wells said when she came back.

She didn't ask what he meant.

"Find someone you love more than yourself, you grab that luck with both hands. I knew I was marrying Ellis by the end of our second date. As what's-his-name from **The Catcher in the Rye—**"

"Holden—"

"Yes. As Holden Caufield would have said, he wasn't a phony. Didn't care about his clothes, his car, just wanted to experience the world. He was so **engaged**. And smart. Could tell me anything about countries I couldn't even find on a map."

"Anything you wanted to know, plenty you didn't."

"Part of his charm. And I knew he loved me right away. Every time he looked at me, his eyes went soft. I was pretty back then."

"You're pretty now."

"He could have told me he wanted to take us to the moon and I would have gone."

"**Grab that luck.**"

"You'll find her, John."

"You think so?" Wells knew Rachel was wrong, but she was too sweet for him to argue.

"Maybe you already have and you won't admit it."

"Maybe. So, what's new?"

"Not much. I don't think of myself as starstruck, but it's strange to think that we know the President. Ellis won't admit it, but I think it's gone to his head a little. We've been there a few times."

There meaning the **White House**, Wells assumed. "Nobody's more dangerous than a revolutionary in charge."

"Drink your tea. I'll call him, tell him you're here."

She returned a few minutes later. "Thinks he'll be home by one. He asked me if you were here about Raqqa and I told him to ask you himself."

They drank tea and talked about their kids for an hour before Rachel went to bed. Wells was still at the kitchen table when Shafer walked in, wired and jittery as a boxer stepping into the ring for the first time. He leaned over, patted Wells's cheeks.

"Anne come to her senses, kick you out?"

"I was never in. How's Vinny?"

"How would I know?"

"Rachel says you're buds."

"Rachel exaggerates."

"How many state dinners?"

Shafer rummaged through the fridge for a beer, popped it, tipped it at Wells. "Cheers, John. I'm not afraid to say I missed you." Shafer drank, wiped his mouth on his sleeve. Wells thought of what Rachel had said: **He didn't care about his clothes or his car.**

"What are you grinning at, John-O?"

"Even now, you've got the manners of an eight-year-old boy."

"I can see the column now: **Ask a Killer.** What brings you to Sodom?"

That fast, they were back to business.

"Oleg Kirkov called me." Wells explained the London trip, how the Bulgarian had played the conversation between the jihadis. Wells expected Shafer to push back, raise the possibility of a false flag.

But Shafer only nodded. "Anybody else know?"

"I think only Kirkov and the guy who found it."

"We lost two operatives in Raqqa today. Ambushed on an exfil. IS knew exactly where they were going, they never had a chance. Seventh floor had a meeting tonight."

"Which you crashed."

"Which I crashed. Ludlow wants to blame the Turks. He's shutting down a bunch of ops in Syria until we sort it out. I spent the night looking at stuff that's gone wrong lately. Plenty to read. Not just Syria, not just our ops. The Saudis thought they had the ISAP commander"— Islamic State of the Arabian Peninsula—"locked down in Jeddah. He disappeared one night last

August, gone ever since. Four months ago, you might remember, the Egyptians hit a Daesh safehouse in Cairo, the place was wired, seventeen Egyptian soldiers and six civvies dead, only two bad guys. We were in on that op, our intel. Problems in Libya and West Africa, too. I haven't even gotten to those reports yet."

"Those hits go bad all the time, Ellis." Wells found himself playing devil's advocate without enthusiasm. "Especially when the locals are running them."

"Then why always the Islamic State? Never al-Qaeda or anyone else?"

Wells wanted to argue, but he couldn't. Though he wasn't sure anyone outside this room would agree. They'd ask Shafer and Wells for actual evidence, of which there was none.

"Has to be someone who sees this stuff as a matter of course. And, from what you say, has access to the prisoner database, too. Very senior."

"What about the tech side?"

"A sys admin?" Systems administrators, who ran the agency's computer networks. "Since Snowden, we're way more careful with them. Except in emergencies, desk heads have to approve or alarms go off."

"But if you run the systems, you can bypass the alarms."

"The software watches for that, too. I don't know enough about it to know how secure it is, but that's a checkable fact."

"So if it's not the tech side, who? DCIA, DDO—"

"Ludlow and Pushkin, yeah. Plus the assistant deputy director for counterterrorism, a guy named Vernon Green, and Walter Crompond, the head of Gamma Station. What we're calling the anti-IS desk these days."

"Green is the ADDO and Crompond runs Gamma." Wells had never met either one.

"Correct. Green is black, ex-military. Crompond's kind of an old-school WASP. Both rising stars."

"Ludlow, Pushkin, Green, Crompond." Wells had hardly slept for forty hours and crossed the Atlantic twice. The blurriness crept in on cat's feet. "Sounds like the world's worst law firm."

"All in the meeting today."

"They get along?"

"You'd be surprised. They know who's running the show. Vinny, Vinny, he's our man. If he can't boss us, no one can."

Wells didn't want to get sidetracked on Duto. "What about the chiefs for Syria and Iraq? Maybe the other blown ops were coincidence."

Shafer sipped his beer as if it might have the

answer. "Doesn't explain the prisoner database. Beer? Or does Allah still say no?"

"What else do you have?"

"Serve yourself, cowboy."

Wells rummaged through the fridge, poured himself a glass of low-lactose milk. It tasted less like milk than he hoped. He poured it out, tried again with orange juice. Maybe it was just fatigue, but speculating about a traitor in Shafer's kitchen suddenly seemed absurd. "I don't know."

"You don't know what?"

"Who's running him? How'd he get hooked up? How's he pass stuff?"

"Any of those guys could set up secure coms. Secure enough, anyway, with nobody looking."

"None of it explains why."

"I'm sure he has his reasons. I'm sure they make sense to him." Shafer stood. "Get some sleep. Tomorrow morning we figure out what to tell Vinny."

WELLS WOKE TO find Shafer beside his bed, sipping coffee from a chipped mug that read **Tanned, Rested, and Ready: Nixon in '88.**

"Should I be creeped out that you watch me sleep?"

"Not unless I crawl under the covers and caress your scars."

"That's a bit specific, Ellis."

"Get dressed. West Wing in two hours."

Vinny Duto, President of the United States. Wells couldn't quite believe it. Duto had been an okay president so far. No surprise, he was a gravel-and-concrete guy. He'd raised some taxes, spent the money on infrastructure, a program he called Rebuilding America.

The biggest risk he had taken was scaling back the war on drugs. He halved the Drug Enforcement Administration's budget and announced that the federal government would no longer enforce marijuana laws because too many states had taken contradictory positions. He expanded needle exchange programs and supported research on medical uses for psychedelics. **Let's focus our law enforcement and military where they'll do some good,** Duto said. **I'm worried about jihadis, not potheads.** Wells expected a backlash, but the move turned out to be Duto's Nixon-in-China moment. His toughness gave him credibility. Congress barely argued.

On foreign policy, Duto kept his promise to be aggressive. He challenged China in the South China Sea and gave Ukraine advanced weapons systems even after Russia objected. He budgeted a hundred-fifty billion dollars to add three new aircraft carrier groups to the Navy's current total of twelve. The move was obviously aimed at the People's Republic, though Duto didn't say so.

Otherwise, Duto stayed away from big moves. He pulled the United States out of talks on climate change, saying he wouldn't sacrifice the American economy to let the Chinese build coal-fired power plants. He rarely held press conferences, kept public appearances to a minimum. He seemed content to rule from the White House. A **Washington Post** columnist had nicknamed him Vinny Dutin, and his governing style did have a Putinesque, **Father Knows Best** quality.

But with the economy growing decently, Duto's approval ratings were in the high fifties. Ordinary Americans seemed to have decided that even if they didn't trust Duto, they trusted him to do a good job.

"Two hours?" Wells said. "That was quick."

"Soon as I mentioned your name, he got hot and bothered."

DUTO HAD KEPT the Oval Office basically unchanged. Wells recognized the furniture, the yellow couches and the heavy wooden desk. But he'd added a sideboard filled with thirty-year-old whiskeys and single malt scotches. Wells was no expert, but he suspected some of those bottles cost as much as cars. He wondered what other gifts Duto's corporate friends had snuck into the White House. Presidents made four hundred thousand dollars a year, but they lived like billionaires.

Duto bounced up from the couch and grinned as they walked in. His handshake was as fierce as Wells remembered, and he'd lost weight. No doubt the White House gym had a great personal trainer.

"John, John, John."

"Here you are."

"Here I be. And you have a daughter now."

"Emmie."

"Congratulations."

"Thank you."

"Evan's in San Diego? Still playing hoops?"

"A senior now. And yes." Evan started at shooting guard on the Aztecs, San Diego State's nationally ranked basketball team. He'd been second-team All-Pac-12 the year before.

"He have plans after graduation?"

Wells wondered if Duto knew that Evan planned to join the Rangers, just as Wells had done after he graduated from Dartmouth. The prospect left Wells equally excited and nervous. "Considering his options."

"I'm sorry you missed the Inaugural, John. Next time."

Next time. Duto spoke with perfect confidence. As CIA director, Duto had learned how to hide his edges, project authority and control. But back then Wells saw the rage that fueled him, the need to win. Now he **had** won. The shell fit him more perfectly than ever. He could even pretend to be charming, ask after Wells's family as if he cared. He had the confidence that this room bestowed on all but its weakest occupants.

Even so, Wells felt a touch of pride on Duto's behalf. The man had worked and schemed for this prize as long as Wells had known him. **What Makes Vinny Run?** Wells hoped he appreciated it. "How's the view from the bridge, Vinny?"

"Sit, please." They sat and Duto arranged himself on the couch across from theirs. He half closed his eyes and faded into himself, like Wells's question was something other than polite chitchat. "A lot of bull, but so much power, too," he finally said. "Still figuring it out. So far, so good, though, right?"

"If you believe the polls."

"Can't even give me that." Duto grimaced, real annoyance. **You won't kiss the ring, at least tell me it shines nice.** "So what's up? This about Raqqa? I heard about the show you put on last night, Ellis."

"Told you," Shafer said to Wells. "Team Vinny." To Duto: "It wasn't a show."

"You think somebody's betraying us to the Islamic State."

"Why don't you listen to John? He saw Oleg Kirkov yesterday."

"Bulgarian friend?"

"None other." Again Wells explained how he'd gone to London, heard Kirkov's recording.

"A two-minute tape," Duto said when Wells was done. "Doesn't name anyone specific. Just enough to get us to unleash the hounds."

"I'd play it for you if you understood Arabic. It was the real deal."

"You don't think these two knew we're taping their prayer room?"

"Even if they did, how could they have planned this?" Shafer said. "They didn't know we'd put them in the same prison, much less the same room."

"But they know they can get rendered. The top hundred guys could all have that little speech planned. **How do I know the Big Bad Wolf won't hurt my family, Mohammed? Don't worry, Abu Abu, we have someone inside.** So this op yesterday went bad. Means less than nothing."

Duto had just reminded Wells why Wells despised him. Less than nothing was exactly how much he cared about those dead operatives.

"It's obvious what's going on, Vinny," Shafer said.

"Enlighten me."

"You don't want to deal with this because you know how bad it looks. Maybe you've got some cognitive dissonance, too."

"Cognitive what, now? So we're clear. You think a senior officer—really senior—is betraying us to the Islamic State. Like who? Reg Pushkin?"

"Possibly."

"You know his grandparents came over from East Germany with nothing, snuck past before the commies closed the border? Insult him this way."

"Not saying it's him, Vinny. Someone with that kind of access. Crompond or Green, maybe."

Duto looked to Wells. "You agree with this nonsense?"

Wells wasn't as sure as Shafer. But the Oval Office was the wrong place to reveal those doubts. Duto would eat them alive. "What I heard, it sounded real."

"Batman and Robin strike again. If he said jump—"

"You ask me my opinion, I tell you."

Duto settled back against the couch. For all his bluster, he knew he couldn't dismiss the possibility out of hand, Wells saw. Too many ops had gone bad. "What do you propose we do?"

"Box 'em, for a start," Shafer said.

"Put our top guys on the poly, ask them if they work for Daesh."

"Should have already."

"Total eff you to guys who have worked their asses off. And it won't work anyway. Those guys can beat the box. No. They get polyed on schedule like everyone else. Next?"

"FBI surveillance."

"How many targets?"

"Four, five maybe."

"Great idea. Thirty agents per guy, that's a hundred fifty feebs." Duto had a CIA veteran's dislike of the Bureau. "We'll tell the D.C. office to quit every other counterespionage job. For how long? What are they looking for? And, by the way, what do we tell Pushkin or whoever when they spot the tails? Which they will, no way can the feds follow these guys without tripping over their own feet. Oh, it was just a training exercise, Reg, don't worry about it. Absolutely not. Out of the question. Next?"

"Tap their phones, computers, run digital traces to see if we can find suspicious emails, downloads, whatnot."

Duto paused. "Work or home?"

"Start with work. That's legal anyway." As a condition of employment, CIA officers agreed to let the agency tape their calls and monitor their computers. "We see anything, we widen the op, you don't argue."

"No way any of those guys would be dumb enough to do anything you could trace."

"Then we won't find anything."

"All right. You can have that. Next?"

"I get their whole files, back to the day they applied, background check, psych records, health, financial, evaluations."

"Whatever's in the records. But you don't talk to anyone. Root through the trash all you like, you're not throwing shade on any of these guys. Next?"

"We'll think of something."

"I don't doubt it." Duto stood up. "I'm meeting the secretary of commerce in fifteen minutes. I have no idea why, but it's on the sched. You two shoo." He flicked his hand at the door to emphasize their unimportance. "Gotta be honest. I missed you idiots. Like old times." As if they were high school buddies he had invited to the White House to prove how far he'd come.

AFTER THE WHITE HOUSE, Wells feared that Shafer would insist that they go to Shirley's. Instead, he led Wells south to the Mall and they strolled alongside the reflecting pool toward the Lincoln Memorial.

"Doesn't want to admit it, but he's worried," Shafer said.

"Don't know if I'd go that far. He's interested. Anyway, how do we find this guy? No way did he leave us an electronic trail."

Shafer didn't answer for a while. They passed the State Department and neared the Lincoln Memorial. Wells wondered again if they were right. He understood the impulse to betray all this for the Kremlin or Tiananmen Square. Those places had their own majesty. But for **Raqqa**?

"Dangle an op, make him jump? Fingerprint it somehow?" Wells was stuck on motive, but Shafer had moved to the practical problem of catching the guy. Dangles were classic counterespionage. Create a fake operation so important that the mole would want to tell the Islamic State about it immediately. Ideally, they would find a way to show each target a slightly different version of the operation and then monitor the jihadi response to see which version had been passed.

Before Wells could answer, Shafer rejected the idea. "No. All those guys see everything. No way could we create a plausible op even if Duto signed off, which he wouldn't."

"Nice of you to consider my opinion, Ellis." They were now at the base of the Lincoln, the greatest tribute in Washington, for the greatest president.

"No dangle. Maybe a depth charge." Another staple in the counterespionage play book, essentially the dangle's flip side. Frighten the traitor into believing that he faced exposure and needed to protect himself by removing the threat. "What'll make these guys think we're close?"

"The recording."

"It shows that neither guy knows who the mole is. Right?"

"Latif doesn't, for sure. The other one, Hani, he says something like only the Shura Council knows, and even though I'm on it, I don't know everything."

"Because this mole, he knows the tricks. We show him something convincing or he shuts down, we never find him."

"Giving him a lot of credit."

"Right, let's assume he's an idiot. We'll put up an index card in the seventh-floor break room—**Mr. Traitor: Come out, come out, wherever you are**—and a little piece of cheese—Gruyère, traitors love Gruyère—he'll come running."

Wells remembered for the thousandth time that arguing with Shafer didn't pay.

Then Shafer stopped mid-stride.

"You having a stroke?"

Shafer sat on a bench between the Lincoln Memorial and the Vietnam Veterans Memorial Wall, muttering to himself, **Okay, okay. No, okay.** Playing a game of three-dimensional chess that only he could see.

"Have to make him think Hani is going to narc him out."

"Unfortunately, as you pointed out, the tape—"

"Forget the tape. The tape is two guys yapping at each other in Arabic. And one's not even there anymore. We don't play the tape. We tell our targets that Kirkov called you because he knows you from back in the day. And told you one of his guys heard Hani telling somebody that he knows something the CIA would kill to find out."

"About the mole."

"No. We specifically say we **don't** know what it is. Maybe it's the bunker where all the top commanders live. Maybe it's some big terror attack. I say, **Hey, maybe it's the traitor**, but everyone shoots that down. That way, Duto can't say we're conducting a witch hunt. Only the mole has reason to worry. Kirkov backs what we say."

"How does that help? Seventh floor will say we should send in an interrogator. And we will. And Hani will tell him to get bent. They'll see those reports and we're right back where we started."

"Correct. That's why we aren't going to use an interrogator. You trust Kirkov? **Really** trust him?"

"Yes."

"Enough to go into that prison undercover?"

Okay, Wells hadn't seen **that** question coming.

SHAFER EXPLAINED. They would tell the seventh floor that standard interrogation tactics wouldn't work. Hani hadn't given up anything so far. Asking him what he knew would only put him on his guard. They had only one choice, putting their own informant in the prison undercover. Wells was the obvious choice. Even now, no other American had spent as much time inside an Islamist terror group.

"With Qaeda. Not the Islamic State. In case you've forgotten, they don't get along."

"Works to our advantage." Wells would pretend to be a mid-level al-Qaeda commander who'd been underground in Afghanistan and Pakistan. He'd just been captured. Hani wouldn't know him, but Hani had never fought in Afghanistan.

"Plus we tell the seventh floor that Kirkov wants you for this. No one else. He has a history with you, you guys trust each other. Don't mention Duto, no need. Everyone knows we're connected."

On that score, Shafer was right. Everyone would know that if Wells wanted to go, the agency couldn't stop him. "So I get dropped in, wave my magic wand, and the next day Hani tells me about their crown jewel secret source inside the CIA. Didn't know you had such a high opinion of me."

"No."

"Again, I'm confused."

"I smell your brain burning. You're forgetting the most important part. **The mole knows you're going.** He's going to feel pressure to react. He doesn't know what Hani knows. And he can't risk you finding out. Maybe he tries to sneak word to Hani. Maybe he goes directly at you."

"Come on, Ellis. He does that, he might as well put a billboard over the seventh floor, **Traitor works here.**"

"How a depth charge is **supposed** to work. Surface or die. Let's say he doesn't do anything. Then you work Hani for a few months, see if he gives you anything."

A few months—Shafer made the pitch as casually as if he were suggesting a vacation in Florida. Hang out on the beach. The full weight of the proposal hit Wells now. To have any chance, he would have to inhabit this new identity completely. The guards would have to treat him like every other prisoner. No mysterious days out of his cell. No visitors. In fact, none of the guards could know. Only Kirkov, and one or two senior prison officers.

Of course he could have no chances to call Emmie or Anne. He would be as lost to them as if he'd fallen into a coma.

"You don't like it, we won't do it. We'll find another way."

"I say I didn't like it? It's good. We're not going to come up with anything better."

"You can say enough is enough."

Wells wondered if Shafer was still second-guessing him for what had happened in that garage in Hong Kong. "Buvchenko deserved what he got, Ellis."

"We don't agree. But it's not about that."

"Tell me what it's about, then."

"Not too many people get another chance, another family—"

Shafer spoke so quietly that Wells had to lean close to hear him. His caution infuriated Wells, precisely because it put into words the thoughts Wells couldn't let himself have. "I didn't come begging for this. You suggested it, all of the sudden you're having an attack of conscience."

"I hadn't thought about your changed circumstances."

"Changed circumstances?"

Shafer stared into his lap. "You can **feel**," he finally said. "Be afraid of missing your family. It's allowed."

After a while, Shafer stood, turned to face him. "This is why they all leave you, John."

"If I'm going to make this work, I need a proper jacket." A backstory.

Shafer's eyes softened in his wrinkled face. He looked at Wells with something like pity.

"Not another word, Ellis."

"Fine. For the jacket, we use somebody real, long as we can be sure he's dead or disappeared so long ago that nobody at the prison could know him. Someone who froze in the Kush five years ago and the body was never found."

Wells nodded. The idea of using a real Qaeda jihadi made sense, if they could find the right one.

"More than that. I want to start in Afghanistan. Put me on a list, let a Delta/SOG team pick me up, give me to the flyboys"—the rendition teams. Wells was proposing he be treated like the al-Qaeda commander he was pretending to be even before he arrived at the prison. "The farther upstream I'm inserted, the better. More time to live it."

"All right."

Shafer agreed so quickly that Wells wondered if he had planned to make the same suggestion. "You think Kirkov and Vinny will sign off?"

"You know Kirkov better than I do. As for Vinny, it's no skin off his back, and that's always his main worry."

Wells couldn't argue. Duto would love this mission, which gave him the chance to catch a traitor without having to acknowledge that the man even existed.

"Fine. I'm going back to North Conway, spend a couple of days there. Then Kirkov. Make sure he's on board before we pitch Vinny."

"I'll talk to the tech guys, make sure we can exclude a Snowden-type breach. Also see if we can find any digital fingerprints, downloads, et cetera. Check back in a couple of days."

"Long as you promise not to talk about feelings, Ellis. Yours **or** mine."

6

RAQQA, SYRIA

MOST doctors and nurses at the National Hospital in Raqqa had fled the Islamic State. Those who stayed were a motley bunch, like the humpbacked anesthesiologist the group had coaxed to remain with the promise of a fresh virgin every month. With staff so scarce, the hospital had closed its top two floors.

But Daesh had found its own use for the extra space.

THAT THE JIHADIS wanted weapons of mass destruction was no surprise. The Daesh commanders had no qualms about killing civilians. Truly, they hoped for the chance, to provoke the West into revealing its hatred of Muslims. The Islamic State also understood the symbolic value of unconventional weapons, which would show the world how technically advanced it had become.

So after the group consolidated its territory in the summer of 2014, its leader, Abu Bakr al-Baghdadi, began the Qiyamah Project, after the Arabic word for **resurrection**. Baghdadi named an Iraqi friend named Omar Haddad as the program's leader.

Haddad was a former colonel in Saddam Hussein's **mukhabarat**. He had strangled his first wife to marry her cousin. He decided to focus on anthrax, among the deadliest of all biological weapons. **Two million, one kilo, one hundred thousand,** Haddad told Baghdadi. For two million dollars, he hoped to produce a kilogram of anthrax spores, enough to kill a hundred thousand people in a crowded city like New York.

Two million dollars was real money for the Islamic State. Baghdadi hesitated. Haddad urged him to imagine dead **kaffirs** stacked five-high outside hospitals, the United States declaring martial law. After considering for a week, Baghdadi signed off.

Then the Islamic State learned what other terrorist groups had already discovered. Growing anthrax sounded easy enough. The reality was different. Every step—from picking the right strains and designing a laboratory to harvesting the spores—brought new difficulties. The Islamic State had engineers in its ranks but no microbiologists or infectious disease specialists. Specialized fermenters and centrifuges were expensive and impossible to buy legally. The group was reduced to smuggling balky Soviet-era equipment from Serbia. Even the basics of the biology befuddled Haddad, who had not taken a science class since seventh grade.

The Qiyamah Project churned through its initial budget in six months without producing a single batch of anthrax spores. Haddad promised Baghdadi he was close. **Another million, that's all.** When the additional money disappeared six months later, Baghdadi shut down the research.

"What now, Caliph?" Haddad asked.

"Now you have the honor of leading a platoon of suicide bombers, Omar."

When Haddad said he preferred a more conventional unit, Baghdadi hung him in Raqqa's main square.

Nuclear weapons proved even further out of reach. Even relatively advanced nations like Iran and Brazil had struggled with them. Producing plutonium or enriching uranium required hundreds of scientists working at massive industrial complexes. The Islamic State had no chance. The group made scattered attempts to steal or buy material. But it found only shady arms dealers who promised plutonium and HEU by the kilo but never had any themselves. They inevitably turned out to be criminals, frauds, or police informants—often all three at once.

Baghdadi put aside the Islamic State's quest for weapons of mass destruction. Until a man who had briefly worked in Haddad's anthrax laboratory asked to meet him "to talk about Qiyamah."

Soufiane Kassani was a thirty-two-year-old Moroccan who'd been a Web designer before joining the jihad five years before. He came from a wealthy family that owned luxury hotels in Morocco and Tunisia. His parents had sent him to the American School in the Moroccan capital of Rabat. He spoke and read English with an almost native fluency. But the West had never fooled him the way it did his parents. He preferred the simplicity of a one-room mosque to the footmen and filigrees at his family's hotels. Rich Westerners saw his people as nothing more than an exotic backdrop for their desert adventures. Their mere presence polluted his country.

Even now, Kassani remembered seeing the World Trade Center towers collapse and thinking, **Good. They deserved it.** He happily joined the men fighting for a new caliphate in Syria. He quickly distinguished himself for his piety— unlike many of his fellow fighters, he didn't have an arrest record and didn't need to be educated in the Quran—and his brutality. Even by the group's standards, he was quick to **go to the knife**, as the jihadis said.

Kassani was small and trim, with strangely gray skin and black eyes. He was not a scientist, but he had taken classes in biology and chemistry at Mohammed V University in Rabat. He had volunteered to help design the anthrax lab, but after a month he asked to be returned to the front lines.

Now he was back in Raqqa, building the group's websites. He was a mid-level functionary, at best, and for him to ask for an audience with the caliph was shockingly bold.

Kassani heard nothing for a month. Then, after dinner one night, his phone buzzed.

"You know Moataz Street?" An unfamiliar voice.

"Of course."

"Come to the coffeehouse at the south end. One hour."

Kassani arrived to find the shop empty but for one man, big, with the cashew skin of an Iraqi and eyebrows so thick they seemed almost painted on his face. The man didn't introduce himself, much less offer the usual pleasantries. He nodded to a door. "Go back there, take off your clothes. All of them."

Kassani didn't argue. He imagined that the Iraqi wanted to be sure he wasn't hiding some kind of tracking device. The American drones were a constant presence over Raqqa.

The back room was a windowless storage area, empty except for a thin mattress speckled with red-brown stains. Kassani undressed, leaving his shirt and pants in a neat pile. As if by treating them carefully, he could ensure he would have the chance to wear them again.

The Iraqi walked in, holding a hypodermic needle. "Sit on the mattress, left arm out." He grabbed Kassani's wrist, inspected the crook of his elbow, lifted the needle. "Want to know what I'm giving you?" Before Kassani could answer, the Iraqi slid the needle into his forearm. An expert stroke, almost parallel to the skin instead of perpendicular. A cool rush spread through Kassani, filled him with a numbing pleasure. His head lolled. The man pinched his cheek hard enough to draw blood.

"You want to hurt the caliph?"

"Of course not." Kassani's voice sounded strange in his own ears.

"You believe in the cause?"

"With all my soul."

"You want to hurt the caliph?"

Kassani tried to shake his head. The man stared at him for what seemed like a very long time. Finally, he laid Kassani down on the mattress. "Sleep."

KASSANI WOKE TO a dull headache, a dry mouth. He felt groggy, dimwitted. He had never tasted even a sip of alcohol, but he guessed he was having what the **kaffirs** called a hangover from whatever the man had given him.

He realized he was no longer in the coffeehouse. This room was painted yellow and had a barred window high in one wall. The sky outside was the grayish blue of early morning. He was still naked. Whoever had moved him hadn't brought his clothes. Instead, a plain white shirt and pants were draped over a chair, along with a bottle of water. Kassani made himself rise and dress. He wasn't surprised to find that the room's only door was locked from the outside.

Kassani wondered if they planned to torture him. The prospect didn't bother him as much as he expected. He'd been on the other side for long enough to know that no one had an infinite capacity for agony. Sooner or later, the body shut down. He would hope for sooner.

Outside, the sky brightened and the calls to prayer began. The sound gladdened Kassani. He washed his hands and began his ablutions.

He had just finished when the door opened to reveal the Iraqi man he'd met the day before.

"Ready for the caliph, Soufiane?"

Words Kassani hadn't expected to hear. He nodded, hoping that his muzzy head would clear enough for him to explain his plan.

"I can't wait to hear this." After that last dig, the Iraqi stared silently at Kassani until Baghdadi arrived twenty minutes later.

The caliph had black eyes and a long, thick beard graying on the sides. He wore a heavy black cloak and simple leather sandals. His face was at once kind and all-knowing. As soon as Baghdadi looked at him, Kassani knew he wouldn't fight back no matter what Baghdadi did. Even if the caliph punched and kicked him until his bones broke. He would trust the man had seen some impurity in him that he didn't recognize in himself. Those lucky Muslims fourteen hundred years ago must have felt the same when they met the Prophet, peace be upon him.

"**As-salaam alaikum**, Soufiane." Behind him, the Iraqi stepped away, stood by the door.

Kassani went to a knee. "**Alaikum salaam**, my caliph."

Baghdadi waggled his fingers and Kassani rose.

"I'm sorry for these precautions, but Ghaith insists."

Kassani nodded. He hardly trusted himself to speak.

"You asked to see me about Qiyamah." Baghdadi's voice was barely a whisper, like he knew Kassani couldn't handle him at full volume. "Speak, then."

Kassani found his voice. He told the caliph he had seen from the beginning that Haddad couldn't succeed. He had asked out because he didn't want to work on a failing project. Ever since, he had researched unconventional weapons, reading all he could online. The Islamic State controlled Internet access even for jihadis. But its rules didn't apply to Kassani because of his Web work.

"You have an idea?"

"Chemicals."

"How can we make those if we can't make the anthrax?"

"Do you know about Aum Shinrikyo? The Japanese?"

Baghdadi looked at his watch, turned and whispered to Ghaith. The Iraqi argued briefly, but Baghdadi shook his head. Ghaith walked out, pulled the door shut behind him, almost slamming it.

"He takes protecting me seriously. But I know I can trust you."

Kassani felt as if the summer sun had filled the room. "Thank you, Caliph."

"Now, tell me about these Japanese."

So Kassani explained the story of Aum Shinrikyo, a Japanese cult whose power had peaked in the early 1990s. Aum Shinrikyo didn't control its own territory, but in every other way it had advantages over the Islamic State. The Japanese police left it alone. It could buy first-rate manufacturing equipment. It had even spent thirty million dollars to build a laboratory.

"Yet these Japanese couldn't make anthrax into a weapon. They tried. They even harvested the spores and released them, but they never hurt anyone."

For the first time, Baghdadi seemed annoyed. "Then why tell me all this?"

"Because with the chemicals, it was different.

They succeeded. They made sarin, and another one called VX. They killed people with both—"

"How many—"

"More than twenty. Injured thousands. They would have gone further, but the police came after them, they ran out of time."

"What happened to them?"

"Some, put to death. Others, still in jail."

"These Japanese spent thirty million dollars to kill twenty people? This is your idea?"

Kassani felt like a fool. But he couldn't quit now. "I think they wasted money on the anthrax, Caliph. Sarin is easier. Safe to store, too, with simple precautions."

"It's a gas?"

"At normal temperatures, a liquid, but it evaporates quickly. Like water."

Baghdadi nodded. "How many people does this kill?"

"Depends how much we make. Four or five liters could kill everyone on a subway train, if they couldn't leave. If you can get it into the air, it doesn't smell, so people don't know what's happening until too late."

"And you understand how to make it? Not in a general way but exactly?"

"I do. Specific chemicals, mixed and cooked

for a specific length of time. Tricky, but not impossible. I can explain, if you want, Caliph."

"That's all right. How long will this take?"

"With money and two or three men, I would guess I can make ten liters in a year. After that, it'll be faster."

"And how much money do you want?"

"It depends on how easily I can get the equipment—"

"A number, Soufiane."

"Three hundred thousand." Kassani was guessing. He had looked online for the gear he thought he needed, but he wasn't sure how much bringing it over the border would cost.

"Dollars?"

Kassani nodded.

"Three hundred thousand dollars. You know what happened to Haddad."

"Caliph, if I fail, I expect you to do the same to me."

"You don't fear dying?"

"Not for Allah."

Baghdadi had big, meaty hands. Now he laid them on Kassani's shoulders and stared at the Moroccan as though he could see not just Kassani's thoughts but his very soul. "Then you'll have the chance. Three hundred thousand and a year to work. No one will bother you. You can do it at the National Hospital, the top floor, the Americans won't ever bomb there."

Kassani couldn't speak. He bowed his head.

"One more thing, Soufiane. Let's not call it Qiyamah anymore. I want a simpler title. How about the Special Projects Division?"

THUS, the Islamic State birthed its Special Projects Division.

As Kassani had said, sarin was relatively easy to make. Scientists at Germany's IG Farben chemical company had found it in the late 1930s while looking for pesticides. It belonged to a class of molecules called organophosphates, but its structure made it particularly lethal. The Nazis had immediately seen its potential as a weapon. They had decided not to use it, fearing that doing so would provoke a massive counterattack.

Despite sarin's deadliness, the process to make it was hardly secret. The second-to-last step in producing it was making a chemical called methylphosphonyl difluoride—which chemists called DF. DF was tricky stuff. It could eat through glass, and if it mixed with water, it released deadly hydrofluoric acid. But if treated with respect, DF could be stored for years.

Until the moment when its keepers mixed it with isopropyl alcohol, what civilians called rubbing alcohol, available in any drugstore. DF and isopropyl alcohol combined to make sarin, no special steps needed.

And sarin was death. Like other nerve agents, it worked by blocking an enzyme called cholinesterase. With cholinesterase unable to work, muscle cells couldn't turn themselves off. They fired until they destroyed themselves.

The best-known recipes to synthesize sarin started with two simple chemicals. The first was methanol, alcohol's lethal cousin, the stuff that contaminated bootleg moonshine. The second was phosphorus trichloride, a common industrial chemical. Heating those together produced a molecule called trimethylphosphine.

Getting from trimethylphosphine to DF took three more steps. None needed advanced technology, though they did require other chemicals. After Saddam Hussein killed thousands of Kurds in 1988 with chemical weapons, industrial countries tried to control trade in what chemists called precursors, chemicals important to making sarin and other deadly agents. The closer a precursor was to an actual chemical weapon, the more tightly regulated it was. Buying or selling DF was impossible, for example.

But governments couldn't stop the export of basic industrial building blocks like phosphorus trichloride. Worldwide, chemical companies made three hundred thousand tons of the stuff every year. Kassani needed only a few hundred kilograms. The Turkish traders who bought oil by the tankload from the Islamic State were happy enough to sell it.

The equipment was harder to come by. But because Kassani was working on laboratory rather than industrial scale, he didn't need Teflon-coated pipes or expensive process control systems. He did splurge on respirators and full-body chemical handling suits. He didn't mind dying, but not until he'd succeeded.

A month after meeting Baghdadi, Kassani stumbled across an auction liquidating the laboratories of a bankrupt Indian generic drugmaker. A lucky break. Through an Istanbul trading company whose owner supported the Islamic State, he bought a mass spectrometer, a diesel-fired electric generator, and two fifteen-hundred-millimeter fume hoods. Plus basic lab equipment like beakers, pipettes, and Bunsen burners. They all had legitimate commercial purposes and faced no export controls. Shipping them to Turkey took six weeks, clearing them through customs and smuggling them to Raqqa another month. By the time Kassani finished buying everything, he had spent ninety percent of his budget. He hoped he hadn't missed anything important.

Meanwhile, he visited the Islamic State oil fields, looking for true believers, men who wouldn't fear the work ahead. He chose three men: a mechanical engineer, a welder, and a tanker driver who had been studying for a chemistry degree at Mamoun University when the war started.

Together, they moved the equipment from the hospital's basement to a ten-by-ten-meter room on its top floor. The space had been the dialysis ward before the Islamic State arrived. Shelves of books and magazines still sat against one wall, reading material for patients. A tourist guide for Italy, a biography of Queen Rania of Jordan. Kassani tossed everything. Whatever this place had been before, it belonged to the jihad now. It belonged to **him**.

Kassani had no money for fancy air filtration systems. He ducted the fume hoods straight to the roof. He put the generator in another room and vented it through the windows. The Occupational Safety and Health Administration wouldn't have approved, but then its inspectors would have faced more immediate problems if they'd visited Raqqa.

Routing the exterior ducts took a week. Finally, Kassani and his men finished and coupled the fume hoods to the blowers. The preliminaries were finished, the real work about to begin.

"Now we pray." Kassani went to his knees. "Allah, we beg You to grant us health with faith, faith with good conduct, success followed by further success, mercy and healing, and Your forgiveness and Your satisfaction."

PRAYERS OR NO, making sarin proved harder than Kassani expected. Reading about the right ways to handle hydrofluoric acid or chlorine gas was easy enough. Following through hour after hour, reactor load after reactor load, was harder. A single mistake could be fatal.

The men learned that truth in the worst possible way. It was a Thursday night, the end of a long week of work. Kassani was looking forward to their day off. Friday was the holiest day of the Muslim week, and they always observed it.

They were slowly making progress. Their most recent cooks had produced a sixty percent yield of trimethylphosphine. Yields were crucial. Even with an eighty percent yield per step, their overall yield of DF at the end of a five-step process would be barely thirty percent, and the DF itself would be impure and unstable.

Normally, they worked in two-man teams, one team at each fume hood. But the generator had shorted the night before, and the truck driver had stayed up all night fixing it. Kassani had given him the day off. Now he and the welder, a Turk named Ahmed, worked at one fume hood while Bashir the engineer was at the other.

Suddenly Bashir screamed. Kassani turned to see him hopping foot to foot, scrabbling at his waist with his polyvinyl gloves. The motion would have seemed comic if not for the sound he was making. The noise filled the room like Bashir was a human air-raid siren.

Bashir tugged down his pants and underwear. His thighs and penis were **bubbling**—no other word would do—the skin furling on itself like a blanket. In the fume hood behind him, a beaker lay half melted. Kassani knew at once what had happened. Bashir had been pouring hydrofluoric acid into a beaker. But he hadn't realized the beaker was glass, not plastic, and vulnerable to the acid.

As the liquid ate through the beaker, Bashir

had foolishly tried to pick it up and throw it into a plastic safety box. Instead, the glass broke and acid poured out. Bashir was leaning forward and couldn't jump back in time. Hydrofluoric acid was among the most corrosive chemicals ever created. The acid hit him waist-high, and his clothes offered no protection. His agony would only worsen as the minutes passed. The acid would eat Bashir's muscles and organs until it killed him.

Bashir staggered for the bathroom, leaving a trail of blood.

Kassani had never told the others, but he kept a 9-millimeter pistol in the backpack he brought to the lab every day. He grabbed it.

"Soufiane—" Ahmed said.

"You think he wants to suffer this way?"

IN THE BATHROOM, Bashir had turned on the taps in a hopeless effort to wash off the acid. His blood was flowing more steadily now, pink-tinted water covering the floor. Kassani had never seen such pain in a man's face. The skin in Bashir's groin was entirely gone, exposing the fat and muscle beneath.

"Help me—"

Kassani lifted the pistol. "Allah will help. Do you want to pray?"

"Please, Soufiane—"

Kassani aimed at the center of Bashir's chest and squeezed the trigger twice. The Iraqi went to one knee. He tilted sideways against the sink, trying to keep himself upright. Kassani put the pistol beside Bashir's temple and shot him once more. Bashir's face stilled instantly, the muscles relaxed, the agony gone. Kassani knew he'd made the right choice.

He closed his eyes and offered the prayer for the newly dead: "Oh Allah, Bashir al-Umrauk is under Your care and protection, so protect him from the trial of the grave and torment of the fire . . ."

THEY STUFFED Bashir's corpse and clothes into trash bags and buried them in a palm grove a few kilometers from Raqqa.

The accident slowed them. Kassani cut their hours, giving them Saturdays off as well as Fridays. The accident had proven the value in two-man teams, so Kassani went back to the oil fields for another worker.

Yet, for all their difficulties, they made progress. Kassani found he enjoyed lab work, the precision and care that handling chemicals required, the breaks when the batch reactors were working and they had nothing to do but trade stories.

Week by week, they increased their yields. The DF that came out of the reactors was clear, with a pungent acid odor, as the textbooks promised. Yet Kassani hesitated to take the final step, to combine the methylphosphonyl difluoride with isopropyl alcohol. To make sarin.

He told himself he didn't want to distract himself with a test. They would need a space that was sealed, with its own vents, and, ideally, a window so they could watch.

But Kassani knew a deeper fear was holding him back, a fear he had overreached, made a mistake somewhere along the way. So they kept cooking, adding to their DF stockpile, until they had almost four liters.

Then Ghaith showed up. The big Iraqi stood in the center of the room, took in the hoods and reactors, the fire extinguishers in each corner, the thick black electrical cable taped to the floor. "The Division of Special Projects." The sarcasm in his voice was unmistakable.

"I've missed you, Ghaith."

Ghaith recited the months that had passed since Kassani met Baghdadi.

"Your year's almost up, Soufiane."

"We're ready."

Ghaith's thick eyebrows rose. "Show me."

They kept the DF locked in a steel cabinet.

Kassani wore the key around his neck as a constant reminder of their work. He extracted it now, opened the cabinet to reveal the bottles inside.

"All your work for **that**?"

"That can kill a hundred people. More." Kassani didn't see any reason to explain that the liquid in the bottles wasn't actually sarin.

"You've tested it, then?"

"We've checked it, we know it's pure—"

"I don't know what that is, but it doesn't sound like a test. Do I need to tell you what a test is?"

"You don't need to tell me anything, Ghaith."

"So have you?"

"We will. Come back tomorrow." He could start with a dog. The wild dogs were gone from Raqqa. The jihadis had shot them for sport. But a few survived in the groves.

"Playing for a year, you don't even know if it works."

"We don't have a sealed space up here. If we just use a regular room, we'll contaminate the floor."

"We can fix that." Ghaith explained.

Kassani wished he'd thought of the idea himself. "Fine. We'll start tomorrow with a dog?"

Ghaith grinned. "This afternoon. And a dog? I don't think so."

THE PRISONERS wore red jumpsuits and had empty eyes. One had a Libyan's dusky skin. The other was local. Kassani didn't know, didn't want to know, what they'd done. Their arms were cuffed behind their backs, but the precaution seemed unnecessary. They stood under the desert sun looking almost bored. Resigned to their fates.

This ravine was eighty kilometers southeast of Raqqa. Kassani and Ghaith had driven separately from the prisoners and their guards. Kassani had left his men in the lab. Success or failure would belong to him alone.

He'd brought a respirator, gloves, an apron, plastic plants. He knew he'd look ridiculous if the stuff didn't work. And he couldn't be sure. It **should**. His mass spectrometer showed these batches of DF were eighty-five percent pure. But he wished he'd tested it. Instead, he would be mixing and hoping.

Kassani tried not to wonder what Ghaith would do if he was wrong. He wasn't afraid. He just didn't want to disappoint the caliph.

He was a little afraid, too, though.

THE CARS were boxy Korean compacts, one gray, the second black. The guards stuffed the prisoners in the front passenger seats, cuffing their ankles, shackling their arms, wrapping one final chain around their waists. The prisoners protested only mildly. Not that it would have mattered. They were test subjects now. **Subject A** and **Subject B**, doing their part to advance science in the Islamic State.

Kassani opened the front passenger door of the gray compact and sliced a ten-centimeter-by-ten-centimeter square off the right shoulder of the prisoner's jumpsuit to expose the skin. Now the prisoner—the **subject**—began to beg. "Please, sir, I am a good Muslim, I pray every day, give the **zakat**—"

The prisoner who died without begging was rare indeed, and the pleas for mercy were always more or less the same, Kassani knew. In fact, the words had a certain rote quality as if the speaker knew they wouldn't help. Kassani taped a gauze pad to the prisoner's shoulder.

"Whatever they've told you about me, it isn't true—"

At the hospital, Kassani had split his highest-purity DF batch into ten smaller bottles, each with about one hundred milliliters—a little less than four ounces of liquid, half a glass of water. He took out a DF bottle now, poured it into a wide-mouthed plastic beaker. He wanted to offer a prayer for success, but there wasn't time.

He opened a bottle of isopropyl alcohol, gently poured the clear liquid into the beaker. The mixture bubbled and fumed as the liquids mixed. Kassani swirled the liquids in the beaker with a long-handled nickel stirrer. He could almost see the chemicals coming together, the isopropyl doing its work, displacing a fluorine atom, bonding with the phosphorus at the center of the DF.

Making something new and beautiful. A molecule that hadn't existed before.

Kassani had learned to love chemistry.

The bubbling increased, though it remained controlled. The prisoner had fallen silent, as if he, too, were an interested bystander. Kassani smiled through his respirator and slowly poured the liquid onto the pad, soaking it completely. When he was done, he threw the empty beaker into the car and shut the door.

By then, the liquid had reached the prisoner's skin. Despite his lack of formal training, Kassani had proven a capable chemist. Standing just outside the passenger's window, Kassani could see the prisoner's pupils constrict pinpoint tight and a stream of clear mucus pour from his nose. He screamed, or tried to, but his mouth opened wide and drool dripped from the corners. The fabric of his jumpsuit darkened at his groin as his bladder failed, the beginning of the sarin's systemic effects. He heaved and jerked against the chains that held him, rocking the seat against its frame.

Kassani stepped back from the window, half afraid that the prisoner might break free and somehow kick through the glass. He stole a quick look at Ghaith. The Iraqi watched impassively from ten meters away, hands folded across his chest.

Sooner than Kassani expected, the prisoner's convulsions slowed. His eyes were open and unseeing. Mucus and blood covered his chin. He'd bitten off his lower lip. Kassani backed away from the car, pulled off his gloves and respirator. He looked down to see how long the experiment had taken, but he'd forgotten to start his stopwatch.

His only mistake. He'd fix it next time.

Ghaith peered inside the car. "You're sure he's dead?"

A silly question, as they both knew. "Not too close. It's not airtight."

Ghaith stepped back, all the proof that Kassani needed of the power of what he'd just done.

"So that's sarin."

"I don't have to put it on the skin either. I can leave it in the beaker and it'll turn into gas on its own. It'll take longer, but it'll work."

Ghaith nodded at the prisoner in the other car. The man's eyes were wide, mouth slack in terror. "Let's see."

7

ANNE HAD baked Emmie a Hello Kitty cake, pink-frosted, with black jellybean eyes and tented purple ears.

"Can I have a piece, Momma? Please?"

"When your friends come."

"A **tiny** piece?"

Even at age two, girls were natural coquettes. Wells had to smile. "She said 'please,' Mommy."

"Don't encourage her."

"A **teeny-tiny** piece—"

"When your friends come." Talking to toddlers: Wash, rinse, repeat. "Come on, help me with the plates."

Emmie looked at Wells, big pleading eyes underneath long eyelashes. A born heartbreaker.

He shook his head. She dropped the protest, followed Anne to the cupboard, stood impatiently with her hands turned palms up in front of her, waiting for Anne to give her paper plates. Little kids did everything with **intent**, no secrets, nothing hidden. Emmie didn't even know how to lie yet. A world in every way the reverse of the one Wells knew.

FOUR HOURS LATER, Wells had cake under his fingernails and an ache in his knees from crawling on the floor. He'd spent the afternoon playing nanny, an easy excuse to stay apart from the other parents, Anne's friends. He was never sure what they knew. Not talking was easier than lying.

Anne washed up as Wells threw away cake-smudged plates. The house was a happy mess, toys under the couch, wrapping paper balled in the corners, a half-finished jigsaw puzzle on the kitchen table. Tonka prowled around, lapping up crumbs. Emmie was already asleep. As the last car pulled away, she'd said, **Can I have my birthday every day?** and conked.

Wells finished cleaning, thought about his own bag of goodies, the one in the safe-deposit box in the Chase branch downtown. He put his hands on Anne's hips. "Can I have my birthday every day?"

She'd been quiet as they tidied. Now she swiveled away, stared at him.

"You don't even know if you're selling or buy-ing, do you? Get home in time for the birthday, so everyone can see what a great dad you are. Pretend you're the happy family man, pretend you're Muslim, pretend you love that girl—"

A sting as real as a slap, and Anne must have seen she was wrong. "That wasn't fair."

"It wasn't **true**."

"I know you're about to saddle up. You spent the party looking at her like she was made of glass. Like you wanted to store every memory you could."

"You must be a detective."

She didn't smile.

"I'll be undercover. First in Afghanistan and then somewhere else."

"Undercover?"

"In the system." Wells knew he was trying to explain without really telling her.

But she wasn't fooled. "Pretending to be one of them, you mean. How long?"

"A month or two." Wells hesitated. "Three, four at the outside."

"You think you can make that work? After all these years?"

"These guys, they're paranoid, but at the same time they want to believe that the cause brings in believers from all over."

"Put on your turban, and welcome to the jihad."

Wells knew she knew Muslims didn't wear turbans. "Ellis and I think there's a traitor at Langley. High up." More than he should tell her. Justifying himself.

"And how does this—" She shook her head: **I don't want to know.** "So you'll be completely dark. Can't break cover."

"Ellis will know how to reach me. If there's an emergency with Emmie or something."

"You think I'd come to you?"

Wells opened his mouth, shut it again.

"What are you planning to tell your daughter?"

"That I'm going to Daddy School and I'll be back soon with presents." The line didn't sound as good out loud as it had in his head.

"What if you don't? You're the only one who knows the rules here, John."

"I'll come back."

Anne wasn't prone to displays of temper or emotion. The winters in New Hampshire chased off or broke anyone who wasn't strong and solid. She wasn't crying, but Wells saw just how much this trip would cost her. He could have said something like, **You don't want me to go, just say so,** but making her ask would have been cheap. His decision. He'd own it.

She searched his face. "Sure you want to do this? I'm not asking for me. Or even Emmie. I'm asking for **you**. It's easy enough when you have nothing to lose. Different now."

A snippet from U2 came to Wells: **All that you measure / All that you feel / All this you can leave behind . . .** And he could. He knew why, too, though he couldn't bring himself to say the words. Spoken, they would sound like a Memorial Day speech. But he'd seen enough of war to know that peace had to be earned.

"I'll come back."

"Keep saying it, maybe it's true. When do you go?"

"Tomorrow." He'd agreed to meet Kirkov in Munich. Then Washington. Then east.

Anne turned to the sink. "I need to finish cleaning," she said. "You can say your good-byes when she wakes up, and I'll do what I can to help, but after that I don't want to see you anymore."

Until I'm ready to get home? Or ever? Wells looked at the set of her shoulders and thought better of asking.

No PARK WALKS this time. To save time, Wells and Kirkov met at the airport Hilton. Wells found the Bulgarian in his room, leafing through papers. The German-subtitled version of **The 40-Year-Old Virgin** played in the background, Steve Carell cursing as his chest hair was pulled off in two-inch-wide strips. No translation necessary.

"Hilarious," Kirkov said.

Wells waited for Kirkov to turn the television off. And waited.

"Didn't know I was here for movie night."

Kirkov reached for the remote with real regret. "I will tell you, I didn't expect to see you again so soon."

Wells walked him through the evidence of a mole, the failed operation in Raqqa, the earlier lost missions. "The pattern's obvious, once you look. We haven't wanted to."

"This proves what I said in London. Whoever it is must be very senior. You have suspects?"

"Targets. People who had easy access to the prisoner lists and the ops details."

"No evidence. Guessing."

Wells conceded the point with a nod.

"Now what? You come to the Castle, ask Hani? It won't work. These Daesh prisoners, I don't know if it's they're afraid for their families or they believe all the nonsense, but they don't help. Ever."

"No." Wells explained Shafer's plan.

When he was done, Kirkov shook his head. "Hani won't believe. Too smart."

"I **lived** this, Oleg."

"A long time ago."

"Exactly. I can tell them stories about fighting Americans while they were knee-high."

"I can't protect you."

"I don't expect you to. Only way it works is if I go in dark. We won't tell the guards, just the warden and one or two others, men you really trust. They bring me in from Afghanistan, my file looks normal, you treat me like a regular high-value prisoner—"

"You know how we treat those men?"

"I can guess."

"Even now, even with the EU watching. Not a hotel. No movies."

"Give me the chance to talk to them. When I get what I need, I ring the bell and you'll let me out."

"Unless Hani figures it out and kills you. Or the guards decide they don't like you, beat you until you can't walk. Or the man you're looking for finds a way to get a message inside—" Kirkov stopped. Wells realized he'd seen the other side of the scheme. "What you want, isn't it? That the traitor knows you're after him, he gets nervous, makes a mistake." Kirkov said something in Bulgarian. "I don't know the word in English."

"**Bait.** Yes. I'm bait."

"You get killed, big mess."

"Thanks for the vote of confidence."

"Why not from your end?"

"Investigate our top guys? Without hard evidence?"

"This should be your last move. Not your first." Kirkov picked up the remote, tossed it idly. He was going to agree, Wells saw. Agree so he could get back to Steve Carell while he waited to fly to Sofia. Or wherever he was going next.

The windows rattled as an A380 took off. "Vinny okays this?"

Wells nodded. **Maybe. Why wouldn't he?** "You've known all along we can't do this the easy way, Oleg."

Kirkov didn't answer for a while. "Crazy, but your choice," he finally said. "But you need to find a way to make them trust you quickly."

"Have any ideas?"

"In fact, yes." Kirkov explained.

"Not bad," Wells said when Kirkov was done, "if you can do it without being obvious."

"Leave that to me. After Vinny says okay, tell

me, we'll work out the details." Wells's face must have shown his surprise because Kirkov smiled. "Of course you come to me before your president."

"Thank you for this, Oleg."

"You tell Vinny that this doesn't just make us even. He owes me now."

SHAFER WAS WAITING at Dulles when Wells landed that night. As he lead-footed his way down 267, he told Wells that his first pass through the electronic records of Peter Ludlow and the other targets had turned up nothing of interest.

"I had a long talk with a woman named Danielle Chen," Shafer said. "DAD"—deputy assistant director—"for operational records management and systems control. A blast at parties, I'm sure. She told me the desks grade active ops into six broad tiers, based on risk and importance. Tier 1 is for stuff like bin Laden, though of course that one wasn't in the system at all. Those stay secret forever—"

"Unless somebody from SEAL Team 6 writes a book."

"Tier 2 includes anything where our own of-ficers are on the ground in what we rather eu-phemistically call uncontrolled territory. Tier 3 is ops in places like China, dangerous but probably not lethal if they go bad. The bottom three tiers are more or less routine. Drone stuff is graded separately because the risk to our officers is lower but the risk of blowback is higher."

"So the Raqqa op—"

"Tier 2."

"Who could see it?"

"Desk heads and senior officers have unlimited access to ops on their own desks. They can see all tier 4, 5, and 6 ops worldwide without leaving an audit trail. Some tier 3 ops, too. Next level up is more closely guarded. Anybody who isn't directly involved needs approval. There's an automatic audit trail, too. The only people who are exempt from all the restrictions, who can see anything at any tier, are the director and the DDO. Ludlow and Pushkin."

"What about the other two?"

"Let me finish, please." Occasionally Shafer spoke with a prissiness that betrayed his age. "I said every op. That includes Russia, wherever. Green and Crompond have unlimited looks at anything classified as a counterterror op. Whether against the Islamic State or al-Qaeda or anyone else."

"Even though Gamma Station goes after IS, not AQ?"

"Correct. There's so much overlap that arbitrarily restricting him wouldn't make sense."

"Do his deputies have that much freedom?"

"No. Crompond is the only Gamma Station officer who sees everything."

Wells thought he understood, but he wanted to hear Shafer say it. "So the final takeaway—"

"After all that, we're back to the big four. Ludlow, Pushkin, Green, Crompond."

"Good."

"I think so. Gives us a place to focus. Meantime, check the back seat."

Wells came up with a thin manila file. Shafer had found a jihadi for him to impersonate, an al-Qaeda fighter nicknamed Nassim al-Beiruti. As his name suggested, al-Beiruti was a Lebanese who had joined the group in 2000. After the United States invaded Afghanistan, he'd fled to Pakistan. He had never been senior enough to rate serious drone attention, a key to jihadi survival.

Al-Beiruti had last shown up in 2004. The Pakistani army arrested him at the Afghan border. By the time the CIA learned of his detention, the army had let him go. Bureaucratic miscommunication, it said. More likely, al-Beiruti had bribed his way out. He'd never been heard from again.

Wells flipped the file into the back. "No.

He's even more likely to get me killed than your driving."

"How is anybody going to say you're not him? He's dead, or so deep in hiding he might as well be."

"Unless he quit and went home."

"Lebanese haven't seen him."

"Because their border controls are so good. Went home, quit, and then unquit. Wound up over the border in Syria. I say I'm him, but these guys know what he looks like. Tough to explain that."

"He was the best candidate, John. By far."

"Then let's make up a file that matches me better and slip it into the databases. Make the guy American or Canadian, so the language isn't such an issue."

Shafer hated to admit he was wrong as much as anyone Wells had ever met. He didn't speak as he made his way through the suburban Virginia streets. But as they turned in to his driveway, he nodded. "Fine. I'll talk to the techs, we'll figure out how to get it in with no fingerprints. You win."

"America wins, Ellis."

WELLS'S GOOD MOOD didn't survive the night. He dreamed he was watching a ten-year-old

Emmie kicking a soccer ball into a tiny net, over and over. **You can do something else,** he told her. **You can do whatever you like.** She ignored him, kept kicking. **Go, Emmie,** a woman shouted behind him. The voice was Anne's, but when he turned to look, he saw Exley. She looked the same as she had when they'd first met at Langley almost twenty years before. Before September 11. Before everything.

How do you know her name?

Of course I know her name. I'm her mother.

You aren't.

If I'm not her mother, how do I know her name, John? Exley smiled at her own irrefutable logic. **Watch your daughter, John.**

Wells turned back to the field. Emmie was gone.

He blinked himself awake in the dark and lay on the lumpy pullout bed, staring at the ceiling, wondering if Anne was right, if love was the enemy of soldiering. And whether Exley would ever leave him. Or come back to him. Then he closed his eyes and thought of the Hindu Kush until he slept.

SEEING DUTO IN the Oval Office the next afternoon was a relief. Duto wasn't big on talking about feelings.

"Miss it that bad, do you?" Duto leaned back in his chair. Relaxed behind the big desk. "I still say you're wasting your time."

"When I come back, you can tell me how wrong I was." Wells didn't bother to point out that if Duto really thought so, he would have stopped them.

"These guys will buy you as an overage jihadi who went AWOL in the Kush?"

"Long as the mole thinks they might—" Shafer said.

"Fine. Kirkov on board?"

"If you are," Wells said.

"Seventh floor won't be happy." Duto quieted for a moment, seemingly calculating the potential agency fallout. "What do you need from me?"

"Two findings," Shafer said. A finding was White House jargon for a presidential memo that explained why a secret operation was either legal or illegal but necessary for national security.

"So much paper, Ellis." Duto liked written records only when their contents suited him.

"One authorizing the mission, the real mission. Two copies, one for you, one for me."

"What, you don't trust me?"

"The second to Langley with the official cover story. I'll keep a copy of that one, too. Wouldn't want John to get lost over there."

Duto had big, heavy eyelids, the heart of any caricature. They sank now as he squinted at Shafer, then Wells. "Long as they both say clearly that this whole thing was your idea."

"Your lawyer's writing them, have 'em say whatever you like. Put in a recipe."

"In that case, done and done. Now what? You go to Langley, talk to the boys? Fun."

"After we get John's identity right."

"Next week," Wells said. "After my hike."

Duto and Shafer looked at Wells like he'd made a joke that they'd missed.

"You'll see."

THAT AFTERNOON, WELLS had Shafer drop him in Harpers Ferry, a tiny town sixty-five miles northwest of Washington, where the Potomac and Shenandoah rivers came together. In 1859, the abolitionist John Brown had raided an armory in the town, then known as Harper's Ferry. Brown hoped to arm local slaves with the stolen weapons and spark a rebellion. His quest turned out to be a suicide mission. He had fewer than two dozen fighters and no way to bring the weapons to the slaves. Townsfolk pinned him and his men in a factory beside the armory. Marines led by Robert E. Lee and J. E. B. Stuart, soon to be famous Confederate commanders, captured Brown two days later. He was convicted of treason and hanged.

Since reading about Brown in ninth grade, Wells had always felt an odd kinship for the man, a big-bearded preacher who gave stem-winding sermons straight from the Old Testament. Wells distrusted that degree of fervor. The jihadi camps were filled with fanatics convinced that they had direct lines to God.

Yet Wells admired the clarity of Brown's vision. Unlike so many prophets, Brown fought alongside his followers rather than staying safe in the rear. He sacrificed his life to make other men free—not metaphorically but actually free of slavery's chains. And he didn't fear death. After being convicted of treason, he asked for punishment rather than mercy, telling the judge, "[If] it is deemed necessary that I should forfeit my life for the furtherance of the ends of justice, and mingle my blood further with the blood of my children"—two of his sons had died in the raid—". . . so let it be done."

Wells only hoped to be as cool when he met the man on the pale horse.

———

AFTER SHAFER DROVE off, Wells stopped at the brick building where Brown had made his last stand. Fittingly, it could have passed for a church. Wells imagined Brown preaching even as Lee moved his Marines into place for the final charge.

Back outside, Wells followed the signs for the Appalachian Trail, the real reason he'd come. Harpers Ferry lay near the midpoint of the trail, which stretched twenty-two hundred miles from Maine to Georgia. Along the way, Wells and Shafer had stopped at a Walmart so Wells could buy a cheap backpack and camping supplies—a tarp, a sleep sack, water purification tablets, caffeine pills, and a box of energy bars.

"That all you're getting?" Shafer said.

"Yes."

"Gonna be cold."

"And hungry." All the years back in the United States had softened Wells, softened his hair and skin and hands. He needed to make himself less obviously American. He could think of no faster way than a hard week in the mountains. He planned to hike to Roanoke, two hundred miles by car but almost three hundred by trail. Forty miles a day was a grueling but not impossible pace. The world record holder had hiked the entire Appalachian in only forty-six days, averaging almost fifty miles a day the entire way. But Wells intended to keep himself to near-starvation rations, twelve to fifteen hundred calories a day. The hiking would burn between six and eight thousand calories a day on top of his core needs. He figured he would lose at least two pounds a day.

HE NEEDED EIGHT days to reach Roanoke, and his weight-loss math proved conservative. He wound up down nineteen pounds by the time he stumbled off the trail. Wells had always kept himself in fighting shape, never had anything close to a gut. Now all the fat had disappeared from his stomach and arms, giving him an almost wasted look. He hadn't been so hungry since his years in Pakistan. Within twenty-four hours of walking out of Harpers Ferry, he had the ever-present ache that most Americans couldn't even imagine, not just in his belly but his legs, arms, and even his shoulders. Worse than the hunger was the sure knowledge that the next meal wouldn't defeat it, only take the edge off for a few minutes until it returned with reinforcements.

He had forgotten the power of hunger and

dirt and exposure and fatigue to grind down the will. He hadn't realized how much his time back home had weakened him. More than once, he wondered if he'd make the week. The John Wells who had survived years in the Kush would have laughed at this man. John Brown wouldn't even have bothered to laugh.

As for the hike itself, Wells remembered almost nothing. He'd passed through beautiful country, Shenandoah National Park and the Blue Ridge Mountains, looking over tree-carpeted valleys and granite escarpments, a quilt of gray and green that stretched for miles to the west. But the trail was less isolated than he expected. For long stretches, it closely paralleled Skyline Drive, the main road through the national park. Farther south, it hung close to the Blue Ridge Parkway, and was only a couple of miles from Interstate 81. The westerly wind carried the rumble of eighteen-wheelers. He had been far more alone in his cabin in the Bitterroots. Anyway, after the second day, Wells didn't have the energy to appreciate the view. He kept his head down and focused on the next step.

The Appalachian was a friendly place, and it didn't have much of a dress code. But Wells had brought only one spare T-shirt and pair of socks.

By the fourth morning, he could smell himself, and the hikers he passed eyed him as if he might be dangerous. Female hikers gave him a wide berth. More than one discreetly reached for pepper spray. Men, alone or in pairs, grunted greetings but kept their heads down. Only groups of men would risk talking to him, **Y'all right** or **Hey, dude, everything okay?** but Wells ignored them, and they didn't ask twice. He found himself hoping for rain to wash away his stink, but none came.

On the second-to-last morning, still fifty miles from Roanoke, he ran out of caffeine pills and went into withdrawal. He hadn't brought aspirin or ibuprofen, and his headache worsened by the hour. With every step he felt the softness leaching, his bones hollowing. **Life is suffering.** Wells wasn't a Buddhist, but the Kush had taught him the truth of those words. This week was a crash refresher. For a while, the pain became its own pleasure. He imagined staying on the trail, to Tennessee, North Carolina, Georgia, walking without food until he collapsed, then picking himself up and walking some more. He was high on his own endorphins, he realized. He was sorry when the haze lifted.

On his last day, a mile before he left the trail and headed into Roanoke, he tripped on a rock and gashed his shin on a gnarled oak root. The blood seeped through his jeans, which were more brown than blue now from all the dirt and sweat. Even the homeless guys gave him space as he waited for Shafer at the Roanoke bus station. Shafer put down the windows as soon as Wells slipped inside.

"Lucky nobody called the cops."

Wells ignored him.

"And that you didn't get sepsis. This is what eight days does to you? I thought you were tough."

"Hush or I'll sit closer."

"While you were busy on the Naturemaster, I was doing real work." Shafer reached into the back seat and after much grunting came out with a manila file, a twin of the one from the week before.

Wells flipped it open, looked at the pages inside blankly, the words dancing. "I need coffee." He didn't think coffee was cheating. Even the poorest villages in Pakistan had coffee and tea, because caffeine suppressed hunger so effectively.

"Let's stick with drive-through."

An extra-large black coffee later, Wells could read again. He was Samir Khalili, born in Toronto to a Lebanese father and a Canadian mother. He had come to al-Qaeda two years before September 11, gone to Chechnya to fight with the rebels, returned to the camps in Afghanistan. After the attacks, he disappeared. He resurfaced in Pakistan in 2003. The National Security Agency picked up his name as a courier for Ayman al-Zawahiri four times over the next eight years. Then Khalili vanished. He hadn't gone back to Toronto—at least, as far as the Canadian government knew. He hadn't turned up in intercepts or detainee reports. He was presumed dead.

"Much better," Wells said. The references to Zawahiri, who had led al-Qaeda since bin Laden's death, ensured that the agency would care enough about Khalili to want to control him even now. Meanwhile, Wells's own experiences in Chechnya and the Kush had plenty in common with Khalili's backstory.

"Glad you approve, Samir. The sys admins say they can put it in the system so it looks real. Some guys at Bagram may wonder why they never heard about you before if you're such a priority all of a sudden, but we're catching a break on that. A bunch of Deltas are rotating out this month. We'll have COS Kabul"—the station chief—"brief incoming units about you. The guys in the birds"—the Special Forces and

SOG operators who helicoptered out to capture high-value targets—"will figure the station screwed up, didn't recognize your importance."

"And is using the changeover to cover the mistake, put me on the target list where I belong."

"You get picked up, they hand you to the mercs, those guys don't care whether you're Zawahiri or some random Talib as long as the paperwork is signed and they get paid."

"Just like that, Samir Khalili is in Bulgaria with a live jacket. Well done, Ellis."

"Yeah, then you have the easy part."

WELLS SLEPT TWELVE hours before the meeting with the seventh floor. He wanted to be rested. This briefing was both a formality and the hinge for the mission. They had to walk a fine line, to set the hook while making the mole believe he was relatively safe. If he knew they were looking for him, he might look for a way to kill Wells before Wells even reached Bulgaria.

Besides, Wells would admit to being interested in Ludlow and the agency's new top officers. Ludlow had helped Wells on his last mission. Wells had never met the others. But they were all his cousins, all children of September 11. The agency's new breed, moving into middle age and authority. Wells might have been one of them if he had been better at bureaucratic infighting. And at giving orders that risked other men's lives.

Even now, he wasn't sure he believed that one of these men could be a traitor. The usual motives didn't seem to apply. Money or love seemed impossible, ideology and blackmail almost as unlikely. Shafer would do the talking, so Wells could watch them, though he didn't expect to see anything revealing. These men were pros.

When Wells followed Shafer into Ludlow's office, all four were already waiting. They made an odd-looking set. Ludlow was compact and unassuming, with quiet eyes. Pushkin had a fleshy face with Slavic features, like an old-school member of the Soviet Politburo. Green was the opposite. He could have come off a Marine recruiting poster, lean and fit. Crompond was an old-school WASP, blond hair and blue eyes, straight from the yacht club.

They greeted Wells with an enthusiasm that surprised him, though Wells sensed nostalgia, too. Like Wells was an All-Pro quarterback coming back to the team for the first time after retirement. **That ol' boy sure could sling it.** Two and a half years away from the field was a long time, and Wells had reached the age where most operators either retired or came inside.

"At last," Crompond said. "The legend."

"Save it for when I'm dead," Wells said.

"Place look different?" Ludlow said. Wells had seen the office more than once when Duto was director.

"Vinny had more junk."

"Give me time. We all know I owe you a finder's fee." Ludlow paused. "Though it does look like you've had better weeks. So, what can we do for you?"

Shafer had deliberately not told Ludlow, or the others, why they wanted the meeting.

"John's heard something you need to know." Shafer recounted the story he and Wells had devised at the Lincoln Memorial and refined since: Kirkov had told Wells his men had overheard Hani, an Islamic State commander detained in Bulgaria, bragging he had crucial information. Shafer and Wells wanted to send Wells to the prison to find out what Hani meant. Kirkov had agreed to the plan. Shafer had created a fake identity for Wells. And finally, Wells believed he had the best chance of success if a Special Ops team captured him in Afghanistan and transferred him back to Bulgaria.

Wells watched the men throughout. He saw no alarm, merely incredulity. Green and Crompond showed the most skepticism. Near the end, Crompond gave Green a **Can you believe this?** eyebrow raise. Pushkin seemed to stop paying attention after a while. He stared at his hands like a guy stuck next to a subway preacher, waiting for the next stop so he could switch cars. Ludlow, who knew firsthand what Wells and Shafer could do—and how close they were to Duto—was less dismissive.

"So we only need your approval," Shafer said. "And to give COS Kabul his part, handle any questions that might come up when John's file goes live."

The room was silent until Ludlow said, dry and quiet, "Anyone have questions?"

"John, did Kirkov mention if this detainee offered specifics about what he knew?" Pushkin said.

"No specifics."

"Was this taped? Anything we can hear?"

"Unfortunately, no. Hani happened to be speaking in front of a guard who knows Arabic and has kept that fact to himself to spy on the detainees."

"Let's hire him, then," Green muttered.

"This could be anything from a loose nuke to nothing at all?" Pushkin again.

"Exactly."

"Why did he pick you anyway?" Green said.

"Why not come straight to us? We pay for that place."

"You'd have to ask him, but he knows me from a couple of years ago."

"Don't even know where to start with this," Crompond said. "You want to get yourself **rendered** under a fake name on the strength of a thirdhand conversation in Bulgaria? How about this instead? We interrogate this guy Hani. We're allowed, you know—"

"And you know he'll never talk," Shafer said.

"Least I understand now why you have that beard," Pushkin said to Wells.

"John, if you're this bored, come work with me," Green said.

"Tell me you're hiding something and this isn't as dumb as it sounds," Crompond said.

"I have a question, Ellis," Ludlow said, and his low voice quieted them all. "I suppose you have the finding already?" **Is Duto on board?**

"Yes."

"Signed?"

"Ask Vinny." Shafer deliberately using Duto's first name to emphasize the relationship.

"In that case, I suggest we wish John the best of luck."

"You can't be serious," Crompond said. "You're rolling over for this?"

"Your concerns are noted, Walter. For the record."

Crompond looked at Wells. "For the record, I want to say this is going to get you killed."

Ludlow pushed himself up from his chair.

"I'll ask the President to send over that finding and we'll talk about next steps, what we'll tell Kabul," Ludlow said. "Thanks for coming to see us, gentlemen."

NEITHER WELLS NOR Shafer spoke even after they cleared the gates at the Route 123 exit. Wells doubted anyone would risk bugging Shafer's car, but this wasn't the moment to be sloppy. As Shafer drove, Wells mulled over the men. Crompond had been the most opposed, Pushkin the most interested in exactly what Hani knew. Green had asked the best question, the one most likely to unravel the scheme, when he wondered why Kirkov hadn't simply gone to the agency with his story.

No real answers.

Shafer parked outside a Safeway and they stepped out.

"Running countersurveillance?" Wells said.

"Going shopping. Fridge is empty."

"What'd you think?"

"I think they more or less bought it. I wonder whether Ludlow wanted to protect Crom-pond or shut him up."

"It's not Ludlow." The words surprised Wells. But he knew as soon as he spoke them that he was right. "You hear him? All he was worried about was Duto."

"I've thought all along he was wrong. He doesn't have the background. There's some-thing"—Shafer paused—"intimate about this kind of betrayal. The others are closer to the Islamic State."

"You can never just admit I'm right, can you?"

"The others are more likely, that's all. Any-way, whoever it is, he's not going to make a move right away. He knows he has time. You ready for this, John? Say good-bye to that cute little girl?"

I better be.

8

LANGLEY

IN THE HOURS after Shafer and Wells came
to the seventh floor, the man who called
himself Wayne did his job with a sullen heart
and a straight face. He refereed a conference
call about a potential operation in Somalia. He
watched three General Dynamics engineers
demonstrate a prototype drone no larger than a
Frisbee. All along, he wanted to drive as far
from the campus as he could. Head for I-66
and a false escape into the so-called heartland.
Like he'd last a week, with every cop in the
country looking for him. He had no cash hoard,
no second passport, and, most important, nowhere to go.

He was learning that knowing the theoreti-
cal risks of his crimes felt very different than
being **hunted**.

Though he wasn't, actually. Or was he? He

had known of Hani even before Shafer mentioned him, of course. Months before, the imam had asked Wayne to find out where Hani was being held. But Wayne couldn't imagine Hani had any idea who he was. The imam understood the importance of protecting Wayne's identity.

In any case, Hani might be keeping a different secret, most likely that Daesh was planning a big attack on the United States. And none of this mattered unless Wells could convince Hani to talk, a prospect that seemed the longest of shots.

Yet Wayne didn't want to underestimate this threat. Shafer and Wells pretended to be cowboys. But history showed they were canny operators. They had set up this plan in secrecy, convinced Duto to buy in, brought it to the seventh floor as fait accompli. They knew Hani might lead Wells to a traitor. Shafer had raised the possibility after the bloodbath in Raqqa.

Wayne wished he could have probed Shafer and Wells further at the meeting, figured out what they knew. But Ludlow had shut it down. **Give 'em all the rope they want,** he'd said afterward. **It's dumb, but if the big man is on board . . .** The director was furious the President had undercut his authority without even bothering to tell him in advance, Wayne thought. Though Ludlow was both too proud and too dependent on Duto to say so.

Along with Wayne's urge to flee, he had an equally counterproductive impulse, to run his own back-channel investigation. Pull every record he could find on Wells, ask the sys admins what Shafer had said when he'd put together Wells's cover identity. But asking those questions would make him a suspect faster than anything else. For the same reason, Wayne didn't see how he could track Wells's progress. Staying in the dark would be maddening, but he had no choice.

His last meeting finally ended. Wayne choked down four Advil, sat at his desk, tried to relax by scanning the most important reports of the last twenty-four hours. They covered everything from chatter about attacks in Istanbul to an analysis of a new Taliban militia. Nothing surprising . . .

Until he found a statement from a Daesh defector who had worked in Raqqa before fleeing to Kurdish-held territory. The defector—codenamed Yellowfin in the cable—claimed that chemists for the Islamic State were making what he called death gas somewhere in the city. The gas was colorless, odorless, and caused death almost immediately, Yellowfin said. The scientists had tested it on two prisoners and killed both.

Yellowfin acknowledges he did not personally witness the prisoner tests, which he says were conducted outside Raqqa. Nonetheless, we consider his report credible. Of special note, he reports a rumor the Islamic State may film further CW tests for release as propaganda. He does not know whether the chemists are able to produce large quantities of poison or only experimental quantities.

Colorless, odorless, and caused death almost immediately meant **nerve gas.** Most likely, sarin. Wayne smiled to himself. **We bring the monster to life and we're surprised he wants to learn our tricks?**

THE OFFICES AROUND his emptied. The agency never shut down, of course. But most senior officers worked relatively stable hours, in by 7:30 or 8 to beat D.C.'s terrible traffic, out between 5 and 6 for dinner at home. Wayne sometimes imagined the agency as an old-time traveling salesman. On the road, anything went. But at Langley, officers faced trouble if they didn't behave. The agency had been hit with enough sexual harassment suits to have developed an allergy to edgy behavior.

Wayne reread the report and then joined the exodus. Just another day at the office. Yet something had changed. One way or another, the end was coming. He couldn't stop Wells from going to Bulgaria. He needed a plan of his own.

By the time he'd reached home, he'd come up with two moves. He needed the imam's help for both.

Luckily, his wife was at her monthly book club. She went out without him once or twice a week. He never asked too many questions. Sometimes he even hoped she were having an affair, a balance to his treason. As if the two could be compared. But he knew the truth. Her life was as simple and open as it seemed. If—when—everything crashed down, he ought to leave her a note, tell her she'd had nothing to do with his crimes, that she hadn't known him at all.

On second thought, maybe skip the note.

He used simple precautions to talk to the imam outside their normally scheduled meetings, burners and standard gmail accounts that he tossed after every couple of uses. He knew firsthand that the NSA could crack anything that he had the technical skills to handle. Better to hide in the weeds of ten billion spam accounts. He hid the burners in a locked toolbox in his garage. His wife wouldn't stumble on them. A thorough search would, but no one would knock on his door with a warrant unless they already had him.

He and the imam had agreed that if they needed to talk face-to-face in an emergency meeting, they would arrange to bump into each other in one of the many shopping centers nearby. Wayne powered up a fresh burner, texted the imam, **S 1105 SA 119.** The message hardly deserved to be called code—location, time, day. The **S** stood for Springfield Town Center, a Virginia mall just outside the Beltway. It was miles from Langley and Wayne's house, far enough that he wouldn't see anyone he knew, close enough that his presence would raise no questions if he did.

The last three numbers were the only un-usual part: **119** was the equivalent of 911 in many Asian countries. Wayne's way of saying the meeting was a priority. His phone buzzed back five minutes later with a single number: 1. **Yes.**

ON SATURDAY, WAYNE spent an hour shopping, buying sneakers for himself, bras for his wife. Acting naturally was the best countersurveil-lance tactic. The mall wasn't crowded. He had plenty of space to watch for watchers. The agency couldn't risk using its own counterintelligence officers to track him. He might recognize them. It would have to rely on the FBI, and despite its efforts to diversify, the Bureau remained heavy on middle-aged white guys who spent too much time at the gym. They'd stand out at Victoria's Secret.

No one raised Wayne's suspicions. At this hour, his fellow shoppers were mostly stealth exercisers. Moms pushed strollers. Retirees power walked. At exactly 11:05, Wayne passed the Starbucks near the mall's east entrance. The imam stepped out.

"My friend. What a pleasant surprise."

"**Salaam alaikum**," Wayne said.

"**Alaikum as-salaam.**"

"What brings you here?"

"My wife has dispatched me to Macy's to buy towels."

"Macy's? Me, too. I'll walk with you."

They strolled the mall's wide corridors.

"What was so very urgent?" the imam murmured, not quite keeping the sarcasm out of his voice.

Wayne felt the slightest chill. **This man is not your friend.** But this man was his only friend. Thus, he had no friends at all.

His own choice. "First, find out if you can pass a message to Hani."

"The one in Bulgaria? Did you let him out?"

"No—"

"Then how can we send him a message? You'd have a better chance yourself."

"Just try."

"What's the message?"

"First find out if you can pass it."

"All right. What else?"

"A defector tells us your friends are making nerve agents. Probably sarin."

"So."

"I need it."

The imam stopped, reminding Wayne that he wasn't a pro, no matter how much he pretended to be.

"Keep walking, please. Two buddies on our way to Macy's."

The imam walked. "What for?"

Wayne felt the bags in his hands, all this **stuff** that he didn't need, that no one needed. Lace bras and hundred-dollar Nikes, useless excess from sea to shining sea. "When the people I work with are choking to death, you think they'll remember all the junk they bought? When their bowels give, you think they'll care if they're wearing Fruit of the Loom or Jockey?"

"**Insh'allah**," the imam muttered.

"That's right, my man. **Insh'allah** all night long." For the first time in months, years, a decade, **since Jane**, Wayne felt free. As though a seed he'd carried had finally found sunlight.

"This stuff, if we have it, how much do you want?"

"All there is."

"A number, please. If you're serious."

The imam's tone suggested that Wayne should put the crazy back in the basement. "Ten liters. If you have that much."

"If we don't?"

"Tell me how much you have, how quickly you're making it, the potency."

The imam didn't answer. Wayne read his mind: **Is he playing me? Was he working for the agency all along?**

"Everything I've given you and you don't trust me."

"And if this sarin exists at all, what will you do with it?"

"Just see if you have it, please."

They'd reached Macy's. Wayne gave the imam a piece of paper, an email address he'd created that morning. "When you know, write me here."

The imam nodded. "Until we meet again."

"Until we meet again."

WAYNE FORCED HIMSELF not to check the email more than once a day. Still, the waiting nearly snapped him, especially since he knew each hour brought Wells closer to Hani. He had come up with one move that might stop Wells even before he reached Afghanistan. He decided to try it, mainly because he was sure no one could connect it to him.

But Wells would probably beat it. Then he'd be on his way. Wayne imagined a History Channel–style red line tracking Wells's progress as he landed in Kabul and made his way east. Wayne wanted to hope the Taliban would catch Wells. But Wells had lived among the jihadis for years. He was a survivor.

He was coming.

Wayne coped with the pressure by imagining the sarin, what he'd do with it.

A week passed before he found a message from the imam: **You were correct. I am told to tell you we have almost 5L of the substance. Still waiting to hear about the other.**

Five liters was more than he expected. Enough to kill hundreds of people. He and his friends had to move it from Syria to the United States, and then into Langley, without being caught. A **non-trivial obstacle**, as the analysts said. But beatable, Wayne hoped. They'd beat it.

Then he would have his fun.

PART
TWO

9

KABUL, AFGHANISTAN

THE WAR in Afghanistan was over. But charter flights loaded with contractors still landed at Bagram Air Base. American soldiers and airmen still launched air strikes against the Taliban to prop up the corrupt Afghan government. Deltas and SEALs still died in ambushes and helicopter crashes, the casualties barely noticed back home.

The war in Afghanistan was over.

But it wasn't.

Wells had come back more than once since the years he'd spent in the Kush as part of al-Qaeda. He'd traveled semi-officially, arriving on military jets, sleeping on bases until he ventured outside the wire. Not now. For this op, he would come as a civilian. JFK to Dubai to Karachi, a bus to Islamabad, one final flight to Kabul. From there, he would find his way into the mountains on the Afghanistan–Pakistan border. Along the way, he'd become Samir Khalili, a veteran al-Qaeda courier whose luck at avoiding capture was about to run out.

Wells and Shafer had not yet figured out exactly when or where the Special Ops team would grab him. Wells needed to find the right village. It had to have a hotel big enough for him to blend in, small enough that the team that picked him up could do so quickly. Wells wanted to minimize the chance that American soldiers would die in a mission whose only real purpose was to establish Samir Khalili's identity. But providing Wells's exact location to the capture team too far ahead in advance would raise questions. Couriers didn't stay long in one place unless they had no choice.

THE FIRST LEG of Wells's trip was easy. Emirates to Dubai, on a fresh passport from the agency in the easy-to-forget name of Mitch Kelly. Wells sat in coach, reading his Quran, recalling the comfort the words had given him in the mountains so many years before: **He is God the Creator, the Maker, the Shaper. To Him belong the Names Most Beautiful. All that is in the heavens and the earth magnifies Him. He is the All-Mighty, the All-Wise. The**

Allah depicted in the Quran had more in common with the Jewish God of the Old Testament than the Christian Father of the New. Like Yahweh, Allah demanded constant homage to His greatness and lashed out against His doubters: **Shall We then treat the people of Faith like the people of Sin? What is the matter with you?**

Wells knew he'd never truly convince himself that God existed—or that He didn't. Some mysteries didn't answer to human understanding. Maybe all of creation existed inside the shell of a hydrogen atom. Maybe, as the old joke went, it was turtles all the way down. Yet the Quran's fierceness resonated with him. A punishing master for a punishing universe. A God who combined infinite power with an all-too-human need to prove His might. Wells wondered sometimes why he couldn't accept the forgiveness that the God of Jesus and Mary offered. The failure was his, he supposed. He couldn't imagine a better world.

The connection from Dubai to Karachi offered Wells the first glimpse of the world that had once been his home. Westerners mostly avoided Pakistan. Wells clocked only two other white faces on the plane, both in business class, of course. He was in coach, which was filled with construction workers coming back from projects in the Emirates. They wore their cleanest long-sleeved shirts and jeans, happy to be returning home. Wells's seatmate eyed him critically, but when Wells opened his Quran and began to read in Arabic, the man's frown disappeared. "Muslim?"

"Nam."

"Salaam alaikum."

"Alaikum as-salaam."

"From France?"

"America."

The man smiled broadly. Wells had almost forgotten that the United States could generate this reaction, along with the reverse. "Do you know Alcatraz?"

"The prison?"

The man cocked his head as though Wells were a fool even to raise the question: **What other Alcatraz is there?** "The Rock. I want to see it. But impossible now. Visas." He had brown eyes, and a tiny scar in the very center of his chin. "I am Faisal."

"Mitch. You like Dubai?"

Faisal shook his head. "The Arabs, they treat us worse than animals." A common complaint among non-Arab Muslims.

Pakistanis were a talky bunch, but even by

those standards, Faisal was exceptional. He spent the rest of the two-hour flight in a near-nonstop monologue, pouring out facts in broken English about Alcatraz and the American penal system. He was a savant of sorts. **You know the Eastern State Penitentiary? In Philadelphia? It opened in eighteen hundreds. Now a museum, you can visit . . .** An odd coincidence, considering the mission. Wells wondered if Faisal knew anything about Bulgarian prisons, decided not to ask.

By the time they touched down in Karachi, Faisal had invited Wells for dinner. Wells was reminded of Islam's power to cross nationalities, the strength of the brotherhood that had first attracted him to the faith.

Too bad he would never have the chance to take Faisal up.

THE IMMIGRATION AGENT in Karachi looked Wells over with distaste. Wells wondered if the man figured him and his big beard and American passport for a private military contractor. "Purpose of trip?"

"Business."

"Traveling outside Karachi?"

"Yes."

"Do you have any weapons?"

Good question. Once he reached Afghanistan, Wells would need a pistol and, ideally, an assault rifle, too, to establish his cover and for protection. He'd also need an expired Canadian passport in Samir Khalili's name and other bits of what the agency called **pocket litter**. Those were the photos, fake identity cards, maps, and trinkets that Khalili would have accumulated over the years in the Kush.

The agency had designers and forgers who specialized in these documents. Before Wells left, they'd made what he needed. The tricky part was bringing it to Kabul. Wells could have carried it, but since he was flying on a civilian passport, he faced the risk of a bag search. Under these circumstances, he would normally have another CIA officer bring the stuff in a diplomatic pouch and deliver it once he'd arrived. But—aside from the necessary step of having the Kabul chief of station brief the Deltas and Special Operations Group on Samir Khalili—Wells and Shafer wanted to keep the case officers in Afghanistan in the dark.

Shafer found the solution: a British MI6 operative would deliver everything to Wells once he came to Kabul, bypassing the CIA. Duto could ask the head of MI6 directly. The move even had a certain symmetry. The prior president had used the British **against** Wells on his last mission.

So Wells had nothing to worry about in his bag. "No, no weapons."

The agent consulted his screen.

"I need to check your luggage." The agent wasn't asking. A second officer had already come to the counter, his right hand touching the pistol on his hip.

The men led Wells to a windowless concrete room, empty except for a portable X-ray machine and a plastic table. They locked Wells inside, returned ten minutes later with his black Samsonite, a stock bag, no hidden compartments.

"Yours?"

"Yes." Wells wondered if they'd planted a gun or drugs inside it. The delay would have given them time. He watched as they ran the Samsonite through the X-ray machine and emptied it so they could tug at every seam for hidden compartments. Wells was glad he'd come in clean. Even the agency's best trick suitcases wouldn't have survived this inspection.

After fifteen minutes, the men grew frustrated. The good news was that they hadn't planted anything or they wouldn't have gone to so much trouble to find it. But they had obviously expected to find something.

"This bag, it has a hidden compartment? Maybe we cut it open."

"Whatever you like."

The search hadn't been random, Wells realized. Someone at Langley had found the name Wells would be using on his new passport, then made an anonymous phone call telling the Pakistani government to watch for Mitch Kelly. Shafer and Wells hadn't told the seventh floor about their plan to use the British. The mole might have assumed Wells would carry his own litter, or even a weapon. If the Pakistanis found it and arrested Wells, he'd be stuck in prison for months. If he asked the agency to help, word would spread to every case officer in Central Asia. His mission would be derailed before he ever reached Bulgaria.

Best of all, from the mole's point of view, the move carried no risk. Wells and Shafer had no good way to chase down the tip, or even prove anyone had made one.

Wells had to give the mole credit. He wondered how far the Pakistani officers would press the issue, if they would hold him without evidence. But after another five minutes of prodding at the suitcase, the agents let him go.

Nice try, Mr. X. I'm still coming.

BECAUSE PAKISTAN AIRLINES was less than re-
liable—it had recently suspended service after
three of its workers died in a riot for higher
pay—decent intercity bus lines connected the
country's major cities. Yet his nine-hundred-
mile ride to Islamabad lasted more than a day
on pockmarked highways. By the time he
stepped off the bus, Wells felt as though the
world's worst masseuse had worked him over.

He found a drab hotel by the station, took a
lukewarm shower to wash the stink off his
body. The cracked mirror displayed an exhausted, dull-eyed man. Good. The Islamabad–Kabul flight had plenty of Western aid
workers and bodyguards. Wells didn't want
them to mistake him for one of them. He preferred they see him as one of the confused ad-
venturers who showed up in Kabul a couple of
times a month. They called themselves free-
lance journalists or directors of charities they'd
invented themselves. Usually Afghanistan
wasn't their first stop. They'd survived Myan-
mar or Egypt and thought they were ready for
the big leagues.

The smart ones saw the dangers and hung

around Kabul's handful of expat cafés for a few days before going back to Dubai. The lucky ones ran out of cash before they could bump into supposedly friendly locals who could lure them from the capital's relative safety. The really lucky ones went straight north and wound up in Tajikistan, where they blog-bragged about their adventures in the Graveyard of Empires. The unlucky ones . . . disappeared. They were kidnapped and held for insane ransoms. Or simply murdered, their torn bodies dumped at the edge of the capital, a wordless warning to every other Westerner in Afghanistan: **Get out. You don't belong.**

The professional foreigners didn't like these guys. Not just because their kidnappings caused trouble. Their Lonely Planet wandering called into question the seriousness of the diplomats and journalists. **To you, Kabul's a hardship post, the center of American foreign policy in Central Asia, a chance to win a Pulitzer. To me, it's a passport stamp and a place to buy a cheap rug.** The pros would have liked to ban them, but the Islamic Republic of Afghanistan had its own rules.

So Wells wanted his fellow passengers to see him as an amateur. And ignore him.

INDEED, ON THE flight the next morning, no one said a word. Wells had booked a window seat on the right side of the plane so he could look at the green hills to the north. Past them, the great mountains of the Kush, their peaks covered in untracked snow, so massive that even from a hundred miles away they erupted into the sky. The sight filled Wells with a nostalgia, real and false at once. Despite the deprivation he'd endured in those mountains, he'd felt a sense of purpose that he'd never entirely recaptured. Stop al-Qaeda before it could attack the United States again. What could be simpler or more important? Ever since, the threats had grown muddier, the missions more complicated. **We were soldiers once . . . and young . . .**

The 737 left the mountains behind and descended into Hamid Karzai International Airport. It had been called Kabul International until 2014, when the Afghan parliament renamed it after the former president, probably to commemorate all the money he'd skimmed during reconstruction. The jet came in in a standard approach, no tactical landing needed. So the airport was safe, for now.

At Immigration, Wells offered himself up as Mitch Kelly for what he expected would be the second-to-last time. The officer flipped to the visa page. "Purpose of visit."

"Tourism. Panjshir Valley." North of Kabul, a mostly Tajik province.

"You come here for drugs?" the agent said abruptly. Wells wondered if the mole had tried the same trick here as in Pakistan. Probably not. He would know that if Wells beat Pakistani Immigration, he was clean.

"Just to see your country."

The agent didn't hide his sneer. "Welcome to Kabul."

As WELLS STEPPED out of the airport, his heart leapt. He wanted to feel sorry that he wouldn't see Emmie for months, and part of him did . . . But he felt more alive in the field than anywhere else.

The threat of kidnapping and terror over-shadowed every aspect of life in Kabul for Westerners. To move around the city, they either had their own drivers or called cabs from a handful of taxi services known to be safe. But Wells needed to get away from the Western infrastructure—and practice his Pashto—as quickly as he could. He needed to **become**

Samir Khalili, even if for only a few days, before his capture.

The first cab he saw was a battered Toyota Corolla station wagon with a **Tax** sign screwed to its roof, the **i** gone. Wells sat up front, shoving the seat back as far as it would go. Photos of two boys and a girl were taped to the dashboard, as clear a signal as Wells could have hoped that the driver was not a Talib. Religious militants didn't show off pictures of their children, especially not their daughters.

"Yes, where to?" the cabbie said in English.

"Just around," Wells said in Pashto, the language of the Pashtuns, who dominated southern Afghanistan and formed the core of the Taliban. Wells had learned the language during his years here. But he'd rarely had reason to use it during his years in the United States. He wondered how bad he sounded. Pashto had a stuttering, rhyming cadence. To the untrained ear, it sounded a lot like Arabic, which Wells **did** speak fluently.

"Nowhere in particular?" The cabbie's words were in Pashto. Wells knew he sounded better than he'd feared. No one would confuse him for a native, but Samir Khalili wasn't a native either.

"I want to see how it's changed. I was here years ago."

"When the Americans first came?" **With the CIA?**

"Your children?" Wells said in answer, pointing at the dashboard.

"Yes. You have any?"

"Two. A boy and a girl."

The cabbie stared at Wells a few seconds more before shoving the Toyota into gear. They spent the afternoon on Kabul's cramped streets. Wells had seen the city during his years as a jihadi. He remembered it as desperately poor, its buildings shell-torn and crumbling, its residents destitute, amputees everywhere. The Russian invasion and the Afghan civil war had shredded it. The Taliban hadn't had the money to rebuild it, and they considered Kandahar their real capital anyway.

But the building boom that came with Western aid after September 11 had swept away the wreckage. Concrete mansions now filled the hills of the Sherpur neighborhood, west of the airport. "This one, forty-seven bedrooms," the cabbie told Wells, pointing to one monstrosity. A block farther on: "This one has nightclub. In basement." The houses belonged to drug traffickers, politicians, and the contractors who had made billions supplying the United States military. Many were empty now, as the Taliban closed in. Their owners had laundered every dollar they could and fled to Dubai.

Southeast of Sherpur was Wazir Akbar Khan, the city's international center. Ironically, the district was named for the emir who forced the British from Afghanistan in 1842, not the first or last time that an invading army had come to grief here. Wazir was home to the American embassy, the Presidential Palace, and the biggest non-governmental organizations. The aid groups had spent years fighting for causes dear to Western hearts, like women's rights and the rule of law. Most locals remained indifferent, if not openly hostile, to those grand ideas. Terror attacks had forced the aid workers behind blast walls and checkpoints manned by Nepali mercenaries, whose grim faces offered stark proof that the NGOs had failed to win over the population they claimed to serve. The checkpoints meant that much of central Kabul was barred to civilian traffic. Delivery trucks and the over-stuffed minibuses that served as the city's public transportation system fought for space on the few open streets.

Meanwhile, outside the center of town, Kabul now sprawled for miles. When Wells had first seen it, its population had totaled about one million. Now it had more than four million residents. Some had come for work during the boom. Others were rural refugees driven from their homes by the war.

The growth had stretched Kabul's limited infrastructure far past its breaking point. The city didn't even have an underground sewage system. Waste drained into concrete ditches alongside the roads. During the dry season, the stuff had nowhere to go except into the air. Meanwhile, slums had grown up the mountains that surrounded the city. To survive Kabul's cold nights, their inhabitants burned waste oil, scrap wood, and whatever coal they could scrounge. On windless days, the smog made a mockery of the pure snow to the east.

Yet the city was wealthier and saner than it had been when Wells had known it. Despite the Talib attacks on hotels, government ministries, and aid organizations, it was mostly peaceful. Women no longer had to wear the veiled blue burqas that the Taliban had required, though many still did. The bustling stores testified to the fact that some Western cash had escaped politicians' bank accounts and reached the streets.

After a half hour fighting the traffic in Wazir, they finally made their way to the highway that led to Pakistan. "Where now?"

"Stay on this a while."

"You want to go to Peshawar?"

"You're full of good advice."

The cabbie laughed. Wells liked this guy. Trusted him, too, for no obvious reason except those pictures on the dash. Wells had learned over the years to go with his first read, positive or negative. Most civilians weren't great liars.

They drove east another fifteen minutes. When Wells was sure they weren't being tailed, he told the cabbie to turn around and take him to Pul-e Khishti, the city's biggest mosque, which was known for its pale blue dome.

"You want to pray?"

"Shop."

For centuries, the streets around the mosque had served as a giant open-air bazaar. The Soviets had demolished the bazaar's wooden storefronts, but the Afghans had replaced them with concrete buildings after September 11. Like the rest of Kabul, the market was uglier but busier now. It sold everything from fresh vegetables to live sheep, burqas to laptops.

"For a kite?" Kite flying had been an Afghan pastime for centuries, made famous in the book **The Kite Runner.**

"A phone." Among other things.

A half hour later, the cabbie parked in the

giant plaza between mosque and bazaar. Between worshippers and shoppers, the spot
looked overdue for a truck bomb to Wells.

The bazaar's streets were crowded and noisy.
A woman in a canary yellow headscarf fingered
a bolt of fabric, murmuring, "Too much, too
much," to a tailor who stood a respectful four
feet away. A chicken squawked as a farmer
shoved it at shoppers walking by. "Nice and fat."

After fifteen minutes of searching, Wells
found the street he wanted, shopkeepers selling
cooking supplies. Including knives and propane
tanks. The stalls in the center looked to have
the best stuff. At one, a green-eyed Tajik sent
sparks flying as he sharpened a carving knife
against a whetstone. Strangely, the stone was
perched atop a massive oak desk that looked
like it belonged in a white-shoe law firm in New
York. Beside the grinding stone, a dozen blades
were lined up neatly.

"My friend," the Tajik said. "Sharpest knife
in Kabul."

Wells saw a forest of tiny white scars on the
Tajik's hands, proof of the dangers of the trade.
He picked up the smallest of the knives, plastic-
handled, the blade barely two inches long. Too
small to be much use at dinner, but handy as a
last-ditch weapon for close-in combat.

"For sheep." The man grinned. "Or whatever else you need to cut."

Wells edged his thumb along the blade—

"Careful—"

Too late. The steel sliced through his skin. "How much?"

"Thirty dollars, very good price. With this, too"—the Tajik reached under the desk, came up with a battered black leather sheath.

Thirty dollars for a tiny blade was an extortionate price in a country where much of the population survived on a dollar a day. Wells picked up a second knife, this one five inches long, with a dagger's sharp tip. And a long-handled plastic butane torch, the kind that Americans used to light barbecues. "Thirty for all of it."

"Sixty. You want junk, go somewhere else."

Knives were a poor substitute for pistols, but until the British made their delivery, the blades would have to do. Wells put three twenty-dollar bills in the Tajik's scarred hand.

WELLS SPENT ANOTHER hour buying mobile phones and **shalwar kameez**, the standard outfit for Afghan men, loose linen pants topped by a matching tunic and a sleeveless vest. As the sun vanished behind the city's western mountains, he found his way back to the cab.

Inside the Toyota, Wells strapped a knife to each leg, under his jeans and just above his boots. Kinda cowboy, he'd admit. "Let's go."

Naturally, Kabul had expensive and well-guarded hotels for executives and aid workers. Wells had instead picked the Winter Inn, a modest guesthouse west of the city center that catered to Pakistani traders.

"How much?" Wells said as they arrived. They hadn't settled on a price for the afternoon.

Greed and fear were visibly battling in the cabbie's face. Wells was a lone American and normally would have been ripe for fleecing. The day's itinerary and the knives on his legs suggested otherwise.

"Four hundred dollars."

Wells shook his head.

"Two hundred."

"I don't think so."

"One hundred. Fair price."

Wells gave him the hundred, plus a twenty-dollar tip, received a torn piece of paper with a phone number in return. "If you need me tomorrow—"

THE BIG HOTELS had blast walls, guards in body armor, airport-style X-ray scanners to check bags. The Winter Inn had three scrawny locals outside the front door, wearing AK-47s and bored faces. Inside, two more guards. One patted Wells down as the other poked through his bag.

"You have guns?" the first said in English. "No guns here. We protect you."

"Naturally."

Halfhearted as it was, the pat-down probably would have found a pistol if Wells had been carrying one. But the knives got through.

The front desk manager gave Wells an insincere, too-wide smile when he saw the Mitch Kelly passport. The smile meant either **I wish you'd picked somewhere else. The Taliban know we don't have Americans, so they don't bother us—**

Or Hello, stranger. I'll be right back, soon as I've called my friends so I can collect a commission on your ransom.

Either way, Wells wanted Samir Khalili's passport and pistol. He wanted to be wearing his new **shalwar kameez** instead of a T-shirt and jeans. Mitch Kelly was bound for trouble. Wells remembered what Shafer had said to him before his very first trip over here: **We've been trying to buy their loyalty since 1980. Every year, the price goes up.**

Shafer said those words almost twenty years before. The price was still rising.

"How long, sir?"

"One night."

"Passport, please?" Wells handed it over, wondering if he would have to argue to get it back. But the clerk merely flipped through, checked the visa page, and returned it.

Rooms started at thirty-five dollars. Wells spent an extra ten so he could splurge for a single with its own bathroom.

"You pay cash, Mr. Kelly? Five-dollar discount."

Wells passed over forty dollars. The too-friendly clerk gave a too-friendly smile and slid across a key attached to an old-style brass plate. "Number 18. First floor"—meaning the second, as Afghans used the British system and called the street-level floor the ground floor.

Number 18 was long and narrow. Its barred window looked out on a chimney-sized air shaft. Its bathroom consisted of a dirty toilet and sink, separated from the rest of the room by a thin blue curtain. The best evidence that the room wasn't a prison cell were the plastic skis glued to the walls, a nod to the hotel's name.

Wells powered up his new phone, texted **Here** to the Afghan number Shafer had given him. The British officer must have been waiting because the response came back in minutes: **Have your kit. Tomorrow 0900 turnoff TV Hill Road. 4R.**

TV Hill, officially named Mount Asmai, was a Kabul landmark southwest of the city center. Dozens of television antennas sprung from its long ridgeline. Though they claimed to love traditional culture, Afghans had a voracious appetite for television. Mud-brick slum houses stretched along the sides of the mountain, but the only road to the top came from the west, near Kabul University.

Wells wasn't sure what **4R** meant. British spy slang? **Read, react, ride, and roll . . .** Didn't sound much like MI6 to him. The rest of the message was clear enough. **K,** he texted back. He was happy enough not to have the pickup at the hotel. Mitch Kelly would walk out of this room in the morning and vanish, never to return.

Wells stretched out on the floor to sleep. No reason to get comfortable. He gave the butane lighter the bed.

HE WOKE TO footsteps coming down the hall, two men at least. His room was blackout dark. He checked his new phone: **02:35.** Outside, a low voice in Pashto. "Eighteen." That fast, his head cleared. The clerk had sold him out. That the kidnappers had come for him inside the hotel surprised him. But unprotected Americans were a rare and precious commodity. These guys didn't want to lose him to someone else.

Now Wells understood why the clerk hadn't made a copy of the Mitch Kelly passport, why he had offered Wells a discount for cash. The clerk hadn't even registered him. The rooms around him were silent. The kidnappers must figure they could take him in the dark, drag him into a car. No one would connect him to this hotel.

How many? Two, three at most. More would be in the way in a room this small.

The footsteps were almost at the door now—

How would they get him out? Blind him with flashlights, control him with a pistol. They knew he'd been searched at the entrance. They'd figure he was unarmed. Still, they wouldn't come at him physically unless they had no choice. The clerk would have warned them that he was a big man. They wouldn't want to risk a fight that might wake the other guests.

The footsteps stopped outside his door. "Remember, let me talk," the first man said.

Then Wells knew. They would tell him that they were **police**. Most Americans instinctively trusted the police. They would expect him to give them the benefit of the doubt. He'd do the opposite. No slow play. He needed to distract them.

Fire.

Wells flicked on the butane torch, waved it at the curtain that separated the toilet from the rest of the room.

A knock rattled the door—

The curtain caught, the flames kissing the filmy blue fabric, throwing the devil's own light into the darkness, the smoke fouling Wells's throat—

"Police," a man said in heavily accented English from outside. "Afghan police." Wells needed to move before the smell of smoke was obvious. He tugged the mattress onto the floor beneath the curtain—

A key scraped in the lock.

Wells pulled the bigger of his new knives with his right hand and crossed to the door. He opened it with his left hand while hiding the knife behind his right leg. Two men stood outside. Wells looked at them, knowing the ball had already been snapped, the players were moving. He had to decide **now** whether to kill them. Without identifying himself. Without giving them the chance to explain themselves. If he was wrong, if they were really cops . . .

They wore the uniform tops of the Afghan National Police, which meant nothing. They had Makarovs stuffed into their waistbands.

Real police would have had Glocks.

The flames grabbed the men's attention. They looked past Wells. "What is this?" the man nearer Wells said in Pashto. He reached for his Makarov. Too late. Wells was already coming. He wrapped his left arm around the Talib's back, pulled him close. With his right hand, Wells drove the knife into the Talib's stomach. The sharpest knife in Kabul ripped through clothing and skin and fat into the intestines underneath and the big blood vessels that fed them. The reason for the phrase **weak underbelly**. The man's eyes popped wide in disbelief. Wells ripped the knife upward for maximum damage and turned to the second Talib, who was trying to pull his Makarov—

Wells didn't waste time going for the pistol. He stepped forward and put all of his two hundred ten pounds into a right cross that caught the Talib flush in the jaw. The man sprawled backward, would have gone down if the hallway wall hadn't propped him up. He reached again for the pistol, but his eyes were cloudy and his movements slow.

Wells used his left hand to pin the Talib's

gun arm and raised his right elbow and slammed it into the man's temple. The bone-on-bone crack echoed in the hall as lightning surged up Wells's arm. The Talib's eyes rolled back in his head and his tongue lolled from his mouth. He slumped to the floor, in a dark world all his own.

The smoke poured from the room's doorway now, but Wells had attacked so fast that the men hadn't had time to yell for help. The first Taliban was trying to pull the dagger out of his stomach but didn't have the strength. His blood-smeared hand came off the knife. He raised his fingers to Wells, a fluttery wave. **Look what you've done.**

Wells stepped over him, looked inside the doorway. The mattress had ignited and the fire was raging. He hated to lose the Afghan clothes and run out of here dressed like an American, but he had no choice. Anyway, nothing would connect him to the hotel. His passport and wallet were in his pocket, and now the clerk's decision not to copy his passport worked for him. The clerk would hardly want to tell the police that he'd tried to sell an American to the Taliban. Not that Wells expected much of an investigation. Most Afghan cops preferred committing crimes to solving them.

Wells stepped toward the fire stairs at the end of the hallway, then realized the kidnappers probably had a car waiting there. Even if they'd come through the main entrance on the way in, why risk it on the way out? A guess, but logical. He grabbed the second Talib's Makarov and bolted down the hall, yelling, "Fire!" in Pashto. Warning the other guests increased his chances of being caught, but the hotel had no sprinklers. Wells couldn't let civilians burn in their beds.

As Wells sprinted down the hotel's front steps, the clerk appeared. He saw Wells, turned to run. Wells leapt down, grabbed the man's scrawny arm, twisted until his shoulder began to pop from its socket. In Pashtun: "Those men, which way were they going to take me?"

"Sir, please—"

Wells put the Makarov to the clerk's temple. "Which way?"

The clerk pointed at the front door.

"If you're lying, I kill you."

"I promise on my father."

Now Wells had to bring the guy with him. If the clerk was lying and the other Talibs were waiting outside the fire door, Wells could use him as a hostage. If he was telling the truth, the Talibs were outside the front entrance, a few yards away, and the clerk would surely run to them and tell them where Wells had gone.

Wells frog-marched him down the hall toward the fire exit. The man squirmed but didn't fight. Footsteps thumped overhead, and the smell of smoke was thickening by the second.

Wells kicked open the unmarked fire door at the end of the hall, pushed the clerk out—

And stepped into a trash-covered alley that ran along the side of the hotel. It was empty.

"See?" The guy seemed to want a medal for telling the truth with a pistol to his head. Wells lifted the Makarov, whipped it down on the guy's skull. The dull thud of Bakelite on bone echoed up the alley. The clerk crumpled.

Wells ran for the back of the hotel, barely squeezing through the rough brick walls that formed the alley. He popped onto an unlit street. He had no idea of the neighborhood's geography or its streets, so he took the simplest possible zigzag, left, right, left, right.

Wells was prepared to make a stand in these empty streets. He would die before he let the Talibs grab him. But he didn't see or hear any-one. The kidnappers in front were probably still trying to figure out what had happened.

Trash piled up and the streets grew shabbier

until he came to a ridge that fell away into a muddy slum. He was alone. No Kabulite with a choice ventured out at this hour. He checked to be sure the Makarov had a round chambered and its safety off, walked down the hill.

The smell of waste was nose-wrinkling here, the houses crumbling mud walls topped with miserable quilts of tin and plastic. Aside from the dim orange glow of fires and the faint starlight that seeped through the smoke, the hillside was dark. The slum was a city within a city, the families inside clustered against the night. Wells wasn't worried about anyone calling the Taliban on him here. No one here supported the group. Or opposed it. For people this poor, survival was the only politics.

On the left he saw a hut that didn't have the usual blue tarp covering its entrance hole. Even the poorest families insisted on that much privacy for their women. Whoever had lived here was gone. Wells stepped inside, found himself in a void. Someone moved against the back wall. "My friend," Wells murmured in Pashto. Afghanistan had a major heroin problem. This hut could easily be the last stop on the junkie downbound.

In response, he heard only paws scrabbling, the whimper of a dog that wanted no trouble.

Wells rested against the mud wall beside the entrance. He left the pistol in his lap but clicked on the safety. He closed his eyes, expecting the cold would keep him awake. It reached into his bones as the adrenaline from the fight faded. If **fight** was the right word.

But he must have drifted, for around him dozens of flowers bloomed at once, roses, waving in a summer breeze, an easy vision—

He leaned close to smell their scent, watched as the roses turned, bone-white stems and blood-tipped petals, each one a man Wells had killed, spindly, nerveless, and growing without end—

The dog barked once, a sudden alarm—

Wells came to his feet, the Makarov in his hand. But he knew even as he lifted the pistol that he had nowhere to aim. This poor mutt feared **him**, no one else. A colossal weariness overcame him. He squatted and ran his hand across the hut's dirt floor, feeling its grit. More men dead, and he hadn't even been picked up for rendition. Maybe he should simply have flown into Bagram and disappeared from there. Maybe he should have avoided Afghanistan entirely, gone straight to Bulgaria with the right papers.

But he'd chosen this route precisely for its

difficulty. What Wells knew better than anyone was that Samir Khalili would feel an unspoken **relief** at his capture, relief at escaping
the mountains at last, relief that a drone strike
hadn't punched his one-way ticket to Paradise.
If he airmailed himself to Sofia, he had no hope
of capturing that feeling, or of being a plausible
Samir.

Again he leaned against the wall. After a
while, the dog came across the hut to him, one
slow step at a time, waiting for a kick to send
him away. Wells didn't move. Finally, the beast
stretched out and lay beside him with a faint
sigh that might have been satisfaction.

Together, they waited for the dawn.

WHEN IT CAME, Wells powered his phone,
called the cabbie. "I need a ride."

"From the Winter Inn."

"No."

"No?" Surprise in the driver's voice.

"Let's say I had an early checkout." Wells explained the path he'd taken, how he'd wound
up in the slum.

"I think I know where you are. Be at the top,
where you came in, in an hour."

"Faster is better." Morning would reveal the
blood that spattered Wells's dark blue sweatshirt

and jeans. He could take off the sweatshirt, but with only a T-shirt underneath he'd stand out even more. Plus he'd have no place to hide the Makarov.

"Half an hour, I'll try."

The dog watched this conversation with concern. Wells figured human voices rarely meant good news for him. He was a hundred different breeds, in better shape than Wells had feared, skinny but not emaciated. He had calm brown eyes and a stump for a tail. Twenty minutes later, when Wells stood and stepped out, the dog tilted his head and rose to follow. Wells shook his head, and the animal whimpered and sat, resigned to his fate.

Wells reached the slum's entrance just as the Toyota rolled up.

"What happened, my friend?"

"Drive."

They drove slowly along the narrow road along the slum's eastern edge.

"What's your name?" Wells said.

"Dilshod."

"I need to be at the TV Hill road at nine a.m., Dilshod."

Dilshod reached across the seat, ran a thick finger down the biggest bloodstain on Wells's sweatshirt, an oddly intimate gesture.

"Looks like the Empire State Building, I know."

"I drove by the hotel on my way here."

"Not sure where you're going with this."

Dilshod put the taxi in neutral and they rolled to a stop. "You have money?"

"I have money."

"Two thousand dollars, I take you to TV Hill."

"TV Hill, then you drive me to Jalalabad, one thousand total." Jalalabad was a hundred miles east of Kabul, the last big Afghan town before the Pakistan border. The Taliban controlled the mountains around it. But the highway from Kabul was relatively safe. At least during the day. At least for vehicles that weren't obviously American military or Afghan National Army. "I need two more shalwar kameez, too. I lost mine."

Dilshod tapped the photos of his children taped to the dashboard like they could help him decide. "One thousand now. Right now. I take you to TV Hill, then I decide Jalalabad."

Wells gave him ten crisp one-hundred-dollar bills. Dilshod lifted his tunic and stuck the money in his waistband like the world's hairiest stripper.

———

ON THE WAY to TV Hill, Dilshod stopped at a tailor's shop, emerging after a few minutes with two **shalwar kameez**, identical and ugly, light brown tunics and dark brown vests. "Only ones big enough." He turned in to an alley, and Wells pulled off his sweatshirt and wriggled into the tunic and the vest and pants. He left his old clothes in a pile. No need to burn them. The Afghan police had a better chance of finding a UFO than connecting the blood on that sweatshirt to the fire at the hotel.

They reached the turnoff to TV Hill ten minutes early. Afghan kids were already lined up at a water station near the road. The mountain slums had no water system, so every gallon had to be carried in. The lucky kids led donkeys. The rest carried plastic jugs they would hump up themselves. In other countries, they would have been described as school-age, but here school wasn't even a fantasy.

Dilshod pulled over. "Keep driving," Wells said. He didn't feel like sitting still. When they returned a few minutes later, a beaten-up Toyota 4Runner sat near the turnoff. So now Wells knew what **4R** meant.

Wells's phone buzzed. **Taxi?**

Y.

Follow.

The 4Runner pulled out in front of the taxi. "After him."

Dilshod seemed about to object, then didn't. The Toyota headed for the highway that ran toward central Kabul. Wells sincerely hoped the British weren't planning to make the handover at their embassy. Nope. They passed the downtown exits and the big blue dome of Pul-e Khishti without slowing.

"Your friend, he wants to go to Peshawar, too," Dilshod said.

After another few minutes, the neighborhoods around the highway thinned out. The 4Runner pulled off beside an industrial park and parked behind a waiting minivan. Wells's phone buzzed: **Park in front. Engine off.**

"Here. And turn off the engine."

"Your friends don't trust you much."

No one trusts me much. A tall man stepped out of the 4Runner and ambled up to Wells's window, holding a short blue duffel bag weighted by the AK inside.

"Lot of trouble to drop off a bag."

"You have a certain reputation." The Brit had a ski-jump nose and thick dirty-blond hair that justified the label **Byronic**. "Also, we thought you might be upset about Hong Kong."

"Not a bit."

"I wouldn't have guessed you're the forgiving sort. Anyway, this is yours." He handed the bag forward.

Wells peeked inside: a short-stock AK and two loaded magazines; a worn Canadian passport that had supposedly expired in 2009; a well-thumbed Quran and a book of the Prophet's sayings; a yellowed picture of an Arab woman; a fake Pakistani identity card featuring Samir Khalili's photo; two expired credit cards; a bundled stack of dollars, afghanis, and Pakistani rupees; and the **pièce de résistance**, a genuine post–September 11 photo of Osama bin Laden. It had never been seen publicly. SEAL Team 6 had found it during the raid on the house in Abbottabad. On the back, the words **safe passage** were written in spindly Arabic handwriting that matched samples of bin Laden's that the SEALs had also recovered.

"Thank you."

"Our pleasure. You don't want your own people to know about this? I can't say I understand the play, but I'm sure it has a logic all its own."

Wells could listen to this guy talk all day. "I could tell you, but I'd have to kill you."

"In that case, I'd prefer you didn't." The Brit leaned in, dropped his voice to a whisper. "Speaking of killing, we're hearing rumors that someone took care of two Talibs at a guesthouse this morning."

"News to me."

"The Talibs are supposedly **very** angry. They've vowed to find the man. Good luck to him if they do. All the SEALs in the world won't get him back." Byron handed back the keys, opened the door. "Be careful out there. You never know who to trust." His eyes shifted to the cabbie.

"**Whom.**" Wells had never been happier to correct another man's grammar.

"Whom?"

"Whom to trust.

10

LANGLEY

FOR WEEKS, Shafer had burned his eyes and brain reading every file that Reg Pushkin, Vernon Green, and Walter Crompond had generated during their agency careers. Every annual evaluation. After-action statement. Background check. Expense report. Email and text.

None of the three had Facebook pages, of course. But their wives and parents did. Shafer checked them all, not just the public posts but the private ones. The National Security Agency had those saved for posterity.

He drove past their houses and kids' schools. He pored over bank statements and tax returns, court filings and speeding tickets. Health insurance claims, too. He had, for now, stopped at getting the details of medical records.

So far, he'd come to one main conclusion, one that only made his job harder.

All three were good officers. Excellent, even.

The relentless pressure of the war on terror meant the agency couldn't afford paper pushers on the seventh floor. And Duto was a keen judge of talent—as his relationship with Wells proved. Pushkin, Green, and Crompond were driven, smart, and brave. All had served with distinction in Iraq.

Pushkin had risen fastest. He'd taken over Moscow after only two years on the insistence of the outgoing chief. **I have never seen a harder-working, more forward-looking officer,** she wrote. **It is my strong recommendation that he become the next COS.** Even more impressive, Pushkin had convinced the deputy he'd jumped to stay and work for him.

Green had run Nigeria, working hundred-hour weeks to support that country's fight against Boko Haram, its own radical Muslim insurgency. **A superior chief who has gained the respect of local intelligence officers with his personal bravery,** the chief of the West African desk wrote in a letter of commendation. In other words, Green had gone into the forests and chased Boko's guerrillas himself.

Meanwhile, Crompond had taken over the

drone desk at Langley, making endless close calls. Twice he had refused to okay an attack despite pressure from more senior officers. Both times the agency's final analysis showed he was correct. **Has uncanny judgment and a keen moral sense,** his boss wrote.

BUT ALL THREE men had red flags.

Pushkin and his wife had government salaries and champagne taste: two kids in private school, his and her BMWs, and almost no savings. Their financial records showed that her parents had sent her four checks in the last two years, forty-eight thousand dollars in all. Without the money, they would have fallen behind on their mortgage. Two other times, they had made ninety-five-hundred-dollar cash deposits, just under the limit that triggered banks to report deposits to the Internal Revenue Service. Shafer assumed that money came from her parents, too, but unless he asked, he couldn't be sure.

Shafer didn't like German iron. One of his many not entirely random prejudices. He was old enough, and Jewish enough, to remember that the Bayerische Motoren Werke had used slave labor to make jet engines for the Luftwaffe. But even in his most cynical moments, he couldn't imagine anyone would betray the United States to the Islamic State for a 528i. Especially since the nineteen thousand dollars in cash he'd found so far would barely cover the down payment.

Still, needing constant help from the in-laws couldn't feel very good. Maybe the pressure had gotten to Pushkin. He also traveled the most of the three. As deputy director, he left the United States regularly to talk with his counterparts. Paris, Berlin, and Cairo, three cities notable for their Islamic State cells, were his most frequent destinations.

Even more surprising was the fact that despite their money problems, he and his wife had taken trips to France in each of the last two years. If Pushkin was passing information to Daesh, the vacations were great cover. As the deputy director, Pushkin had full-time bodyguards. Freeing himself from them in northern Virginia wouldn't be easy. But **I'm going to Paris with my wife and we want the week to ourselves** was a solid excuse.

Or maybe the Pushkins just liked the **Mona Lisa**.

MEANWHILE, GREEN HAD divorced three years before. His wife wound up with their kids. He hadn't contested the ruling. The split looked relatively friendly to Shafer, at least from the court filings. Yet only Green knew how it felt to him. His bank account showed a half-dozen three-hundred-dollar checks to one Ben Appelbaum, a psychiatrist near Baltimore. But going to a shrink didn't make you a traitor. Neither did trying to keep the agency from knowing about it by picking a guy an hour away.

Green's emails and texts revealed that in the wake of the divorce, he had what might politely be called an active social life. Shafer could hardly fault him for taking advantage of the perks of being a single, handsome, successful African-American man in Washington. However, the sheer volume of his conquests bespoke a certain lax attitude toward risk.

Green also had a potential connection to the Islamic State. He was Christian, but he had a cousin in Baltimore, Ali Shabazz, who was a Black Muslim. Shabazz was highly devout, according to a brief file that the agency's counter-intelligence desk had compiled. He served as an imam at a storefront mosque in West Baltimore. He'd even made the **hajj**, the ritual trip to Mecca that all Muslims were supposed to take at least once.

Green had never hidden his connection with

Shabazz, though he claimed he saw his cousin only a couple of times a year. Nor could Shafer find any evidence that Shabazz had an actual, as opposed to potential, relationship with Islamist terror groups. But, like Pushkin's trips, Green's cousin might be a backdoor route to funnel information to the Islamic State, which actively recruited Black Muslims.

ON THE SURFACE, Crompond was the most stable of the three. He was married, with no financial problems. But he, too, showed signs of fraying. He'd picked up three speeding tickets in three years, and his wife's insurance records showed several prescriptions for Valium and other anti-anxiety drugs. She might be filling those so they didn't show up in his records.

Crompond had his own unusual connection to a prominent local Muslim. A couple of years before, he'd had a parking lot fender bender with Aziz Murak, an imam at a large northern Virginia mosque. In a note he sent to the counterintel desk, Crompond said he had recognized the imam and seen a chance to develop the relationship.

Imam Murak was pleasantly surprised I knew of his prominence in the Muslim-

American community. I provided him my DoS [Department of State] business card, identifying me as James Jones, Deputy Assistant Secretary for South Asian Affairs. We spoke for several minutes. I believe that I can develop him as a source. However, given the sensitivity of this contact, I felt I should inform CI immediately.

Despite his prominence as an Islamic activist, Murak didn't appear on any watch lists, and, after a short investigation, the counterintelligence desk encouraged Crompond to develop the relationship. He met with Murak several times but reported that the imam was not willing to provide valuable information. Murak remains polite but continues to resist efforts to develop him as a USGOV source. I will continue to meet him from time to time but will not pursue actively.

Like Shabazz, Murak might have connections to the Islamic State. But Crompond hadn't needed to report the contact. If he were really passing information through Murak, why draw attention to their relationship?

On the **other** other hand, maybe Crompond wanted to insulate himself by explaining the contact in advance. That way, if the FBI happened to stumble across the meetings,

Crompond would already have an excuse in place. He'd be hiding in plain sight.

HAVING LEADS ON all three men gave Shafer the hope that he would find the mole before Wells did, maybe even before Wells wound up in Bulgaria at all. Both pride and his desire to keep Wells out of that particular briar patch were driving him.

You don't talk to anyone, Duto had said when Shafer and Wells had first proposed the plan. **You're not throwing shade on these guys.** A clear enough warning. But Shafer decided Duto meant it to apply only inside the agency, not out. Talking to someone's cousin or mother-in-law hardly counted as throwing shade.

Shafer rubbed his eyes, forced himself to ignore the pain in his back and sit up straight. Not even noon, and he was exhausted. He was staying too late too often, grinding himself down. He knew why. He wanted to share the discomfort that Wells faced. Stupid. He wouldn't help himself or Wells if he made himself a zombie.

But he couldn't stop himself.

He wanted to check Pushkin's finances again. He'd looked for accounts that carried Social Security numbers belonging to Pushkin. But

Pushkin might have gotten tricky, setting up accounts with shell companies. Through the NSA, the agency had access to state tax and corporate records. Those nearly always contained the tax identification numbers of the shell owners.

In truth, Shafer thought the odds were against Pushkin stowing money in a shell account. The man didn't seem like the type to keep his savings tucked away. But detective work meant chasing a thousand leads.

He was just about to log in to the corporate records database when his computer pinged:

KABUL STATION/URGENT: SUICIDE ATTACK ON WEST KABUL HOTEL

AFGHAN NATIONAL POLICE REPORT TWO DEAD, SEVERAL INJURED, AT WINTER INN HOTEL; NO REPORT OF IED OR SUICIDE ATTACK BUT HOTEL SEVERELY DAMAGED BY FIRE OF UNKNOWN ORIGIN.

ATTACK OCCURRED APPROX 0300 LOCAL TIME; NO US/ALLIED CASUALTIES REPORTED ... MOTIVE UNKNOWN/ UNCLEAR; PLACE AND TIME OF ATTACK CONTRARY TO TALIB CALLS TO FOCUS ON

WESTERN TARGETS; TALIB HAVE NOT YET
CLAIMED RESPONSIBILITY.

NO OTHER ATTACKS REPORTED AT THIS
TIME, BUT RETAIN HIGHEST SECURITY
POSTURE . . . UPDATES AS NEEDED . . .

No U.S. casualties. So Wells was fine. Unless somebody had mistaken him for a Talib. Shafer hadn't heard from him.

Shafer's phone buzzed. A blocked number.

"Ellis Shafer?" A woman. "Hold for the President."

"I have to?"

By the time Shafer had finished asking, Duto was on the line.

"Hear about your buddy?"

Shafer's heart pulled tight in his chest, the pain sudden and terrible. He'd known this call would come—

"He's already making a mess."

Shafer barely managed not to say, **You scared me, Vinny.** "This about that hotel, the Winter Inn? Just saw the cable. What happened?"

"Brits tell me he killed a couple of hostiles last night."

"Then they know more than we do."

Duto let the question hang, all the answer Shafer needed. What happened was what always happened. Wells was a one-man ambush.

"I'm having lunch with Mark Cuban and he's ruining it." Duto sounded as petulant as a grounded teenager.

"Why are you having lunch with Mark Cuban?"

"Because I want to." Left unspoken, barely: **And I'm the president, you idiot, so I can.** "So now the Talibs are looking for an American who killed two of their own. He'd best not plan on staying in Kabul."

"I'm sure he's figured that. He get his package?"

"Indeed. SIS reports he's **hale and hearty.** Their words."

"There'll always be an England."

"I'm worried he's overestimated his ability to go undercover."

"I always knew you cared, Vinny."

"What you know is, I'm right. Better hope he gets his Muslim mojo back—"

"Muslim mojo?"

"Before he winds up with his head on a stick in Kandahar."

"Speaking of, I wanted to ask—"

But Duto was already gone. Shafer was talking to an empty line.

"Good. I'll take that as a yes."

SHAFER SPENT THE afternoon scouring files, without success. He needed to escape the office. He decided to start with Ali Shabazz.

He called home. "Sweetie."

"Husband. Will I see you soon?"

The hope in her voice made Shafer hate himself a little.

"I have an errand. Not too late. Maybe nine."

"Okay," she said, after staying quiet just long enough to let him know it wasn't.

Shabazz lived in West Baltimore, a mile from the harbor. Not the worst neighborhood in the city. Those were on the east side of town. Still, the streetlamps looked to be mostly for target practice, and the potholes were big enough to form the foundations of a newer, happier city.

As he neared Shabazz's house, Shafer noticed stores advertising **halal** meat—in English and Arabic—along with South Asian women in headscarves walking side by side. Maybe the Black Muslims and the Muslim Muslims really had found one another. A white supremacist's worst nightmare.

An oversized white flag with the Muslim credo emblazoned in black hung over the stoop of Shabazz's house. The flag wasn't that of the Islamic State. Those were black with the credo in white. But a casual observer could easily have mistaken the two. Shafer suspected the chance for confusion was precisely the point.

No wonder Green didn't talk much about his cousin.

A new pickup, a black Nissan with a **PBUH** sticker plastered to its shiny chrome bumper, sat in the driveway. The letters stood for **Peace Be Upon Him**, the words devout Muslims used when they referred to Muhammad. Shafer parked inches from the sticker and creaked his way to the front door. Stomach bleeding had made him cut down on his anti-inflammatory pills, but his joints hadn't read the memo. Being old was one lousy choice after another.

The door swung open as he reached it. A tall black teenage boy wearing a neatly coiffed Afro looked at him with undiluted contempt.

"My name's Ellis Shafer. I'm looking for your dad—"

"Dad! Whitey's here! An old one."

"You can't be serious."

As an answer, the kid shut the door in his face.

"Nineteen sixty-seven called," Shafer yelled. "It wants its hair back."

A minute later, the door opened again, revealing a stockier, older version of the teenager. He wore a flowing white robe, a skullcap, and a frown. Shafer put out a hand. The man let it hang.

"Ali Shabazz?"

"Who wants to know?"

"I'm with Publishers Clearing House, and you may have won a million dollars—"

"If you're trying to serve me—"

"If I were trying to serve you, I would have already."

Shabazz started to close the door. Shafer stuck his foot in the jamb.

"Dummy. You know I can shoot you for that. Entering my domicile." Shabazz gave Shafer a sardonic smile at the fifty-cent word. "Even if you do look like every Jew lawyer in Baltimore"—**Bal-more**. The agency's file said Shabazz had grown up in the Bronx, but somewhere along the way he'd acquired the mumbly local accent, words creased together. "Not the good ones. The cheap ones who hang around all day looking for clients."

"I'd rather you didn't. Shoot me, that is."

"Get your fool foot out of my door."

Shafer did.

"And what are you doing blocking my driveway?"

"I didn't see any spaces."

In fact, the curb directly in front of Shabazz's house was open.

"Now you're just being provocative."

"I'm not the one with the pretend ISIS flag. You're gonna play, you might as well go all the way."

Shabazz rubbed his fingers over his carefully trimmed goatee, the hairs salt as much as pepper.

"Last time I checked, I'm allowed to tell people I'm Muslim. Anyway, I see a man at my front door who's too mouthy to be FBI. And too old to be a cop. You get one minute to explain what you want."

"Name's Ellis Shafer. I work for the CIA."

"Am I supposed to be impressed?"

"Like your cousin Vernon."

Shabazz didn't blink.

"You're not surprised. He tell you?"

"Doesn't matter what he told me. Me personally? I think signing up for the **armed forces**"— Shabazz put a sarcastic emphasis on the last two words—"is about as Uncle Tom as it gets. Shoot colored folk all over the world until you hit your twenty, and massa gives you a pension, VA **benefits**. Still and all, I admit Vern making the Deltas was cool. Gonna be a soldier, might as well be the baddest. Then he quits, tells us he's going to work for the State Department. Please. Wasn't one of us didn't know what that meant."

"So he didn't explicitly mention the CIA?"

"You trying to get him in trouble, Mr. Ellis? Don't like black people in your precious agency? Especially up top? Don't like taking orders from a man young enough to be your son?" Shabazz smirked. "Though if Vern was your son, you might need some words with your **wife**."

"Subtle. You see him a lot?"

"What's it to you?"

"You two ever talk about religion? Your pilgrimage? Casting stones at the devil?"

"Don't move, please." Shabazz stepped away from the door. When he came back, he was holding a big black pistol in his right hand. "This is a .40 caliber Glock 19, legally registered in the state of Maryland. Now, remove yourself from my front step and your car from my driveway or I will exercise my Allah-given right to protect my homestead and put a cap in your ass."

Shabazz grinned, a smile that said, **Yeah, I'm posing, and I'm enjoying myself . . . but give me the excuse and I might shoot you.**

Shafer raised his hands, backed away. Shabazz watched him into his car. Only when he was inside with the doors locked did he risk giving Shabazz a thumbs-up. Shabazz responded with a different finger.

After a few blocks, Shafer pulled over to think through the conversation. Sprinkled among his threats and his bluster, Shabazz had given up two crucial words: **taking orders**. A hint that Shabazz knew Green was at the very top of the agency. He shouldn't have. Green was a stickler for rules. The rules said you didn't tell family members that you worked at the agency, much less what you did. So why had Green told Shabazz? They were cousins, not husband and wife.

A small clue, sure, but small clues were all Shafer had.

On the other hand, would Shabazz really act so over the top if he had something to hide? Would Green risk using him? Most likely, Green had just talked too much after a couple of beers.

Maybe, maybe, maybe. Shafer wished he could bounce these clues off Wells, or even his old friend Lucy Joyner. He felt faintly disappointed as he found 95 and turned south. He'd driven up here hoping to clear Green somehow so he could focus on Pushkin and Crompond. Turn three targets into two and have an excuse to call Wells home. He couldn't, though.

He was stuck with three. And Wells was still going inside.

11

LANGLEY

THE ORIGINAL Headquarters Building, where the director and his deputies had their offices, had two permanently staffed entrances. The main lobby, with its wall of stars honoring dead officers, was the CIA's public face. It had appeared in countless movies. But the headquarters had another, semi-private entrance a floor below, accessible via a tunnel from the garage reserved for senior officers.

The second entrance gave foreign leaders, the heads of rival spy services, and even corporate executives the chance to enter headquarters discreetly. Just as important, it served as a status symbol. Theoretically, any employee could use it. But the guards knew who belonged, and they weren't shy about discouraging those who didn't.

Wayne belonged.

So as he approached the gate, agency identification in one hand, gym bag in the other, he didn't expect questions. He put his card to the gate and its glass barriers swung back—

"Sir."

Wayne shot the guard an annoyed look. The real threats were on the edge of the campus, where troublemakers could snipe at vehicles waiting to enter or blow themselves up. No would-be intruder had come close to the headquarters buildings in at least a generation. Watching these gates was a cushy job for security officers in their forties and fifties, a last stop before retirement. This guard was wearing a boxy gray suit that didn't hide how much weight he'd added in middle age. Wayne had exchanged pleasantries with him hundreds of times. His name was—

"Frank. What's up?"

"I hate to bother you, but I need to scan that." He nodded at the bag in Wayne's hand, blue nylon, the faded words **Washington Athletic Club** faintly visible in white.

"I'm in a hurry, Frank. You really need to see my gym clothes?"

"Afraid I do." The guard held out his hand.

Wayne hesitated, then handed over the bag.

An X-ray machine was mounted behind the

counter where the guards sat. Frank put the bag on the conveyor, watched the screen as it rolled through. Wayne did his best to look annoyed, not angry—**You know our security guards, they have to dot every** i **and cross every** t—

"Can I look inside?"

They both knew the guard was asking only to be polite. Security officers had the right to inspect every package that everyone, no matter how senior, brought in or out of headquarters. As David Petraeus had learned too late, no one was exempt from the government's strict rules on secrecy.

"Sure. You may want to wear a mask."

"Sir?"

"I have a couple of old T-shirts in there."

"Of course."

Trying to joke with the guards was always a mistake. Frank unzipped the bag, poked through the T-shirts and shorts, came out with two bottles of Gatorade, one full and unopened with red liquid inside, the other about three-quarters full of clear liquid.

"Can't bring these in."

"Come on, Frank. You've never seen me at the gym"—the agency's new fitness center had free weights, treadmills, even a climbing wall—

"but if you did, you'd know I'm a **sweater.**
Buckets of it. Gotta stay hydrated."

"I'm sorry, sir. I don't make the rules." The
guard unscrewed the cap to the bottle with the
clear liquid, sniffed it. "In fact, would you mind
taking a sip for me right now? This doesn't look
like Gatorade."

Wayne gave the guard a **Know your place**
stare. "It's water."

"You don't have to, but, in that case, I have
to confiscate the bottle and maybe send it to
the lab—"

"You've got to be kidding."

"Afraid not, sir." The guard looked at Wayne
with the first hint of real suspicion and Wayne
realized that he'd pushed this game as far he
could. The guard waggled his fingers—**Here**—
and handed it over, and Wayne looked at it like
it might be poisoned—

And took a long sip of what he knew was
plain Virginia tap water.

"Happy now, Frank?"

"This one, too."

"The Gatorade? I know you're just doing
your job, but look at it. It's not even open."
Wayne's annoyance was genuine now. The
guard backed off slightly.

"All right. Look, that one you can take back to your car, if you want—"

"I've wasted enough time. Just give it here."

He unscrewed the bottle, took a swallow.

"Can I take these up to my office now, Frank? Or do you want to swab them for DNA, too?" Without waiting for an answer, he flashed his identification at the turnstile scanner and marched through.

But he couldn't even make a clean exit.

"Your bag, sir—"

Frank handed it over. Wayne rode to seven, holding the bag in one hand, the bottles in the other. He wanted to put a hole in the wall of the elevator, but the feeds from its cameras went straight to the guard stations. He kept himself calm until he reached his office, closed the door, where he could safely curse under his breath.

How was he going to bring the sarin inside Langley? Though the chemical was incredibly toxic, it wasn't a biological weapon like anthrax that was lethal in quantities so minuscule they could barely be seen. He had done some basic calculations and realized he would need to bring in at least ten liters of DF, the liquid precursor to sarin, to have a realistic chance to send lethal quantities through the seventh floor's ventilation system. Plus an equal amount of isopropyl alcohol.

He'd also have to figure out how to tamper with the vents without being caught. The agency was well aware of the risk of a chemical or biological weapons attack, and its engineers closely watched its heating and air-conditioning systems.

But Wayne couldn't even overcome the first hurdle of sneaking the liquid inside. Three days before, he had tried the same test at the main lobby gate in late afternoon, hoping the crush of employees leaving for the day might distract the guards. It hadn't. They stopped him there, too, though that time they just sent him back to his car.

Worse, the guards were supposed to log unusual incidents at their stations. He doubted his test three days before had reached that level. Today's run-in probably would. And that little troll Shafer was surely looking for incident reports with his name. Bringing in a couple bottles of Gatorade was hardly suspicious, but to get written up for it more than once would be notable.

He needed a new plan. At this point it didn't matter if the Islamic State brought him a thousand liters of sarin. The only CIA officer he could poison was himself.

WAYNE CALLED THE imam, scheduled another meet, this one at a Lowe's in Fairfax, a few miles outside the Beltway. He was pushing his luck by meeting again so soon, but he had to take the chance.

Again Wayne made the meeting part of a normal Saturday run for groceries, dry cleaning, an oil change. The usual suburban nonsense that distracted his fellow Americans from the horrors they fueled. No. They didn't need distraction. They didn't think about their sins. Just went about their merry business.

By the time he reached Lowe's, he was sure he didn't have anyone on him. The imam was out back, nosing around the garden supplies area like he couldn't decide if he wanted Kentucky bluegrass or genetically modified fescue. He was dressed in a T-shirt and jeans, nothing to attract attention, and nobody was within thirty feet of him.

"My lawn's getting raggedy," Wayne said. "Any advice?"

The imam didn't smile. "I thought you were the expert. Now I'm wondering."

Wayne picked up a bag of ryegrass. "Thirty bucks for ten pounds? Seems expensive."

"Didn't you say we should meet as little as possible, **habibi**?"

"It couldn't be avoided. First. There's a chance that a man named Ellis Shafer may contact you. He probably won't, but he might." Wayne had debated whether to mention Shafer. He didn't want to set the imam off unnecessarily, but Shafer hadn't stopped poking around. By now, Shafer probably was aware of Wayne's contacts with the imam, and Wayne couldn't rule out that Shafer would try to push the imam himself.

"What do I tell him? If he does?"

"He may know I've approached you. Just stick to our old cover story."

"Who is this man Shafer anyway?"

Another reason Wayne hadn't wanted to mention Shafer. "Nobody. He doesn't have any real authority, he doesn't know anything, he just asks questions." **And talks to the President.**

"Why me?"

"He decided to look at prominent Muslims who have contact with senior folks, even if we've properly reported them." A safe lie.

"The truth. Do I need to worry?"

"He's fishing, that's all."

"Fine. What else?"

"The stuff we talked about. I don't see how I can get it inside. Without that, it's useless."

"Maybe I should invite your friends for a prayer session. **Please, leave your gas masks at home.**"

Wayne looked at the stacked bags of fertilizer beside the grass seeds. Maybe a truck bomb? No, exactly the wrong idea. Sarin worked far better in a confined space, why he'd wanted to get it inside.

"To be honest, I'm not sure we can get it to the United States," the imam said. "Europe, yes. But not America. So unless you want me to give a sermon at the Vatican, invite all your friends—"

A sermon at the Vatican. That fast, Wayne saw the outlines of a plan. The operation would be tricky and complicated, but he could use the agency's own security protocols against it. And if it worked, the carnage wouldn't be hidden in some conference room in Langley. The whole world would see it live—

Wayne turned the idea over in his mind. Yes. It was possible.

Carefully, he outlined it for the imam.

"Can we get to him?" the imam said when he was finished. "He must have protection."

"Not as much as you think. Nothing like our people. I'll find out where he lives, pass it to you." Though Wayne would have to be careful.

Pushing too hard would set off alarms. "Then you just need men who don't mind dying—"

"Martyrs aren't a problem. Especially over there."

"After that, the second part flows naturally."

"You're sure you'll know where it'll be."

"I'll figure it out."

"If you're wrong?"

Wayne shrugged. "The first part is worth doing anyway."

"You make it sound easy."

"Not easy. But possible."

"Insh'allah."

"Yeah, Insh'allah."

12

NANGALAM, AFGHANISTAN

WELLS WAS about to make a mistake. He couldn't help himself.

It was past midnight in Nangalam, a tiny eastern Afghanistan town where the Pech River flowed out of the mountains into a valley green with alfalfa. During the early years of the Afghan war, this district had been hotly contested. The United States had put a base called Camp Blessing a half mile away, complete with an artillery battalion to launch giant 155-millimeter shells into the mountains—a rarity in an age of drones and smart bombs.

But even with all its combat power, the United States never truly controlled the area. The tribes here were ornery even by Afghan standards. Not only could they not be bought, they couldn't even be rented. As far as they were concerned, only the flags changed with each new invader. They happily took the radios and blankets the United States offered them. Then they let the Taliban rain mortars on Blessing. In 2008, Talib fighters nearly overran a small American base a few miles north of Nangalam. Only massive air support had stopped them.

After 2010, the United States moved its soldiers out and focused on controlling Kandahar and south-central Afghanistan. The choice made sense. As the heartland and spiritual center of the Taliban, the south was more important strategically. It was also friendlier tactically. Desert bases didn't need helicopter resupply, and air support was easier on flat ground.

The mountain tribes and Talibs saw the withdrawal as a victory. Ever since, the jihadis in the area had moved back and forth to Pakistan's North-West Frontier at will. They faced occasional Special Forces raids, but the Afghan National Army didn't even try to contest them.

So Nangalam was a perfect place for Wells to become Samir Khalili. As long as the Taliban didn't find him first.

AFTER GETTING HIS gear in Kabul, Wells convinced Dilshod the taxi driver to give him a ride to Jalalabad. More precisely, an extra two thousand dollars from Wells convinced Dilshod.

The drive turned out to be nearly as dangerous as Wells's night at the Winter Inn. The highway to Jalalabad was among the deadliest in the world. Just east of Kabul, the road cut through a narrow ravine, stark, beautiful, and lethal. The Kabul River bubbled hundreds of feet below. Crumbly cliffs soared a thousand feet above. The slopes spat rocks down in bad weather and good.

But the real danger came from the other drivers on the road, which carried the grand name of the Afghan National Highway. In reality, it was one lane in each direction without even a yellow centerline. Thanks to hundreds of millions of dollars in Western aid, it was paved nearly for its entire length. But the asphalt was as much curse as blessing. Wells remembered Afghans as aggressive drivers, but they had reached a new pitch of insanity in the last few years. Maybe they'd been at war for so long that they no longer cared about life at all. They passed on blind curves. They passed trucks into **oncoming** trucks.

The fruit of this testosterone tree lay along the river below, wrecks that would never be cleared. At the worst curves, scrawny kids stood on the side of the road, yelling, **Go!** or **Stop!** seemingly at random, their hands cupped, begging a coin or two in payment for their advice.

Halfway through the gorge, the road briefly straightened, and Wells watched as an SUV passed a pickup that was itself trying to get by a sedan, the three vehicles side by side by side, all honking as wildly as geese in November.

Dilshod drove coolly, but he couldn't escape the madness. On the last blind curve before the highway escaped the gorge, an oncoming pickup forced the taxi so far over that it popped onto the highway's low stone curb. The jolt threw Wells against his belt. Through his streaked window, he glimpsed the football field drop to the right. The river surged below, foamy and white. Wells thought they would go over. But Dilshod braked and downshifted and spun the steering wheel all at once, hands and feet moving in tandem like he was coming out of Turn 4 at Daytona.

The taxi popped back to safety as the Hilux edged by. Dilshod turned to Wells and grinned.

An hour later, at a gas station at the edge of Jalalabad, Dilshod pulled over. "Here, yes?"

The guy had done enough. Wells didn't want him to press his luck further. Anyway, if Wells couldn't find the bus station on his own, he ought to give himself to the Talibs right now. He slid twenty one-hundred-dollar bills to Dilshod. "Go home, forget me." Wells almost added **Kiss your kids**, but the sentiment wasn't very Afghan.

"You think I need you to tell me?"

"Don't suppose you know any hotels I can trust in the mountains."

"Those people"—Dilshod shook his head with a city dweller's disdain for the hicks up-state—"they keep goats in their beds. Not only to stay warm. You see?"

Wells smiled.

"Too many Taliban up there. Whatever it is you're doing, Mr. American, I hope Allah is with you."

Allah and an AK . . . "Drive safe, Dilshod."

IF UNGUARDED AMERICAN civilians were un-likely sights in Kabul, they were as rare as uni-corns everywhere else in Pashtun territory. Wells planned to use that fact to his benefit. No one was looking for Americans. Thus, no one would wonder if he was American. He would speak Arabic first, Pashtun only if necessary. Big-bearded Arabs were known to be trigger-happy. He didn't expect questions.

Even so, the Winter Inn might haunt him. The clerk would remember Mitch Kelly's name even without a copy of the passport. The jihadis might have someone inside the airport who could run the name and find Kelly's passport picture, complete with Wells's photo. By then, Wells needed to be laying low in the hills, waiting for the men in the black helicopters to come get him. **Even paranoids have enemies.** He was aiming for Asadabad, a town of fifty thousand, northeast of here, close to the Pakistani border.

Under a clear blue sky, Jalalabad was bustling. Wells followed a muddy road crowded with minibuses and trucks and 100 cc motorbikes, two-wheeled lawn mowers. Russian tanks, American jets, and Talib suicide bombers had all left scars here. But the Afghans were still doing what they loved best, gossiping and trading. **If we would just leave them alone for twenty years . . .**

No one ever did. For a country that had no oil, no ports, no gold or diamonds, no real strategic relevance, Afghanistan attracted more than its share of attention. The great powers almost seemed to want to send their armies into this unforgiving land just to prove they could.

JALALABAD'S BUS STATION was misnamed, a gravel lot where brightly painted vans and minibuses parked in haphazard rows, their drivers shouting destinations and fares. The passengers were mainly families with five or six children and sometimes chickens, sheep, and goats. They tied duffel bags and suitcases onto the roofs, stuffed themselves and their livestock in. Wells found the next ride to Asadabad, an orange Kia minibus, and handed over a one-hundred-afghani note—about a dollar-fifty.

"By yourself?" the driver said in Pashtun.

Wells nodded. The driver handed him a five-afghani coin in change, waved him on board without looking twice. Wells felt himself shedding his American skin.

The Kia pulled out an hour later, a twelve-seater with eighteen passengers on board. Fortunately, no animals. The Asadabad road was less crowded than the Jalalabad highway, and though the minibus's brakes squeaked, the driver avoided near-death experiences. The kids around Wells chattered nonstop. He thought of Emmie and the luck she'd had to be American. It was early morning in New Hampshire now. She'd be sleeping in her bed, her mother one room away, her belly full. She was healthy and happy and lovely in her innocence, not yet aware the world could be anything other than peaceful.

He missed her.

The bus passed two police stations on the way to Asadabad. The first was abandoned, windows shot out, bricks crumbling. The second was filled with white pickup trucks that looked to Wells like they belonged to the Taliban, not the Afghan cops. Afghanistan's official black, red, and green flag was nowhere in sight. Neither the driver nor anyone else in the minibus commented. Talib control was a fact of life here, not worth mentioning.

Just outside Asadabad, two Hilux pickups formed a makeshift checkpoint. A white flag emblazoned with the **shahada**, the Muslim creed, flew overhead. A bearded jihadi stepped into the road and waved the bus over. The driver sighed, pulled to the side, turned off the engine.

A Talib with a pistol on his hip walked close. "How many?"

"Four men, three women, eleven children."

"Fifteen for the men, ten for the women, five for the children." The math was apparently beyond the Talib. After a few seconds, the driver made the mistake of speaking.

"One forty-five."

"Two hundred, yes." The Talib grinned.

The driver pulled two one-hundred-afghani notes from his pocket, handed them over.

"Did you see anything worth telling?"

"No, Commander."

"No Americans, no ANA?"

"No, Commander. I swear on Allah's name."

"All right. Go on."

As the driver turned on the engine, the Talib spied Wells. He chopped his hand in front of the windshield, yelled, "Stop!" He muttered under his breath, and two men stepped up and put their AKs on the van.

Wells realized he should have stuck himself in the middle of the bus along with the kids. He would hardly have been seen.

So the moment of truth had come sooner than he expected. He wasn't worried that these Talibs were looking for the man who'd burned the Winter Inn. Even in Kabul they couldn't know about Mitch Kelly yet, much less have a picture. But if he couldn't pass as Arab, this ride would turn messy very fast.

Samir Khalili. No one else.

The commander pointed to Wells, crooked his finger—**Get out.** The United States had decimated al-Qaeda and killed bin Laden. But Arab jihadis still looked down on the locals. Wells didn't plan to be too deferential. He strolled to the side of the road.

"What's your name?" The man's Arabic was rough but understandable. He had thick black hair, heavily oiled.

"Samir, Commander. Samir Khalili. And yours?"

"Where from?"

"Lebanon. Many years ago." Wells wanted to avoid mentioning Canada, though he knew he was taking a chance. If they searched his bag, they'd find the passport.

The commander looked around, playing to his men. "Is there sea here?" The jihadis shook their heads. "This doesn't look like Lebanon to me."

"I'm on my way to the Swat." The Swat Valley was in Pakistan, home to a few hardy al-Qaeda refugees who after all these years were practically locals.

"Why?"

Wells didn't answer. The commander looked at the men beside him and suddenly Wells had two AKs pointed at him. He hesitated long enough to make sure the commander knew he was **choosing** to answer. "I have a message."

"For me."

"Your Arabic isn't bad, Commander. Did you learn from men like me?"

The Talib smiled at a joke Wells hadn't told. "Not too many like you left here. They've gone home. Or died. Some fell in love with poppies. Is that you? Don't you know my men will shoot you right here if I say so and throw your body there"—he nodded at the road just as a truck rolled past, belching diesel smoke—"for the trucks to squash?"

"You're right, there aren't many of us left, but I was in Afghanistan with the sheikh before the Americans came. And, truly, I believe that Allah will give us our revenge, if we keep our faith and don't give up. If I have a message for someone, he hears it, no one else."

The Talib nodded, and Wells knew that he'd scored. "Did you really know bin Laden?"

Strange to think bin Laden's name still carried weight. But, then, September 11 remained the most successful terrorist attack. "I didn't know him, but I saw him. He was a lion. When he spoke, we thought anything was possible."

The commander pulled a camera from his pocket, stood next to Wells, snapped his picture, a two-man selfie. "Go on, then. Peace be with you."

Wells ignored the stares of the other passengers as he stepped back into the minibus. He'd sold himself a little too convincingly. He hoped the picture wouldn't come back on him. He couldn't stay in Asadabad tonight either, not after telling the man he was headed for Pakistan.

When the bus stopped again, he found a rickety taxi. "Where to?"

"Nangalam." Twenty miles west of Asad-abad. Wells remembered hiding there in early 2002 as the jihadis fled east toward Pakistan. The town had about five thousand people. Big enough to have a hotel, or at least a guesthouse, but small enough that the Talibs would hardly care about it.

Wells hoped.

NANGALAM'S ONLY HOTEL was a mix of wedding cake and Motel 6, four stories that formed a U around a central courtyard. Its concrete walkways were held up by pillars tiled with intricate geometric patterns. The place had seen better days. Harsh mountain sun had faded its yellow paint almost to white. Trash littered the courtyard. No doubt the hotel had been built to serve the Afghan contractors who supplied Camp Blessing. With the Americans and their money gone, it limped along.

At the front desk, the clerk's eyes were half closed in an opiate trance. He told Wells that the rooms were two thousand afghanis a night, payable every day in advance. No identification required.

"Can I pay for more than one night?"

The clerk looked at Wells like he'd asked if the place took Discover cards. "If you like."

Wells handed over eight thousand afghanis. "And give me a room on the top floor." The operators would come by helicopter. A top-floor room would make the capture much easier.

"Are you sure? There's no one up there."

Even better. "I'm sure."

"Some space to yourself, I understand." The clerk handed over the key to room 404.

The room had a narrow metal bed and a knotty prayer rug. Wells knew he'd found the right place. The last place anyway. From here he could only go into the mountains, villages that didn't even have guesthouses.

Outside, the sunset call to prayer sounded. Wells went to his knees, made his devotions. He didn't feel much like praying this night. He couldn't help but think of the **shahada** on the Talib flag, the way jihadis used the Quran's words to justify all they did. Maybe he'd been away for too long. Maybe he couldn't go back.

But as long as he was here, he had to pray. Samir Khalili would pray whenever he could.

The string of Arabic soothed him, as it had so often. When he was done, he unzipped his bag. Laid the AK and the Makarov on his cot. Stripped and rebuilt them both to be sure they were working. Tucked them away, found his new phone, dialed a Kabul number. A high-pitched chirp answered, another, then silence. Fifteen seconds later, Shafer picked up. The agency had arranged a local relay so that if the Taliban were monitoring local cellular towers they wouldn't see a call to the United States.

"John."

"**Nam**"—**Yes** in Arabic.

"Long speak no time. Tell me you're not still in Kabul."

So Shafer had heard about the Winter Inn. "Nangalam," Wells murmured so quietly he could barely hear himself. Even with no one around, he didn't like speaking English here.

"My knowledge of Afghan mudvilles is not exhaustive."

"West of Asadabad."

Faint clicking came through the line. "I see it. There's only the one hotel, right? U-shaped, looks like a palace for the criminally insane?"

"Room 404."

"Four-zero-four. Top floor?"

"**Nam.**"

"Good. Don't suppose you want to tell me about last night."

Wells didn't answer.

"Guessing you don't want to **talkee** the English much, but the big man and I agree that the quicker we get you to your final destination, the better."

"Nam."

"But it's at least two nights away. You cool for that long?"

"Nam." He would stay in his room, leaving only enough that his lack of movement wouldn't seem suspicious. Afghanistan's drug problem would work in his favor. The clerk would assume he was a fellow junkie.

"Fine. Now that we know where you are. COS Kabul has a meeting at Bagram tomorrow. He'll put you at the top of the capture list. Say we have new intel from the ISI"—Pakistan's Inter-Services Intelligence agency—"on a high-value target with knowledge of Qaeda networks in Pakistan. The ISI's been looking for you for a while, too, just got its own report that you're in Nangalam."

More or less what Wells and Shafer had talked about before. But sourcing the report to the ISI was smart. Every CIA officer knew that Pakistan was—to be polite—an unreliable ally. The ISI could have protected Samir Khalili for many years, not even telling the United States that he existed, and for its own reasons decided to give him up now. Maybe it was sacrificing him to protect someone else. Maybe he'd angered a Pakistani Taliban leader who had asked the ISI to make him disappear.

In other words, the ISI provided the perfect excuse for the fact that Khalili hadn't been on the CIA's target lists before. Better yet, Wells and Shafer wouldn't even have to invent a reason why Khalili had come to Nangalam. If the Pakistanis decided to toss Khalili aside, they would do so in just this way, shuffling him over the border and telling the United States to come for him. The ISI wouldn't care if Khalili ultimately told his American capturers that he'd worked with them for years. It would simply deny what he said—and take credit for helping the CIA catch another jihadi.

Best of all, the chief of station wouldn't have to explain these subtleties to the operators on the rendition team. They already knew.

The most effective lies answered questions that hadn't even been asked.

"**Nam.**" Wells wondered if he could get away with saying only **Nam** for the rest of the conversation. Maybe the rest of his time in Afghanistan.

"Glad you like. Only one problem. All three takedown teams at Bagram are on the hook for an op tomorrow night near Ghaznī. We can't resched it without raising too many questions. So the night after tomorrow is the earliest. Then they process you for a couple of days."

Process. A polite word for not letting him sleep more than fifteen minutes at a time, until he would do whatever his captors said if they would just let him rest. The travel teams liked their prisoners docile.

"Then they kick you to the travel team. You should be in Bulgaria a week from now. Ten days at most. Bet you never thought that idea would sound so good. Okay?"

Wells heard footsteps shuffling up the concrete stairs.

"**Nam.**" He pulled his pistol.

Shafer didn't catch his urgency. "Okay—"

The steps stopped outside. His door was little more than plywood. An AK would tear it up.

Wells hung up, went to the door, pulled it open with the pistol low at his side—

Instead of Talibs, he saw only the clerk, pupils pinprick-tight, head wobbling on his skinny neck, a half smile creasing his lips. "I bought what you wanted. Do you want to pray with me?"

Wells was having lousy luck with hotel clerks. After Wells asked for the top-floor room, the guy had decided Wells had given him the money to buy drugs for them both—even though Wells specifically said that he was paying for extra nights. Another cultural cue missed, another mistake.

This one he could turn to his benefit.

"You know what the Prophet, peace be unto him, told us about drugs?" Wells shouted in Arabic, making sure everyone else in the hotel would hear. **"Satan's plan is to sow hatred among you with drugs and gambling. Haram, haram, haram"**—Forbidden, forbidden, forbidden.

"You—"

"I paid you in advance. So you wouldn't bother me. Because I saw what you were." Wells pushed his pistol into the clerk's chest. "Do you know the penalty for drugs? For abusing the body that Allah has given you? Death. Then eternal torment."

The clerk's head bobbed metronomically as he looked at the pistol.

"Eternity in hell. Pray that Allah forgives you." Wells shoved him with the flat of the pistol. The clerk stumbled back, almost went over the railing, whimpered like a kicked dog.

"Don't bother me again."

The clerk was still mumbling as he turned for the stairs and his next fix.

Wells watched him run. Guy probably hadn't moved so fast in years. One problem solved. And everyone else staying here would have heard him yelling. Samir Khalili, who quoted the Quran and hated heroin. An aging Lebanese-Canadian jihadi who had become more trouble to his Pakistani handlers than he was worth.

Soon enough, men would come for him. He would hope they were American, not Talibs.

He went to sleep as Samir Khalili.

BUT WHEN HE woke, he was John Wells again. He wanted more than anything to hear his daughter's voice. Not even to speak, just to hear her call him **Daddy**.

His phone told him it was 2:12 a.m., the emptiest hour. Dawn a dozen dreams away. The room was cave dark and cold. Wells stared at the ceiling, reminded himself why calling New Hampshire would be a mistake. Nothing would take him farther from the place he needed to be. Emmie would be confused and upset. Anne would be furious. And if the Talibs did happen to be monitoring the mobile networks—

He found himself reaching for the phone, thumbing in the number, deleting it, thumbing it in again, like a sixth grader who couldn't decide whether to call his crush—

Enough.

As long as he had this phone, he had a lifeline. To Langley, to New Hampshire, even to Dilshod the cabdriver. A way out.

The last time he'd been undercover here, he'd given himself no escape.

Destroying the phone would be a mistake. He should check in with Shafer once a day, make sure the chief of station had briefed the capture team, that the plan was moving ahead. He should have a way to tell Shafer if he changed rooms or had to leave this hotel to escape the Taliban.

But Wells no longer cared about the practicalities. The team would come for him, in two nights or in two weeks. He would stay until it did. If the Talibs came for him, he'd have no way to escape anyway.

So a mistake, yes.

But the **right** mistake. The only way to leave Emmie where she belonged. To leave John Wells, too. He laid the phone on the floor, smashed it until its screen darkened and its shell cracked and it gave out a sad electronic sigh and fell silent. Then he had the pistol beside his bed and slept.

THE NEXT DAY PASSED. The next night. He didn't leave his room. Neither the clerk nor anyone else bothered him. He prayed, read the Quran, stared at the photos and identity cards and Canadian passport that were no longer pocket litter but instead the proof of the life he had lived as Samir Khalili. He wondered why his Inter-Services Intelligence handlers had left him in Nangalam. He had known them for years and always trusted them, but this trip felt different.

On the second day, he wandered to the town's grubby outdoor market, which had a no-name restaurant selling plates of lamb and rice. At noon, the meat tasted fine. By sunset, he knew it wasn't. John Wells's stomach had forgotten the rigors of these mountains. Samir Khalili would pay the price.

He tried to read the Quran as he waited for the ache to pass. Instead, it twisted on itself, doubled him over. The minutes piled like bricks. He couldn't keep anything down, not even water. Finally, he pulled off his **shalwar kameez** and lay naked and shivering on his bed, dreading the ten-foot trips to the toilet. By the early morning, he was flushed and dehydrated and feverish all at once. The little room stank like an outhouse in July.

The part of him that was still John Wells knew that the illness might help him if the capture team came tonight. The operators would see he wasn't a threat.

But he couldn't count himself lucky.

He thought he might be hallucinating when he heard the helicopters sweeping overhead. He dug his fingernails into his palms, made himself focus. The copters seemed to be gone, if they'd been real at all. He staggered up, turned on the tap, wiped down his face with a dribble of cold water.

Now he heard them again. This time, he was sure. So the Americans and not the Talibs had found him first. **After your adventure-filled trip to Afghanistan, what's next for you?**

I'm going to Bulgaria!

Above him, the helicopters closed until their engines set the room vibrating. They weren't as loud as he expected until he realized that they must be the modified Black Hawks the Special Ops teams flew, with special cladding to keep their engine noise down.

SAMIR KHALILI DIDN'T care about cladding, though. He wanted out. He stumbled for the door, then realized he was naked. The ultimate humiliation. He reached for his underwear and pants, hoping his gut wouldn't betray him yet again. But it did. This time, he barely reached the toilet.

Why had Allah visited this stomach curse upon him tonight of all nights?

Above he heard the chick-chick of ropes kissing the roof. The Americans would slide down those ropes. They were coming for him. After so many years. Why had the Pakistanis betrayed him? He'd always done what they asked. He wondered if he should reach for his AK, let the Americans make a martyr of him, take one or two with him. But he had no chance. They were barely even human in their armor and their night vision goggles.

Besides . . . he didn't want to die in this room. He sat helpless as the thumps began above, men sliding down the ropes to the roof. How long had passed since he'd first heard the helicopters. Two minutes? Three?

They were outside his door now. For the first time, he wondered if they'd just shoot him and be done with it. He heard three low puffs. The lock gave and the door inched open and a grenade rolled inside.

Oh, come on, not another flashbang, they're the worst—Wells now.

Samir Khalili squeezed his eyes shut, clapped his hands over his ears, and the room exploded in lightning and thunder, as though Allah Himself had come to express His displeasure.

When he opened his eyes, the door was open. The flash from the grenade had nearly blinded him. But he could make out shadows. The men were inside, the Americans. They swept him onto the floor. They pulled his arms behind his back, cuffed him tightly, sat him up. They were speaking, but he couldn't hear them. A thousand calls to prayer filled his ears. They held him fast and pulled a bag over his head.

The darkness swallowed him. He closed his eyes and didn't fight as they pulled him to his feet and looped fabric straps to him, under his arms and between his legs. They dragged him out, a man on each side. When he was outside, they clicked hooks to the harness they'd made. The metal swiped his chest and back.

His ears cleared just enough for him to hear them laughing, the last sound before the harness tightened and he rose, dragged though the air like a puppet in the hands of a child, naked, his humiliation complete. He rose toward the helicopter, which would take his freedom, and he hated these Americans, hated them, hated them—

————

THE ROUGH, GLOVED hands bundled him into the helicopter, and Wells knew Samir Khalili was real to him, and always would be. The men in Bulgaria would believe him, too. He smiled under his hood as the Americans trussed him in a blanket and threw him to the floor and the Black Hawk rose and turned west, to Bagram, his first stop on the long journey home.

13

RAQQA

NEITHER GHAITH nor Soufiane Kassani spoke much on the drive back to Raqqa the afternoon after what Kassani thought of as **Experiment No. 1**. Ghaith handled the SUV more carefully. Like he wanted to be sure he wouldn't have an accident. Every so often, his eyes strayed to the bags in the back seat that held the bottles of DF.

For himself, Kassani couldn't stop remembering how that first prisoner had died. How his body flailed like he was trying to escape his own flesh.

Kassani was surprised the death bothered him at all. He had killed men in terrible ways before. He had once filled his stomach with lamb and rice an hour after burying a Kurdish prisoner alive. But the apparent lack of cause and effect with sarin made its effects harder to take. When you shot a man, or hit him over the head with a shovel and poured sand in his mouth until it came out his nostrils, his pain made sense. But this stuff looked like **water**. Yet there was no stopping it, no hiding from it.

The human body was a miracle. That it could be erased so quickly by the product of a few chemical reactions seemed proof of the devil's existence.

Nonetheless.

Nonetheless, from a practical point of view, Kassani's experiment had succeeded. The sarin **worked**. And even after the experiment, Kassani had nearly four liters of DF.

Viewed one way, four liters wasn't much. Bashar al-Assad had tons of the stuff stockpiled in bunkers in Damascus, a final insurance policy if the Syrian army crumbled and the caliph's men came to his gates.

Still, spread through a rush-hour subway train in New York or London, four liters of sarin could kill hundreds of people. The horror would be unimaginable. If Kassani couldn't get his mind off the dying men, what hope did soft-headed American civilians have? Smartphones would carry the images everywhere.

In its own way, September 11 had been a fluke. Pilots would never again open their cockpit doors to hijackers. A jumbo jet would never again be turned into a flying missile. But for all their power, the **kaffirs** couldn't stop what Kassani had unleashed today. Not even if an American drone killed him or bombed his laboratory to rubble. Kassani had saved his work for posterity. He made digital videos of each step. He kept meticulous notes. Of course he had hidden all the files. He didn't want to tip the Americans to his progress. But someday—probably after the first attack, probably **soon**—he would put everything he'd done online. It would live forever in the cold bosom of the Internet.

Even if it didn't, even if the Americans made all the videos and the records disappear, they could never hide the attack itself. Other **mujahids** would know what Kassani had done. They'd know that without giant factories, they, too, could create sarin.

So would their targets.

"Now what?" Kassani asked, as Ghaith pulled up at the hospital's front entrance.

Ghaith reached across Kassani, opened the front passenger door, his big arm touching Kassani's chest. The Iraqi stank of stale sweat and sour milk. He seemed more comfortable now that they'd left the desert behind. "What do you think? Get back to work. And faster."

―――――

KASSANI DID. WHEN his men asked him how the experiment had gone, he told them, **As expected**. No one asked more. He was tempted to bring in more workers, but he didn't want to take time to train them. Instead, he pressed his team. He hadn't forgotten the carelessness that had killed Bashir. But he saw at the same time that he and his men had fallen a little in love with playing chemists. He told them to quit trying to improve the process and instead put as many batches through as they could.

A week later, he had just added a new and nearly full liter bottle of DF to the others in his locker when the stairwell door swung open and slammed against the wall. Even before he looked, Kassani knew he'd see Ghaith. The Iraqi treated the lab like it belonged to him.

"Get enough for one prisoner. Time for another test."

Kassani grabbed one of the hundred-milliliter bottles he had poured the week before, went to the cabinet where he kept the safety equipment—

"None of that."

"You want me to mix it without a respirator?"

"When it's time to use it, whoever puts it out isn't going to be wearing one of those, right?" Ghaith didn't wait for an answer. "Come on, the caliph wants to see."

Kassani tried to remember how quickly the newly mixed sarin had begun to fume the week before. A few seconds. And that had been in the heat of the desert. He'd use a long-necked beaker, fill it a quarter of the way. He should be all right. The Aum Shinrikyo cultists in Tokyo had punctured plastic bags filled with **premixed** sarin inside subway cars and walked away uninjured. The sarin hadn't become airborne in lethal quantities until they were gone. Though their preparation was much less pure than his.

Kassani had bought thick plastic bags for this eventuality. He had ampules of atropine, too, an injectable drug that blocked sarin's effects. Atropine wasn't risk-free. In high doses, it could cause heart attacks. But it beat the alternative.

GHAITH LED KASSANI to the basement of the hospital and pulled open a black-painted door to reveal a concrete tunnel barely two meters high. Kassani hadn't known it existed, though now that he did it made sense. The Americans knew the Islamic State brought fighters here.

Their drones would surely monitor the hospital's entrances.

The tunnel was warm and stale. Dim emergency lights stretched backward into darkness. Claustrophobia was Kassani's secret fear. He stopped short, bumping into Ghaith.

The Iraqi shoved him ahead. "If I can fit, you can, too." Ghaith pushed past him, then pulled the steel door shut behind them both.

Kassani couldn't help feeling that this tunnel led nowhere but to his own funeral. Still, he silently followed. After five minutes, the tunnel crossed another, a four-way underground junction. Ghaith turned right.

"A whole maze under here."

"You think the caliph would be alive if the Americans could see his face?"

Two more tunnels later, Ghaith led them up a flight of stairs to another steel door. He rapped until it swung open. Kassani expected an empty building or garage.

But they stepped into an ordinary living room, with a couch, a coffee table, a big-screen television. A sullen young Iraqi wearing a pistol stood by the tunnel door. "**Salaam alaikum—**"

Without a word, Ghaith raised his massive right hand and slapped the Iraqi so hard that the younger man went to one knee.

"Uncle—"

Ghaith shoved the man onto his back, put a knee on his chest. "Ask the password **before** you unlock the door. If you don't hear the right answer, you make sure you're ready to shoot if you open it."

"I'm sorry, Uncle. Truly."

"You're protecting the caliph. Next time, I won't just hit you. You understand?"

Abu Bakr stepped into the room. "Everything all right?" Without waiting for an answer, he turned to Kassani. "Ghaith says that Allah has blessed us. That you've succeeded. I'd like to see for myself."

Once again, the caliph's **presence** struck Kassani. "Of course, Your Eminence. But I must warn you, it's dangerous."

"I didn't mean in person. There's a shed in the yard. After you're done, we'll pour gasoline on it and burn it. That'll destroy the gas, yes?"

"It should." Muslims weren't supposed to be cremated, but considering what they were about to do, whoever was inside the shed had bigger worries. "But how will you see?"

Abu Bakr turned on the flat-screen to reveal a color feed from a wireless camera. A figure in a black robe sat trussed to a chair.

Not a robe. An **abbaya**. At first Kassani

couldn't make sense of what he was seeing. "A woman, Caliph?" She turned her head to look at the camera. She had long black hair and bruises under her eyes. She was beautiful. And she wasn't a woman. She was a girl. Maybe fifteen.

"A Yazidi whore. She injured one of our men."

Ghaith laughed. "Grabbed his—"

"Enough," Abu Bakr said. "I personally have considered the evidence. She looks innocent, but she belongs to the devil. Don't let her tempt you, Soufiane."

If the caliph says so—

"Where is she?"

LIKE MANY ARAB houses, the home had a small backyard enclosed by high concrete walls, a chance for women to get air without being seen. In the middle was a small wooden shed, maybe three meters on each side. Kassani had never seen one like it anywhere in Syria. Where had it come from? No matter. He realized that he was trying to distract himself.

He opened the door. He hoped the girl didn't speak Arabic.

Not a girl. An apostate whore who deserved this punishment.

Inside, the air was hot and dry. An extension

cord powered a lamp and a camera pointed at her chair.

She hardly looked as he stepped close. Her face was shiny with sweat, but her eyes showed no fear, only the dull certainty of pain. "If you're going to do it, you'll need to unlock me," she said. "Unless you're so small that it fits even with my legs closed. I've seen a few of those."

"Don't speak this way."

"Why not? Will you convince me it's my **duty** to let you rape me?"

"How old are you?"

She laughed, the sound a skeleton's rattling bones. "I used to be thirteen. Now I'm nothing."

Kassani wondered if he could find another way. Maybe Abu Bakr had another prisoner nearby.

"Soufiane," the caliph said. "Trust in Allah." The voice came out of nowhere. Kassani needed a moment to see the camera had a speaker attached. Then he knew he would have no reprieve. He needed to choose. The Yazidi or the caliph.

"Soufiane—" the girl said.

"Quiet."

"Are you sure? Some of your friends liked me to moan—"

He knelt beside her, reached out, squeezed her neck until her eyes bulged and her tongue hung out. She smelled foul, infected. The caliph was right. "I said **quiet**, whore."

Now that he'd decided, he felt better. He'd planned to use a bowl, put it under her chair and run for the house. But as he looked at her devil eyes, he found a better way.

He flipped her chair on its back. The girl's eyes were wide now. She muttered to him, but he no longer cared what she had to say. Behind him he heard the camera moving to follow the girl. Good. He pulled on two sets of gloves, laid out the bottles of DF and isopropyl alcohol, the tall mixing stick, the long-necked beaker.

The girl devil squirmed in the chair and began to speak more loudly, not Arabic, words he couldn't understand. He clouted her hard enough that she groaned and went still. He no longer cared what she said, but he needed her not to move.

He poured the DF into the beaker. Then the crucial step, the isopropyl. He stirred the potion quickly but delicately, like the bartenders at his family's infidel hotels. The liquid bubbled as it turned to sarin. He lifted the beaker, holding it by its base, as far from his body as he could.

He tipped the clear glass over and poured the liquid on the girl's face.

BY THE TIME Kassani escaped the shed and kicked the door shut behind him, he realized that he'd gotten a whiff of the stuff, too. His nose was running wildly, and he could see straight ahead but not to the sides. Like a curtain was being pulled over his eyes. He threw off his gloves, reached in his bag for the needle loaded with atropine. But he couldn't seem to pick it up, his fingers wouldn't listen. Now a spastic pain hit him behind the eyes. Maybe he'd gotten more than a whiff—

He made himself relax. He was walking, breathing, he just needed that ampule. He didn't understand what had happened. He'd left quickly. He found the needle again, wrapped his fingers around it, went to a knee. He tried to pull off the plastic cap. But his hands trembled, and the ampule slipped away.

He reached down, knowing he had to have it, the poison was taking control, his throat was tightening—

He couldn't see it—

Suddenly Ghaith was beside him.

"Calm. This?" Ghaith held the needle before his eyes. Kassani nodded, he wasn't sure he could speak, and pounded his right thigh to show Ghaith where to inject him. Ghaith grinned, and for a moment Kassani thought the Iraqi was going to walk away. **He's always wanted me to die—**

But Ghaith pulled the cap and jabbed the needle through Kassani's pants and into his thigh. A moment later, the relief came, spreading up Kassani's legs and then everywhere. Kassani's hands rested, and the curtain over his eyes opened, though his head was aflame. Ghaith pulled him up and tugged him inside, into the kitchen.

"What happened?"

Kassani wiped his chin. He didn't trust himself to speak. He didn't have to ask about the girl. He could hear her screams and the wild clanking of the chains coming through the speakers in the living room. She didn't sound like the devil now. She sounded like a dying thirteen-year-old. Amazing to think that he had been only a breath or two from joining her. Though he didn't understand. He'd left the shack—

Then he saw the wet spot on his left thigh. **Off. Take it off.** He pulled down his pants, tossed them into the backyard. "Those burn." He forced out the words though his tongue felt loose in his mouth. His heart fluttered, a side effect of the atropine. "Thank you."

"Thank the caliph. He told me to check."

Kassani closed his eyes and waited for the girl's screams to stop. When he opened them again a few minutes later, Abu Bakr sat next to him. Was it only his imagination or did the caliph smell of cologne?

"It works." Abu Bakr patted him on the shoulder. "Almost too well, I'd say."

"Thank you for sending Ghaith."

"You see, I chose her to test you."

Relief filled Kassani, relief and the understanding that he had given his soul to this man. He'd proven his loyalty. He was already forgetting about the girl. Who was she? Nothing. A test. One he'd passed.

"You told Ghaith last week you had five liters, Soufiane."

"Yes."

"For a big room, maybe two hundred people sitting, a high ceiling, how much do we need?"

Two hundred people, a high ceiling. A strangely specific question. The caliph must have a target in mind already. "Can you tell me more about the place? Is it everyone packed in close?"

"Close, yes."

Kassani waited for more information, but the

caliph was done. "A room like that, the sarin will need a while to spread. If people can leave quickly, most of them will run as soon as they feel symptoms. Can we lock them in?"

"Assume yes."

"Then it would depend how quickly we can get it into the air. If there are pipes, ducts, if it's coming from more than one place. To be honest, Caliph, these are engineering questions. Beyond me."

"But we'd need more than we have now."

"Yes. Twenty liters would be better. Fifteen is the minimum."

Abu Bakr nodded. Kassani sensed someone else had given him a similar answer.

"How quickly can you do that?"

"This week, we made almost a liter. We're nearly at six."

Bakr shook his head.

"If we work every day, even Fridays, twelve hours, we could make two liters a week." **If we don't kill ourselves trying.** "Maybe two and a half." Kassani felt as though he were negotiating with Allah Himself. "That's ten in four weeks. Plus what we have now. Four more weeks and we'll have almost sixteen."

"Four weeks." The caliph nodded. "And you can move it without too much trouble?"

"Yes. As long as it's DF, it's safe. Easy for a man to carry. Even a man pretending to be a refugee. Though it might look odd, why does one refugee have so many water bottles?"

"You just worry about making it."

14

NEAR TROYAN, BULGARIA

THE CASTLE suited Wells better than he expected.

A fact that might not say much for his mental health.

HE'D ARRIVED IN Bulgaria after a long week at Bagram. The Black Hawk touched tarmac. The operators dragged him to a cement room and hosed him clean. A Delta medic showed up with a wide-gauge needle and a rehydration bag. They held him down while he screamed they were poisoning him.

The next morning, the interrogators asked him what he'd been doing in Nangalam, how long he had been a courier for al-Qaeda, what he knew about the Pakistani Taliban. He shrugged and grunted like he'd forgotten how to speak. **We found your passport**, they said. **We know**

your real name. We know you speak English. Why waste our time pretending you don't?

They didn't torture him—not exactly. But after the third interrogation session where he wouldn't answer questions or even confirm his name, they moved him to a windowless cell that had bright fluorescent lights and loud atonal music that never turned off. For his protection, they said. Sleep was impossible. Time stretched until it snapped. After a day, maybe two, Wells left Khalili and the cell behind. He found himself home in Montana, sitting at the kitchen table with his parents. His mom ladled overcooked spaghetti. His dad sipped from a highball glass. A typical supper. His folks had loved him, but they were World War II babies, not exactly emotionally aware.

They didn't notice him now, not even when he tried to tell them how much he'd missed them. He'd been undercover on his first mission in Afghanistan when they died. Hadn't even known they were gone until he came back to Hamilton to see them. One of his great regrets. Now they were growing old again. This time, he had no choice but to watch. The minutes were years. His mother turned stooped and frail, his father jowly and soft. All along, he couldn't make them hear him.

Finally, the kitchen was empty, and Wells felt the strange warmth of tears on his cheeks. Real or a dream, he didn't know.

The interrogators came for him then. They asked more questions he wouldn't answer and moved him back to a regular cell. A cell where he could sleep. When he woke, the guards told him he was being taken to another prison, one that wasn't in Afghanistan. They didn't say where. He didn't ask.

FIVE GUARDS FLEW him west on a Gulfstream. They shackled his hands and legs to his seat but otherwise treated him decently. They didn't hood or sedate him. They let him use the toilet, as long as he left the door open. They even offered him the same energy bars they were eating. Wells thought about turning them down, decided not to bother. Samir Khalili had already proved himself, and he had no idea when he'd get his next real meal.

You don't know how good you've got it, the head guard said, as Wells crunched his third PowerBar. **Free snacks. If we had some near beer, it'd practically be cocktail hour. In a week, you'll be begging to come back, buddy. Too bad the rides only go one way.**

Wells closed his eyes. He woke to find the

plane already on the ground. The guards hooded him, tightened his cuffs, pulled him out. The European air was cool and clammy, nothing like Afghanistan, with a chemical tang Wells couldn't place. His hood was not quite blackout dark. Through its fabric, he saw blue police lights flashing on a black van. Behind him, the Gulfstream's engines spooled down.

Enjoy your stay, Sammy, the head guard said. Two men grabbed him, wrenched him toward the van. Even before they spoke, Wells knew they weren't American. One smelled of cheap perfumed soap, the other of plum brandy and cigarettes.

They threw him into the cargo compartment, slammed the doors. The van stayed motionless, and a guard beat him, steady as a lumberjack chopping a log, grunting with each strike, sending spikes of pain through Wells's arms and ribs.

The beating stopped. Started again. A different guard. The rhythm now was slower, smoother, the blows aimed carefully at his knees and shoulders and shins, vulnerable spots. Wells didn't try to defend himself. They'd hit him harder if he resisted.

To pass the time, he counted the shots as dispassionately as if he were watching someone else take them. **Fivesixseveneight** . . . Nothing to see here. Wells had never thought of himself as a masochist. Maybe he'd become one without even knowing. How many beatings had he endured over the years? **Twelvethirteenfourteen** . . . Did he seek out this abuse as punishment for his own violence?

Wells wished he understood himself. **Twentyonetwothree** . . .

Or maybe he was glad he didn't.

After an even thirty strikes, the beating stopped. The van rolled away. Then—surprise!— a hand pulled off his hood. Wells found himself looking at a tall, fleshy man in a dark blue uniform. The guard was in his thirties, but his cheeks and nose were covered in the angry red pimples of an unlucky teenager. Mother Teresa would have hated the world if she'd had to live in that skin.

"Samir." He was the one who stank of brandy. "Speak English?"

"Yes." The guard probably knew. Wells saw no reason to lie. Irritating these men would only increase his misery and might interfere with Kirkov's efforts to keep him close to Hani.

"You'll find out sooner or later, so I may as well tell you. This is Bulgaria. Europe. Even if the Germans and French don't think so. We hold you for the Americans. Lucky you."

"I don't talk to Americans."

"Your business. I don't care if you're Osama bin Laden or some farmer they caught by accident. Take it up with them. But you don't complain to me or my men. This prison, we call it the Castle. But no kings here. Only fools. Understand?"

Wells nodded.

"When I ask you a question, you answer."

"I understand."

"Not nice, the Castle. Not nice for our own people, so why should it be nice for jihadi scum? Some of you think you're Allah's warriors. Make trouble. Like it's our fault you're here. Don't do that, Samir. The reason I come on these rides, to give all of you this warning. Make trouble, this place will be hell on earth. You understand?"

"I understand."

"You do what we say. Otherwise, we throw you in a hole that's dark twenty-three hours a day, feed you rice that even the worms spit out. Understand?"

Wells nodded. The guard clouted him across the cheek hard enough to send a crescent moon streaking across his eyes.

"Answer."

"I'm sorry. Yes. I understand."

THEY DROVE FOR an hour at highway speed before turning onto a rougher road that rose and twisted into what Wells assumed were the mountains east of Sofia. The guards, who sat on a rear-facing bench attached to the partition, laughed as Wells bounced around the cargo compartment. The road finally straightened and smoothed out.

Minutes later, the van halted. Wells heard a gate creak up. The van rolled ahead, turned right. The strangely suburban sound of a garage door opening followed. The van inched inside, stopped. The pimply guard popped open the door, led Wells into a loading bay. Through the open garage door, Wells glimpsed the prison's outer walls, ten meters of old-school brick topped with coils of razor wire that spotlights painted silver and mean. A corner guard tower was embedded with long, narrow windows, archers' slits.

At least Wells knew why they called it the Castle.

The guards led him to a low-ceilinged intake room where four uniformed men played cards. The stink of stale smoke suffused the room to its very pores. Hell's perfume. Pictograms warned against bringing in weapons and contraband. A dust-covered desktop computer from the 1980s sat on a desk.

The guards fingerprinted Wells with an old-style ink pad. They stood him against a wall and photographed him as he held a slate pad chalked with Samir Khalili's name and a six-digit identification number. Then the humiliations began. Two guards held him in a chair as a third sheared his hair and chopped his beard with a dull single-blade razor. With his hair gone, they photographed him again. They stripped him naked, made him stand with his legs spread wide and his hands flat against a wall as they tugged and poked him. Every procedure was rougher than necessary. Wells knew the indecency was not accidental but the point. They wanted him to feel his helplessness.

When they were done amusing themselves, they walked him to a shower that had the filthiest graffiti Wells had ever seen. After a minute, the water cut off abruptly, and Wells shivered in the locked stall for half an hour before the guards brought him to a counter where a tiny man sat in front of shelves of uniforms. Without a word, the man reached under his desk and handed Wells grayish underwear, a powder-blue uniform smeared with grease stains, and leather sandals that miraculously fit perfectly.

Samir Khalili had to stand up for himself, even after the guard's warning.

"Dirty." Wells pushed the uniform back. The clerk shooed him away. Wells tried again. This time, the guards grabbed him, wrenched his arms behind his shoulders. After a minute, the commander with the pimples arrived.

"Making trouble?"

"It's dirty—"

The commander popped his baton and took a vicious short swing at Wells like a batter fighting off a two-strike fastball. The blow caught Wells in the ribs, doubled him over.

"Hands against the wall."

Wells complied. And felt the cool steel of the baton against his groin.

"You've been good so far. The only reason I'm not hitting you there. Understand?"

Wells started to nod, stopped himself. "Yes."

"Turn around. Let me see that uniform." The commander pretended to examine it. "You're right. It does need a cleaning." He cleared his throat, spat a gob of tar-colored phlegm at the uniform's chest. He stuck his hand down the back of his pants, rubbed with the exaggerated vigor of a kid who'd just learned how to wipe himself, and massaged the spittle into the fabric with his dirty hand. "That should do it." He let the uniform slip from his fingers like the world's worst seductress. "Shall I clean your underwear, too?"

"No, thank you." He'd find a way to clean it before he put it on.

"Very good. Get dressed, then. **Now.**"

So Wells pulled on the spit-stained uniform, trying to keep the fabric from touching his head. When he was done, the commander gave him a mock salute. "Your palace awaits."

THE COMMANDER LED Wells and the other guards down a corridor to a steel gate, electrically controlled and watched by cameras.

"Most important rule, Samir. This side, guards only. Always. You never come through here unless we bring you. Understand?"

"I understand."

The commander waved at a camera, and the gate squeaked back on its metal rollers. He pushed Wells through. The other guards followed, but the commander stayed on the guards-only side and gave Wells a mock salute as the gate slid shut.

Thirty feet down, the corridor intersected another. Wells sensed they'd reached the prison's central axis. Arrows pointed ahead to block a/b, right to food/yard, left to special block. All in English, for whatever reason.

No surprise, they turned left. This hallway led to an old-fashioned mantrap, twin sets of gates separated by ten feet of corridor. The lead guard fished on his belt for an oversized key ring. He unlocked the first gate, ushered Wells inside, locked it behind them. A guard appeared at the second gate, pulled it open, waggled his fingers—**Come on down.**

Wells found himself in a brick shed the size of a small warehouse, twenty-five feet wide, a hundred feet long. Narrow barred windows were set near the ceiling. The cellblock itself was a single concrete tier set five feet back from the walls. The individual cells were not even four feet wide, maybe seven feet deep. Wells guessed there were about twenty-five. Their lights were out, but they all seemed occupied. He saw only three guards, the one who'd let him in and two others sitting in a booth beside the entrance. Elevated sentry platforms had been built at the building's four corners, but they all seemed to be empty.

So the Castle was . . . an ordinary prison. Nothing high-tech about it. Or even medium-tech. Aside from that single remotely operated lock separating the cellblocks from the guard quarters, the place belonged to another century. Wells supposed he shouldn't be surprised. Not after the crudity of the intake. Still, he'd somehow figured they would keep the jihadis in a purpose-built cellblock.

This place was the opposite. The air stank of sewage. The only illumination came from dim bulbs that hung from ceiling rafters. As his eyes adjusted, Wells saw rats popping in and out of holes in the concrete floor. Suddenly his open-toe sandals didn't seem so great.

But hadn't Kirkov told him that the annex for the jihadis was new? No. He'd said only that the Bulgarians had built a new **prayer room**. Ever since, Wells had deliberately avoided learning more, wanting Samir Khalili to come in cold.

As the guards walked him along the block, men stirred and muttered in Arabic.

"What's your name?"

"Where you from, brother?"

"Who got you?"

They walked him around the side of the block. Wells saw what he should have already realized. It actually consisted of two rows of cells that backed against each other. The back side was a crude high-security area. Some cells had steel plates welded to their bars, leaving only a couple of inches at the top and bottom for air. But only one cell appeared to be occupied. It was at the far end, with a plate attached.

A cadaverously thin guard slept in a folding chair in the corner. The men with Wells kicked at him and he startled awake with an exaggerated jump. He led Wells to a cell in the middle and slid open the gate. No steel plate on this one.

"Go on." Wells stepped in. The belly of the beast. The guard clanged the gate shut and locked it. "Have fun, Osama." They walked off, leaving him to his new home.

As Kirkov had warned, no one would confuse the Castle for the airport Hilton. This cell was worse than the ones Wells had glimpsed on the other side. It had no cot at all, only an inch-thick mattress covered with a thin gray blanket. He would have to hope the heat stayed strong. The concrete walls were flaking; and a rusty piece of rebar stuck out of the ceiling. Worst of all, the cell had neither a toilet nor a faucet, just a bucket that didn't have a top or even a handle. If he went through another bout of intestinal misery . . . The thought was too filthy to contemplate. He had been in more dangerous places. But he wasn't sure he'd ever found himself anywhere so gross.

Yet as he lay on his mattress and listened to the rats skitter, his spirits rose.

Samir Khalili's trip had paid off. Kirkov had come through. Hani was almost surely in the cell at the end of the block. The sound-deadening plates on his bars might make talking difficult, but Wells would find a way.

As he drifted off to sleep, he felt the mission taking shape.

HE WOKE TO metal banging metal, a guard shouting in Bulgarian. The block was dark. Wells wondered if a prisoner had escaped. But the clanging had a regular rhythm and the guard's steps were unhurried. Wells realized it was a late-night bed check, timed to ensure that the prisoners never fell fully asleep.

The guard, the thin one, reached Wells's cell, hit him with a flashlight so bright that it must have been surplus American military—and shouted, "Up, up—"

As Wells jumped to his feet, the guard unzipped his fly and sprayed the cell like a dog marking territory—

"Faster next time."

These guards had an unhealthy fascination with bodily fluids. At least the guy didn't have much of a stream. He walked off, and Wells turned over the mattress and tried to breathe through his mouth and ignore the smell. **Thanks for the warning, buddy.**

He was nearly asleep when he heard a prisoner sobbing on the other side, no words, just a low, crazy-making moan. Men yelled in Arabic—**Fakr, enough! Wake up!**—but the moaning continued for another few minutes, until it stopped as abruptly and creepily as it had begun.

Still later, Wells woke to a dog panting outside his cell. A dream, he thought, but when he opened his eyes, the animal was real enough, a muscled Doberman, staring at him. The Dobie's teeth were bared, his breathing fast and excited. Wells was glad for the steel between them.

"Likes you," a new guard said in English. "Wants to be your friend." Wells wondered why all the guards assumed that he spoke English. Or maybe they just knew that he didn't speak Bulgarian. The dog turned away, dragged the handler down the corridor, lunging for a rat. "Maybe later."

The next time Wells woke, dawn rays were fighting their way through the grime in the windows, and the **Fajr**, the morning Muslim prayer, was beginning. The first of the day's five devotions. Wells waited for the guards to clang their batons and overwhelm the Arabic. They didn't. Apparently, the prisoners were allowed this much. Wells joined. He didn't think anyone would hear him, but the words made this place a mosque, and Samir Khalili wanted to be part of it.

FOR FOUR DAYS, nothing happened. Nothing useful anyway. Two guards brought him to the bathroom twice a day, morning and evening. They watched as he dumped his blue bucket and washed his hands. No shower, though. Most disappointingly, they brought him by himself. Wells heard the guards come to Hani's cell. But Wells never saw him.

Wells heard the prisoners on the other side coming and going for meals, but the guards delivered his food. It was the same every day, and it was terrible. Moldy white bread slathered with a brown peanut butter paste for breakfast. A grayish stew with potatoes and half-black carrots for lunch. A gristly brown lump of meat for dinner. Everything tasted of the same sour chemicals. Wells devoured it all. He needed every calorie they saw fit to give him. He made himself exercise until his muscles burned, push-ups and sit-ups and crunches and reverse lifts against the bars. He waited for the guards to stop him, but they didn't seem to care.

Along with the morning prayer, the prisoners could pray, just after lights-out, the evening prayer, or **Isha**. But not during the day, when a dozen or so guards roamed the unit.

Wells catalogued everything he saw. He wasn't bored. If living in the Kush all those years had taught him anything, it was how to keep his mind alive without books or television or even much conversation.

On the fifth day, his first chance at Hani arrived. After the dawn prayer, the guards pushed a threadbare towel and a beige-brown bar of soap into his hand. "Prayer day."

Shower day, too, apparently. The water was warm, the pressure surprisingly decent. Wells let himself relax and scrubbed himself with the soap until he decided that it smelled worse than he did. When he was done, the guards led him out. Waiting in the hallway was a handsome fortyish man with deep-brown eyes and beige skin. He had the relaxed, magisterial air of a Gulf Arab.

Hani. At last.

"**Akhi**," Wells said. Brother.

Hani looked at Wells with bored, superior eyes. "You're the new one. What's your name?"

"Samir. Yours?"

"What did you do to get put on my side?"

A guard shoved Wells ahead.

"See you in prayers," Hani said.

Back in his cell, Wells wondered why Hani had been so cold, if he had spotted something wrong. But he wasn't a comic-book supervillain who could recognize Khalili as an impostor with a single look. Probably he considered himself the ward boss and wanted to put this new arrival in his place.

The morning dragged. Wells felt like a quarterback on Super Bowl Sunday, waiting for the stadium to fill and the coaches to finish their speeches. **No.** Samir Khalili couldn't have cared less about the Super Bowl. He simply wanted to meet this man, to speak in the Prophet's tongue with another believer.

The guards came a few minutes after noon. The prayer area was tucked at the end of the cellblock. Twenty feet square, with white plaster walls, newer and cleaner than the rest of the prison. It felt like a real mosque. It even had a **mihrab**, the semicircular notch in the wall that indicated the direction of Mecca, which Muslims faced for their prayers. Wells understood better why Hani and Latif had spoken so openly here. Kirkov and the Bulgarians had created a perfect trap, a room that unconsciously made the **jihadis** believe they were safe.

A dozen men, including Hani, stood in a loose circle. "Brothers," Wells said. The word itself brought him back to Afghanistan, to men praying on dusty ground with the mountains on every side.

"Do you pray, Samir?"

He remembers my name. Like a good boss. "Of course."

"Stand with me." Hani led Wells to the room's back wall and they prayed. Hani was judging him, his accent and his fluency. Samir Khalili didn't care, because he knew every prayer and had fought the Americans far longer than this man next to him.

After the second verse, Hani touched his arm and leaned in.

"You asked my name, Samir." His voice was low, confident. "It's Hani. Do you know where you are?"

"In the van that brought me here, the guard with the face said Bulgaria."

"The guard with the face." Hani nodded. "He's trouble. Don't ever say anything about"— he touched his cheeks. "One of the Iraqis did,

Fakr, and they took him for a week. He won't say what happened, but now he screams in his sleep. Where did they catch you, Samir?"

"Afghanistan."

Hani tapped his chest. "Syria."

"With the Islamic State? Or Nusra?"

"Of course the Islamic State. Are you with us, brother?"

The question that Wells had hoped his own question would provoke. He wanted Hani to think of him as a Qaeda **jihadi**—a potential opponent, at least for now. "I fight for the sheikh and I always will."

"Always? Until Allah raises him from the ocean where the Americans dumped him?"

"Don't joke about this."

Hani's smile said **You'll see the truth soon enough**. "How did the Americans catch you?"

"In a town called Nangalam." He didn't want to give too much too soon.

"Not where. How?"

"Why would I tell you?"

"I already know. Someone betrayed you. The Pakistanis, yes?"

They locked eyes. Wells blinked first. "How—"

"Al-Qaeda is finished, Samir. Don't you see? Those Pakis give you a little money, keep you busy, let you pretend you're putting something together. Then when they need to make the Americans happy, do something to distract from their own business, they sell you out. When was the last time you did anything that mattered?"

Samir Khalili didn't want to hear this bitter truth. "And what have you done but chop the heads of other Muslims? Make them hate us? The sheikh may be dead, but he was right. Concentrate on the far enemy"—the United States and the West. "Killing other believers doesn't help the cause."

"Except that while you've been in the mountains, we created a **caliphate**. Our own government, land, money. Our own **Sharia**"—Islamic law. "We don't depend on lying Pakistanis or anyone else. The Americans keep saying they're going to destroy us, but they haven't." Hani was a braggart, as Wells had heard on that very first tape. Wells wanted to let him spout on, but Khalili felt differently.

"We're the only ones to have attacked the United States."

"For now." Hani spoke so confidently that Wells wondered if the cover story that he and Shafer had invented for the seventh floor was true after all, that the Islamic State had a big attack planned. Hani was practically daring Khalili to ask more, too.

Instead, Wells stepped forward to finish his prayers. Now that they'd connected, he didn't want to seem too interested. Nothing frustrated a boaster like a story left untold.

When prayers were done, the door opened and a guard waved the prisoners out. Wells wondered if the rest of the prisoners would be waiting to use the room, but apparently they had already done so.

"Exercise time," a guard said. "Single line, two steps apart."

Wells felt his pulse speed. The moment was coming.

THE GUARDS LED them out of the cellblock and past the intersection that led to the electrified gate. The prisoners seemed excited now. Time outside must be a luxury. Still, they stayed in line. Their docility didn't entirely surprise Wells. Prisons were strange places. A few convicts would die before being broken, like the Irish hunger strikers who had starved themselves to death in Britain in the 1980s. But most prisoners, here and everywhere, did what they could to get along with their captors and make their lives easier.

They turned left down a short corridor, stopped in front of a steel door. The lead guard said, "Remember, forty minutes. And if you climb the fence, you will be shot without warning."

The yard wasn't much, a rectangle fifty feet long, seventy feet wide, surrounded by tall cyclone fencing. The high exterior walls of the prison stood ten feet back from the fence, creating a no-man's-land where four Dobermans ran. The dogs barked wildly and bared their teeth as the jihadis walked out. Two guards, both slinging AKs, watched from a post on the wall. A light rain seeped from the gray sky, but the prisoners didn't seem to mind. They tilted their faces skyward to the drizzle.

Twenty or so Bulgarians were already inside. They wore dark green uniforms instead of the powder blue of the jihadis. The local prisoners were a dull-eyed, brutish bunch. Blurry prison tattoos striped their hands and faces. They didn't seem pleased with having to share the space. They formed a loose cordon that stretched diagonally across the yard, backing the Muslims into a corner, yelling in Bulgarian.

"They always like this?" Wells muttered to Hani.

"Mostly."

"Let me ask you, Hani. If the Islamic State is so powerful, what are you doing in here?"

"My own fault. Went to Turkey and the Americans picked me up. They knew who I was right away."

"They were waiting for you."

"Yes."

"Someone betrayed you. No different than me."

"My traitor, we've already dealt with him." Hani sliced a hand across his throat. Where Wells had hoped he'd go. "And his family."

"I hope you had the right man."

"Don't worry about that. We don't make those mistakes. The ISI who gave you up, you'll never touch them," Hani said.

"After I get out of here, I'll go back to those mountains, find them."

"I'm surprised you lasted so long, Samir. You seem . . . confused."

Wells stepped close to Hani. "Say it again—"

Suddenly three other Arabs were tugging at Wells.

"He doesn't mean trouble," Hani said. "Right, Samir?"

Wells nodded. The other jihadis backed off.

Two Bulgarians had taken advantage of the distraction to edge closer. "Move," Hani said to them. In English.

"Arab scum." The prisoner was short, muscled-up, eyes as faded as his tattoos.

"We don't bother you, you don't bother us."

The Bulgarian muttered but stepped away. Hani turned to Wells.

"Your little dream about the ISI. First of all, if the Americans move you out of here, it'll be to bring you somewhere else."

"They send people home now."

"Not you. If they've put you on my side, they think you're high-value. Why, they only let us out with the others once a week. I can't imagine what they think you know—"

"And you never will."

Hani didn't answer for a while. "First smart thing you've said," he finally said. "Anyway, if they think you know something important, they'll hold you forever."

"You, too."

"No, because eventually they'll have to recognize the Islamic State, talk with the caliph. They'll want peace, and part of peace is letting prisoners of war go free."

You call me **delusional.** "How often do the Americans come for interviews?"

"For me, once every few weeks. They don't hurt me or anyone else. They offer bribes, a transfer to a better prison. I won't talk to them at all. They always give up after an hour or two."

"This place could be worse."

"Yes. They let us pray, and they don't bother us if we don't make trouble for them. It's not political for these guards. Not like Guantá-namo. The Americans give the Bulgarians a lot of money to keep us and the guards get some. That's what they told us."

"But some brothers must want to fight."

"It doesn't do any good. I haven't been here that long, but when I came, I told them I wanted my own Quran and they laughed at me. Then they dumped me in a punishment cell for two days, no food."

"So we stay here forever? Like sheep?"

"You have a better idea?"

"Find a way out."

Hani tilted his head at the guards outside the tower. "The walls are ten meters high, razor wire, dogs, they put us in concrete cells, no place to hide anything. Tell you what, Samir, you see a way, you let me—"

But Hani didn't have a chance to finish his thought. Suddenly the little prisoner who had called them **Arab scum** yelled in Bulgarian, and he and the other local convicts were on them—

———

HE'S AS TALL as you, and even bigger. Bald. A scythe on his cheeks, a skull on the back of his head.

Sure I'll recognize him?

Kirkov didn't smile. **He'll be in the yard. The first or second time you're out there.**

The play Kirkov had suggested to Wells, back at the airport in Munich. Have a Bulgarian prisoner attack Hani so Wells could defend him and prove his loyalty in the most visceral way possible.

The very first time? Won't that seem obvious?

Sooner will be better because, after, you'll be on lockdown for at least a few days. And, believe me, the way this man and his friends come, no one will think it's a setup. You'd better be ready.

I was born ready.

It's no joke, John—

IT WASN'T.

The Bulgarians had the numbers. And boots instead of open-toe sandals, a big edge in a scrum like this. The little guy was pumping his right arm low and fast in a way that suggested he had a shiv. Wells had only one edge. Knowing what might be coming, he'd put himself and Hani at the outside edge of the jihadis, near the fence. He could move. The best chance to win a melee like this was to attack quickly, take out the other side's leaders, before everyone else fully engaged.

Wells stepped into the scrum, pushed aside two men, went for the little guy, who was facing away from him, stabbing furiously, focused only on drawing blood—

Wells wrapped his big left hand around the guy's forehead to line him up and pulled back his right arm and hit him with an open-handed chop in the neck just below the skull. A rabbit punch. He felt vertebrae buckle. The guy screamed and dropped. A toothpaste handle with a three-inch razor blade taped tight came out of his hand and Wells reached for it—

Above them, the guards shouted—

Wells turned, saw the big man ten feet away, the tattooed skull on the back of his naked head staring balefully. The guy was going for Hani. Three jihadis had lined up to protect their leader, but the guy was bashing them with a piece of concrete. Wells stepped toward him—

Staggered as a blow caught him below his left

armpit. Not a fist, something harder—wood, maybe. If not for all those crunches, it would have knocked him down. As it was, he felt a rib crack, but, no matter, that's what ribs were for. He turned and swung the shiv at whoever had just hit him, aiming high.

The man leaned back, but Wells stretched his arm and the shiv dug a red straightaway on the man's cheek. He yelped. Wells stepped up and kicked him between the legs, and the yelp rose to a full-on **castrato** scream and the man doubled over.

Wells spun again, saw the big Bulgarian had taken out the first two jihadis guarding Hani. Now he clouted the third with a sweeping two-handed shot. Whatever else he might be, he wasn't subtle. The Arab dropped like a spent round.

Hani had his hands up. But he was pinned against the fence, nowhere to go. The convict lifted his big right fist, a piece of concrete jutting out. Wells saw he couldn't reach Hani in time to stop the blow. Instead, he threw the shiv, sidearm, spinning it, hoping for enough torque to keep it in line. The razor caught the Bulgarian low in the back of the head, between the skull's grinning teeth—and stuck in his heavy flesh. The giant reached for it, pulled it out, roared, turned around.

Let's dance. Wells felt the frenzy of hand-to-hand combat surge through him, the best drug in the world, and he and the big man raised their fists and stepped toward each other—

Then, above, the rip-rip-rip of AKs on full automatic. Wells, the big man, and everyone else looked up. Two guards fired into the air, brass jackets pouring out of their rifles. Three others aimed their AKs into the yard—

The shooting stopped. An amplified Bulgarian voice yelled from speakers above the yard door.

The Bulgarian convicts looked at one another, raised their hands and backed away. Wells couldn't help himself, he felt nothing but disappointment, and he knew the big man agreed.

The guy whom Wells had rabbit-punched couldn't walk. He crawled, awkwardly, on two hands and one leg. The big man went to him, picked him up, something almost tender in the gesture.

"On your knees, Arabs," the voice shouted in English.

"Thank you, Samir," Hani murmured.

"Brother for brother. Muslim for Muslim. I'd kill them all, if I could."

The strange alchemy of close combat. At that moment, Samir Khalili and Wells both meant every word.

15

ALMOST TWO weeks since Shafer's trip to Baltimore to see Vernon Green's cousin Ali Shabazz. To his surprise, Shafer had heard nothing from Green. No late-night phone call. No knock on Shafer's door. Not even an email telling him to get lost.

Maybe Shabazz hadn't told his cousin about the meeting. Though he didn't seem like the type to keep his mouth shut. Maybe Green had decided the best play was to lay low, for whatever reason.

In any case, Shafer had waited long enough for a response. He still couldn't exclude Pushkin, Crompond, or Green, much less decide who was the most likely traitor. Under normal circumstances, he would have gone to them by now, tried to force the issue. But Duto would be furious. Maybe furious enough to fire him.

Shafer had no choice but another sideways play. He'd shake Aziz Murak, the imam at the Islamic Center of Northern Virginia, the guy whom Walter Crompond had tried and failed to cultivate. Going at Murak carried its own risks. The imam appeared regularly on cable talk shows to defend Islam and even argue that American Muslims shouldn't be prosecuted for fighting in Syria. "Nothing wrong with Muslims standing up for fellow Muslims," he'd told Fox News. "The war over there, there's been atrocities on all sides. We shouldn't criminalize people who may just be trying to save their families, their homes."

So Shafer knew that his visit might lead Murak to complain, both to Langley and in public, that the CIA was hassling him. But he had to take the chance.

THE ISLAMIC CENTER was an attractive complex of modern white buildings in Alexandria. It included a school, a community center, and of course a mosque. Tens of millions of dollars from Saudi Arabia had helped build it. The Kingdom gave money to mosques and madrassas around Washington to project a positive image of Islam. The grants were neither hidden nor illegal, but Shafer didn't like them. He

wished the Saudis would worry less about how
they looked in the United States, more about
the crisis that radical Islam was causing in their
own society.

It was just past noon on Friday. The week's
most important prayer and sermon were happening inside. The center's parking lot was
nearly full. The call had sounded fifteen minutes before, but discreetly. The blocks nearby
were residential, and the Islamic Center didn't
advertise its presence too aggressively. **We're
good neighbors. Part of the community.** An
American flag hung from a pole in front of the
parking lot, though Shafer cynically noted it
had been put as far from the mosque as possible.

The cars, too, belonged to the broad upper
middle class—new Hondas and Fords, a few
Mercedes and BMWs sprinkled in. The BMWs
made Shafer think of Reg Pushkin. He wondered if he dared approach Pushkin's in-laws
about the money they'd given him.

Shafer had come a few minutes before the
call to prayer and watched men and women
hurry to the mosque. Now that the cars around
him were empty, he stood out. Five minutes before, a trim Arab man in a suit walking through
the lot had spotted him, stopped, and discreetly
ducked his head toward the mike on his shoul-

der. Shafer was not entirely surprised when two Alexandria police cruisers rolled into the lot and turned his way, their light bars flashing a silent warning. **You protecting me from them or them from me?** An officer stepped out, a young guy wearing wraparound shades despite the overcast sky. Shafer lowered his window.

"Sir. We've had a complaint."

"I get that a lot."

"Sir?"

Shafer liked to talk back to cops, not his finest habit. He reminded himself to save his energy for Murak. Getting old meant choosing your battles. He handed over his driver's license and CIA identification.

The cop pulled his shades, squinted at the agency ID. "People who really work there don't normally show us these."

"Cutting to the chase."

"This is official business?"

Shafer shrugged: **Draw your own conclusions.**

"You need to go in, talk to someone? Do it," the cop said. "You want to watch them from across the street? Do that, too. But they don't want you just sitting here. I have to ask you to leave."

Stickler for procedure, this one. "I know somebody at your HQ can make a call, make sure I'm real." The agency and FBI had programs in place with police departments for these situations. "You want to run me? I won't get you in trouble—"

"How would you get me in trouble—"

"But no more questions."

The cop hesitated. Shafer thought that he might simply hand back the ID and go. Then he walked to his cruiser, holding the identification card and license. "Be right back."

Too polite or well-trained to say so, but he doesn't buy the story because he thinks I'm too old.

The Arab guy at the gate had watched this interaction with open interest. As the cop stepped away, the guy pointed a finger at Shafer: **Busted.**

"We'll see," Shafer muttered.

The cop returned ten minutes later. His face was vaguely puzzled as he handed Shafer the license and identification. "How much longer do you want to stay, Mr. Shafer?"

"Not too."

"I'll tell them—"

"Do me a favor. Don't say anything. Roll out, and let whoever called you wonder."

"I—"

"You did your job. Let me do mine."

———

WHEN THE CRUISERS were gone, Shafer walked to the front gate. A frown replaced the guard's smirk.

"Sir? Here for the service?"

Shafer shook his head.

"You'll have to leave."

"Funny, I think you saw the cops let me stay."

"This is private property."

"I have business with your cleric."

"What kind of business?"

"Why don't you run inside, tell him when he's done talking about how great Allah is, and was, and always will be, there's a government-issued **kaffir** who needs a moment?" Shafer was enjoying himself now. "I'll keep an eye on things out here. Make sure there's no trouble."

The man was clearly torn between his desire to toss Shafer and his awareness that the police had just let Shafer go. He muttered some Arabic in his mike, and after a couple of minutes another guard arrived. This one was more obviously muscle, a bruiser who barely fit into his suit.

"You want the imam? Go with him."

As the big guy led him around the mosque,

Shafer heard murmured prayers in Arabic. He would never understand what Wells saw in this religion. Of course he was an atheist, so none of this voodoo meant much to him. As far as he could tell, it was all a failed effort to make people feel better about the big dirt nap everyone took sooner or later. **Grandma's in the big blue sky with angels and trumpets, Junior! You can see her if you squint hard enough.**

But Islam seemed particularly pointless, a mash-up of Judaism and Christianity, with some desert hocus-pocus on top. At least Christians had Jesus to run interference for their sins. But the faith seemed to give Wells comfort, and Allah knew he needed all the comfort he could find.

A ONE-STORY OFFICE building was tucked behind the mosque. **Islamic Center Administrative Offices**, a sign read. The place was empty, everyone at prayers. The bruiser tugged him into a conference room embellished with expensive Arabic calligraphy, one of the few types of art that devout Muslims permitted themselves, along with black-and-white photos of Mecca's Grand Mosque, the holiest site in all of Islam.

"Sit."

"I have to take a piss."

"Not in our bathrooms."

"Come on, this is bush league." Though not one one-thousandth as bad as the indignities Wells had just suffered. The Kabul chief of station had passed Shafer the capture reports:

PRISONER REFUSED TO DISCUSS MEDICAL CONDITION BUT SHOWED SYMPTOMS OF CONCUSSION, POSSIBLY RELATED TO FLASHBANG GRENADE USED IN CAPTURE. UPON ARRIVAL AT BAGRAM, PRISONER ALSO SHOWED SIGNS OF SEVERE GASTRIC DISTRESS BUT REFUSED REHYDRATION TUBE, CLAIMING IT WAS POISON; MEDICAL PERSONNEL FORCIBLY INTUBATED PRISONER.

He'd refused the feeding tube. Though he must have known how badly he needed it. Crazy. Except Samir Khalili would have done the same. Not for the first time, Shafer glimpsed how Wells had survived so long undercover and why he believed he could convince the Islamic State commanders of his bona fides. But what a price he paid:

AFTER STABILIZATION AND INITIAL INTERROGATION, PRISONER WAS PLACED UNDER TWENTY-FOUR-HOUR OBSERVATION.

Twenty-four-hour observation being bureaucratic code for **Just** try **to sleep**—

INTERROGATION WAS UNPRODUCTIVE. PRISONER
REFUSED TO ANSWER QUESTIONS, AND ALL EFFORTS
AT OUTREACH, INCLUDING OFFERS OF A QURAN AND
POTENTIAL FAMILY CONTACT.

BASED ON MATERIAL FOUND WITH PRISONER AT TIME
OF CAPTURE (SEE APPENDIX B), PRISONER RECLASSIFIED
AS EXTREMELY HIGH-VALUE. UPON RECOMMENDATION
OF KABUL COS, PRISONER WAS PREPARED FOR TRANSFER
TO ALLIED FACILITY FOR FURTHER PROCESSING . . .

Prisoner, prisoner, prisoner. The reports
avoided a name or even a number for Wells, another way to dehumanize him.

Now Wells was in Bulgaria, facing new indignities. Shafer would live with a full bladder.

HE AND THE GUARD passed a half hour in silence before the conference room door swung
open to reveal Aziz Murak. Murak wore a long
white **thobe**, the flowing gown Saudis tradi-
tionally wore. He was a tall man with a round,
second-trimester-pregnant belly. Shafer figured
he'd ease in, try for background first.

"I didn't know you were Saudi, Imam."

"I'm not. Egyptian."

"The **thobe**—"

"Many years ago, before I came to America, I spent two years in Mecca. Learning Islamic law at the Umm al-Qura University."

"I thought that was only for Saudis." Shafer had no idea, but as long as Murak was feeling chatty, he'd press.

"They allowed in a few of us outsiders every year. Quite an experience, being a poor Egyptian in Saudi Arabia back then."

"They didn't mind you dressing like them?"

"As long as we didn't wear the **gutra**. I grew to like the traditional Saudi dress. Surprisingly cool in the heat."

"Are those pictures from back then? Mecca must have been very different."

"It wasn't as crowded." Murak glanced at the pictures and all at once seemed to remember that he hadn't invited Shafer. "You come to my mosque on a Friday afternoon. Bother my brothers, interrupt prayers."

"I didn't interrupt anything."

"Your name, please."

Shafer slid his agency identification across the table.

"Ellis Shafer, Central Intelligence Agency.

Am I meant to be impressed?" Murak flicked the identification back. "Unless you're here to tell me you know of a threat to my mosque, you'd better go."

"Are you pretending you don't know why I'm here?"

"I'm not pretending anything."

"Then get rid of this side of beef so we can talk man-to-man."

"I don't have anything to talk about. Except the lawsuit that the Islamic Center will file if you harass me. I don't do business with the American government. I've told the FBI that I want nothing to do with them. I say the same to you."

"Say whatever you like."

"You think I don't know my rights?"

"You don't need to put on a show for me. James Jones sent me."

Murak shook his head in apparent uncertainty. "Is that the one who works for the State Department?"

"Don't pretend you don't know. Come on, Imam, he hit your car." Though Crompond had claimed in his reports that he hadn't seen Murak in months. Murak might not remember Jones's name, despite the fender bender.

"You know about that? Then you know it

was a scrape. Years ago." The imam flapped his hand to show Shafer how minor the accident had been. "What does any of this matter?"

"You're going to make me say it in front of him?" Shafer nodded at the guard.

"He knows better than to trust a little old Jew," Murak muttered under his breath in Arabic, provoking a laugh from the guard. Shafer didn't need a translator to understand.

"I understand it's embarrassing to talk about, but we need to formalize our relationship." Shafer had tucked an envelope into his jacket for just this moment. He pulled it out now, tore it open, unfolded the single sheet of paper inside. Throughout the Cold War, the CIA had tried to make its foreign agents sign contracts. **This protects both sides . . .** The biggest lie ever told. Though Soviet and Eastern bloc agents, who were used to bureaucracy, had agreed surprisingly often. The agency had largely given up the practice after September 11, but the contracts could still be a useful prop.

"What is this?" Murak's confusion seemed genuine.

"Can't have you off the books anymore. Too sensitive."

"Is that what this man Jones tells you? That **I** work for **you**?"

"Why do you think I'm here? And I know you two meet all the time—"

"Another lie."

"You think we don't have video?" Shafer pushed one step further. "You think we can't hear you? Maybe you think you've been clever, you've tricked him into passing you information, not given any of your own . . . **Please.** Don't you know how this works? You think you can fool the Central Intelligence Agency?"

"Are you threatening me? With what? A leak? You tell my congregation I work for you if I don't sign this?"

"Call it what you like."

"I thought Jews were supposed to be smart. You tell me that if I don't work for you, you'll tell the world I do? Enough. This center, it's peaceful, and I want it to stay that way. You leave." He said something in Arabic. The guard stood, moved toward Shafer.

"Can't get away from this, Imam." Shafer handed Murak his card. "When you're ready, you call me."

"Why wouldn't I just call him?"

The better question is, why are you so willing to believe Walter Crompond, a/k/a James Jones, works for the CIA when a minute ago you barely seemed to remember him? And

that he supposedly told you he works for the State Department. And that he reported he never did more than make a soft approach to you that went nowhere.

But Shafer had pushed Murak enough. Especially since Murak's guard was now edging closer. "Go ahead. Call whoever you like. It was a pleasure meeting you—"

"Come back here again, I'll call the police myself, make sure you're arrested."

Shafer pushed himself from the table. If this meeting didn't provoke Murak into calling Crompond, nothing would. "Oh, Sheikh. And here I was, hoping for some kind of interfaith understanding."

He walked out, feeling he'd lit a fuse. He hoped it wouldn't blow up in his face.

LANGLEY

FRANCE'S CIA was called the DGSE, the general directorate for external security. It reported to the Ministry of Defense. But its leaders were rarely career spies. They were mostly former ambassadors who had spent their careers at France's Foreign Ministry.

In the United States, officers rarely shifted from State to CIA, or vice versa. But France had practical reasons to let diplomats run its spy agency. The French had long made economic interests the cornerstone of their foreign policy. Throughout its history, the DGSE had specialized in corporate espionage. It set honey traps for American executives and broke into Paris hotel rooms to steal laptops. Meanwhile, the Ministry of Foreign Affairs helped French companies win contracts with unsavory regimes all over the world. The two agencies worked hand in glove in a way the CIA and State Department rarely did. In other words, French diplomats already acted more like spies than their American counterparts.

At the same time, most senior French bureaucrats came through a handful of elite universities in Paris, notably the Sciences Po and the École Nationale d'Administration. France's foreign policy community was small enough for personal relationships to overcome institutional rivalries in a way impossible in Washington.

But the fact that the DGSE's top officers didn't have hard-core espionage experience had hurt France in the new age of Islamist terror. For too long, the Parisian elite imagined French opposition to American foreign policy would save them from the jihadis. For too long, they believed in **realpolitik** and French exceptionalism. While most Americans supported Israel against the Palestinians, many French felt the opposite.

Those distinctions had carried weight with old-school Arab nationalists, who focused their anger on the United States and Israel rather than France and the rest of Europe. But to the new breed of jihadis, the French were no different than other **kaffirs**. In fact, many Muslims disliked France more than the United States because France was so avowedly secular. Wearing a burqa was more acceptable in New York than in Paris. Yet France had the largest Muslim community in Europe, mostly from the North African countries that it had once ruled. Nearly seven million French citizens were Muslim, ten percent of the population, compared to only one percent of Americans. Most were under thirty.

Slow economic growth meant that those young Muslims had little chance at decent jobs. They were isolated, unhappy, unemployed, and looking for meaning. Many found it in radical Islam. Thousands traveled to Syria to fight for the Islamic State. Many had now returned. Not everyone who came back was a budding terrorist. Daesh's savagery had turned some against the group. But those who remained loyal now had the training and experience to carry out deadly assaults. They were supported by thousands more—even tens of thousands—who had not traveled to Syria but secretly sympathized.

So France faced a threat of Islamic terror more serious than any other Western country, even the United States. Along with the November 2015 massacre in Paris and the Bastille Day 2016 truck attack in Nice, dozens of smaller attacks had hit France.

The DGSE had struggled to catch up. The agency had dithered for years whether to build a new headquarters big enough to house both its senior staff and its operational arm, the Action Division. For now, the two groups worked from complexes several kilometers apart, not exactly a model of efficiency. And though the agency—and its counterpart the DGSI, the French equivalent of the FBI—had added hundreds of new officers, they still had only a couple of thousand frontline agents in all. Even with help from the Paris police, they couldn't begin to track every potential jihadi. Worse, many potential terrorists lived in Belgium or Germany, where European rules meant the DGSE could work only with difficulty. The agency's technical division had solid surveillance capabilities within France, but nothing like the worldwide data collection that the National Security Agency provided to the CIA.

Most important, at least from Wayne's point of view, the DGSE provided only limited protection for its officers, even the most senior. Wayne knew just how much security they had, because Western intelligence services traded tips on what the United States called force protection. The DGSE's director traveled with just two bodyguards and a driver, a tiny detail by

CIA standards. The agency regularly urged the French to tighten up. Extend the perimeter around DGSE headquarters in northeastern Paris. Add chase cars for its director's limousine. Use helicopters whenever possible. **You can't protect anyone if you and your people aren't safe. You need to see that you're the ultimate target.**

The French brushed aside the suggestions. The DGSE's reluctance partly resulted from manpower and cost concerns. But attitude played a role, too. **Yes, we have risk,** its director had said. **So does everyone who gets on the Métro. All those people checking in at CDG every day. Why should we be in a bubble? Why should I ride in a helicopter like a superhero? Anyway, a low profile is the best defense.** A pessimist might call the view fatalism. An optimist, bravery.

The director's name was Antoine Martin. He'd run the DGSE for almost three years. Before taking over, he had served as France's ambassador to Russia. Wayne had met him in Iraq, where he'd been the undersecretary of the French mission during Wayne's final tour. Wayne remembered him as a good guy, clear-eyed about American failures but not too dogmatic, knowing the CIA's officers were stuck with policies set ten thousand kilometers away. Like many French spies and diplomats, Martin looked professorial, not soldierly. He was trim and narrow-shouldered, with rimless glasses that emphasized the intelligence in his blue eyes. He carried himself with an aristocrat's casual confidence. Wayne vaguely remembered hearing that his father had been a grandee in the French Foreign Ministry, too.

Now Wayne was going to give Martin's address to the imam so the Islamic State could kill him. And his family, if necessary. Martin had a wife and three teenage sons.

Wayne wished he cared. But he didn't. **Can't make an omelette without breaking some oeufs . . .**

THE CIA HAD the mobile numbers of the top officers at the DGSE and other European spy agencies. No NSA voodoo necessary. In an age of coordinated terror attacks, the world's top intelligence officers needed to be able to reach each other without delay.

But the information sharing didn't extend to home addresses, and Wayne worried that asking the seventh-floor admins to contact Paris for Martin's might seem odd. **We forgot your birthday present this year! I want to mail your**

present personally. A nice California red. Alternatively, Wayne could have asked the NSA to locate a batch of French phone numbers and thrown in Martin's. Odds were, no one would have noticed. But Wayne didn't want to take the risk. Not with Shafer nosing around.

He found a more subtle way. The agency didn't have home addresses of its senior counterparts, but it did keep a database of the names of their spouses and children, an easy way to break transatlantic conversational ice. **How's Isabelle?** Martin's sons were Simon, Remi, and Damien.

Martin didn't have a Facebook page. Neither did his wife. But the boys did, all three. Two had Twitter accounts, which they had thoughtfully created in their real names. Wayne supposed he understood the mistake. Martin was the most common last name in France. And French news agencies had never publicly named his children. Martin must have figured his kids could use the Internet because no one would connect them to him.

He hadn't counted on having to worry about Wayne.

Now all Wayne needed was a single home photo with embedded geolocation information. He found it on Remi's Twitter account, a picture of the family bulldog raising his leg beside the front door. Caption: **Attendez, Rousseau!** Yes, the Martins had named their dog after an Enlightenment intellectual. How very . . . French. Wayne's golden retriever was named Pinkie.

A few hours googling, and checking French baptismal, wedding, and funeral records at ancestry.com, provided the rest of the information Wayne needed. The agency's researchers could have answered his questions, but, again, he preferred to leave no trace. He was pleased to find his memory correct. Martin came from a family of diplomats. His father had served as the French ambassador to Cambodia. And for as many generations as Wayne could trace, the Martins had held their religious ceremonies at the same Paris church.

Perfect.

Now Wayne was seeing the imam once again. He had decided on an official meeting this time rather than pushing his luck with another accidental bumping-into at the mall. **Glad you called, James,** the imam told him. **I need to ask you something.** His tone suggested that the **something** wasn't good.

They agreed to meet the next morning, 7 a.m.

at the Islamic Center. If Wayne slept, he didn't remember. After hours staring at the ceiling, as his wife snored quietly beside him, he gave up. He spent the rest of the night rereading **A Bright Shining Lie**, blanketing himself in his government's sins. In the morning, he drove straight to the mosque. A countersurveillance run would look odd, considering he was visiting on official business.

The mosque guard led him to a conference room next to the imam's office. The man himself showed a few minutes later. "James." His tone suggested Wayne had announced he was writing a book called **Prophet Muhammad: World's Biggest Loser.**

"Imam. Good to see you."

"You told me you work at the State Department."

No small talk today. "And I do."

"Your friend Ellis Shafer visited a few days ago."

As we both know, I told you he might. "Don't know anyone by that name."

"He says he works for the Central Intelligence Agency. And you do, too."

Wayne wondered why the imam was acting so strangely. Had Shafer rattled him, made him think maybe Wayne was using him instead of the other way around? Hard to believe, considering how much information Wayne had passed. But, then, Wayne knew firsthand that Shafer was an expert provocateur.

The situation was even trickier because Murak was acting as if this room might be wired. Wayne could hardly launch into a full-throated defense of his own betrayals. **No, habibi, I am a traitor. Truly. Think of all the missions I've compromised.**

"Maybe I do. Maybe I've been trying to recruit you for the CIA. In that case, I failed, as we both know."

"He said the CIA videotaped our meetings."

Wayne's heart hopped against his ribs like it wanted to make a break for Mexico. No wonder Murak was spooked. "Nonsense."

"He knew we'd met recently."

"Months ago, yes—"

"But—"

Wayne put a finger to his lips. The imam was about to make his first real mistake by confirming the off-the-books meetings to anyone who might be listening. If anyone was. Wayne was sure there was no surveillance.

Almost sure.

Finally, the imam saw. "Yes, months ago. But this man Shafer threatened me. He said I had to keep working for the agency—which I **don't**—or he would tell my congregants. He said we needed to formalize our relationship. He brought in a **contract** for me to sign."

Wayne wanted to laugh at the brazenness of Shafer's scam. The agency didn't even use written contracts anymore. "What did you tell him?"

"The truth. That we don't have any relationship. That we met in a car accident, you told me you worked for the State Department. I made him leave. Nasty little man."

"I'm sorry, Imam."

"This Shafer, he spoke the truth? You work for the CIA?"

"On behalf of the Central Intelligence Agency, I apologize. We don't blackmail religious leaders. Mr. Shafer acted inappropriately. I will make sure he's disciplined." **Ideally, Soviet-style, with a bullet to the back of the head.**

"What's your real name?"

They both knew the imam knew, of course. But he would ask, under these circumstances. And Wayne would answer.

"Walter Crompond."

Strange to say it aloud. A freedom in taking back his own name. In bringing the pieces of himself together. Walter Crompond. Princeton graduate, husband, father, CIA officer. As American as a Form 1040. And traitor.

"You need to leave, Walter. You and Shafer, you profane this mosque with your lies."

Crompond nodded, beckoned the imam to follow. All this, and he hadn't passed along what he'd come to say. Shafer had made them both paranoid, yet Crompond would bet he didn't know anything.

In the hallway, Crompond leaned close. "Somewhere we can be sure no one's listening."

The imam led Crompond outside, along the side wall of the mosque, to a door with a combination lock. He spun it open. Inside, a closet-sized room, empty but for five pairs of men's shoes, as well as a few hats and umbrellas.

"Lost and found. From the services."

A smart choice. If the NSA or FBI were listening in this room, then nowhere was safe. Crompond and the imam might as well turn themselves in. "People leave shoes?"

"Mainly, they grab other people's, then the ones who go later realize the mistake."

"They take shoes by accident?"

"We have three thousand worshippers on Fridays . . . Is this what you came to me to talk about, Walter?"

A flush rose in Crompond's cheeks. "Sorry.

Shafer doesn't know anything. He was guessing. Trying to make you think we were taping. If he had anything, he wouldn't be here. He'd pick you up at your house in the middle of the night, bring you to Langley. He'd tell you to come clean or spend your life in jail. He wouldn't be by himself either."

Murak nodded.

"You still haven't asked why I wanted to see you." Crompond handed the imam a piece of paper on which he'd inked a Paris address. "Antoine Martin lives here."

"An apartment building."

"With a doorman. He doesn't have half as much security as our director, but he's no fool. An armored limousine picks him up every morning—a driver, two bodyguards. I'm only guessing, but probably the police watch the building at least part-time and have a response team on call. I don't know if he varies his routes to the office, your people will have to figure that out." Wayne realized he was talking too much, a residue of his nervousness.

The imam pocketed the card.

"As for the church, it's called Notre-Dame—"

"Notre-Dame—"

"Not the famous one. There's a bunch of churches with that name in Paris. This one is

Notre-Dame de Bonne-Nouvelle. It's in the Second Arrondissement. The Right Bank."

"Bonne-Nouvelle."

"Yes. I checked it out online. Couldn't ask for better."

"Why do you smile?"

"**Bonne-Nouvelle** means **Good News**. The Annunciation. When the angel Gabriel told Mary she was going to have a son even though she was a virgin. Fitting, no? We'll have an announcement of our own."

The poetry—if **poetry** was the word— seemed to be lost on the imam. "You're sure that's the place."

"His family has used it a long time. His grandfather was married there, his father, his brother—"

"All right."

"What about the stuff? Are you close? How much do you have?"

The imam didn't answer. Finally, Crompond realized. "Need-to-know basis, huh? And I don't need to know."

The imam nodded like a judge about to pronounce sentence. Just another infidel. Crompond doubted they'd see each other again. So be it. No one outside this room would understand, but in his own mind he'd benefited from their arrangement as much as the jihadis.

"If this man Shafer comes back—"

"Send him away, and tell me. It's best if he thinks you haven't talked to me. Or at least can't be sure. If he knows you have, then sooner or later I'll have to confront him about what he did to you. If I don't, it'll look suspicious. I'd rather not have that conversation. But if I do have to have it, I'll let you know."

"He seemed so sure of himself."

"I'm telling you he doesn't have anything, and even if they come down on me, they can't prove I went through you. And I'll never tell them."

"You have a family, too, Walter."

Is that a threat? Of course.

The imam extended a hand and, in the lost-and-found closet at the Islamic Center of Northern Virginia, Walter Crompond shook it. "Aren't you going to try to convert me? At least give me an **Insh'allah** or a **hamdilillah**?"

The imam looked at Crompond as if from a thousand feet away. "I can't convert you, Walter. I can teach you the words, but Allah opens your heart. Do you want me to teach you the words?"

Crompond opened the door and stepped into

the sunlight. He didn't look back as he walked. He'd cleared Earth orbit, another stage left behind on his journey to the center of the universe.

HE KNEW HE ought to go straight to Langley, but he found himself driving toward Shafer's house, rage in his blood. At least John Wells put himself on the line. Shafer . . . Shafer was content to sit home, lying and meddling.

Worst of all, he knew better. He wasn't an agency drone. He knew how the CIA had behaved over the years. He knew that what Crompond wanted was **just**. Yet he insisted on interfering. Simply to prove his own cleverness.

Crompond rolled slowly past Shafer's gray house. The old Ford wasn't in the driveway. Shafer must already be at work. Crompond kept a pistol under his front seat. Just in case. He turned the corner, pulled over. He reached down, felt its grip. Solid and comforting as life.

He could walk to Shafer's front door, ring the doorbell, shoot whoever opened the door. Shafer's wife, no doubt. How long would he need? Ten seconds? Fifteen?

The thought made Crompond's fingers twitch. Let Shafer's phone ring. Let him speed home, find the police cruisers outside, the house taped off, cops canvassing the neighbors. He would know even before the detectives told him.

Crompond would shoot her in the chest, give Shafer that small courtesy, the chance to see her face one last time unspoiled, touch her cheek.

Then he saw the woman across the street. Pretty, a redhead, fortyish, pushing a stroller. A double-wide. Twins. Courtesy of some fertility doctor, no doubt. The pistol was still under the seat, but she was looking at Crompond like she could read his mind. She saw him looking back, didn't smile. He let go of the pistol like it was on fire, gave her a halfhearted wave, and eased away from the curb.

Lesson learned. No shooting anyone. Not today. He didn't have a silencer, and neighborhoods like this had stay-at-home moms, cameras where they wouldn't be noticed. The police would find him quick. And his arrest would destroy his bigger plans, the plans that really mattered. Shafer's wife was nothing.

First things first. Let the imam give Martin's address to his French friends. Let them move.

He'd handle Shafer if he saw the chance. He turned on the radio, low, found an adult contemporary station to play him some Taylor Swift, drove the speed limit to Langley. He rolled into the campus, smiling and cool. No need to rush. No need to panic. Soon enough, he'd make his announcement.

17

THE CASTLE

LOCKDOWN GAVE Wells the chance to learn every inch of Samir Khalili's cell. The Florida-shaped crack in the back wall's concrete. The rust-brown stain in the floor that looked like blood, except when it didn't. The barely visible deformations in the bars, as if the cell's previous occupants had tugged the steel until their hands shed skin. Not because they believed they could escape but so they remembered they hadn't given up.

Wells understood.

Since the fight, the guards had run the block more nastily. They brought in oversized speakers and blasted '80s hair metal bands like Def Leppard when the jihadis tried to pray. They threatened to sic their Dobermans on prisoners who spoke Arabic after curfew. They turned off the heat, then cranked it far too high.

The crackdown didn't surprise Wells. The jihadis might be their meal ticket, but the guards sympathized with their fellow Bulgarians. And they obviously knew what he'd done during the fight. They treated him more harshly than anyone else. For the first week of lockdown, they allowed him only one meal and latrine visit a day. They came to his cell four or five times a night and made him stand at attention, shivering in his thin uniform.

Not so long ago, Wells had been imprisoned in an aircraft carrier, its brig far belowdecks. That cell had been cleaner, but here he could watch the sky lighten and darken. He'd take the trade. Still, he hated losing these precious days, especially since he didn't know what was happening at Langley. The warden obviously planned to leave the lockdown in place long enough that no one would question the reality of the reprimand, much less the fight that had sparked it. But as a second week passed, and a third, Wells wondered if the brawl had been worth the trouble, the lost time.

Finally, exactly twenty-one days after the fight, he heard booted footsteps echoing along the cellblock. He came to the bars, found himself looking at the angry pimpled face of the commanding guard. Wells hadn't seen him since that first night.

"Boss went soft on you throat slitters. Says you get time to pray this week." The commander unlocked Wells's cell, slid open the gate. "If it was my choice, you'd be praying for me to stop beating your head in."

"Glad it's not up to you."

The commander's mouth became a slit.

"Stand in the doorway. Grab the bars on either side and spread your feet."

Wells knew he shouldn't have talked back. Arguing would only anger the commander further. Wells squeezed his hands around the bars. The guard popped his baton, whacked him once in the ribs, twice—

"You have kids? Hope so—" He dug low and came up between Wells's legs. An underhand strike. Sun fire. Agony. Wells gasped, staggered, the weight of his body hanging from his arms.

"Might be tough now."

Wells could only moan. **Scale of one to ten, what's your pain level?** Ten. Billion. Slowly, the pain faded enough for him to stand upright. The guard stepped close.

"You broke a bone in Gruv's neck. Lucky he can walk."

Wells didn't speak, sure that the wrong answer would earn another beating.

"A rat, that one. Nasty with a knife. Maybe I'm not so mad you taught him a lesson. But do anything like it again, I'll slit your throat. Don't forget it."

"Yes."

"Now come, dirty Arab, play with your brothers." The commander smirked. "I meant **pray**."

Wells tried to walk. Gravity was more powerful than he remembered. He went to his knees. Somehow, he forced himself to his feet and staggered for the prayer room, walking bowlegged, clownish. Maybe he wasn't a masochist. Maybe he was only a fool.

WITH ITS calm white walls, the prayer room felt like a hospital. The other jihadis half carried him to the back wall. He slumped down. Hani sat beside him, looked at him with respect and worry both.

"What did they do to you?"

Wells ran his hands up his thighs, gingerly touched himself, wished he hadn't. He'd be pissing blood for a week. He needed an ice bath and Vicodin more than anything, but asking for those would only earn him another blow.

He wouldn't know if the shot had done any permanent harm until a real doctor looked at him and he wouldn't have that chance until he left this place.

He stayed very still as he listened to the prayers. "Can we help?" Hani said.

"You were right about that guard."

"They're animals."

"They think the same of us."

"Someone hits you between the legs, now you're a philosopher?" Hani squeezed Wells's hand. "I didn't have the chance to say it properly before. Thank you. That big one, he would have—"

"The knife came to me, I threw it."

"They hate you more than me. They know you're dangerous."

"I thought I was a philosopher."

"In Afghanistan, did you kill?"

"Everyone killed."

"Americans?"

"**Nam.**" The truth, for Samir Khalili and Wells both. "Think they'll ever let us into the yard again? I want my chance at the big one."

"Not a good idea right now. Unless you can knock him down with your swollen balls."

"I like that idea."

"But I hope you heal fast. I hear the **kaffirs**

have a price on us both," Hani said. "Five thousand euros."

"Only five?"

"For a thousand, those pigs would cut their
own mothers in half."

"Doesn't matter. Unless the guards open the
gates for them, they can't get to us and we can't
get to them."

"Truly, I'm surprised they even let us have
this meeting."

"Maybe the Americans said they had to let
us pray once a week."

"Maybe."

The prayers washed over them. Wells didn't
want to push, but he worried that once this session ended, he wouldn't see Hani for another
week or longer.

"Tell me, Hani. I've thought about it a lot in
the cell."

"What's that?"

"The Islamic State has more men than we
ever did. Especially in Europe. How come you
haven't been able to make a big attack like
September 11?"

"Back to this? You're obsessed. You were
lucky that day, that's all."

"Allah smiled on us." **Did I just say that?**
No, Samir Khalili did.

"Maybe you didn't notice living with the goats in the mountains all these years, but everywhere has more security. Not just jets. It's hard to surprise them."

"Is that it? Or is it that your leaders are all in Raqqa? The brothers in Europe only look for easy targets. Nightclubs to shoot up. One week they dance, the next they come back with an AK. What good is that?"

"That guard scrambled your mind, too. I shouldn't say this—"

"Then don't." Wells was taking a chance, playing back. But Hani liked to brag.

"Under their noses in Paris—"

Wells willed Hani to go on. He didn't. Wells would have to risk pressing once more. "What, you have a big man there?"

Hani raised his eyebrows. A painkiller better than Vicodin. An actual lead.

"Let me guess. A cousin of yours. Snuck in from Syria a few years ago, before anyone ever heard of the Islamic State. Married himself to a French girl, who had convinced herself Arabs are the best lovers. Did she take the **hijab** or does he keep her locked in a closet so he's the only one who sees her?"

"Not my cousin."

"Or maybe one of those Algerians whose parents were dumb enough to think the French were serious about making them citizens? With those silly names, half French and half Arab, which makes them nothing at all, Jacques Hamidou, whatever." Still, Hani didn't answer. "Don't tell me, then."

"Call him Abu Najma." Father of Najma. The name meant **star** in Arabic.

"Such an original nickname." Every Islamic State fighter seemed to have a **nom de guerre** that started with **Abu**—the Arabic word for **father**. "Abu Najma, Abu Bakr—"

"Fine. Call him the Puma."

Puma. Wells had won another clue for the NSA databases. If Hani hadn't made up the nickname Puma on the spot for his own obscure reasons. If Wells beat whatever the Bulgarian convicts had planned for him and escaped. If the mole hadn't already shot up the seventh floor by then. He wondered for a moment if he should break cover to pass the aliases to Shafer.

But a million Muslims lived in Paris and its suburbs. Even if Wells excluded every woman, and every man under twenty-five, he would be left with hundreds of thousands of potential suspects. Two aliases wouldn't be enough. To have a real chance at the guy, Wells needed at least one more tidbit. His last name would be best, though Hani was very unlikely to give that up. His job, if he had one. Where he lived. Some unusual physical trait.

"Call him whatever you like. Call him Prince Charles. I don't see the point."

"The point is that this Puma, the French, they trust him, see? They think he's one of the good ones." Hani laughed.

"Because he's educated. Mouths all the right words." Hani didn't contradict Wells, but he didn't offer more details either. "A scientist? A politician? An imam?" Nothing. Wells gave up. "Like the **kaffirs** can see our hearts. Like they have any idea of what we believe. When they can't imagine Allah's glory."

"You **are** a philosopher, Samir."

"In the mountains, I had time to think. But I'm glad to hear you have this one in France. That's something that we never had, a commander in America who could bring the war to the **kaffirs**. If we had one like that—"

Wells hoped Hani would take the bait, brag about the Islamic State's man in Washington. Nope. "Soon, **Insh'allah**, we'll do something in France that makes September 11 look like nothing."

But was Hani serious? Or bragging? He'd

been in here a while already. Any big attack he knew was coming would probably have happened by now. Wells suspected he was blowing smoke, trying to impress Samir Khalili. Wells decided to frustrate his impulse to brag, and, not coincidentally, try again to shift the conversation. "France isn't America. When we hit those towers, we started another world war."

"A world war? Samir—"

"Why are you here, then? And me? How many countries have the Americans attacked since then? They're more powerful than the rest of the world put together. Their army, their CIA"—the three magic letters. He hoped he hadn't shoehorned them too obviously.

"The United States is much harder to, but you know that. Even if—"

But Hani stopped there, seeming to think the better of whatever he was going to say next.

Even if we have someone inside the CIA?
"Even if what?"

Hani didn't answer. Wells knew he had pushed as far as he dared.

The men finished their prayers. Wells pushed himself up. The sudden movement inflamed his groin, and he groaned and leaned hard against the wall. No need to playact.

"Careful, Samir. We need you."

"And I you, brother." Wells, thinking, **Wish I could tell you how much.**

IN HIS CELL he sat on his too-thin mattress, trying to find a position that didn't amplify the ache between his legs. Without Hani to distract him, the pain was worsening again.

Wells saw now that the guards should have put him closer to Hani's cell so they could have talked more easily outside of the prayer room. Maybe the warden had thought interfering that way would be too obvious. Maybe he **had** given that order, but the guards hadn't listened. Or maybe he had a prison to run and hadn't even considered the idea.

Whatever the reason, at least seven precious days would pass before his next conversation with Hani. Wells could almost see the sand slipping past.

PART
THREE

18

PARIS

THE GUIDE led Soufiane Kassani over the border at dawn. A kilometer inside Turkey, three sedans waited, white and anonymous. Kassani spread the bottles among them, as the caliph had instructed. Eleven one-liter bottles in two trunks. Twelve in the third. Each bottle half full. Seventeen liters of DF in all, ninety percent pure on average. Enough to pack a subway train or concert hall with corpses.

Kassani watched with something like nostalgia as the cars pulled away and bumped along a dirt track to parts unknown. A year's work in those trunks. He wondered if he'd see the precious cargo again. He knew his next stop, but not much more.

A pickup arrived, a new Nissan with leather seats, air-conditioning. The drive turned out to be long but straightforward, no roadblocks to bypass or bandits to outrun. The pickup's driver kept to the speed limit. He had obviously been told to defer to Kassani. He barely spoke as the hours passed.

Darkness had fallen by the time they pulled off the E80 in Gebze, an eastern suburb of Istanbul. The driver wound through an industrial neighborhood, parked beside a low concrete building marked by a discreet sign, white letters on a dark red background: **Five-Star Mehmet Import-Export.**

Inside, the office was dark and stank of smoke. An old man sat on a soft brown couch, his face lit by the glow of a movie playing on an Apple laptop. **"As-salaam alaikum."**

"Alaikum salaam."

"Is Adnan here?" Adnan was the trader who'd bought the lab equipment for Kassani. They'd spoken three times, emailed dozens more, never met.

"Brother." The man creaked to his feet. He was in his seventies, his pouchy cheeks marked with black moles that even Kassani's untrained eyes recognized as cancers-in-waiting.

"You're Adnan?" He'd been so aggressive about finding the equipment. Kassani had imagined him young, a fire-breather.

The man wrapped skinny arms around Kassani's shoulders. "Not what you expected?" He led Kassani into a cluttered back office. Blue binders were stacked along a wall, samples of carpet spread over a desk.

"You made good use of what I sent."

"You have the stuff?"

"Don't worry about that. It'll be waiting for you in Paris."

Paris. No one had mentioned Paris. The caliph had told him only that he'd meet Adnan in Istanbul. Ghaith had told him to pack light, leave his Quran but bring his atropine syringes. Neither man had said, **You won't be coming back**. They hadn't needed to.

Kassani wondered if he'd have to take a boat from Turkey, pretend to be a refugee. Plenty of Islamic State fighters had returned to Europe that way. With so many migrants, European nations couldn't run decent background checks. Countries like Italy hadn't even guarded their refugee camps before the Paris attacks in 2015. Now some countries had tightened up. But even in the best-run camps, a determined refugee could sneak off.

Still, going in as a migrant would be inherently risky. The Greeks no longer simply waved refugee ships through. What if they sent Kassani's vessel back to Turkey? Or he wound up in a camp he couldn't escape? Too many variables he couldn't control.

"They didn't tell you about Paris?"

Kassani shook his head.

"Beautiful. If only the French weren't there to ruin it."

"You've been?" Kassani had, too, as a child. His parents had taken him and his brothers to a hotel industry convention. He vividly remembered a boat ride on the Seine, passing under bridges with a breeze in his face, so unlike Tunisia.

"When I was young. Before I understood." The old man shook his head, at his own youthful mistakes or the sins of the French or both. "You're tired. A long journey today." He nodded at the back wall of the office, where a passport photo camera pointed at a blue curtain. "I need your picture."

Kassani stood before the curtain and offered the pained half smile a billion travelers knew.

The camera clicked. "There's a room in the back. Sleep. It's a narrow bed but clean."

Kassani dreamt he was floating down the Seine, pouring isopropyl bottles into a river of pure DF.

HE WOKE TO the smell of good strong coffee, impossible to find in Raqqa these days. He was pouring himself a cup when Adnan appeared, carrying a black plastic bag.

"Like it here, Soufiane? Want to stay? Drink my coffee?"

Kassani found himself charmed by this tumorous old man. "They'd miss me in Paris."

Adnan handed him a passport with a dark purple cover and golden letters: europese unie. koninkrijk belgië.

"Belgian."

"**Nam.** And valid."

Kassani flipped through the pages, wondering if he'd see the photo that Adnan had taken the night before. He was no expert, but the passport seemed real. It had a biometric chip in the cover. Its end pages were slick-coated paper, covered with holographic seals, hard to tamper with or re-create. It was less than two years old and had only a few stamps. The most recent was from Istanbul immigration four days before. It carried the name of Beji Nounes, whose birthday was exactly two months after Kassani's.

The picture was the surprise. It was close. He and Beji could have been cousins. But it wasn't his. Even a sloppy immigration officer wouldn't miss the differences.

"Memorize the birthdate, the place of issue," Adnan said.

"I don't understand. How do I use this?"

"You don't." Adnan took back the passport, tore it in half along the spine, a satisfying rip. "The Belgians are going to give you a new one. With your face in it."

He reached into his bag, came out with an official-looking form, two pieces of paper covered in Turkish. "A police report. You reported it stolen yesterday. You were in the Grand Bazaar, and when you went back to your hotel, it was gone. Someone bumped into you, maybe your pocket was picked. Not your wallet—that was in your front pocket—just the passport. The truth is, maybe you dropped it. But you'd never admit that."

Kassani held up the papers. "I can't read this."

"No one expects you to. Repeat what I said back to me."

Kassani did. And twice more, on Adnan's prompting.

"Good. You don't have to be perfect on every detail, Soufiane. You're upset." Adnan laid a fresh piece of paper on the table. "You're supposed to be back in Belgium tomorrow night. Here's your itinerary."

He—Beji—was booked on a Turkish Airways nonstop, leaving Istanbul at 3:30 p.m., landing Brussels 6 p.m.

"You have to catch it. You don't have the money for a new ticket, and you need to get back to work."

"Where do I work?"

"A café in Molenbeek."

"They'll accept this?"

Adnan spread a handful of cards across the table. "Once you show them these, they will."

A key card from a Turkish hotel. A bank card for Beji Nounes. And the crowning touch. A mint-green piece of plastic with four languages across its top, including English: BELGIUM / identity card. It looked real to Kassani, and it carried Beji Nounes's name. All the details matched the passport. Except the photograph. It was the one of Kassani that Adnan had taken the night before.

"You made this?"

"Not me. But, yes. The passport is hard to fake, this is easy. Now, this morning, we walk around the Grand Bazaar for a few minutes, so you see it, see how you lost your passport there. Then to the Belgium consulate. You tell them Beji Nounes of 18B Rue van Mulder, Sint-Jans-Molenbeek, Brussels, needs a new passport by tomorrow."

"They'll be suspicious."

"Maybe, but Beji doesn't pray at the mosques

they watch. He's not a troublemaker, not on their lists. Otherwise, they wouldn't have let him on the plane to come here. So he lost his passport. People go to Istanbul and get pickpocketed and lose their passports. Even Arab Belgians."

"I don't speak much French."

"Lots of brothers don't."

"Are there other names I need to know?"

"What do you mean?"

"Is Beji married? Does he have children?"

"No. And they won't ask. They won't be thinking of this, that you're not him. Not once they see your identity card. Their main concern, are you in the jihad? Did you see the brothers in Syria? But you've only been here four days, so they won't be too worried. They'll ask, you tell them no, that's it. At worst, they'll give you a temporary passport for a single trip. Good enough. But probably they give you a full replacement. Then you can travel all around Europe, no problem. Even the French police, if they stop you with that, they'll just let you go."

"Because I'm Beji."

"Because you are Beji. And Beji is very nice. Too bad you can't meet him."

"What's going to happen to him?"

"He'll go to Syria. Don't worry about him.

Worry about Brussels. You'll wear this when you come out of the airport there." Adnan dumped out the last goodie in his bag, a brand-new cap, powder-blue, a golden double-headed eagle embossed across the front. The logo of the Manchester City Football Club. "Someone will pick you up. After that, I don't know. But it's been arranged."

Kassani grinned

"Why do you smile?"

"How lucky we are to have Beji here." But even as Kassani spoke, he realized his mistake.

"He came to Istanbul for this reason only, to give you his name. Come on, you didn't think we would put you with the refugees?"

KASSANI SPENT the morning at the consulate, answering questions. The Belgian clerks didn't like the missing passport. But their annoyance seemed to have as much to do with the extra work it caused them as with any suspicion about him. They asked if he was sure he hadn't left it at his hotel. They warned him processing a new one overnight would cost ninety euros in extra fees. They sent him away for lunch, and when he returned, they brought him to an office he hadn't seen before. No tourist posters in here, just a metal table, bare except for a single folder.

Standing behind it, a thirty-something Belgian with an interrogator's hard eyes and short hair. Kassani wondered what he'd done wrong, how they'd found him.

"I'm Bernard. Sit, please."

Kassani sensed the name was as fake as his own. "Beji."

"You're sure you've lost your passport." He spoke excellent Arabic.

"Yes."

"In the Grand Bazaar?"

"I think so."

"How?"

"A pickpocket, I assume."

"They didn't take your wallet."

"It was in my front pocket."

The man who called himself Bernard leaned close enough for Kassani to smell the cigarettes on his breath. "Did you throw it in the Bosphorus? Was there a stamp you don't want us to see?"

"I don't know what you mean."

"You went to Lebanon this week? Iraq?"

"**Non, monsieur.**"

"Syria? To see your Daesh friends?"

Kassani didn't point out that he probably wouldn't get a stamp in that case. "I've hardly even seen Istanbul."

"Why come here at all?"

"I've always wanted to visit." He waited for Bernard to trip him up, ask what he'd seen, pry into the last few days, with questions he couldn't answer.

Bernard said only, "Such a long trip. Why not London? Paris?"

"Men like me aren't always welcome in London right now."

"Tunis, then? Go home?"

"Belgium's my home."

Bernard flipped open the file, pushed photos across the table. Surveillance shots of Arab men. "Recognize anyone? From Molenbeek or here?"

Kassani studied the photos, wondering who these men were, if he'd meet them. "Sorry. I wish I could help."

Bernard gathered the pictures, riffled through Kassani's forms. Suddenly he seemed weary, and Kassani understood why Adnan was so sure the Belgians would give him the new passport. This man must be trying to track dozens of men. He had no more time for the curious case of Beji Nounes.

"Do you support the Islamic State, Beji?"

"No. They don't do us any good."

Bernard waved his hand at the door. "Come back tomorrow, you'll have your passport."

———

Two DAYS LATER, Kassani found himself in the Père Lachaise Cemetery in northeastern Paris. The graveyard stretched across a hundred acres on a low hillside that offered beautiful views of the city. It had hosted hundreds of thousands of burials in its two centuries. But it was best known as the eternal home of Jim Morrison. The Doors' lead singer lay in a grave protected by barricades and strewn with flowers.

Kassani walked past it now, wearing the light blue cap that had become his calling card.

"YOU'LL HAVE an hour to walk around this graveyard," his driver had said that morning as they drove south through the French country-side. "Wander. Make sure no one is watching. Be at Jim Morrison's tomb at one p.m."

"I don't know who that is."

The driver passed Kassani a map of the cem-etery, a number circled near the center. "I don't either, but it's marked here. A tall man in a white shirt will be there. Long sleeves. He'll ask you about Napoleon's tomb. If you're sure you aren't being followed, you say, 'The other side of the river.' If you're afraid someone's watch-ing, you say, 'Invalides, I think.'"

"Invalides, I think."

"Yes."

"Why all this? How could anyone be watching me? They'd have to be following us now."

"I know. But you're both too important to take chances."

A TALL MAN in a long-sleeved white shirt walked toward him.

"Do you know where I can find Napoleon's tomb?" He had a long nose, eyes deep in his face, sandy desert skin. A North African like Kassani, Algerian or Tunisian.

Kassani was sure no one had followed him. Or even noticed him. "Napoleon? That's the other side of the river."

"I must be lost." The man stepped closer. "Walk with me, Soufiane."

They left the tourists gawking at Morrison's grave and tiptoed along narrow paths through the tombstones until no one was within thirty meters. Only the dead were crowded in this place.

"As-salaam alaikum."

"Alaikum salaam."

"I'm Raouf. My real name, in case you're wondering. I lead the believers here."

"All of them?"

"All of them."

Now Kassani understood the precautions. "If I'm meeting you, Paris must be my last stop."

"There's something I want you to see."

L'ÉGLISE NOTRE-DAME DE Bonne-Nouvelle—the Church of Our Lady of Good News—was a wide, squat stone building at the top end of Paris's 2nd Arrondissement, a mile or so northeast of the Louvre. Bonne-Nouvelle had been erected in the 1820s to replace an older church that had been wrecked during the French Revolution.

In a nod to that angry history, the church had been rebuilt sturdy and solid. Easily defensible. It had none of the flourishes that marked its famous medieval namesake. No towers topped with gargoyles. No big stained glass windows. In fact, its front wall had no windows at all. The columns that supported its central pediment were its only ornamentation. It could have been a bank, a courthouse, even a jail. And though it faced north into a pocket park, Bonne-Nouvelle had no real estate of its own. Narrow single-lane streets, glorified alleys, encircled it on three sides. Its eastern wall merged with an apartment building.

Inside, Bonne-Nouvelle had been built in

what architects called neoclassical style. Arches and simple stone pillars separated the central nave from the side aisles. Its ceilings stood thirty feet above the aisles, forty above the nave. The lack of ornamentation and high ceilings gave the church an open, airy feel and made it seem larger than it was. In reality, Bonne-Nouvelle was no larger than a big hotel ballroom.

Still, the church was never crowded. Surveys showed that fewer than a quarter of French Catholics considered religion important to their lives. The percentage was even smaller in Paris, where God had to compete with the city's pleasures. Bonne-Nouvelle's regular Sunday services drew fewer than twenty worshippers, mostly women past sixty, white-haired and stooped. Yet the church's priests tried their best. They officiated at baptisms, communions, weddings, and funerals. They sat for confession every day in case anyone showed up.

So Raouf and Kassani found the church's front gate unlocked this afternoon, its tall front door cracked open. Inside, narrow wooden chairs were arranged around a long table in the center of the nave. On either side of the table, fat candles burned dimly, streaking smoke into the hall. At the end of the main aisle, the ceiling rose into a dome painted with eye-catching dark hexagons. Clear glass in the dome's center sprayed the church with sunlight. Along the walls were paintings of scenes that Kassani imagined came from the Christian Bible.

Mosques were austere and simple. Houses of prayer, nothing more. This place was—

"Pretty."

"A pretty place for their pretty god. A museum where they can see how they used to believe." Raouf spoke in a whisper. "I don't know if you'll see it again, so take a good look. I have photos and a plan of the inside, but your own eyes are always best."

"What am I looking for?"

Raouf opened his hands—**Don't make me say it**. Kassani was embarrassed. He looked again at the space. Imagining it as pure geometry, nothing more than an open room. Imagining it as a target.

The lack of windows would help. As would the fact that the windows the church did have were high in the walls. Sarin was a big molecule, heavier than air. It tended to fall rather than rise.

Kassani circled the walls, pretending he was interested in the Christian frippery. He was checking the ventilation system. Air-conditioning hadn't existed when Bonne-Nouvelle was built. Its architects had counted on stone walls and high ceilings to keep the church cool. For winter, the building had a primitive heating system, grilles scattered across its stone floors. The lazy drift of the smoke from the candles showed how slowly the air was moving.

The lack of modern vents meant that the poison wouldn't clear easily once it became airborne. But it also would need time to spread from wherever they hid it. Kassini wondered if they'd have access to the heating vents or the ductwork under them.

Kassani believed seventeen liters of sarin would be enough to kill most of the people inside this space. If they couldn't run out. Though there, too, the church's age might give them an advantage. Bonne-Nouvelle had been built long before building codes required emergency exits. As far as Kassani could tell, the church had only one secondary exit, a little door tucked in the back right corner. A panicked rush to escape could jam it. If Raouf could somehow block the front door.

If, if, if. Lots of questions. Including the most important. Out of all the churches in Paris, why this one? He'd have to ask later. As Kassani finished his circle and came back to the center table, a fiftyish man in a dark blue sweater walked toward him. The priest, no doubt. He wore a puzzled smile as he chattered at Kassani. Kassani froze. He understood only basic French, hardly enough to handle a conversation. How would he explain his wanderings?

Suddenly Raouf was beside him, speaking as smoothly as the priest. After a minute, the priest nodded, smiled, pointed to the church's back right corner.

"He says he understands your difficulty," Raouf said. "The toilet's over there."

"Ahh, merci. Merci beaucoup."

RAOUF AND KASSANI walked toward the Gare du Nord, the big train station that connected Paris with its northern suburbs and points beyond.

"Impressive, how you handled the priest."

"I've lived here a long time. And these French, they're all the same. They imagine there's a certain way of doing things. The right way. The **French** way. To speak, to buy groceries, to dress. They're not afraid to tell you if you're doing it the wrong way. In fact, they **like** to tell you. They're so proud of themselves, of their country."

"It sounds tiresome."

"The Americans, they blow us up, but at least

they don't order us around. Tell us how to speak English."

"But I don't see, how does that help you with them?"

"I know what they want. I let them give their speeches—priests, mayors, everyone. I nod, listen—"

"Promise you'll do it their way."

Raouf shook his head. "Too obvious. And they don't think an Arab can be French—not exactly. But without saying so, I admit that their way is better."

"That's what they want?"

"That's all they want. From us anyway. So?"

"You mean the church?"

"Of course."

"The stuff is here already?"

"Some coming today. The rest tomorrow."

"Adnan—"

"Yes, Adnan. What do you think?"

Kassani saw that for all his protests, Raouf had internalized the French attitude about correction. **We're not talking about Adnan now. We're talking about the church.** "For that space? We have enough. I think."

"Come, let's sit a minute." Raouf led Kassani into an empty café. A waiter brought them lemonades in the Parisian style, fresh-pressed lemon juice, a cool pitcher of water, and another, smaller pitcher with simple syrup. "A tiresome country, **oui**, but they do know how to eat."

"We can talk here?"

"These are the best places. A couple of Arabs talking about our mistresses. Just keep your voice low. Now, what's wrong?"

"This stuff, it's not what you imagine. You don't just pour out a few drops and **poof**—" Kassani lifted his hands. "I'll have to premix it."

"Like this." Raouf poured a dollop of lemon juice into his glass, mixed it with a long silver rod, added the sugar.

Watching the juice turn to a cloud in the glass brought Kassani back to the caliph's backyard. "You can't imagine how dangerous it is. Unless you want me to get killed while I'm mixing, I need the right gear and plenty of space. With its own ventilation."

"I have that."

"Then, once I'm done, I have to seal it tight. If it leaks, it'll kill anyone it touches. So let's say that works—the mixing. I assume you're planning to leave it under the grates. In that case, we need a way to puncture the plastic and release it. A needle or a knife, with a mechanism to make it stab."

"Is that all?"

"No. The stuff, it starts as liquid. It aerosol-izes at room temperatures, but we have to blow it up into the vents."

"How much space will it take?"

"For the liquid alone, imagine a box half a meter square." Kassani outlined the shape. "Heavy, too. Twenty kilos, not counting the container. Or the knife. Or the fan, or whatever we're using to blow it. And—"

"There's more?"

"It would be better if we had it coming from at least two or three places. With the doors closed, the air doesn't move fast in there."

Raouf nodded. "But if we get inside and set the boxes in place, underneath, in the heating."

"If, sure. But all of that takes time, and I saw the front door has an alarm."

"Let me take care of that."

"Magic again."

Raouf leaned in. "The French can't be both-ered to clean their own sewers, water pipes, the cables underground. They like Arabs for that work."

"But where the sewer meets the church, it must be an alarm—"

"We've checked. A locked gate, that's all. That place is two hundred years old, and no one cares about those Jesus paintings anymore. My men go in the basement, leave the boxes, get out—"

"Paint the boxes black, too, so no one can see them from above, they can stay until we're ready."

Raouf sipped his lemonade. "Once the boxes are in place, could dogs find them?"

"Do the sewers in Paris have dogs?"

"I mean, trained dogs, like the ones they use to sniff for bombs."

Kassani considered. "It's possible. But I can promise they wouldn't be nearly as good as the kind that find explosives. These chemicals are rare. No one's going to spend a lot of time training dogs to find them. And they couldn't possibly train them with sarin, so they'd have to teach them to find what's called a precursor."

"Something the dogs can smell without getting killed."

"Yes. But we'll load actual sarin in those containers. Even if they do pick that up, they won't know what it is." Kassani hesitated. "I don't understand why you're expecting dogs. At **that** church."

Raouf took one last long sip of lemonade. "Last question. After the gas starts flowing, will anyone have any advance warning?"

Kassani could answer this one with absolute assurance. "No. It doesn't smell, it doesn't taste, you can't see it, you can't feel it. Until it gets inside you. But if we want to be sure it's lethal, we have to be sure no one gets out for at least a minute. Two would be better."

"That long?"

"When they used it in Tokyo, in the subways, they killed twenty people, but hundreds more took a few breaths and didn't die. They got to fresh air in time. Ours is more dangerous, but one or two breaths won't be enough. People can run for a few seconds after they feel the effects. The longer we can pin them, the better."

Kassani waited, but Raouf didn't say anything more. "I understand, there's only the one big door at the front of the church. Are you expecting people will jam it in the panic?"

"**Insh'allah**, they won't go for the door at all. They'll stay right where they are. Until too late."

19

THE CASTLE

ORCHIDECTOMY.

Strange word. Wells would always remember the first time he'd heard it.

Eighth grade. Starting to play football seriously. His talent was already obvious, his speed and strength and most of all his slipperiness. Fast feet, the coaches said. A single tackler could rarely stop him. He was there, then he wasn't. The trait would serve him well in the years to come.

In his memory he lay in bed, reading **Sports Illustrated**, boxing, a beast of a heavyweight named Mike Tyson, only a few years older than Wells himself. Or maybe **Time**. Hard to imagine now, but back in the pre-Internet era, in Hamilton, Montana, weekly magazines and the nightly news broadcasts were the primary sources of information. His parents subscribed to **Time** and **Newsweek**, encouraged him to read both. **It's a big world. You need to know what's going on, John.**

Wells didn't believe the past had been better or worse. People had always been people, cruel, kind, or both at once. But he was pretty sure it had been simpler. More contained.

That night, he heard the front door creak, his dad shout greetings upstairs. Herbert was a doctor, a surgeon. They'd expected him for dinner, but a nurse called, said he was stuck in the operating room, an emergency. It happened.

Wells heard the rattle of ice in a glass as Herbert poured himself a drink. After a minute or two, more rattling. Slow steps upstairs. The second drink and Herbert's heavy tread meant the surgery had been rough. Though not that it had failed. Herbert gave himself completely to his patients, win or lose.

Herbert tapped lightly on Wells's door. "Awake?"

"Hi, Dad."

The door opened a crack. "Promise me something. Every time you play ball, you'll wear a cup."

"Of course—"

"Not **of course**. Make sure it really fits. Don't be embarrassed, get the right one, one that doesn't slip—"

"This is why you're home so late?" Though Wells hardly needed to ask. His father wasn't a talkative man. The surgery must have been ugly.

"Ever heard of an orchidectomy?" Herbert closed the door without waiting for an answer. Wells found it in his dictionary. **Orchidectomy**, also spelled **orchiectomy**: surgical removal of one or both testes.

THE WORD came back to Wells on the afternoon after his encounter with the guard commander. His scrotum swelled to the size of a baseball and turned so tender that the slightest touch jumped tears from his eyes. Blood, fire-engine red, flavored his urine.

That night, Wells lay on his side, pants pulled to his knees, lips sucked against his teeth. The fire radiated down his legs, some accident of nerves. The pain heightened his senses. He picked up a faint stink of diesel fuel, a radio playing Bulgarian pop, a horse neighing outside the Castle's walls.

He didn't know the sun would ever rise. But it did, and when he stood for attention for the dawn count, the guards smirked.

"Gorilla balls," the cellblock's head guard said. Playing to his men. "Too bad the rest of it didn't grow the same way."

"I need a doctor." Wells had wondered about asking, but why not? He **did**. Even a Qaeda detainee wouldn't want to endure this.

"Needs a doctor. Poor baby."

Wells realized a sentence too late that he should have begged, not demanded.

"Today's Saturday. Doctor's not here today. Or tomorrow."

"Even a bag of ice, then. **Please.**"

"Next, he'll want us to make him a cozy fire. Cook him breakfast." The guards walked off.

An hour later, one came back with a garbage bag of ice, a quart of milk, a bag of oranges, and a chocolate bar. Wells hadn't known food like that existed in here. The kindness was proof that he looked as bad as he felt. He covered himself in ice, closed his eyes, imagined his high school cheerleaders trying a new routine: Gimme an **O**! Gimme an **R**! Gimme a **C**! Gimme a . . .

What's it spell?

Eunuch!

THE ICE HELPED. The swelling subsided, slowly. His urine faded from red to brown. The pain barely budged, but Wells was used to pain.

On the third night, he slept deep enough to dream. Emmie paid a visit. She pulled him through the woods in North Conway. Fall, late afternoon, the sugar maples glowing yellow and red, weirdly neon in the slanting sun. Emmie stayed a step ahead, her legs kicking up leaves. **Come on, Daddy! Let's go!** He couldn't see her face no matter how hard he tried.

He sent her away, but she returned the next night. And the next. Until now, he hadn't truly understood the hold his daughter would have. Another distraction, another danger. He had to push her aside, even if doing so left pain his only companion.

Friday came, and Wells readied himself to meet Hani. But the guards told him and the others that they had canceled prayers. "Next week, if you roaches behave." Already a month had passed since Wells had arrived at the Castle. Now he was losing another week. He knew he ought to protest, but he couldn't find the energy. Not just because the guards wouldn't care. Under the circumstances, having seven more days to recuperate was a relief.

HE KNEW he'd healed, or healed enough, when he woke up on Monday ready for push-ups and tricep exercises. No sit-ups, though. He would let that part of his body be. Along with his strength, his impatience came back. He needed a way to talk to Hani. But his imagination failed him. In a jailhouse movie, he would have figured out a clever trick for the prisoners on the other side of the block to run messages. Morse code through the walls. In reality, he would have had to shout even more loudly to talk to them than to Hani.

He gave up, focused instead on his next conversation. How could he lure Hani into revealing more about the commander in Paris? Or the mole? What if Samir told Hani about his own fights against the Americans? Would Hani brag in return?

Then another idea came to him. A long shot, but maybe it would get Hani talking . . .

The week dragged until the wheel turned Friday. The morning passed with no word. Wells wondered if he could afford to wait another week. But, just before noon, he heard the echoing steps of the guards. The prisoners on the other side murmured as their cells clanked open. Finally, they came for him. Once again, the pimpled commander led them. His skin seemed worse today. A full-on boil crested his nose. Wells pitied him, and then he saw the baton.

"Samir."

"Sir." Wells was glad for the bars that split

them. He wanted to put his hands on the commander's throat, whatever the punishment.

"I'm sorry we couldn't get you a doctor." The commander grinned. "Though you seem to have recovered on your own."

He unlocked the gate, slid it back. Wells understood. The commander was playing, trying to provoke him. He made himself relax. "I'm feeling much better. Sir."

"Now you'll have the chance to thank Allah for your quick return to health."

The commander muttered in Bulgarian to the other guards. They trotted away. When they were out of sight around the corner, the commander pulled a knife from his pocket. A shiv, with a rough-hewn wooden handle and a whet-sharpened blade.

Wells tightened up, waiting for the strike, wondering if he could take away the knife without hurting the commander too much. Instead, the man offered the shiv to Wells.

A new trap, far more dangerous. Wells shook his head.

"Take it—"

"So you call your guys back, tell them you found it on me?"

"Take it. Or I'll stick it in you."

No good choices here. Wells extended his

arm unwillingly, an inch at a time, until the commander pressed the handle of the shiv into his palm. Wells waited for the man to snap the baton over his head or yell that he'd found a weapon. But he only stared until Wells eased the shiv into the single pocket of his uniform pants. "You probably want to lose it. Don't."

"You say so." **Why this? Why now?** Wells knew he couldn't ask.

"Come on, Samir. You'd better pray."

HANI WAITED in the prayer room. **"As-salaam alaikum."**

"Alaikum salaam, my friend." They sat against the back wall as the others began their ablutions. Wells felt the knife pressing against his thigh. He decided not to mention it. For now.

"Are you all right? You were moaning in your sleep."

"As long as I'm alive, I'm alive."

"Tougher than a stone." A famous Arab proverb.

"Stupider than a camel." **Not** a famous Arab proverb.

"I asked them to let me see you. They said no, the beasts."

Even before the commander pressed the shiv

on him, Wells had planned to turn the conversation to escape. Now Hani had given him the chance. Wells leaned close. "We need to get out."

"I told you, impossible. Concrete cells. No tools."

"We're not always in the cells."

"Then the guards are with us."

"I could take out a guard. Or two. I'd **like** to take out a guard or two. Say, next Friday, on the way over here."

"And we're still inside the block."

"We climb the walls. They're brick. Plenty of handholds. To the windows and out."

"Eight, nine meters up. Jump down, even if you don't break your legs, you land in barbed wire. You're not **outside**. There's another wall to climb, higher, and it's concrete, not brick. Now you try to climb it with the guards shooting at you. This isn't a plan, Samir. It's fantasy—"

"Maybe for you."

Hani gave Wells the smile of a doctor humoring a mad patient. "Say you get out, somehow. In the middle of Bulgaria. No money. Don't speak the language. Wearing a prison uniform. Every soldier and policeman chasing you. What then? You sneak on a plane, go back to Afghanistan. So the Americans can catch you again?"

They'd wound up where Wells had hoped. "Not the mountains. I've changed my mind. We're in Europe, we stay in Europe."

"I didn't know you knew so many people in Europe."

"You do."

"So, what, I take you to Sevran, introduce you, he used to be Qaeda but now he's one of ours?"

"Why not? Anyway, what's Sevran?" Though Wells knew. Sevran was a poor Paris suburb, one of the most troubled of what the French called the **banlieues**, its residents nearly all Muslim, North African, and Middle Eastern.

Wells knew, but Samir Khalili didn't. So he asked.

"Sevran? Paris. On the train to the airport."

"Paris. This is where your friend lives? The one you called the Lion?"

"Puma."

"Right. Puma."

Hani had just given Wells as big a clue as he could have hoped. The target area wasn't the Paris metro area anymore. Or even the **banlieues**. It was a single suburb. Wells didn't know how big Sevran was. But even if it had twenty thousand Muslim men, Hani had shrunk the target pool for the Islamic State's commander by ninety-five percent. He'd turned the search from impossible to manageable. Difficult but manageable. And if the Puma—a/k/a Abu Najma—had any extremist history at all, he would be in an NSA or CIA or French database. Maybe all three. If not, Wells would go to Sevran himself and find him.

"Puma, Lion—I was close."

"Have you ever seen a lion?"

"Have you? So the Puma-Lion-Rhinoceros— after I escape, I go to his kebab stand in this place Sevran and tell him you sent me."

"Not a kebab stand."

"**Shawarma**, then?" Wells hoped to annoy him into giving up more.

"Forget it, Samir. This is stupid. No one's escaping."

"You Gulf Arabs don't have any sense of humor."

"Maybe if you didn't joke so much, the guards wouldn't hit you."

Wells decided he'd reached the moment to press hard. Even at the risk of raising Hani's suspicions. The Islamic State's commander in France was a huge prize, worth aborting the mission to uncover the mole. Anyway, the knife in his pocket suggested that his time in the Castle would be ending soon, one way or another.

This might be his last chance to find the mole.

"Maybe they'd hit me harder. Anyway, I wonder if the guard hurt me more than I thought two weeks ago. I don't remember much of what we said. Weren't we talking about September 11? The Americans?"

"Your favorite subject."

"How we fought them? And the CIA. How they'd attacked us, it was time for us to attack them—"

Hani tilted his head, gave Wells a searching look. More puzzled than suspicious. As if he'd just realized how little they knew about each other. "For someone who says he can't remember, you remember well."

"So we **were** talking about that?"

"Mostly, you. Just like now. Tell you what, when you see the Puma, you can ask him." Hani laughed. "Come on, let's pray—"

Hani stood, stepped away from Wells. He didn't turn back, didn't offer Wells a hand, and Wells knew that he'd blown his shot. Maybe he had pushed too hard. Or maybe Hani was just being cautious, especially since Latif had guessed at the mole's existence so quickly.

Hani's new suspicion gave Wells another reason not to hang around much longer. Not that he needed one.

BEFORE the mission began, Kirkov had told Wells that if he needed to get out, he should tell a guard, **Samir Khalili must speak with Colonel Zogrin about Radka and Bilyana.**

"Which guard?"

"Any guard."

"Zogrin's the warden?"

"Yes. Don't worry, we can trust him."

"Radka and Bilyana?"

"His daughters. Which isn't something any of the prisoners know. That's how I'm sure the guards will pass the message, even though they don't know who you are."

"Beat me to bits, too, until Zogrin hears it and stops them."

"Never. They're softies. Anyway, they'll pass it quickly."

Kirkov's blasé confidence in the guards no longer seemed funny. Yes, they probably would speed Wells's words along. No one would want to endanger the warden's kids. But the message would need an hour or two to move up the chain of command. More, if Zogrin happened to be away from his office. Plenty of time for the guards to hurt Wells.

Yet Wells had no other way to reach Zogrin. The guy wasn't exactly hanging out on the cellblock.

THE GUARDS ordered them out, lined them up at the block's main gate.

"Outside for you. Even insects need fresh air." Two guards took their places at the front of the line, one behind. They led the jihadis into the corridor. The guard at the cellblock gate smirked at Wells at he passed and slammed the gate shut behind them. "Have fun," the guard muttered under his breath.

That fast, Wells understood why the commander had given him the blade.

"Hani. It's coming. Pass the word."

"What?"

"It. In the yard—"

Wells was wrong. It came before the yard.

As the jihadis turned left down the short corridor that led to the yard, Wells saw that the door ahead was open. Suddenly the two guards in front ran for it. At the same time, Wells heard a rumble behind them. He looked back to see a dozen Bulgarian prisoners piling down the wide tiled hallway. The big one with the scythe on his cheek led the way, holding something silver and shiny, a short metal bar that looked to have come out of a weight room. The rear guard had disappeared. He must have peeled off into the corridor that led to the administration wing.

"Run—outside—" Wells yelled in Arabic.

But the guards ahead had vanished into the yard. Instead, more Bulgarians were coming through the door at them. Wells turned back again. The big man was locked on Wells, running hard, nearly out of control, the same brute-force attack that he'd used in the yard. Wells squared his shoulders, kept the knife low where the guy wouldn't notice it, hoping he would aim high, and not low, with the club.

Five feet away, the Bulgarian raised his right hand. Wells lifted his left arm, not trying to avoid the blow, only trying to deflect it from his head. He wanted the guy close.

As the man brought the bar down onto his forearm, Wells stepped forward, the move no one ever expected.

The metal rod crunched into the meat of his left arm and shoulder, muscles and bone that had taken shots before. But Wells's adrenaline was flowing. The pain was pleasure to him now. He brought up his right arm, drove the knife into the man's neck, not a slash but a single deadly sideways strike. They locked eyes for a moment before the man tried to jerk his head away, but too late. Wells forced the blade deep into the muscle, and a jet of arterial blood covered his hand and he knew he'd severed the carotid.

The giant screamed. The metal bar clattered from his fingers. He reached for his neck and tried hopelessly to stanch the blood. Wells pulled the blade, shoved it into his chest, wrenched it out. Death shaded the Bulgarian's eyes then like a squatter walking through an empty house. The man tilted sideways and toppled, slowly, grudgingly, his blood painting the wall.

Wells stepped away and looked for someone else to attack.

But the other Bulgarians weren't coming anymore. They stared at Wells as if he were the devil himself. Behind him, the fighting went on. But even without turning his head, Wells knew that it had slackened into a scuffle. The giant's collapse had shocked everyone around him, made their battles seem tame and childish.

They stood that way a few seconds, in suspended animation, as the big man's blood streamed and his hands fluttered and he flew to a land only he could see.

Until a guard ran from the central junction

toward them and pulled a gate shut, the hard clank of metal on metal echoing down the hall. Now the only way out was behind Wells, into the yard. But even as the prisoners turned, the door slammed shut and heavy bolts slammed home.

The prisoners muttered in two languages, their fight, and even the giant's death, already subsumed in this new threat. A minute later, four new guards appeared in the hallway behind the gate. They wore gas masks, the full-face black kind that made aliens of their wearers. Three carried yellow canisters with long black hoses. The fourth had an AK. He pointed it at the mass of prisoners. He lifted his mask and shouted in Bulgarian and fired at the ceiling, three quick pops. Then he yelled some more. Wells didn't need a word of Bulgarian to understand: **No more warning shots**.

The local prisoners went to their knees. Wells and the jihadis followed. The guard with the AK pulled his mask on tight and nodded to the three guards holding the canisters. They pointed the hoses through the gate and fired a yellow-orange mist. It wafted toward the prisoners, and when Wells took his next breath, his throat caught fire.

For a few seconds, Wells couldn't breathe at

all. He lay on the floor, closed his eyes, forced air into his lungs. Around him, men coughed and gagged, Bulgarian or Arab, Christian or Muslim, no matter. Whatever this chemical was, it made pepper spray seem like perfume.

After a while, the gate slid open. A guard yelled a name—**Samir! Samir!** Finally, Wells realized it was meant for him. He crawled forward, smeared his hands in the dead Bulgarian's blood. When he reached the open gate, the guards kicked him, sent him sprawling. Then they cuffed his hands and pulled him up and dragged him away.

THEY BROUGHT HIM into the administration wing, threw him into a shower fully dressed. The freezing water washed the mucus off his face and the blood off his hands, so he didn't complain. He wanted to feel something other than empty. Lucky to be alive, maybe. Or sorry to have killed once more.

Empty was all he could manage.

The water slowed to a trickle and the pustule-faced guard commander came to him.

He unlocked Wells's cuffs. "Clothes off."

When Wells was done, the guard looked him over with a butcher's appraising eye. "Don't move." The water blasted him again, and by the time the commander came back with a gym bag and a towel, Wells was as cold as he had ever been.

"I need to see Colonel Zogrin. About Radka and Bilyana."

The commander handed him the towel.

"Please. He'll understand—"

"Don't you get it?"

Then Wells did.

Kirkov had told him at least one person at the Castle besides the warden would know about him. Wells had figured on someone senior. A deputy warden. The commander of the jihadi cellblock. But this guard was senior, too, and he spoke Arabic. Wells imagined him divorced, sleeping inside the prison, listening to tapes of the prisoners to pass the nights.

"You?" Wells felt the ache in his groin. All this pain inflicted by the man meant to be watching out for him.

"It worked, didn't it? No one suspected. Not even you."

Yeah, you should have killed me. Really topped up your cover. Why had the guard hurt him so badly? To make Wells pay for having a face that wasn't covered in boils? For being American, having the chance to leave this place after a few weeks, while the guard was stuck here forever?

We are all just prisoners here, of our own device . . . "Such a lovely place," Wells said.

"I gave you what you needed."

So the guard had known the fight was coming. Why hadn't he stopped it instead of letting Wells and the other prisoner fight to the death, dogs in a cage?

Slowly, the answer dawned. "You hoped I'd kill him for you."

The guard shrugged.

More than ever, Wells wanted to throttle this man, to squeeze his ruined face until pus flowed down his cheeks. He knew he had to control his anger, but he was glad for it. It swept away the fatigue and the pain and whatever remorse he felt for killing a man at another man's whim.

"How did you know I'd win?"

"I didn't." The guard grinned. "But he didn't know you had the knife. And you're tough. My money was on you. Want to see what I bought with the winnings?" He unzipped the gym bag. Inside, civilian clothes and shoes. Plus a Bulgarian identity card and passport, both with Wells's photo. And ten crisp one-hundred-euro notes. "Want to keep talking or would you rather get out before somebody arrests you for killing him?"

AND Wells's time in the Castle was over.

He believed he'd found all he could. Convincing Hani to tell him more about the mole would have been next to impossible. Still, he felt he hadn't been given a fair shot. If he and Shafer had insisted Kirkov be more involved . . . if the warden had put him closer to Hani . . . if the commander hadn't been such a sadist . . .

But Wells couldn't worry about his mistakes anymore. Even without the mole, he had a strong lead on the head of the Islamic State in France. The most important terrorist in Europe. Even better, Hani had implied that the man knew who the mole was. **Tell you what, when you see the Puma, you can ask him.**

At least he had no doubt about his next move. Paris.

20

SHAFER watched Duto's aides enter and leave the Oval Office in precise five-minute intervals. Rarely did more than a few seconds pass between the exit of one visitor and the entrance of the next. A president's time was his most valuable resource. Duto didn't waste his.

He did enjoy wasting Shafer's, though. At least today. **Could be a while,** Duto's senior admin, a fortyish man who had a pickpocket's roaming eyes and a too-pretty suit, had said when Shafer checked in. **Big man's running late.** An obvious lie.

Admittedly, Shafer had called only that morning, telling Duto, "It's about Wells."

"He's out." Duto wasn't asking. Kirkov must have told him already, Shafer realized.

"And he's got something."

"Come by at eleven."

Now it was past noon. For as long as Shafer had known Duto, he'd swung between treating Wells and Shafer as his equals—near equals, anyway—and as problems to manage. Their knowledge of his secrets annoyed him, Shafer thought. Duto knew better than anyone that secrets were power. Maybe they'd grown even **more** precious in the age of Twitter and TMZ because keeping them was so hard.

Or maybe Duto was just being a jerk. In Shafer's experience, power and money made people more of what they already were. The generous became philanthropists. The mean became bullies, using lawyers instead of their fists to pummel their enemies. The vain found plastic surgeons and tried to age in reverse.

As his wait stretched, Shafer wondered if Duto had another motive. A delay this long was more than simply pulling rank. Then Peter Ludlow walked into the anteroom.

"Director."

The naked surprise in Ludlow's blue eyes shaded quickly into distaste. "Shouldn't you be across the river, Ellis? Working?"

"Vinny and I are having lunch."

"You're not. He's having lunch with the Chairman of the Joint Chiefs."

"Look at you. Putting that espionage expertise to good use."

"DCIA is here, sir," the admin murmured into his phone, with the hushed self-importance of an announcer at the Masters. To Ludlow: "He'll see you now."

Ludlow walked in without another word to Shafer. But Shafer saw now why Duto had made him wait so long. He'd wanted Ludlow to know he was meeting Shafer. More, Duto had wanted Ludlow to know that he would meet Shafer afterward, give Shafer the last word. Always an advantage. But why? Did Duto want Ludlow to think his job was in jeopardy? Or was he stirring the pot and causing trouble for no reason other than that he could?

This meeting went fifteen minutes. When Ludlow came out, he wasn't smiling.

"See you soon, Ellis."

"Not if I see you first."

SHAFER found Duto at his desk.

"Sit."

"What's eating Ludlow?"

"Chatter."

Chatter was the worst way to predict a terrorist attack. Suspicious emails, texts, tweets, and phone calls waxed and waned on their own schedule. Worse, terrorists knew the United States monitored them and would increase the tempo to try to fool their listeners. NSA analysts liked to say spikes in chatter had forecast a hundred out of the past three attacks.

Still, the agencies had no choice but to watch and react. And some combinations were particularly worrying, notably when the groups spiked volume on semi-public channels while decreasing it on private channels that their leaders used. A drop in communications was perversely dangerous. It could mean that an attack was now too sensitive for anything but face-to-face discussion.

"Anything specific?"

"Europe."

"That narrows it down. How serious?"

"We'll find out when the bombs go off," Duto said. "So, Wells . . . ?"

"Talked to him this morning. He's got something."

"The name of the mole."

"If he had that, you think I would have sat out there like an idiot for ninety minutes? Not the mole. He thinks he's got a line on the guy who runs Daesh in France. He said he doesn't think the French know about this guy. I'm not sure we do either. I checked before I came over and I couldn't find his aliases in any of our databases."

"What about the mole?"

"Forget the mole—"

"We sent him there to find the mole."

Not the reaction Shafer had expected.

"You know what happened in Bulgaria today, Ellis? He share that with you?"

Shafer wondered what hot mess he'd stepped into.

"There was a little riot. Wells killed another prisoner. A Bulgarian."

"And?" The word leapt out of Shafer's mouth before he could help himself.

"We didn't send him over there to put knives in locals."

"Vinny, you want to be pissed he didn't get this mole that you keep telling me doesn't exist, fine, but it's awful late for you to pretend to care about some Eastern European convict. Kirkov will handle it—"

"And make sure we pay."

"Didn't know it was **your** money."

"The whole point of this nonsense was to get a name. Or, at the least, convince the so-called mole to jump, to take action against Wells and thus confirm his existence. Was that not the point? Tell me."

Duto had always had a mean stare. This office amplified it.

"Yes."

"But nothing happened. No one jumped. No one tried to stop Wells in Afghanistan or Bulgaria."

Wells had run into that unexpected trouble at Pakistani immigration in Karachi. But Shafer didn't think mentioning that incident would help his case. Especially since it was now two months old.

"Thus, you and Bat Boy are no closer to finding the mole—or even proving that he exists—than you were when you started this whole game."

"If you'd let us run proper surveillance—"

"Please. Despite the agency doing just what you asked to make this crazy scheme happen. Despite me lying to my top officers and them lying to the guys on the ground in Afghanistan. A whole avalanche of crap steaming downhill on your insistence. None of it worked. All you've done is waste time."

"We didn't get what we came for, but we got something else. This new lead, it's real, it's specific—"

"You have a name? You know who this guy talks to in Syria? Or who in Paris talks to him?"

"You know that's not how it works."

"Interesting definition of **specific**." The contempt in Duto's voice was worse than a shout.

"If Wells says it's good, it's good."

"Sounds like you had a real in-depth conversation today. Considering you didn't even know he killed someone."

"I know he's going to Paris," Shafer said. "Actually, Sevran, that's a **banlieue**—"

"I know what Sevran is, Ellis. Please don't tell me that Wells is looking for more favors at this point."

"Favors? He just went to prison to find a traitor."

"Want to know the other reason that Ludlow came in here with his hair on fire? You. Crompond and Green are complaining you harassed them."

"I haven't even spoken to them."

"You've spoken to their families. And you gave up Crompond's real identity to a guy he was trying to recruit, which causes problems on about five levels."

"By his own account, he'd already failed." Shafer's defense sounded lame in his own ears. At least now he knew why Crompond hadn't challenged him directly after Shafer met the imam.

Duto put a finger to his lips. "Quiet time now. Think hard. Did all this scuttling around, all these **interviews**, for lack of a better word, get you anywhere?"

"They were productive."

"Did they **produce** any actual leads?"

"Not leads, per se—" Shafer clamped his mouth shut before he could embarrass himself further. The announcer in his head chimed in, sounding exactly like Jim Lampley: **A left! Another left! A vicious jab, and Ellis Shafer is stumbling, out on his feet! How much longer will the refs let this go on?**

"I don't think you realize how much rope I give you and your friend. Ludlow wants you gone. Seeing you today set him off."

So much for Duto making him wait to give him the last word. "Like you hoped it would."

"Said he couldn't tolerate you fishing anymore. Called you the second coming of Angleton. Said he would quit if I didn't deal with you. You hear that? There may be an attack coming, and my handpicked director hates you so much he's more worried about you. You understand what a problem you've become?"

Shafer straightened up, spoke with a confidence he wished he felt. "I understand I walked in here with the biggest intel breakthrough we've had this year. Especially if the chatter's right and this attack in Europe is real. Instead of thanking me, you whine to me about Peter Ludlow's hurt feelings. I'm going to assume this is just you playing some game, Vinny. If it's not, it's pathetic."

"Hope you and your loyal sidekick can find this guy, Ellis. If not, I'm giving Ludlow what he wants. Time for you to kick back anyway."

You can't. But of course Duto could. What leverage did Shafer have? To blackmail Duto with their shared secrets? Revealing the details of the most important covert American operations of the last decade wouldn't do him or the country any good. Somewhere along the way, Duto had realized what Shafer was seeing only now. Some secrets were too big to come out. Having too much leverage could be as useless as having none.

Duto had just reminded Shafer what everyone who walked into this office learned sooner or later. In the end, they all served at the President's pleasure.

"We'll find him."

"I'm sure you will. Now, go on. Out."

"Bastard," Shafer muttered under his breath.

"What did you say, Ellis? Say it again. Out loud."

Duto might fire him on the spot if he repeated the word, Shafer knew. If he didn't, he could never look Duto—or himself—in the eyes again. Easy choice.

"I called you a bastard, Vinny." In for a penny . . . "Shall I spell it? **B-A-S-T-A-R-D.**" With every letter, Shafer waited for the explosion.

But when he finished, Duto grinned, the smile of a man who knew not just that he owned all the cards but the table and the casino, too. "I love it when you talk dirty, Ellis."

21

THE DAY'S last nonstop to Paris had taken off before Wells reached Sofia Airport late Friday afternoon. He was stuck flying through Frankfurt and didn't land at Charles de Gaulle until almost midnight. He decided to find a hotel close by, go to Sevran the next day. He saw no advantage to wandering the **banlieue**'s empty streets tonight.

"I warn you, it's late, we have only singles," the check-in clerk at the Comfort Hotel said. "Quite small."

Wells had to smile. "Long as they have toilets." And beds.

ROOM 310 was not much larger than his cell. But its door opened from the inside. Wells tried three times to be sure. He shucked his clothes, stepped into the shower. Turned the water hot as it would go, leaned against the smooth plastic wall, closed his eyes, and seared the prison off his skin.

When he was done, he wiped off the steamed mirror and looked himself over. The meat of his left shoulder had turned blue-black. Prison meals had cost him another five pounds. He was okay, more or less. As for his other injury, the one between his legs, he'd decided not to think about what permanent damage he might have suffered.

He dug out the phone the guard had given him, thumbed in Shafer's number. Then deleted it, dialed Anne instead.

"John?"

"Yes'm."

She didn't speak. Wells was happy to listen to her breathe. "Where are you?"

"Paris."

"Sounds nice. Not that I've been. Eiffel Tower?"

"Line's too long."

"You're in one piece?"

"I'm fine. I missed you."

"Your daughter, too, I bet. She's right here."

"Anne—"

But she'd already handed off the phone. "DaddyDaddyDaddy—"

"I missed you, little girl."

"A thousand days, Daddy—"

"Slight exaggeration."

"A thousand **million** days. I'm three now—"

"Not quite."

"Yes! I! Am!"

Toddler logic. Wells had forgotten toddler logic. Conversational diversions were the best answer. "How's Freddy?" Her favorite toy.

"Who?"

"Freddy Bear, from the mall, with the backpack—" Wells wondered if he had really put a knife in a man's neck twelve hours before. **Tonight on A&E: Killer Dads!**

"Freddy's boring, Daddy. And Tonka ate his foot. I like Peppa now." Delivered in a **Don't you know anything?** tone.

She'd already forgotten Freddy? "Who's Peppa?"

"Peppa Pig! Mommy said I could watch a video tonight—"

Wells didn't like that idea, but he was hardly in a position to question Anne's parenting.

"Are you outside, Daddy?"

"Outside where? No, I'm in a hotel—"

"Outside our **house**— Hey!" Her voice rose.

"Okay, enough." Anne.

"Tonka ate Freddy Bear's foot? Why wasn't I told?"

"We'll see you tomorrow?"

"Not tomorrow, but soon."

"Be safe, John. We miss you."

Somehow, those easy words twisted the knife more than anything else would have.

"Say good-bye to your dad—" In the background, Emmie began to scream.

"Bye, little lady. I love you—"

Her wails were all Wells heard before Anne hung up.

HE CALLED SHAFER. Who didn't even say hello.

"What is wrong with you?"

"The question on everyone's lips."

"Everyone's favorite POTUS bent me over his desk this afternoon."

"Save the dress."

"Didn't think to tell me about your little knife fight?"

Oh, goody. "Open line, Ellis—"

"Please. Saddest part is, I know why you didn't. You didn't care. He didn't register as a problem, so he didn't register at all. Roadkill."

Wells blinked, found himself in an apartment in the Bronx. A backyard in South Africa. A factory in Turkey. Everywhere, and always leaving death. The faces changed, but the empty eyes were the same. He needed to write down whatever he could remember. Their names, if he had them. Or the details he knew, if he didn't.

He owed the kills at least that much.

"Forgot the good news," Shafer said. "You're right. Nobody cares. No warrants, no Red Notice, no nothing. Doesn't matter. All God's chillun got wings. You gave him his."

A great black bird swooped from the ceiling and dug its claws into Wells's spine. "I'll call you back."

Shafer grunted like he'd only now realized how far he'd pushed. "No. I am not letting you hang up so you can beat yourself about the face and neck for this. Tell me the truth. Him or you, right?"

Wells saw the Bulgarian stomping down the corridor, knew he would have painted Wells's brains on the walls if Wells had given him the chance. "So?"

"So everything. Should have kept my mouth shut. Duto tore me up, I sent it downhill. Manly of me. Leading from across the ocean. Please, John, let's forget it." Real urgency in Shafer's voice.

What Wells wanted to say: **I don't deserve to be anyone's father.** What he said: "Apology accepted."

SHAFER WAITED a few seconds, cleared his throat like a radio jock who'd just finished reading an obituary and now had to go to an ad for a car dealership. "Good. For what it's worth, my meeting today wasn't entirely useless. Our headwaiter gave me the special of the day."

"And?" Wells forcing himself to play along, leave the acid bath of the last five minutes behind.

"We've picked up some chitty-chatty about red team nastiness. Probably in Europe. Before you ask, no particular country."

"Sounds—"

"Useless?"

"I was going to say non-specific."

"That it is. Think it's connected to your little class trip?"

Wells considered. He and Shafer had assumed the traitor would respond to Wells's mission either by attacking him directly or finding a way to pass word to Hani. Maybe their guy had gone with choice C: **Kill 'em all**. Instead of trying to stop Wells, he had decided that the end was nigh and he would help the Islamic State put together a major attack. "Timing's awfully coincidental."

"Question is, what could our friend have given them?"

Almost anything, as both Wells and Shafer knew. "Bet the Puma can tell us," Wells said. "Especially if it's happening here."

"On that note, I ran another search on what you gave me not just our databases but everyone's. Didn't find much. No **Abu Najma**. No **Puma**. There's a guy in Marseilles who goes by **Tiger Junior**."

"That ain't him."

"Agree. I've even gone through French school and birth records to look for girls named Najma in Sevran and the surrounding **banlieues**. Only found two. One of the fathers died in a car accident a few years ago. The other is a junior maintenance worker for Électricité de France, twenty-three. He's worth a look if everything else misses, but I can't believe he's our man."

"What about Sevran? Anything pop up?"

"Not enough to matter. The French think it's mainly recruiters there, nobody senior. They say the guy running the network lives in Bondy."

"Another **banlieue**, right?"

"Yeah, five miles nearer Paris. Any chance your prison friend could have gotten them confused?"

"He was very clear."

"Also, this Puma is smooth, right? Fits in. The guy the French are looking at barely got out of high school, done time for drugs, et cetera."

"Not him."

"Again, we agree. You want anything from us? Technical support?"

Wells couldn't talk anymore, and not just because the line wasn't secure. "Ellis, I gotta go."

"It'll look better with some sleep."

"More rear echelon advice."

Silence. "Had that coming," Shafer finally said.

UGLY DREAMS tossed Wells. He woke with the certainty that he should mention the Puma to the jihadis of Sevran only as a last resort. How would Wells have heard of the alias? Even bringing up Syria too directly would be risky. The Islamic State's recruiters were hungry for new men, but with French security services cracking down, they would be wary of outsiders. Even if Wells overcame their suspicions, the recruiters would hardly send him to their senior commander right away.

Still, he had to find the mosque the jihadis preferred. He wouldn't do anything as obvious as offering to head to Raqqa. He would simply show his face and hope they let him hang out until he could put together an answer that fit the clues Hani had given him. Wells believed that Hani had told the truth. Why lie to another jihadi, especially one who had saved him from a vicious beating?

Of course if Wells was wrong, he'd blown the last two months. He'd find out soon enough.

He worked out for two hours in the hotel gym, covering himself in honest sweat, reminding himself he could justify all he'd done if he found the commander and the mole. Survive and advance.

Back in the room, he shaved and washed his face but didn't shower. He put on the same clothes he'd worn the day before. They, and he, smelled funky, almost ripe, right for this cover. At a drugstore a block from the hotel, he bought a pair of knock-off Ray-Bans. They made him look younger, and slightly sleazy, like so many European jihadis.

He carried neither pistol nor knife. If he needed either for this trip, he had already failed.

Paris had good public transportation, including a commuter rail system called the RER. Line B ran northeast through the city, ending at the airport. Along the way, it served the city's most notorious **banlieues**. These suburbs had once been industrial and Communist. Now they had lost their factories and belonged mainly to Muslim immigrants.

Wells wondered who he would be in Sevran. He didn't need an elaborate cover story. But he would have to know his identity well enough to handle a few minutes of conversation. He had left his Bulgarian passport in his hotel room. It would raise questions he couldn't answer.

As he stood on the platform of the airport station awaiting the train, he decided to remain Samir Khalili. This version of Samir had fought in Afghanistan long before, come home in the winter after September 11. Ever since, he'd wondered if he was a coward for leaving. Now he had come from Canada to France to find a way into this new war.

A train rolled up and Wells stepped on. Ten minutes later, it slid into a tunnel and eased to a halt. "**Sevran-Beaudottes,**" a recorded voice announced. The station was cold, high-ceilinged, concrete. Wells slouched up the steps to a dismal gray plaza. A dozen Arab men clumped near an abandoned movie theater. He wandered past them into the maze of apartment buildings west of the station.

The French government had built housing

projects called **cités** for the immigrants who crossed the Mediterranean beginning in the 1960s. Instead of the ugly high-rise brick towers that marked American public housing, these buildings were mostly mid-rise and white, accented with shaded balconies and brightly colored panels. Yet the **cités** would not have been out of place in the South Bronx. Even if Wells hadn't already known this one was public housing, he would have recognized it instantly. Its buildings were neglected equally by the government that owned them and the tenants who lived in them. Cheap clothes dangled from balconies. Unwatered trees drooped sadly. Wells picked up a faint odor of marijuana, the sweeter scent of hashish. Most tellingly, the residents projected an effortless unfriendliness. Chattering women went silent as Wells walked by. Men stared. Wells understood. Outsiders rarely came to these places, except for the occasional social worker or cop.

As Wells walked the concrete paths, the scope of the complex became clear. A dozen buildings, ten floors each, say twelve or thirteen apartments per floor. Fifteen hundred apartments, averaging four or five residents each, most stuffed into one or two bedrooms. Six or eight thousand people in this **cité** alone, and

Wells saw another across a six-lane road to the west. And Sevran was one **banlieue** of dozens. No wonder the French security services had so much trouble. Without whispered help from the locals, they faced a near-impossible task. But in the **banlieues**, as in American inner cities, snitches were despised.

Wells turned in to the middle of the complex. The buildings here were more cocooned, even less welcoming. An Arab man in a black T-shirt and mirrored sunglasses stood outside the building at the very center, arms folded, staring at everyone who passed. Like the doorman of the hottest club in Paris. Wells walked toward him. The man pretended not to notice.

"**As-salaam alaikum.**"

"**Alaikum salaam.**"

"Nice sunglasses," Wells said in Arabic. He raised his. The man didn't follow. "I'm Samir."

"Are you lost?"

"I'm exactly where I want to be."

"Are you French?"

"Does it matter?"

"**Nam.**"

"Then, no. I'm not."

Now the man raised his shades. "What are you, then? German?"

"No one's ever called me German before. I'm Lebanese but live in Canada."

"And what are you doing in Sevran?"

"I came to pray."

"For peace? One of those?"

"For strength. Strength for the believers."

The man's eyebrows narrowed. "No offense, brother. You look a little old for that kind of prayer."

"Experienced."

"Where?"

"Afghanistan. And Grozny." The capital of Chechnya. The man looked at Wells with new respect. No surprise. Even more than Afghanistan, Chechnya was the cradle of modern jihad. The homegrown Muslim insurgency there during the late 1990s had presaged the Islamic State's horrors right down to the execution videos.

"This isn't something to joke about."

"I'm not joking. Many years ago. Even before Putin."

The man opened the door of the lobby, nodded Wells inside.

The ceiling lights were out, and yellow tape covered an elevator. "Hands against the wall." The man patted Wells down quickly and efficiently. "If you're serious about praying, I'll give you a mosque to visit. Tell them Hamoud sent you. But I warn you, if you're not who you say, best to turn around and walk away."

WELLS CROSSED the boulevard he'd seen before, walked through another **cité**, uglier than the first, more like American projects. Boarded windows were scattered across tall beige buildings. Trash overflowed garbage bins. Wells wondered why Hamoud had opened up so quickly. Maybe Wells had sold himself perfectly. Maybe he'd had some luck to make up for the kidnappers in Kabul and the rest of the trouble he'd found this mission. Years in the field had taught him the bounces usually evened out.

Or maybe Hamoud had decided he was lying, an informant for the French, and was setting him up. No matter. Wells wasn't trying to infiltrate just to see the mosque. For his purposes, he would win this round even if the men here told him nothing at all.

A big hospital complex rose just east of the **cité**. The dismal streets were named for France's greatest medical researchers. The mosque was at 85 Rue du Docteur Fleming, Hamoud had said. The building was another project, the most run-down yet, loose concrete hanging from its balconies. Its ground-floor apartments had doors that opened to the street. At its north end, two North African men stood outside an apartment whose windows were curtained tightly.

Wells's pulse quickened, his journey near an end one way or another. "Brothers."

They regarded him without much love.

"I've come to pray."

"Then you're confused. The mosque is that way"—the man pointed down the street Wells had just taken.

"Hamoud sent me."

"What's your name?"

"Samir."

"Wait here." The man disappeared inside the apartment.

A minute later, the door opened. "Come."

Inside, Wells found that the curtains hid a white-painted wall. It blocked the windows and made the apartment's living room into a single enclosed space, a reasonable facsimile of a mosque. Fifteen or so men stood facing southeast toward Mecca. Behind Wells, a deadbolt snapped in place. The men looked him over, their faces hard. They were in their twenties and early thirties. Two wore long Salafi beards while the others had tightly trimmed goatees.

Even after Hamoud's warning, their open menace surprised Wells. He had expected that, at worst, they'd kick him out, maybe rough him up. But they seemed riled. Maybe the chatter was right. Maybe an attack was imminent.

A slim North African wearing dark blue jeans nodded at him. "Samir, yes?"

"**Nam.**"

"We were just starting. Pray with us."

Wells slipped off his shoes and lay them with the rest, washed his face, hands, and feet, and took a place in the back row.

Prayer was always a performance of sorts, for Allah if no one else. Today, Wells had a more corporeal audience. He knew that even if he prayed with a believer's fervor and precision, these men might not trust him. But if he failed, they surely wouldn't.

Still, he ignored the pressure, found himself in the rhythm of the Arabic. By the time he and the rest of the men finished, the tension in the room had faded. Wells knew he had passed this first test. He turned to the man beside him. "Peace be upon you, brother."

"And you."

The leader walked over. "You're English?"

"From Canada." Wells unrolled his cover. He didn't mention Syria or the Islamic State. Neither did anyone else. The only glitch came when the leader asked for his mobile number.

"Don't have one." Like a Bulgarian passport, a phone with a Bulgarian country code would raise too many questions. Then Wells saw how to spin its absence. "Left it in Toronto. I wanted to make a fresh start."

"No one with you, then?"

"No."

"Where do you sleep?"

He'd planned for this question. "A hostel near the Gare du Nord. Called the Peace and Love Hostel. If you can believe it."

"How'd you end up there?"

"It's cheap. Filled with backpackers. Unpleasant place."

"Too many **kaffirs** drinking and smoking?"

"I'm used to **kaffirs**. But I hate feeling old. I'll find somewhere else."

"You plan to stay in Paris a while?"

"At least a couple of weeks."

The leader glanced at his watch. "Come back next week, pray with us again, Samir. We can talk more then. True brothers are always welcome."

"Thanks be to Allah." Wells turned to pick up his shoes . . .

And **saw**. Mixed among generic leather sandals were four pairs of sneakers that would have made a Brooklyn hipster proud. Old-school Air Jordans, their leather worn but clean. Blue Chuck Taylor All-Stars. Vintage black Adidases with shiny white stripes. And the capper, a set of low brown suede sneakers, puma etched on their sides in gold capital letters.

Not a lion, not a rhinoceros. A calling card, subtle and obvious at once. If Wells hadn't happened to see them lined up near one another, he wouldn't have noticed.

Happy gibberish filled his head. **It's gotta be the shoes . . . Be Like Mike . . .** And Bruno Mars, strutting, and warbling his uptown funk: **Got Chucks on with Saint Laurent / Gotta kiss myself I'm so pretty . . .**

"Nice shoes."

"My friend owns a store."

Bet he's got a daughter named Najma, too. Wells wondered how Shafer had missed her. "You get discounts?"

The leader shook his head in irritation. These Arabs might be alienated from every other part of French culture, but not its distrust of cheap retail.

"Anyway, I'll come by Monday?"

The man shook his head. "Say, Friday. **Ma'a salama**, Samir."

"Ma'a salama."

On the way back to the RER station, Wells stopped to pick up a bottle of water and a halal chicken sandwich. And check for surveillance. He didn't think anyone was following him, but he planned to proof his cover by going into Paris before doubling back to the Comfort Hotel.

No mistakes now. He'd worked too hard, come too far. He was so very close.

22

ARLINGTON, VIRGINIA

WALTER CROMPOND hadn't expected to see the sheikh again. Much less standing outside his front door on a bright Saturday morning. Yet when Crompond opened it, there was Aziz Murak, large as life, hands crossed over his Santa Claus belly.

"Sheikh."

"Mr. Crompond." Murak offered a formal nod. "Is anyone watching us?"

Crompond found his eyes tilting to the sky, looking for black helicopters or God. "Don't think so." Not even his wife, who had left a few minutes earlier for soccer practice with the kids.

"Won't you invite me in? Just a moment or two?"

Inside Crompond's front door, Murak reached into his shirt pocket for a black key fob, squarish, with lock and unlock buttons. "This arrived yesterday. From Paris. I'm told either button will work."

Crompond held it in his palm, an unlucky charm. If the jihadis had sent the trigger, then they must have placed the sarin. And the attack must be imminent.

"It's ready? The church?"

"**Suitable.** That was the word my friend used. And one final piece of advice. Make sure you're inside early. We're not going to wait for the service to start, and you'll want to push that button exactly two minutes after you hear the first bombs."

"You're expecting me to set them off from inside."

"Of course, **habibi.** I thought that was understood."

There was understanding, and then there was **understanding**. With this little black box in his hand, Crompond could no longer escape the reality that in days, a week or two at most, he would die.

"It's all right to be afraid. Even believers sometimes have a hard time at this moment."

How would you know? Don't see you wearing an XXL bomb belt.

Murak seemed to read his mind. "If you can't do it, let me know. We'll find another way."

Murak leaned in close. "But it will happen, Walter, and you know better than I what comes after."

"I thought I was headed for witness protection. Put me in a burqa, send me to a harem in Raqqa."

Murak didn't smile. Crompond wouldn't miss his humorlessness. Time to split his life into stuff he'd miss and stuff he wouldn't. Anyway, Murak was right. Nowhere to run, nowhere to hide.

"Don't you worry about me, Imam. I crossed the river a long time ago. So, okay, I get inside early—"

"Yes. And wait for the attack."

"You've never told me why you're doing this, Walter."

Crompond thought of Jane O'Connor's long white neck. Suddenly he wanted Murak gone. "If there's a God, He knows."

"There's a God—"

"If there isn't, I suppose it doesn't matter. I'll miss you, Imam." A lie, but it did the trick. Murak squeezed his shoulder, walked out.

Crompond leaned against his front door like he was trying to keep monsters out and held the key fob an inch or two from his face. A black box blurred to infinity. Strange. He couldn't hide the truth from himself. What he was about to do was wrong. Immoral. Pick a word. **Unthinkable.** He wanted to walk away. Better yet, ask for forgiveness. Mercy.

But he knew he wouldn't. He had pledged himself to his hate. He couldn't forsake that now.

He closed his eyes, dug his thumb into the button. Soon enough, he'd know the secret his government had taught Jane and the Iraqis and Vietnamese and Afghanis and all those Japanese in Hiroshima and everyone else in the world who had the bad luck to stand in the way of the United States.

"See?" he whispered to the walls. "Doesn't hurt a bit."

23

PARIS

WELLS left the RER at the Gare du Nord, wandered until he was sure beyond sure that no one was on him, hailed a cab. Back at the hotel around 3 p.m., he dug his phone out of the room safe.

"Mao had it backward, Ellis. A journey of a thousand miles ends with a single step," Wells explained.

"You looked for local stores yet?"

"Not yet. But it's right, Ellis, I know it . . ." Though Wells wished he'd looked **before** this call. If the shoes were a coincidence, if the Puma had earned his nickname some other way, Shafer would never let him forget.

"Not saying it isn't. Smells like Teen Spirit to me. Next question. Say you're right. What now?"

"DGSE, yes?"

"And tell them you saw some sneakers? They've got ten thousand guys to track."

"Least ask them if the guy who owns the store is on their radar."

"Once we have his name, we can check that ourselves. And I'm guessing he won't be, not in any meaningful way. That's what Hani told you, right?"

Wells felt his elation fade. Shafer was right. The pieces might fit for him and Shafer, but they weren't going to convince the French.

"You're going to have to pay this guy a visit all by your lonesome," Shafer said.

"Just show up at his store, then, you're thinking? Ask if he's the famous Puma?"

Shafer went quiet.

"What do we know about him?" he said eventually.

"Not much."

"I mean, psychologically?"

"In that case, nothing."

"Wrong again, honey. Lots. He's proud of his store. Proud of his shoes. He **nicknamed** himself after them. Probably a control freak, a micromanager. How else did he keep this network secret? And he likes operating right under the noses of the French. Gets off on it."

The guesses made sense. "I'll buy it."

"Guy like that, whatever he's planning, he's going to keep his stuff close."

"At the store."

"Maybe not that close. I'll bet he's got a little storage place close by. Where he keeps his shoes. And his guns and everything else, too."

"Good, then, I'll knock on his door, ask him where."

"Try this instead." And Shafer explained.

"Not bad," Wells said when Shafer was done.

"You're not arguing?"

"It's better than nothing. Under the circumstances. So I'll need money. And man's best friend."

"The kind that's shiny and black and pokes holes in things?"

Wells waited, but Shafer seemed to want an answer. "Is there any other kind?"

"How many inches we talking, then? Eight? Ten?" Shafer chuckled at his own joke. "I knew you were in that prison too long."

The man was seventy going on thirteen. "Can you set it up? Without involving the station?" The seventh floor would know if Shafer used any CIA officers here. Wells preferred to have the mole believe that he was still in Bulgaria.

"I think so. Our friends and neighbors."

Wells assumed Shafer meant the State Department. Though he might have meant the
British again. No matter. Wells would find out
when the pistol and the cash arrived.

"Give me the hotel, the room number, I'll get
you what you need. May take a few hours, it
being Saturday and all."

"I'll be here."

"Even do a little research while you wait.
Make sure this guy actually exists."

"Hadn't thought of that."

WELLS HAD neither laptop nor smartphone, but
the hotel did have a free computer in its lobby.
Wells typed in **vintage sneakers banlieue**,
hesitated, finally clicked **Recherché Google**.
He hoped he wouldn't wind up scrolling
through a hundred pages, feeling like a greater
fool with each one.

The very first listing was **SuperSneaks Sevran.** The store's website featured pictures of dozens of shoes, prices listed in euros, dollars, and
pounds. The most expensive were photographed
in 3-D. A click rotated them from heel to
toe. **Email for special sizes! Many available!
Climate-controlled storage!** a banner announced
in English.

The search also revealed stories in French

and English about SuperSneaks. The store's unfortunate name belied its Europe-wide reputation for selling hard-to-find vintage shoes at fair prices. Its owner was Raouf Bourgua, a first-generation immigrant in his early fifties who had come to France almost thirty years before. The photos attached to the articles showed a man who fell just short of handsome and who liked immaculate sneakers accented with brightly colored socks.

"This year, Bourgua expects about one million euros in annual sales, mostly through his website," the **Times** of London had reported a few months before. The profiles unsubtly presented Bourgua as a good Arab, a not-too-religious man who had built a profitable, culturally relevant business. One mentioned that he had three children, a boy named Alaa, and two girls, Juliette and Stella. When he saw the third name, Wells felt a surge in his blood, a cold high real as a drug.

Stella. As in **star.** Like Najma.

Wells sent the article to Shafer, no comment necessary. Shafer would search every database for Bourgua and the store. Nobody was better at those deep dives. If Bourgua's storage facility existed—and the reference to climate-controlled storage suggested it did—Shafer might well find it before Wells did.

Meanwhile, Wells read everything else he could. Bourgua showed no hint of radicalism. After the 2015 attacks in Paris, he hung a sign outside his store, **Tous Nos Fils et Filles**. All Our Sons and Daughters. "Some kids who died, I'm sure they were my customers, they wore my shoes," he'd said when **Time Out Paris** asked about the sign. "I feel a special connection."

A special connection. Wells imagined Bourgua smirking at his own cleverness.

According to its website, SuperSneaks closed at 6 p.m. on Saturdays, but it was open Sunday afternoons, a break. Wells would have no chance tonight, but he should tomorrow. Around 7 p.m., his phone buzzed, a text from an American number, 703 area code. **How's your diet?**

The knock came two hours later. Wells opened the door, found two twenty-something men, one black, one white, both medium height, stocky, with brush-cut hair. Marine embassy guards. They might as well have worn uniforms. The black one carried a backpack. Their eyes held respect, with a little hostility. **Whoever you are, you must be important, but we don't appreciate being your errand boys. Especially on Saturday night.**

"Word of the day?"

"Diet." The password was a junior varsity move, but Wells understood.

The Marine handed over the backpack.

"Thank you."

"Thank the ambassador." He saluted and turned away.

Inside, Wells found ten thousand dollars in a neat brick of hundred-dollar bills. Ten thousand euros in various denominations. Under the money, the real prize, a 9-millimeter Sig Sauer. Plus two extra magazines and a concealed carry holster like the one that had saved his life in Hong Kong not so long ago. Wells shoved the extra mags and most of the money in the room safe, strapped on the holster, walked to the train station.

THE PLACE DE LA REPUBLIQUE was a broad, hectic, traffic-clogged square in eastern Paris, the heart of the city's hippest neighborhoods. On those not-so-rare occasions when the students of Paris wanted to protest, they came here, to set up banners and barricades around the statue at the center of the square.

Wells saw no rallies this Saturday night, just a thousand teens and twenty-somethings hanging out, drinking and smoking. He realized as he walked around that making this pitch would be trickier than he'd imagined. His inability to speak French wouldn't help. A creepy old **American** dude was even worse than a creepy old dude.

He saw a skinny white guy, maybe twenty-one, sitting alone on the bottom steps of the statue, a cigarette flaring between his lips. Wells sat beside him. The guy eyed him with distaste, scooted over.

"Hey, man. What's going on?"

Without a word, the guy stood, walked off.

A couple of minutes later, Wells saw another potential mark, this one leaning against a lamp. He was older, maybe twenty-five, a Kronenbourg 1664 tallboy in his hand, two empties between his legs. Best of all, he wore expensive-looking yellow sneakers. Good. An aficionado.

He eyed Wells without much interest. "Nice night," Wells said.

"You know it, bro." In an exaggerated American accent.

"Cool shoes."

As an answer, the guy chugged his Kronenbourg.

"Hey, can I ask a favor?"

"Got no more beers." He let out a tremendous belch. "You can buy some over there." He nodded across the avenue.

"It's not that. And you can make some money."

"Sorry, **bro**. Don't play that way—"

"No, no—"

This guy muttered in French to two other guys a few meters off. They stared at Wells. He shook his head, backed off, left the square for the Boulevard du Temple. Where he called Shafer.

"Anything?"

"Your friend looks clean," Shafer said. "The store, too. And I don't have the warehouse, so that's on you. How goes the recruiting?"

"It's not going to work, your idea. These kids won't let me get to first base."

"Bad analogy."

"It's no joke, Ellis. It's not like I can order them—" Suddenly Wells had the answer. "Call the embassy."

"Now? It's almost midnight over there."

Wells waited in silence for Shafer to think about everything Wells had given already for this mission.

"Fine. And?"

"Tell them to send the coolest Marine they have to Café Canaille. On Boulevard du Temple. Now."

"Yes, sir. Anything else?"

"Tell them to make sure he doesn't dress like a Marine."

INSIDE THE CAFÉ, Wells ordered **steak-frites** and watched the kids around him drink and smoke and enjoy life. Ninety minutes passed before the black Marine who'd brought Wells the knapsack walked through the door. He wore a black T-shirt, black pants, and a black Yankees cap. He didn't look like a Marine anymore. Wells watched girls' heads swivel as he passed. He'd do fine.

He sat across the table from Wells. "Don't know who you are, sir. But you have juice by the gallon." His voice was low, with a hint of a Texas accent.

"What's your name?"

"Winston Coyle."

"Rank?"

"Staff sergeant."

"Are you, in fact, the coolest Marine in Paris?"

For the first time, Coyle smiled. "Sir. I'm the coolest Marine east of Oceanside."

"Glad to hear it. I have a simple job for you, Sergeant Coyle. You're going to buy some shoes."

Now that Wells had found a buyer, the play

was simple enough. Coyle would show up at SuperSneaks the next day with the money he'd brought Wells. He'd demand every pair of Air Jordans that Raouf Bourgua had in his inventory. A cash deal, now or never. Maybe Coyle would ask for a little discount for buying in bulk, but Wells told him not to push.

"I have to warn you, I don't speak French, sir. Only Spanish."

"You're American. He won't expect you to. He probably won't ask why you want them. If he does, just tell him you have buddies at home who are into Jordans."

"My homies. Hanging on the corner."

"Don't push it."

"Don't suppose you want to tell me the point?"

The point was to convince Bourgua to send someone to his warehouse to pick up the inventory. Wells would track the deliveryman. Maybe he'd follow the guy inside, maybe he'd come back later. If he could find even a single weapon inside, he'd have the proof he needed.

"I want to see where he keeps his extra shoes."

"You can't just ask him."

"It's for a good cause."

"Isn't it always?"

"I wouldn't know, Sergeant." The rank to remind Coyle that Wells was ordering, not asking.

"Yessir."

"Be at the hotel at eleven a.m. And it goes without saying, but I'll say it anyway, keep this to yourself."

"Better get my beauty sleep."

Coyle walked out. No salute. He'd make a good operative, Wells thought. He'd listened carefully, asked only one unnecessary question. He hadn't pushed Wells for personal information. Maybe when all this was done, Wells should try to steer him to Langley.

First things first.

THE TABLES around Wells cleared out. Paris was not a truly twenty-four-hour city. The Métro shut not long after midnight. Few restaurants stayed open all night. Wells paid and left to find the Boulevard du Temple was notably quieter than it had been when he entered. Perfect.

He walked south two blocks, turned left on Rue Commines. Like so many streets in Paris, it was narrow, one-way, hemmed in by solid five- and six-story apartment buildings with Juliet balconies and lushly planted flower boxes. The storefronts, closed now, mixed hip boutiques and tiny restaurants. Even Wells, hardly the world's greatest romantic, could see the city's appeal. A block ahead, a man and woman strolled side by side, their heads close, tittering to each other in French.

He walked slowly until the lovers turned right two blocks ahead and he had the street to himself.

He didn't know how long he would have to wait. But his luck held. Not five minutes later, he heard the low rumble of a motorcycle engine echoing behind him. Wells stepped to the curb, looked. Small, maybe 250 ccs, but a real motorcycle, not a moped. It moved slowly down Rue Commines, weaving a bit. The rider was probably drunk. And alone. Perfect.

Wells stepped into the street, waved both hands. He was ready to jump aside if the bike didn't stop. But it did. An old Suzuki. The rider wore a cheap helmet, no face shield. He was in his early twenties, skinny. He said something in French.

"Sorry. I don't understand." Wells stepped closer, half staggering, making sure to put himself on the rider's left side.

"English?"

"American. I'm sorry, I'm so lost, my hotel's on the Left Bank, I got confused on the Métro—"

The rider smirked. "I know, Paris is so **complicated** for Americans." So pleased with himself that he didn't notice Wells closing on him, closing—

Without breaking stride, Wells brought his right arm into the guy's left shoulder and chest, a shiver that sent the rider sprawling sideways over the seat. His legs kicked high as his helmet thumped pavement. Meanwhile, Wells grabbed the bike's left handlebar, squeezed the clutch, holding the Suzuki upright and keeping it from stalling.

"Hey—" The kid sounded more shocked than afraid. Civilians almost always needed a few seconds to process violence that came out of nowhere, understand they were in trouble.

Wells pulled his new Sig. **"Shht."** Not **Shh— Shht**. Like he was talking to a dog. "Take off your helmet, put it on the seat. Don't stand up."

The kid's hands trembled, but he stayed quiet, did as Wells ordered. Wells reached into his pocket for a wad of bills, twenty-five hundred euros, more than the bike was worth. He riffed through the one-hundred-euro notes so the kid could see, tossed the stack on the pavement twenty feet up the road. "Yours. Do me a favor, don't call the police."

"Yes, okay, please."

"Now, crawl to it. Don't walk, crawl."

The kid went to his hands and knees. Wells pulled on the helmet, mounted the bike, disappeared into the night. Behind him, the kid began to yell. No matter. The Paris police had bigger problems than motorcycle thieves.

As Wells rode through the Paris night, a grin sliced open his face. He should feel guilty for stealing the bike. Scaring a civilian. Maybe he could have found another way. But he was short on time. And the kid would drink free for a month telling the story.

Anyway, the criminal in Wells knew the truth. Sometimes taking was so much easier than asking.

24

IN THE months after he took over the DGSE, Antoine Martin had made the mistake of believing his agency was winning the fight against the Islamic State.

Then came the terrible night in November 2015 when the jihadis blotted death across his hometown. The French called the attacks Bataclan, for the nightclub on Boulevard Voltaire where the worst carnage occurred. One hundred thirty gone, and even now the public didn't appreciate its luck. At least two suicide bombers had blown only themselves up. Another had lost his nerve, tossed his belt. Daesh could have killed two or three times as many.

After Bataclan, the DGSE went to war. At Martin's request, the French president ended restrictions on the agency's surveillance. It now monitored every call, email, and text in France and used what it found without judicial oversight. Elsewhere, the DGSE relied on the NSA, which had turned out to be a more-than-willing partner. The **quid pro quo**, unstated but real, was that France would stop complaining about the NSA's other surveillance, terrorism-related or not—and do its best to shut the rest of the European Union up, too.

The extra monitoring helped. So did the officers Martin moved to Belgium to aid that country's troubled security services. The DGSE had cracked a dozen cells and imprisoned hundreds of jihadis and sympathizers, often on vague charges of "conspiracy to support terrorism."

Still, Martin was certain more attacks were coming. Worse, the DGSE was picking up rumors of a secret Islamic State network called al-Zalam, Arabic that translated as **The Dark**. The agency's sources claimed the cell included six to ten highly trained jihadis unknown to any Western spy service. Some of Martin's analysts believed the threat was real. Others argued Daesh lacked the sophistication to keep such an important cell hidden and had invented al-Zalam to increase the stress on France's police and intelligence officers.

If that was the group's goal, it had already succeeded.

The Père Lachaise Cemetery was not far from the DGSE's headquarters, which occupied a small, heavily fortified compound in north-eastern Paris. In early 2016, Martin had found himself visiting the burial ground over and over. Even in that city of corpses, the Bataclan gravesites were obvious. Candles and flowers overran them. Seashells, rocks, well-thumbed paperback novels. Stuffed animals, their fur wet and matted in the winter Paris rain. Pictures, too—pictures most of all. These were the tributes the young left one another, and the Bataclan victims were so young. Pretty girls and handsome boys out for a night of dancing and drinking. A little screwing, if they were lucky. The harmless, febrile pleasure vices of youth.

Every trip exhausted Martin. Finally, he made himself leave the dead to themselves. Mourning the last attack was less important than stopping the next.

He had always been dedicated to his job. Since Bataclan, he slept five hours a night, worked six days a week. Still, he did his best to keep his Sundays inviolate. One day to rest. Most weeks, his driver brought him to his family's estate in the western suburbs. Maybe **estate** was too strong a word, but the house did have a tennis court of cracked red clay. Martin had learned to play there as a child, never lost his love for the game. Even in Iraq, he'd played. Tennis kept him sane in the Green Zone. But that trickster Time had worked its dark magic even before the DGSE grabbed his life. One by one, his sons learned to beat him. He couldn't compete with Simon or Remi anymore. He feared that soon enough even Damien, his youngest, would refuse to give up his Sundays for these trips.

For now, Martin could drag Damien along. The beautiful teenage sisters who had moved in three houses down didn't hurt either, he suspected.

So at 1 p.m. on this pleasant Sunday afternoon, he and Damien grabbed their rackets. With two bodyguards in tow, they made their way to Martin's armored limousine and the chase car that he had accepted a month before as an unfortunate necessity.

TWENTY KILOMETERS northeast, Raouf Bourgua and Soufiane Kassani watched the black American put the last bundle of shoe boxes into the trunk of his waiting Uber. Bourgua offered a friendly wave as the Peugeot rolled off.

"Wish we had more like him."

"I don't know how you can even be open today," Kassani said.

"Just another day. Nothing unusual. If I closed, it would be unusual."

"And him coming in, wanting all those shoes. Does that happen often?"

"A band came three months ago and bought fifty pair. British. But, yes, unusual." He peeled off a twenty-euro note. "Go on, Soufiane, get us lunch." Bourgua wanted to be alone for a few minutes. He wasn't as relaxed as he pretended. He'd waited a very long time for this day.

Then he was alone. As he preferred. It was strange. As a rule, he didn't like people much, but **they** liked **him**. Especially the French. He knew how they saw him. The perfect Arab. Cool but not challenging, successful but not political. They managed to fawn over him and talk down to him at once. **If only the rest were more like him.** They never noticed that he hated how they put him on parade. He hated even more the nickname his hipster customers had given him: the Sneaker Pimp.

The Puma. That was what his friends called him.

The stories the DGSE was hearing about the secret Islamic State network weren't entirely right. Bourgua called it al-Hadi—**The Quiet**—not al-Zalam. More important, it was platoon-rather than squad-sized. Bourgua oversaw five lieutenants, each of whom commanded six jihadis. Including him, thirty-six Quiet Men in all.

SuperSneaks gave him the perfect cover. Even potential terrorists were allowed to buy shoes. Anyway, three of his lieutenants had never shown up on any terrorist screens. The French services knew of the other two, but not how important they were.

Bourgua understood the dangers of DGSE and NSA surveillance. He passed messages face-to-face whenever he could. But he mostly let the networks run themselves. Imams and recruiters didn't need him to tell them how to raise money or bring men to Syria. He had known the Bataclan attacks were coming and been happy enough for the distraction they caused. But he hadn't ordered them or managed them. The jihadis behind them hadn't known he existed.

The hands-off attitude was the only way to keep him and al-Hadi secret. The network had taken him more than five years to build. But he'd stayed patient, trusting in Allah, knowing the power of his creation, knowing he'd most likely have only one chance to use it.

That moment had come.

KASSANI WAS SMILING as he walked through Sevran. He didn't know exactly what Bourgua was planning. But Bourgua seemed convinced they'd succeed. And Kassani had stopped doubting him.

Their preparations so far had gone smoothly. French customs hadn't touched the bottles of DF that Adnan the Turk sent to a grocery store in Toulouse. No one stopped the Quiet Man who drove them to the air-conditioned garage in Sevran where Bourgua stored his most valuable sneakers, two hundred fifty thousand euros of inventory.

Then the real work began. First, Kassani and an electrical engineer named Firas had to design and build what they called the ventilator, the combination of fan and heater that would aerosolize the liquid sarin and blow it into the ducts of L'église Notre-Dame de Bonne-Nouvelle.

"This stuff, do I need to boil it?"

"Not necessarily. It's volatile. As long as we heat it enough to get it into the air, it's fine."

"Does it corrode? Metal or plastic?"

"Only people."

"Easy enough, then."

Eighteen hours later, Firas and Kassani brought Bourgua a prototype. It was a steel box the size of a cake pan with a flat heating element beneath the base, a narrow fan on top, twin batteries on the sides. Admittedly, the device had a certain college science fair quality. But it worked.

"We can turn it on from a distance?" Bourgua said.

"Of course. I'll attach timers. Like a bomb. The alarm goes, triggers the circuits, the heater and fan."

"What if we can't be sure, exactly, when we need it? If we have to put it in place before we know?"

"A mobile, then. It's a bit more complicated, but no problem."

"Say, mobile is out. Out entirely."

Firas frowned. "You mean, someone's shut it down?"

"Exactly that."

"In that case, a short-range radio transmitter."

"Like Wi-Fi?" Kassani said.

"Basically, yes. It doesn't run through the

mobile network. It's a little complicated because we need a timer to turn the radio receiver on at a certain time. Or if it's only going to be a few days, we could leave it on standby, trust that the battery won't die. Sure, it's possible. But someone will have to be close. Twenty, thirty meters at most."

"**Insh'allah**, that should be all right," Bourgua said.

"Then, yes, I can," Firas said. "I'll make a key fob. It'll look like the kind that unlocks a car."

"Could security people jam that radio signal?"

"They can jam everything. But I don't think they would. They'd have no way to use their own radios."

"Then let's do the radio, add the timers as a backup."

A day later, Firas showed them a working prototype. Kassani tested it with twenty milliliters of sarin and a stray mutt that a Quiet Man picked up near Orly Airport, on the south side of Paris, far from Sevran. The dog died less pitifully than Kassani's human subjects, probably because it didn't have time to be frightened before the sarin kicked in. But it died nonetheless. Bourgua insisted on watching. Kassani gave him a gas mask and kept the atropine close.

They decided to build four ventilators for the best coverage inside the church. Firas put them together as Kassani oh-so-carefully mixed the sarin and transferred the lethal liquid to plastic tubs that fit neatly inside the boxes.

At each step, Kassani feared they'd face some insurmountable technical obstacle. But a week after Kassani arrived in Paris, he and Firas had four working ventilators, with radio controls. Kassani wondered who would trigger them. A jihadi? Someone who was going to be inside anyway?

For three days, the ventilators sat squat and lethal in the garage, surrounded by orange boxes of Nikes. **Swoosh.** Then they disappeared.

Forty-eight hours later, Bourgua came to Kassani. "Done."

"In the church? Already?"

"Already."

"I'm starting to believe Allah wants us to succeed."

"Of course He wants us to succeed."

Ideally, they would have tested the ventilators **in situ** with a harmless chemical. But breaking into the basement twice would double the risk of being caught. More important, Bourgua's men would then have to pour out whatever liquid they'd chosen to test and replace it with the sarin. Kassani didn't trust them to make that transfer safely, certainly not in a dark and cramped basement. The earlier experiments would have to do. Still, he found himself puzzled.

"There must be a hundred churches in Paris, Raouf."

"More."

"This one, it's not famous. Not like the other Notre-Dame, or even that big white one on the hill you see from the train."

"Montmartre. No, that's true."

"So how can you be sure that all of Paris will show up there?"

"Not just Paris, Soufiane." Bourgua offered Kassani the thinnest of smiles.

"Please, Raouf, I know you love your secrets, but without me you wouldn't have any of this."

"I'll tell you this, then. You'll find out Sunday."

THE AVENUE DES Champs-Élysées might have been the most famous street in the world. Two kilometers long, it sloped gently uphill from the Place de la Concorde to the Arc de Triomphe. Tree-lined gardens flanked its eastern half. Souvenir shops, tourist trap restaurants, and the world's most expensive brands mingled in the buildings farther west. At night, after a glass of wine, when taillights and headlights blurred into a red-and-white kaleidoscope, the Champs could feel like a three-dimensional dream.

But the avenue played a more prosaic role in Parisian life. In a city filled with narrow and winding streets, it was a vital traffic artery, offering four arrow-straight lanes each way. It carried an endless stream of cars and trucks between western Paris and the heart of the city. To avoid taking it required a special effort.

So the driver of Antoine Martin's limousine saw no reason not to use it for his fifteen-kilometer trip from Martin's apartment to his parents' house. The same route he had followed the Sunday before. And the Sunday before that, just days after the quietest of the Quiet Men first set his eyes on the address that Walter Crompond gave to Aziz Murak.

Though the Champs carried as much traffic as many highways, it lacked a center median. Vehicles heading east and west passed within a meter of one another. The lack of a barrier usually didn't matter. Parisiens drove as they lived—aggressively, even rudely, but within the law. Even taxi drivers rarely ran lights or sped.

Martin's limousine had emergency lights and

sirens, of course. But Martin had told his driver not to use them as long as traffic was flowing. He thought doing so would only call attention to the limo. And Sunday traffic in central Paris was usually fine. Aside from tourist-focused businesses, the city more or less shut down. This morning was no exception, with traffic on the Champs heavy but moving easily between the lights. Martin's limousine eased along at forty kilometers an hour in the left lane. The chase car, a Renault that wasn't armored, followed directly behind.

Martin hadn't wanted the second car, but today he didn't mind. His second bodyguard rode in it, giving him and Damien the limo's back seat to themselves, a chance at a normal conversation. Martin found those harder and harder. When he escaped the secret world, he wanted to think about trivial matters, mainly sports. Nadal versus Federer versus Djokovic . . . This job had made him a lousy father, a worse husband. He consoled himself with the fact that at least he wasn't having an affair.

"How's school?"

"Eh, fine."

"Chemistry this year, right?"

"Right." Damien's half-open eyes pleaded, **Don't interrogate me**. Martin winced. He'd become the sort of father who didn't know how to talk to his sons.

"How about girls?"

"I don't know."

"You don't know?" Lately, Damien had insisted on wearing his hair in an almost military cut, an unflattering look for his narrow face. But he was handsome enough. With his brothers to teach him the ropes, Martin expected he'd have no problem finding a first love. Or two. "You must know."

"What if I don't like girls?"

"Of course girls will like you—"

"That's not what I said, Dad. You don't **listen** anymore."

His son was right. His son was thinking about coming out, or trying to come out, or just plain coming out. Martin hadn't even heard. Now he had no idea what to say. All these years as a diplomat, no idea what to say. He patted Damien's shoulder, received a single grave nod back. **Listening now?**

"Are you sure about this? What about the sisters?"

"Sisters?"

"The twins, the pretty ones who live down from Grandma and Grandpa, I thought that was half the reason you came with me to play . . ."

Damien smiled hopelessly, and Martin felt like a fool. Too late, he remembered the sisters had an older brother, too, a real specimen who liked to run with no shirt.

"Have you told Mom?"

"No, but I think she knows."

And didn't tell me. "And your brothers?"

Damien never had a chance to answer.

THE PUMA'S Quiet Men watched the limousine from the moment it left Martin's building. A moped rider on Rue Saint-Sébastien, a bicyclist on Rue des Archives, a taxi driver on Rue de Rivoli. One by one, they sent word to a white Nissan Pulsar hatchback making a slow loop through the sleepy streets of the 16th Arrondissement. The chase car actually helped the watchers do their job. The two vehicles moved in tandem, making them easy to track.

So just as the limousine turned off the Place de la Concorde, the hatchback made its own turn, leaving the traffic circle that surrounded the Arc de Triomphe, entering the Champs at its western end.

The vehicles were two kilometers apart, closing at eighty kilometers an hour. Thirteen hundred meters a minute. Simple math suggested they were a minute and a half from meeting.

The traffic lights added two minutes, giving Damien Martin enough time to tell his father what had been so much on his mind.

The Pulsar traveled in the leftmost eastbound lane. Two men inside, driver and passenger. In the hatch they'd stowed three big wooden crates that held three hundred twenty kilograms of RDX, military-grade plastic explosive. They'd chosen a relatively small, lightweight vehicle. The limousine's driver was less likely to notice it. It was more maneuverable. Most important, it wouldn't muffle the power of the RDX.

The men knew that in a matter of minutes they would die. They felt anticipation, not fear. They understood the importance of what they were about to do.

The Pulsar's passenger received texts every few seconds on the location of Martin's limousine. These were not street names but numbers, each corresponding to a traffic light along the Champs. He spoke them as they arrived, allowing the driver to keep his eyes on the road. In the last few days, the two men had driven the boulevard over and over, memorizing where its lights were located, how long they lasted, how much time driving between them required.

"Three," the passenger said. "Four." In his lap he held the detonator, a gray box the size of a garage door opener. It was already armed. To prevent it from going off accidentally, a plastic shield protected the single white button in its center. A thick black wire ran from it to the crates.

The driver saw the limousine now. A hundred meters ahead. He eased off the gas, gave space to the car ahead. When the limo was forty meters away, he jammed down his foot. The Pulsar surged. He swung the steering wheel left, cut into the westbound lanes, narrowly avoiding the yellow BMW in front of the limo.

"Allahu akbar—"

THE WHITE HATCHBACK came out of nowhere.

Martin's driver slammed his horn, pulled the limousine's steering wheel sideways, too late.

The two vehicles bent together, grille to grille, engine to engine, the Nissan at an angle to the limo.

Air bags exploded from the limousine's steering wheel and dash, cocooning the men in front. The limo's ballistic-glass windshield starred but didn't shatter. In back, Martin and Damien were jolted onto the floor, arms and legs tangled.

"Dad—"

"C'est bon. C'est bon." But Martin knew it

wasn't. He was furious with himself. For underestimating the threat. For failing to insist that his men follow proper countersurveillance, vary their routes, keep their eyes up. His sloppiness and stupidity might be about to get his son killed. **Merde, merde, merde.**

In front, Martin's bodyguard pulled himself out of the air bag, reached for his door.

"Sirens and go, just go," Martin yelled. The driver and bodyguard hadn't been in Iraq. Martin had. He knew they were deep inside what the Americans called the kill zone, knew what was coming, **vehicle-borne improvised explosive device**, the phrase strangely French in its length and complexity.

BEHIND THEM, the chase car skidded to a stop. Martin's second bodyguard threw open his door, reached for the Heckler & Koch 416C in his lap.

Their only chance.

THE PULSAR'S windshield had cracked, its air bags popped. Black smoke seethed from its engine block. But the passenger still cradled the detonator. He reached for the cover that protected the button.

Stuck. It was **stuck.**

MARTIN's second bodyguard stepped out of the chase car as a minivan swerved past, honking.

He lifted the H&K. The pandemonium began, drivers yelling, tourists staring open-mouthed from the sidewalks.

The bodyguard locked onto the Nissan, two men inside, their faces hidden by windshield and air bags.

He raised the H&K—

But he had no angle, the limo was in the way, and he had to see them, Sunday morning on the Champs-Élysées, maybe the crash had been an **accident**, he couldn't light up two men without at least seeing if they were Arab or not. He ran forward, looking for an angle, yelling.

"Sortez! Sortez!"

THE DRIVER of the chase car had no such qualms, he'd seen the Nissan accelerate and swerve across the road. He knew. He shouldered open his door and stepped halfway out, keeping the door frame as cover, pulling his pistol. Unlike the bodyguard, he had a decent angle. He lifted the pistol, aimed.

And a Mercedes SUV in the eastbound lane flew past and knocked the Renault's door into him. The door pinned him, bent his wrist. He yelped, dropped the pistol onto the roof of the sedan.

IN THE NISSAN, the driver didn't understand why they were alive. "What's wrong?"

The passenger raised the detonator. "It's locked somehow, I can't press it—"

"Give it."

IN THE LIMOUSINE, Martin's driver freed himself from the steering wheel air bag. Barely ten seconds had passed since the Nissan rammed the limousine.

"Back up, get clear," Martin yelled. "Now!"

The driver triggered the sirens, put the limousine in reverse, stamped on the gas. Metal ground metal. But the fact that the cars hadn't hit head-on worked for the jihadis. The limo's front axle was bent, its brake rotor wrapped around its left front wheel. As its engine moaned, the limo lurched back, tugging the Pulsar with it.

THE CHASE CAR'S driver found his pistol and fired one, two, three wild shots up the Champs. The men and women who were watching from the sidewalks turned and ran.

———

A HUNDRED fifty meters down the hill, a Honda CB650F began to accelerate.

THE ROUNDS came through the Nissan's windshield. The driver ducked. He saw the problem. The crash had mangled the plastic teeth that locked the detonator's shield in place. Pressing harder wasn't the answer. He needed to **angle** it. And he did. It popped free.

He flipped it up to expose the button and, without hesitation, thumbed it down.

IN A FRACTION of a second, three hundred twenty kilos of RDX exploded, creating an overpressure wave, a man-made tornado, tiny but massively powerful. The men in the Nissan vaporized. **When flesh becomes air.** The vehicle itself didn't do much better, though bits of its engine block survived.

MARTIN'S LIMOUSINE was big and heavy, more than three tons of steel and reinforced glass, built to take bullets and grenades. But three hundred twenty kilos of RDX was enough explosive to flatten a house. On this Sunday morning on the Champs, the carnage was enormous. Seven vehicles around the Pulsar were destroyed. A tourist bus one lane over flipped on its side and caught fire. Shrapnel and blown windows killed four people on the sidewalks and grievously wounded fifty-three more.

Closer to the hatchback, the explosion pulverized the limousine's windshield, sending a million glass daggers at Martin's driver and bodyguard, killing them instantly. Fragments from the Pulsar's engine shredded the second bodyguard. The pressure wave picked up the limousine and flipped it over, neatly, exactly on top of Martin's chase car. Roof on roof, an accident of physics. It crushed the Renault. It would have killed the driver, too, but he was already dead.

Inside the limousine? When the blast came, Damien and Martin were on the floor of the passenger compartment. The worst of the explosion traveled over them. And the limo's steel skeleton remained intact, testament to the skill of the welders who had reinforced it. Son and father survived, Damien with a fractured skull, Martin with a punctured lung, both with a dozen broken bones, their blood mixing from a thousand cuts.

Martin opened his eyes first, felt rather than saw his son.

"Damien." Martin couldn't do more than

murmur. Each breath set his chest on fire. He forced himself to stay calm. He could save the boy.

Damien's body was heavy against his father's. When Martin pushed him, he didn't push back. Deadweight. Martin slapped Damien's face, hard, pinched the boy's ear. In the darkness, Damien groaned. Good. He was alive.

Martin tried to orient himself. They were lying against the roof, which meant the limo had somehow flipped over, which meant the doors were upside down. Hard to open from the inside. Maybe the windows?

He reached for the windowsill, whimpering from the pain in his legs. He'd been hurt even more badly than he thought. Glass pebbles had sliced open his fingers, he couldn't get himself out. He would have shrieked if he could have drawn breath, but he made himself try again, why wouldn't someone help—

The door of the limousine wrenched open.

"My son," Martin whispered.

Through the swirling smoke, he saw a mirrored visor peering at him. A hand reached inside and almost gently tossed a ball at Martin's feet. The hand disappeared. The ball clanked against the limousine's roof, metal on metal, and Martin knew. **A grenade.**

His last thought, not a prayer. For like so many French, he was a rationalist, an atheist. Even now, God didn't come to him. Instead . . .

All those trips to Père Lachaise, I never guessed at the evil in this world.

25

SEVRAN

TWENTY minutes later. Wells hadn't heard. He called Shafer from the hotel. "Found it. A kilometer from the store. 279 Allée Richelieu. Concrete building, freestanding on a narrow lot, security grates on the windows, razor wire fence, and an alarm."

"Lot of security for sneakers."

"Even cool ones. No sign, nothing that identifies it."

"I'll see what I can find. I assume you're hitting it tonight."

"If I can beat the alarm."

"You care because . . . ?"

"Didn't I just get out of prison?"

"I doubt the French police scramble for Sevran burglaries. Plus, if your friend has anything funky in there, he probably has the alarm company call only him so he can see what's going on for himself before he brings in the cops."

"Hope so. If he comes a-calling, we'll have a nice late-night chat."

Shafer paused. "Hold on—"

Even from four thousand miles away, Wells heard the sudden tension in Shafer's voice. "What's up?"

"You near a TV? Turn it on."

THE FIFTEEN-SECOND delay after the accident and before the bomb went off gave witnesses plenty of time to pull out their phones. Now CNN was cutting between live shots of the Champs, where firefighters were hosing down smoldering cars, and video of the moments before the blast. Off-camera gunshots and a siren were audible before the bomb blew.

Beneath the images, the crawl: MASSIVE EXPLOSION HITS CHAMPS-ÉLYSÉES IN HEART OF PARIS . . . "NUMEROUS" CASUALTIES, POLICE SAY . . . NO CLAIM OF RESPONSIBILITY YET, BUT TERROR ATTACK SUSPECTED . . .

Another video, shot from a couple of hundred feet down the avenue, captured the aftermath. Smoke obscured what was left of the limousine, but not enough to hide the motorcyclist who tossed a grenade through its back door. The image erased any doubt that the attackers had targeted the limo.

"Gotta be gov," Shafer said.

"What?"

"The limo. French government. It's a Renault. Who with a choice picks a Renault limo?"

"I get it." Wells wondered who was inside. A person important enough to merit a chase car. And a bomb that left a ten-foot-deep crater in the Champs-Élysées's asphalt. But not a motorcade or closed streets. So not the President or Prime Minister. Even a senior cabinet member, like the Minister of Defense or Justice, would have had more protection. Maybe a judge who oversaw terrorism trials. A central banker. The mayor of Paris.

The CNN crawl changed: BREAKING: FRANCE DECLARES HEIGHTENED STATE OF EMERGENCY NATIONWIDE . . . EXPLOSION ON CHAMPS-ÉLYSÉES WAS "CERTAINLY" TERRORIST ATTACK, MINISTER OF INTERIOR SAYS . . . PRESIDENT TO SPEAK LATER TODAY . . . FRANCE: STATE OF EMERGENCY TO INCLUDE RANDOM SEARCHES, BORDER CHECKS . . . PARIS AIRPORTS TO REMAIN OPEN BUT MAJOR DELAYS EXPECTED . . .

"That was quick."

"I think they already know who got hit,"

Shafer said. "And that it's bad. They'll have to tell us soon. They're not going to be able to hide much. Too big, too many witnesses."

And bodies. "I'm going to Sevran. Trace the route I'm using tonight." Wells had another stop, though he was keeping it to himself. He feared Shafer would tell him not to go.

"I'll be at Langley. See what Paris Station has for us."

"One more thing. Get me Bourgua's birthday and his kids'. And wedding anniversary."

"For the alarm? Now you're thinking."

"You couldn't be more condescending if you tried, Ellis."

"Believe me. I could."

AN EERIE CALM had settled on the **banlieue.** Ninety minutes before, when Wells tailed the guy from SuperSneaks to the storage depot, he'd passed a park where shirtless teenagers lazily played soccer and old men hunched over chessboards. Now the park was empty. So were the streets. Many of these people had lived under authoritarian Arab governments. They knew soon enough the police would come, angry, looking for revenge and broken bones.

Wells rode his stolen Suzuki past the depot. The garage was south of Sevran's downtown,

in a mixed residential-industrial neighborhood. A plumbing wholesaler occupied the
building to the north. An electrical supply
store lay to the south. Both were closed on this
Sunday. Trees and a concrete wall shielded the
apartment complex behind them.

Coils of razor wire laced the fence around the
garage. But Wells could handle those easily
enough. France had its own version of Home
Depot, a chain of home improvement stores
called Leroy Merlin. The nearest outlet was in
Gonesse, a suburb five miles west. Wells would
pick up a flashlight, a canvas bag, garden shears,
gloves, a claw hammer, rope . . . everything a
good burglar needed. Everything but a pistol,
and he already had one of those. No doubt the
checkout clerk would smirk when he laid out
his purchases. Smirk and take his money.

The alarm was still a problem. The agency
had devices that could neutralize standard commercial alarms, but Wells couldn't ask the Paris
Station for help. And Sevran would have far
more cops than usual tonight. On the other
hand, they would have their own priorities,
probably focused on the cités around the train
station.

Wells put the bike into gear and wended
through the neighborhood around the garage,

memorizing the street grid. It was simple enough. A big surface road called the N370 lay one block west. In turn, the N370 connected to the N2, a divided arterial that ran south of the airport. Left, right, right, left, and Wells could be at his hotel in twenty minutes.

For now, he had another destination.

He rode through Sevran's empty streets until he reached SuperSneaks. In the **banlieue**'s drab downtown, the store stood out. Hundreds of old sneakers jutted from its exterior walls, in every color and size, from gray running shoes to bright green high-tops.

Wells expected SuperSneaks would still be open, a subtle rebellion against the approaching cops. It was. He left the bike in front, walked inside. He wanted to see the Puma for himself.

The walls were covered with posters of indie bands and rappers. Someone had added thought bubbles over their heads: **J'aime Chuck! Adidas Pour Toujours!** The most expensive sneakers were displayed under glass serving dishes, as though they were truly precious objects. A pristine pair of what Wells assumed were first-generation Air Jordans sat in a cage, rotating slowly. No wonder the French hadn't bothered to look at the man who owned this store. They might suspect an imam or a lawyer, no matter

how many times he mouthed the proper plati-
tudes. But they had mistaken hip, sly Raouf
Bourgua for one of them.

Televisions hung from the store's four corners. Wells guessed that they usually played
music videos, old movies, maybe NBA high-
lights. This afternoon they were tuned to France
1, broadcasting live from the Champs. Two
men stood looking up at the television in the
back right corner. Wells had followed the first,
a small, thirtyish Arab with oddly gray skin, on
the run to the storage shed. The second man
was older, and both less and more familiar.
Wells had never met him before, but he had
seen a dozen photos.

Raouf Bourgua.

Now he turned, smiled at Wells. **"Bonjour."**

"As-salaam alaikum."

"Alaikum salaam." Bourgua switched to Arabic. "You prefer Arabic?"

"I don't speak French."

"I wasn't sure."

"It's all right. Nobody knows what to make
of me." Wells immediately sensed Bourgua's vi-
tality, his self-assurance. He had the easy charm
of a politician. His face was smooth, his hair
black, his eyes deep-set, slightly hooded. Underneath the charm Wells sensed a watchfulness,

calm and dark. A summer lake at midnight, a nest of water moccasins lurking three steps from shore.

Wells nodded at the television. "What's happened?"

"You didn't hear?"

Wells held up his helmet. "No radio on the bike."

"A terrorist attack. On the Champs-Élysées. They say a car bomb."

"That's"—Wells paused—"too bad." A flipness in his voice suggesting the opposite.

"Dozens dead, they say. Maybe more than fifty. The Right Bank hospitals are filled."

Did Wells hear a touch of triumph? "They'll blame us. Like they always do."

"Us?"

"All of us."

Bourgua gave Wells his full attention. "Not French. Where are you from?"

"Canada."

"You don't know these people. Believe me, they'll make it miserable up here. They love to remind us who we are."

Not exactly what Bourgua had told **Time Out Paris** after Bataclan.

"Maybe this time it'll be different," Wells

said. "Maybe Allah wants all of us to live through a little misery. To wake up."

"Don't worry about that," the second man said.

Bourgua's head snapped from Wells to the man with gray skin, and Wells knew he'd heard something he shouldn't have. **Don't worry about that.** Why?

Because another attack was coming. And soon.

"I try not to argue with my customers, but I don't think Allah wishes misery for anyone, Soufiane," Bourgua said primly. Stuffing the genie back in the bottle.

"Even the **kaffirs**?" Wells said.

Bourgua gave Wells a shopkeeper's smile, deferential and false. "Even them. Looking for anything in particular, **habibi**?"

Wells wished he could stay longer, see if Bourgua's buddy Soufiane dropped more hints. Maybe Wells should mention Pumas were his favorite brand. Just to see. But he'd pushed his luck already. Time to go. "I wish, but this place is too cool for me."

"You change your mind, we're here."

Beside Bourgua, Soufiane gave a tiny grunt. Hardly audible. The laugh of an inside man at an inside joke. **Because you won't be here very long, Soufiane? That what I'm hearing? Or did you have a piece of air caught in your throat?**

WELLS WAS in Gonesse, putting a pair of shears into a shopping cart, when his phone buzzed. Shafer.

"Antoine Martin was in the limo."

"Who?"

"DGSE director. His son, too. Get ready for an avalanche. They're already talking about bringing in the army. You want to hit that garage, better be tonight."

"Avalanche sounds right. Any leads?"

"Doesn't sound good. They've asked the NSA for everything, but so far we're coming up blank."

"Can't believe he only had one chase car," Wells said.

"Guess he didn't think they knew where he lived. Stupid, but it's a very common name."

"You think our guy gave them Martin's address?" Anyone on the seventh floor could have figured out where Martin lived easily enough.

"Great minds think alike."

"His last play."

"Looks like it. I asked the NSA to put a trace

on Bourgua. Nothing so far. Anything comes up, I'll let you know."

But Wells knew nothing was likely to come up. Bourgua was too canny to use phones or email at this stage. They needed real surveillance, bugs in the house and store, a dozen men to track the Puma's comings and goings. The French no doubt had a hundred or more high-end targets and the manpower to watch ten at most. No way would they kick Bourgua to the top of the list based on what Wells had found.

"You run the garage address?"

"Yeah. Nothing. I have the birthdays, too. I'll text you."

"I went to Sevran, Ellis. I saw him."

"Dumb."

"Maybe. But a guy was with him, the one who picked up the shoes, and he said something. No details, but I'm pretty sure more's coming. And soon."

As WELLS rode back to the hotel, a bag of gear in his lap and another strapped to the back of the bike, he saw a convoy of high-sided Renault police vans speeding south. Toward Sevran and the other **banlieues**. Minutes later, three black sedans, emergency blue lights flashing from their grilles. DGSI or DGSE. The vanguards of the approaching army.

Chasing what? Wells didn't think they knew. Not yet. For now, this was a show of force. But little in life was as pointless as a show of force without a target. A hurricane in the middle of the ocean.

Though the police would have targets soon. Clues, at least. No matter how carefully the attackers had covered their tracks, Paris was a modern city. Modern cities had cameras everywhere. The investigators would start by identifying the license plates of the car and the motorcycle used in the attack. Their owners would face very unpleasant questions. If car and bike had been stolen, the police would focus on the thefts. The bombers themselves, or what was left of them, might be another clue. Forensic technicians would have the gruesome job of scraping DNA from the bits of the bomb for genetic matching.

The investigators would figure the killers had tracked the limousine from Martin's apartment. They'd scour cameras, looking for anyone watching the building. They'd go another step back, try to figure out how the attackers had found Martin's address. They'd scrutinize his friends, the admins at the DGSE, his household help. Though probably not senior officers at Langley.

Most of all, the investigators would offer every Muslim in France a lifetime get-out-of-jail-free card for help catching the attackers. Forensic evidence grabbed headlines and the television shows, but in the real world informants broke most cases.

The French would move as fast as they could. They knew the Islamic State preferred to attack in bunches for maximum psychological impact. But if Wells and Shafer were right and the Puma was behind the attack, the French were in trouble. The DGSE didn't even know the guy existed. Only an informant could help them in time to matter, and why would the Puma's men crack? They'd just pulled off the most important terrorist attack since September 11. They had proven they could strike anytime, anywhere. If the head of the DGSE wasn't safe in an armored limousine on the Champs-Élysées, no one was.

Whatever they were planning next had to be even bigger. The jihadis sold terror, their only product. Like all smart marketers, they saved the best for last.

BACK AT THE hotel, Wells split his time between watching the news and imagining how he'd attack the garage. The French President announced the death of Martin and his son in a grim speech around 7 p.m. "Antoine Martin served with distinction and pride. We will honor his memory by finding the men who killed him and bringing them to justice. Meanwhile, I call for the citizens of the Republic to remain vigilant and strong." Exactly what kind of justice the French planned, and whether they had suspects, were questions that would have to wait. The President took no questions.

At 9 p.m., the Defense Ministry announced that funeral services for Antoine Martin would take place on Tuesday at 11 a.m. at L'église Notre-Dame de Bonne-Nouvelle, in Paris's 2nd Arrondissement. Damien would be buried the next day at the same church. Besides the French President and Prime Minister, Martin's funeral was expected to draw the leaders of every big Western spy service, including MI6, the CIA, and even the Mossad.

"Security at the church will be extraordinary," CNN's Erin Burnett reported. "Police are already blocking off the streets and alleys nearby. There will be snipers, bomb-sniffing dogs, and a small army of police and bodyguards. The various services are already coordinating to make sure they don't step on one another's toes." Good idea. Trigger fingers would be psoriasis itchy on Tuesday, and friendly fire on the Paris streets would hardly inspire public confidence.

An hour later, Wells's phone buzzed. Shafer.

"Anne called me. Wanted to know if you're okay."

Wells silently cursed himself. He had forgotten Anne knew he was in Paris. Of course she'd wondered if he'd been caught up in this.

"I lied. Said you were. You ready?"

"In the wee small hours of the morning."

"Ol' Brown Eyes. That's my boy. I'll be waiting by the phone. And I'll see you Tuesday either way."

"You're coming?"

"It's a hotter ticket than **Hamilton**."

"Think it's the next target?" Wells couldn't imagine a bigger bull's-eye.

"The obvious play. Probably means it's wrong. Besides, they'd need a Panzer division to get close. Have you seen that church?"

Wells had, on Google Maps. The streets around Our Lady of Good News were narrow and easy to block. The building itself looked solid. A car bomb a hundred feet away wouldn't do the trick. Even with attackers who were willing to die, a conventional ground attack would require hundreds of well-trained men and be obvious long before it began. But ground attacks weren't the only way to go.

"What about a cruise missile?"

"They have Tomahawks, we're in even more trouble than I thought. And if you're thinking plane, Paris airspace will be closed to civilian traffic all day. If you made me wager, I'd say they'll take advantage of the fact that every cop in the city is in the Second to do something else."

Wells didn't answer. He was seeing Raouf Bourgua's cool eyes. Bourgua struck Wells as a man who didn't care much for silver medals.

"John?"

"Maybe the answer's in the garage. At least enough to get the DGSE to bite."

"If it looks impossible tonight, tell me. We'll have a face-to-face with the frogs after the funeral. By then, maybe they'll have run through their best leads and be ready to listen."

"If it's not too late."

"It won't be."

"From your lips to Allah's ears," Wells said.

"Allah listens to Jews?"

"As much as anyone."

THREE A.M. Wells bungeed his gear to the Suzuki and saddled up. He'd already checked the bike's engine, chain, brakes, and tires. He didn't need a flat on this run.

The night air was calm, clear, fresh against his skin. Sevran was among the **banlieues** farthest from Paris. Much of the land between it and the airport was surprisingly rural. Wheat, barley, and oat fields stretched to the perimeter of Charles de Gaulle. Hard to believe that the center of the great city was not even twenty miles away. Past the empty lands, the airport had mostly shut for the night, a slumbering beast with lights twinkling. Wells spotted a pair of helicopters several miles south, their spotlights faint at this distance, circling over Bondy or another close-in **banlieue**. He rode steady down the empty road at ninety kilometers an hour. The Suzuki didn't have the power of the 1000 cc monsters he favored, and its engine labored when he wound down the throttle. He was used to bikes that jumped almost before he gave them gas. Still, he was making decent time.

On the left, the farmland ended. Wells passed a big industrial park, presumably put here to be close to the airport and the big highway called La Francilienne. The French had meant it as the third big ring road around Paris, though they'd never finished it. The N2 gained a lane here as the two roads briefly merged.

Wells felt as strong and clearheaded as he had in months. Motorcycling always agreed with him. As the bike thrummed, he imagined exactly how he'd attack the garage. He should have at least sixty seconds before the alarm went off, several minutes more before anyone showed up. Shafer's theory that Bourgua had arranged for the alarm company to notify him first made sense. If it was wrong, then Bourgua probably didn't have anything interesting in the garage anyway.

So. Clip a hole low in the fence . . . Take a few fast chances with the alarm, remembering to enter the birthdays in the European style, day-month-year . . . If they didn't work, shoot out the lock . . . He'd brought a pillow from the hotel . . . During his long-ago training at the Farm, some soulless Cold War pro had called pillows the husband's silencer . . .

And inside. **The bear went over the mountain, / To see what he could see** . . .

Ahead, the highway divided. Wells stayed in the right lane. The off-ramp rose to become an overpass. Beneath him, La Francilienne made a sweeping right, turning northwest, an empty river. The N2, his road, continued tracking west-southwest. About a mile or so ahead was the traffic circle where the N2 met the N370. The overpass peaked, eased down.

Too late, Wells saw the lights twinkling at the traffic circle. A half dozen. More. Only one explanation. The French cops had set a roadblock. In the middle of the night. In a lockeddown **banlieue**. Damn their diligence. And Wells had nowhere to go. The N2 had no exits before the circle. Should he ride on, try to brazen his way through the checkpoint? No chance. He had a pistol on his waist and a bank robber's worth of gear in his bag. Ditch the bike, cross the highway, and disappear into Sevran?

No. Back. He turned the Suzuki around, glad for once he'd stolen such a dinky bike. The headlight was barely worthy of the name. Probably they hadn't even seen him, a speck in a sea of darkness. No cars coming. He would go the wrong way over the overpass. At the merge with La Francilienne, he'd make another U-turn, follow the big highway away from Sevran. He'd circle, come at Sevran from the rural roads to the east. An hour's delay, nothing more.

As long as he could get to the La Francilienne.

Wells wound down the throttle, scrunched over the handlebars, begged the bike for speed as the little engine yipped. He heard the thrum of a helicopter behind and knew they were hunting him, these French. Probably the helicopter had infrared cameras and been tracking him even before he'd seen the cops. The U-turn would have been obvious. Now they would have him if they could.

The bike's speedometer was stuck at one-forty kph, not even eighty-five miles an hour. It rattled madly despite the smooth asphalt. Why hadn't he stolen a BMW? Or a jet pack? Wells eased off the throttle—he feared blowing the engine—and then wound it down once more. He topped the overpass. Ahead he saw the N2 off-ramp come together with La Francilienne, his life running in reverse. He raised his head, chanced a look at the helicopter. It was a couple of miles out. Police sedans were no doubt chasing him, too, but the traffic circle was a couple kilometers away. Even at one hundred sixty kilometers an hour, they wouldn't make up ground quickly.

Wells knew from memorizing the maps that just after the big highway turned right, it offered an exit into Villepinte, the last **banlieue** before the airport. If he reached the surface roads, he'd have the advantage, he could ditch the bike. He knew how to disappear—disappearing was his specialty—he still had a chance.

Except . . .

Screaming down the highway, west, toward

him, two new sets of police lights. Maybe three
kilometers away, but coming fast. And Wells
was working for them, actually closing the gap
with them, as he rode the wrong way down the
ramp.

By the time he reached the point where the
ramp met the highway, he knew he had no
chance. The police cars were barely a kilometer
out. He would have to slow to make the U-turn
before he accelerated again. If he didn't stop,
they might kill him, accidentally or intention-
ally. His best chance now, his only chance, was
to tell the truth. Maybe he could convince them
to look at the garage.

Not much of a plan, but he couldn't think of
a better one.

At the merge, he pulled the bike to the edge
of the road. Dismounted. He couldn't do anything about the bag of gear, but he could at least
get rid of the pistol. He threw it off the highway, into the woods. Then he went to his knees,
raised his hands, waited for the police.

THEY PILED OUT of their sedans with assault
rifles drawn. Wells's eyes bled tears under the
spotlights, but he kept his hands high. A police
officer, thick in a Kevlar vest, walked over to
him, screaming.

"I don't speak French."

"No French? What are you doing here?"

"I'm American. I work for the CIA—"

"Name?"

"John Wells."

"Identification."

Wells shook his head. The officer walked behind Wells and Wells heard him unzip the bag of gear. "What is all this?"

"There's a garage in Sevran—"

The officer reappeared. "Lie on your stomach."

"Please, there's a man you need to look at, a Tunisian named Raouf Bourgua—"

"**On your stomach.**" The officer kicked Wells, a quick one-timer that popped the air from his diaphragm. Wells groaned and lay flat, feeling the asphalt kiss his cheek. So much for convincing them.

"You want to make fools of us? After yesterday? Whoever you are, you won't see America for a long time."

Oh, the irony. After he'd gone to so much trouble to get sent to prison.

The officer put a knee in Wells's back, grabbed his wrists, laced handcuffs tight on his skin.

"Up. On your knees."

"Please. If you'll just let me talk to someone."

Another cop stepped forward, black hood in his hands.

The darkness slid over Wells's eyes. And, with it, the bitter knowledge that he'd failed.

26

LANGLEY

WHERE was Wells?
He hadn't said when he planned to hit the garage. But Shafer figured he'd head out around 3 a.m., the black heart of night. He should be back at the hotel in two hours, three at most. France was six time zones ahead of the East Coast. Thus, Shafer expected a call by midnight at the latest.

But midnight came and went. One a.m. By now, the sun was up in Sevran. Shafer stopped waiting, started calling. Wells's Bulgarian mobile went to voice mail. The phone in his hotel room rang without end. **Where, where, where?**

He'd had an accident. The cops had picked him up. Or, after all those years dancing on the edge, he'd finally slipped. Raouf Bourgua had caught him at the garage, shot him, stuck his body in storage.

No. Shafer refused to believe some French-Tunisian sneaker salesman could beat Wells.

Two a.m. Shafer headed for Langley, hoping at least to catch up on the classified traffic. Paris Station reported the French had found the motorcycle used in the attack in the 7th Arrondissement, the Left Bank. It had been reported stolen a week before. No fingerprints. The cops were looking at cameras in the area to see if they could trace where the rider had gone. But the bike, probably not coincidentally, had been parked on a quiet, surveillance-free street.

Meanwhile, big surprise, the Islamic State had claimed responsibility for the attack. It promised so-called martyrdom videos from the bombers within a day. Jihadi websites and Twitter feeds were cheering, and promising more.

The most notable news came from the DCIA, a cable issued four hours before: all europe/africa/me stations orange status; dgse may ask aid. Orange was the CIA's second-highest readiness level. It meant canceled vacations and mandatory overtime. All case officers had to be ready to be report to duty within two hours.

In forty years, Shafer had never seen the agency raise its alert level at the request of another country's intelligence service. The attack had obviously stretched the DGSE and the internal French security services to their limits. The American ambassador was even now headed to the Élysée Palace, the French president's residence, to offer condolences from the White House and whatever help the French needed. Duto understood allies cemented their bonds at these moments.

After an hour reading cables, Shafer realized that he was only distracting himself, hoping Wells would call. He needed to get to Paris. But a look at airline timetables revealed that he had no options until late afternoon. The commercial flights from the East Coast were all overnights. United had the earliest. It left Dulles at 5:25 p.m., touched down Charles De Gaulle at 6:55 a.m. local. Shafer couldn't do better unless he convinced Duto to charter a jet. Ludlow and the seventh-floor officers were taking a CIA plane to the funeral. But they were leaving later, planning to land around 9:45 at Le Bourget, a private airport closer to Paris than CDG. The French police would escort them in. Afterward, they were heading to DGSE headquarters for an emergency meeting that Shafer planned to crash.

Shafer booked the United flight. With the help of his diplo passport, he ought to be on the ground in Sevran by 8 a.m. local time tomorrow. Almost twenty-two hours away. What about today? Paris Station didn't know Wells was in France. Shafer didn't want to tell them. Anyway, given everything else they had to do, the case officers would help only if Duto personally insisted. And no one woke the President of the United States at this hour unless ICBMs were inbound.

No. Shafer needed someone on the ground now. Someone who could go to hospitals and police stations and jails around Sevran and ask questions that would only be answered in person.

The Marine. Coyle. Wells had said he was good. And he was the only one who had any inkling what Wells was doing. He might not know much, but he knew more than nothing. Shafer spent a few minutes putting together a list of the hospitals and police stations where Wells was most likely to be, then reached for his phone.

"Staff Sergeant Coyle."

"Who's this?"

"Ellis Shafer. I work with John Wells."

Coyle didn't answer.

"You bought shoes for him yesterday."

"Yeah, we're on alert here. Talk to my commander, Mr. Shafer."

"Call me Ellis. And I need your help."

"Help to what?"

"Find him." Shafer explained how Wells had disappeared overnight.

"That's not even six hours ago."

"This mission, he would have called as soon as he could."

"You think he's where they keep the shoes? Those Arabs caught him breaking in and they're holding him there?"

"Maybe."

"I don't even know where that is."

"I do. I'll give you the address. If he's not there, maybe a hospital, a jail."

"Jail? Why would the French— You know what? I don't want to know. I have to go, sir."

"Give me one day. No more. I'll be in Paris tomorrow."

"You're CIA. The station—"

"If we could have used them, we would have already. I promise, I'll get this cleared for you. Officially. Just like Saturday night and yesterday. But I have to talk to the ambassador and he's in a meeting with the French president, so that's going to take some time and I don't have that luxury. I need you now."

"I'm sorry, sir—"

"You have my word you won't get in trouble."

"Your word? I've never even heard your name. Call me from Virginia at four in the morning over there, ask me to go AWOL when the embassy's on lockdown—"

"There are fifty Marines guarding the embassy. You're the only one who can do this. The only one who knows what Wells looks like now. Who knew where he was."

"It's that important?"

"Sergeant, you have no idea."

Coyle sighed in defeat. "All right. My girlfriend would tell me I'm a fool, but I'm trusting you, sir. Please don't get me dishonorably discharged."

"Thank you." Though Shafer knew if this mission went sideways, a dishonorable discharge would be the least of Coyle's problems.

"So where do I look?"

"The garage first."

"Don't ask me to break in."

"No. If there's been trouble there, it'll be obvious. Blood on the wall, a cut in the fence. You see that, you call and sit tight. Do not go in."

"If I don't."

"There's a local hospital near the garage and a big medical center close by. If he got hurt somehow, they would have taken him to one of those two. I'll give you the addresses."

"They won't tell me anything."

"I'll email you a copy of his passport, his real one, and a PDF of some kind of official-looking letter. Tell them the truth, he's an American who's gone missing. Might have been brought in overnight. You don't need any details, but his family's worried and has asked you to find out if he's a patient."

"Then what?"

"Back to his hotel, see if his motorcycle's in the lot. Probably not, but I want to be sure. Knock on his door, too. After that, the **flics**. The police stations in Sevran and Villepinte, maybe they're holding him."

"Why don't you just call the cops yourself and ask? Or the DGSI?"

"I'll try, but they're up to their necks, and they don't know me, and I don't speak French. And, the thing is, he may not even be in the system yet. He probably wasn't carrying ID."

"What about the DGSE?"

"I'll try, I promise." But Shafer had never been posted to Paris. His last decent DGSE contact had retired fifteen years before and died six months later of lung cancer. The French and their Gauloises.

"So what do I tell the police?"

"Same song, different key. He's American,

his family's worried he's been arrested, you work for an American law firm in Paris—"

"And I don't speak French?"

"All you need to know is if they have him. If you strike out all those places—last stop, there's a prison in Villepinte—"

"A prison? They just arrested him. He'd be at a station for sure—"

"They may want him in a higher-security facility."

"Because they think he plays for Team Jihad?"

"It's possible."

"What am I into here, Ellis." Not a question. Coyle knew.

FOR THE REST of the morning Shafer waited as Coyle worked his way through the target list. After each stop Coyle checked in to tell Shafer what he'd found, or, more accurately, hadn't. The garage hadn't been touched. The hospitals took a while, but eventually Coyle found the right people to ask. Wells wasn't in either one. The motorcycle wasn't at the hotel. No one answered when Coyle knocked on the door to Wells's room.

As Coyle ticked off the alternatives, Shafer found himself increasingly sure that a police or counterterror unit had run across Wells and snatched him up. He called the DGSE, the Police Nationale headquarters, and the Ministry of the Interior. The mid-level officers on the other end of the line didn't even bother to hide their indifference. **We are very busy, Mr. Shafer . . . This man, if he has no identification, we can't confirm his identity, you understand . . . You're coming to Paris tomorrow for the funeral? Good, we sort out the problem then . . .**

The cables from Paris explained exactly why the French had no time for Shafer this day: dgse sources report second strike may be imminent . . . islamic state possibly targeting tuesday funeral with large-scale suicide-style attacks . . . The NSA reported picking up identical text messages on a dozen phones it had targeted, brothers gather for prayer service . . .

Shafer hadn't believed the jihadis would throw themselves into the maw of security that would surround the funeral. But Wells had disagreed. Maybe he was right. Maybe the jihadis thought they could break through somehow. Or maybe they didn't care how many men they lost because they knew an attack on this funeral would receive worldwide attention.

Coyle called from the police station in Sevran.

"Nothing. The prison or the station in Villepinte next, you think?"

"Prison first. The station will be open all night."

"All right."

Then nothing. The minutes turned into an hour, the hour turned into a second hour. Shafer busied himself by putting the documentation he'd need to convince the French that both he and Wells were who they claimed to be and getting retroactive clearance for Coyle's mission from the ambassador.

But by 2 p.m. in Virginia, he couldn't escape the realization that Coyle had vanished, too. The **banlieues** were turning into the Bermuda Triangle. The only reasonable explanation was that Coyle's questions about Wells had triggered the prison guards' suspicions and they'd hauled him inside.

Shafer hoped so anyway. Because otherwise he had no idea what had happened. And without Wells, he had less than no chance to stop whatever Raouf Bourgua planned for tomorrow.

27

PARIS

NOTRE-DAME DE BONNE-NOUVELLE lay inside a natural urban perimeter, a triangle about one hundred meters per side formed by three streets that by Paris standards ran straight and true: Rue Poissonnière to the west, the Boulevard de Bonne-Nouvelle to the north, and Rue de Cléry, which connected them.

The Interior Ministry announced Monday that only people who lived inside the zone could enter or leave on Tuesday. No parking would be permitted in the triangle beginning at midnight. After 7 a.m. only emergency vehicles would be allowed to use the roads inside. The mayor of Paris "strongly encouraged" stores and businesses in the zone to close for the day. "Normal operations will be impossible."

The area closest to the church faced even

tighter restrictions. Rue de la Lune and Rue Beauregard, which ran past Bonne-Nouvelle, would be open only to residents on foot on Tuesday but closed even to them after 10 a.m. Essentially, the people who lived within a block of the church would have to stay in their apartments during the funeral. The police promised temporary shelter for residents who were too infirm to leave on their own and feared being trapped.

To patrol the perimeter, the Interior Ministry was deploying seven hundred officers from the CRS, France's infamously tough riot police. A hundred and thirty officers from the GIGN would provide security for the church itself. The GIGN was the most highly trained police detachment in France, the equivalent of the FBI's Hostage Rescue Team, with its own helicopters, snipers, and bomb squads.

The security wouldn't end at the perimeter. No trucks or vans would be permitted within fifty meters of its edges. The police at those outer checkpoints had orders to shoot to kill any driver who disobeyed.

Meanwhile, the French army had moved two companies of light infantry to the grounds of the Hôpital Saint-Louis, a mile east of the church. An entire infantry regiment, twelve hundred soldiers with helicopter support, waited at the Stade de France, four miles northeast. They would do double duty as a quick-reaction force for the church and an anti-riot unit in case of trouble in the **banlieues** in the other direction.

In all, the French would have more than a thousand police officers within two hundred meters of the church, and that didn't include the soldiers in reserve, or another two hundred or so bodyguards and security officers from the CIA, MI6, and the rest, inside the perimeter. Standard military doctrine held that attacking forces should be three times as large as the defense they hoped to breach. According to that math, the Puma needed at least four thousand jihadis, an impossibility. A force that size would be obvious from miles away and required professional military command and control.

In reality, the Puma had his Quiet Men and another fifty jihadis. Eighty-six men in all. Some were known to the French and might be arrested on their way. No matter. The extra jihadis knew nothing but where they were supposed to meet. Once they did arrive, they would simply serve as foot soldiers.

In its own way, the plan was straightforward. The jihadis would attack a few minutes before the funeral was set to start. The timing would be easy to synchronize. Every news channel in the world would carry the ceremony live. As the final and most important dignitaries were still entering, twenty men and a bomb-loaded van would attack from the south, trying to reach the Rue Beauregard and the back of the church.

Simultaneously, another thirty men and another van would hit the checkpoint north of the Boulevard de Bonne-Nouvelle on the Rue d'Hauteville. Their goal would be to cross the boulevard to a short pedestrian walkway that led directly to the front of the church.

Four men who were already in a hotel inside the perimeter, would come up Rue de la Lune on foot from the west. The last group of jihadis and the third van would attack from the Plaza Saint-Denis, to the northeast.

The Puma didn't expect any of the explosive-filled vans would get through the outer perimeter. The CRS cops would block all the intersections with their own big vans and Renault Sherpas, and they would shoot to kill as soon as his drivers refused to stop. No matter, as long as the explosions caused confusion and did enough damage to let even a few of the jihadis through.

Once they broke the outer perimeter, and the

scope of the attack became clear, with men coming from every direction, the GIGN and the bodyguards would utter three magic words. **Shelter in place.** With its thick, nearly window-less stone walls, Bonne-Nouvelle would seem to be the safest place for the dignitaries to wait out the attack. No one would fear an attack from inside. The Paris police had locked down the church even before the Interior Ministry announced it would be used. Dozens of bomb-sniffing dogs had been through it. So the GIGN officers and bodyguards would herd everyone **into** the church.

The attack and the dozens of new people coming through the front door would lead to massive confusion. And as they streamed inside, the mole would trigger the ventilators. Even after the sarin claimed its first victims, the people in the church wouldn't understand what was happening. In the chaos, some would imagine the new arrivals had brought the poison with them. Others would realize the truth. But even then they'd have to fight their way out while the GIGN officers were trying to push others in through the single door in front.

How long would it take those officers to sort out the truth, put on their chemical weapons respirators, and begin to evacuate the people inside? Two minutes? Three? Five? Even two would be long enough for most of the men and women inside Bonne-Nouvelle to get a few breaths of sarin. Five minutes would be enough to kill all but the luckiest.

By the time the officers entered, the church would be a house of the dead. The President of France, Prime Minister of Germany, director of the Central Intelligence Agency, chief of MI6, a hundred others. Dead, dying, gravely wounded. A terrorist attack without parallel. The West would have no choice but to bring its armies into Syria and Iraq.

This time, the men of the Islamic State would be ready for them. Crusader blood would stain the desert red. The war between the Dar al-Islam and the Dar al-Harb would be joined in earnest.

Shelter in place.

28

MIDAIR, OVER THE ATLANTIC OCEAN

ON THE Gulfstream from Langley, Crompond kept to himself. The others didn't bother him. He knew that they knew he'd been friendly with Antoine Martin in Iraq. No doubt they assumed he was taking Martin's death hard.

In his own way he was. He hadn't anticipated how these hours would feel, this between time. Knowing the tidal wave was tumbling toward them. Knowing he'd set it in motion. He'd killed Martin as surely as if he'd thrown the grenade. Martin's son, too. An innocent.

What of it? The drones killed innocents all the time, though the agency pretended otherwise. Somehow, the bombing only confirmed his choice. If he walked away now, he would have sacrificed Damien Martin for nothing. **Winners never quit . . .** And the ease with which the jihadis had pulled off the attack sawed off Crompond's fear that nothing would happen after he pressed the button. If these guys said the sarin was ready, it was ready.

He wanted nothing more than to land in Paris. Reach the church. Be done. The key fob seared his fingertips whenever he touched it, yet he had to fight the urge to take it out and play with it.

He looked up to see Ludlow walking down the aisle toward him.

"You okay, Walter?"

A pained smile. "Been better."

Ludlow squatted beside him. "Ever play tennis with Martin? Over in the Green Zone? Heard he was great."

"Once. I couldn't compete. He started taking it easy. He told me he wasn't, but I knew he was. A gentleman. I told him to play for real. He stomped me." **Then I gave his address to the Islamic State so they could blow up his limo. That'll learn 'im.**

"You know what kills me, Walter?"

You'll find out what kills you soon enough. Crompond with two conversations going. Best keep the one in his head separate from the one on his tongue. "What's that?"

"It was so avoidable. If he'd just taken his security seriously."

"He didn't like bodyguards."

"Nobody likes bodyguards. I want to take a piss, I have to tell them so they can go in first. Stand next to me the whole time. At home, they hear everything. No way around it." Ludlow paused. "Man, I hate them."

"**Hate?** That seems like a strong word."

"Sorry. I'm tired, too. Not the bodyguards. These guys. A year ago, my son showed me this black-and-white picture of a spray-painted banner. All caps. Know what it said?"

High on the list of stuff Crompond wouldn't miss: Peter Ludlow's rhetorical questions. "I do not."

"STOP KILLING PEOPLE, YOU FUCK-ING TWATS. That's about right. I mean, we're professionals, we get the geopolitics, Sykes–Picot—whatever—but enough is enough. Stop killing people. Just stop."

What about us, boss? When do we stop killing people?

"Get some rest, if you can," Ludlow said. "Gonna be a long day tomorrow." He turned away, wandered back down the aisle.

Crompond knew he couldn't sleep. But when he closed his eyes, he did.

29

SEVRAN

WHEN the cops pulled off his hood, Wells found himself looking at yet another prison cell. This one was almost pristine, no graffiti, the toilet gleaming steel. A four-inch-square window set high in the exterior wall. A porthole of thick glass in the door, a slot for food trays down below. A standard iso cell, slightly bigger than most. Probably designed to hold two men, if necessary, though it had only one bed, a metal pallet welded to the wall.

He was becoming quite the expert on confinement.

They pushed him inside, slammed the door.

As their footsteps disappeared down the hall, Wells wondered how long Shafer might need to find him, pull him out. The drive from the N2 had lasted only a few minutes. He had to be in

Sevran, or very close. A break. Shafer would start searching within hours. And the police stations around Sevran would be among the first places he would try to contact.

But the cops hadn't processed him before they threw him in here. No photos, no prints. They hadn't even asked basic biographical details. As far the French government was concerned, John Wells didn't exist. Until he was in the system, Shafer would have no chance of finding him from four thousand miles away, much less convincing the police to release him.

Wells watched the windows brighten as the sun rose. Monday morning. The funeral was Tuesday at 11 a.m. Thirty hours, give or take. How many hours would he dribble away inside these blank walls? The Puma might even now be clearing the garage, erasing clues.

Later. A tray through the slot. An egg salad sandwich, orange juice in a plastic cup. Lunch. Lunch meant afternoon. Less than a day left. Wells wondered if he should attack the cell, tear the bed off the wall. Flood the toilet. Break the tray and cut himself with the shards. Anything to make them notice.

But they'd just throw him wherever they put troublesome prisoners. He reminded himself he was in France, not some dictatorship. These cops had to have rules on how long they could hold him incognito. Eventually they'd have to register him, let him make a phone call.

Eventually. Unless they'd suspended those protections for the state of emergency.

Later. The tiny windows darkening as the sun weakened. The cell door swung back, revealing two new officers. They wore deep-blue uniforms, handsome and simple, with big Police Nationale chevrons. Regular cops. Wells stood. The one nearer the door raised a hand: **Stay back.**

"**Parle-tu français?**"

"I do not."

"Name?"

"John Wells."

The officer pulled a notebook. "Spell, please. And date of birth."

"Can I talk to a lawyer?"

"You're American?"

"Yes."

"A terrorist?"

"No. I have information. I need to speak to someone senior." Wells hoped he sounded urgent. Not unhinged. "DGSI, DGSE, it doesn't matter—"

"What do you know about the DGSE? You helped kill the director?"

"Of course not. I used to work for the CIA."

The cops conferred. "You know about a plot, an active plot? Better tell us—"

There was the rub. "Not exactly."

"Then what, exactly?"

A sentence too late, Wells realized he should have lied. At least they would have brought someone more senior to talk to him, someone who might have understood. "There's someone you need to look at. Here, in Sevran—"

"This is Villepinte." The cop shook his head. **Stop wasting my time.** "Someone will come after the funeral. If you haven't noticed, we're a bit busy."

After the funeral. Raouf Bourgua wouldn't wait until after the funeral. "One call—please—"

The **flic** was already closing the door. Wells stood nose to porthole and watched his freedom walk down a plain white hall. He felt his frustration taking over, his fists clenching involuntarily.

He made himself sit before he did anything truly stupid. They'd asked his name and date of birth. He had to trust they'd done so because they planned to add him to a prisoner roster. Breaking his hand against the wall like some twenty-year-old frat boy wouldn't help.

Just a soul whose intentions are good / Oh Lord, please don't let me be misunderstood . . .

MINUTES LATER, the door opened. Wells found himself looking at Winston Coyle. Somehow, he wasn't surprised. Three big French cops shoved Coyle into the cell, slammed the door home.

Coyle looked at Wells. "You are trouble, my friend."

"You only figured that out now."

"I mentioned your name, they got all nice. Told me to come on back. Then this. I showed them my Marine ID. They didn't care."

"Quick to judge, these French."

"Said they'd let me out as soon as they made some calls, but I think not. Anyway, I guess sooner or later I'll get to tell your buddy I found you."

"Shafer sent you?" Good news at last.

"Ellis, right? He called me from Virginia, talked me into it. Even though he sounds like he's about nine hundred. Idiot."

"He's hardly that."

"I meant me. For listening."

"So he knows you're in Villepinte."

"Yeah. But there's a prison here, too, he might

think I'm there." Coyle explained how he'd searched for Wells, and how on his last call with Shafer he'd said he was going to the prison. "Then I looked again, this place was on the way. I decided I'd hit it first. Stupid. Should have told him."

"He'll figure it. He'll be here tomorrow morning."

"Unless they arrest him, too."

"If Americans keep showing up, they'll have to listen." But Wells saw Coyle's point. The guards at the prison wouldn't have heard about Wells. Shafer could be abrasive. And the guards would be on edge. They might hold Shafer on general principles, at least until the funeral was done.

On the other hand, Shafer would have his diplo passport and CIA identification, and he'd surely be on his best behavior. Wells wondered at the odds, gave up.

"I think I've earned a full explanation, Mr. Wells."

"Fair enough." Wells walked him through the last months, holding nothing back.

"You get your money's worth," Coyle said when Wells was done.

"I try."

"You really think you're going to find the answer in this garage?"

"Shafer's theory about the Puma wanting to keep his stuff close makes sense. And I think they're going for the funeral. The world's fattest target."

"With security to match."

"They must have some trick." Though Wells couldn't imagine what.

They sat in silence, the grim companionable silence of fighting men stuck behind the lines.

Outside, the sun disappeared. Wells made his ablutions and prayed. Coyle stared at the wall. He seemed embarrassed.

"You a Christian, Staff Sergeant?" Wells said afterward.

"I used to play baseball, Mr. Wells. Center field for the Long Beach State Dirtbags. Our actual name." Coyle looked around the cell like he was back in California, waiting to shag flies. "I was good, too. I mean, I was never going pro, couldn't hit a slider to save my life, but I was all right. I was twenty, my little brother was twelve. Lincoln, real old-school Negro name. Worse than Winston. I don't know what my parents were thinking. Sweetest kid in the world, and he loved me. Came to every game.

This old bike he'd bought himself with his chores money so he didn't have to beg rides. Always there in time for my first at bat."

Coyle's voice was a whisper, but his dark eyes screamed a thousand decibels. "See where I'm going with this?"

Wells waited.

"Some jackass in a Buick. Three blocks from the stadium. Ran a yellow." Coyle spoke in telegraph rhythm now, a price on every word. "Said he wasn't texting. I know he was. Nine-month suspended sentence."

"I'm sorry."

"My parents got churchy. God's plan. Not me."

"You quit baseball, too?"

The question seemed to break the spell on Coyle's voice. "As a matter of fact, I did. Week after we put him in the ground, I found a recruiting station. My parents asked me not to. I told 'em God would look after me same as Lincoln."

"You shouldn't have said that."

"I know." Coyle closed his eyes. "I don't normally tell people, especially ones I've just met. You struck me as the kind who could hear it without saying something stupid. Worst is when they ask me if I have other brothers."

"So? Do you?"

Coyle's eyes snapped open.

"That would be way better. Spares. Am I right? Tell me I'm right."

"Go to hell, Mr. Wells." But Coyle was smiling. Sort of.

"Too soon?"

"'Til the day I die, it'll be too soon." Wells watched Coyle stuff the pain deep down. The only place for it, as far as Wells was concerned. "Gonna pull rank, make me sleep on the floor?"

"I think that story won you the pallet."

"If we get out of here tomorrow, I'm coming with you. If you'll have me. Time for a little R and R."

"Long as you're not just one of those pretty embassy Marines."

"Three tours in Helmand"—the bloodiest province in Afghanistan. Nearly a thousand Marines and British soldiers had died fighting the Taliban there.

"Good enough."

WELLS WOKE TO the clatter of a tray in the slot. Coyle was doing push-ups against the wall.

"Sleepyhead."

"Save your energy, Marine."

"How much does it take to pull a trigger?" But Coyle stopped.

"Shafer tell you when he'd get in?"

"Six fifty-five."

If the plane landed on time . . . Shafer cleared immigration fast . . . and had a car waiting . . . he could be here in forty-five minutes. Maybe. But what if he went to the prison first? What if they held him?

They would need to break into the garage and hope the Puma was running late, or had left some clue to his plans. Then they'd have to deliver whatever they'd found to a commander who understood its importance and was senior enough to act on it. Which meant fighting through the traffic and the police cordons and getting to the church itself.

An hour later, two hours, he didn't know, the door swung open. The cop who'd taken his name yesterday. He stared at Wells with the mix of irritation and respect that seemed to be this mission's signature. Even before he spoke, Wells knew they were free.

If only they weren't too late.

In the lobby, Shafer, twitchy and rumpled from the overnight flight. Beside him, a forty-ish brunette, wearing a black suit and a stylish pageboy haircut. Lively hazel eyes. Wells assumed she was French until Coyle saluted her.

"John." Shafer tapped Wells's cheek. "The pleasure is yours. Please meet our secret weapon. Deputy Head of Mission Jean Simmons."

"I just do what I'm told," Simmons said.

"You can thank her for freedom. Her French beats mine. Possibly her people skills, too."

"Thank you, Ms. Simmons."

"Call me Jean, please." She had a soft Virginia twang. Wells bet it played nicely over here. "Shall we?"

Two men with bodyguard haircuts waited outside the station, along with two Chevy Yukons with diplomatic plates, both black, their bodies thick with armor and ballistic glass. A single French police motorcycle waited, too. Wells looked around, realized the N2 was no more than fifty meters north. He'd been arrested barely five hundred meters away.

"What time is it?" He should have asked already.

"Nine-ten. My flight was half an hour late, and we had trouble at the prison—"

Wells didn't care. "Can you spare an SUV, ma'am?"

"She can't," the taller bodyguard said.

"Done," Simmons said.

"Ma'am, a chase car is a necessity, especially now."

"I'm a State Department functionary, not the Queen of England, Eddie. No one cares about me. And I've got an official escort."

"Ma'am—"

"Enough. Let's go."

"One more question—" Wells said.

"You want guns, that's a no," the guard said.

"Actually . . ." Simmons said.

The guard stared at Wells with real anger and plucked a key ring from his pocket. Two keys. "The little one unlocks the center console. Spare Sig in there. The big one, there's a shotgun in back."

"Thankee."

"Hope you know what you're doing, cowboy."

Me, too.

A COUPLE of kilometers southwest, at 279 Allée Richelieu, Soufiane Kassani finished cleaning the last of a dozen AKs. Firas the engineer threw spare magazines into a canvas bag. A white Mazda sedan waited in front, its nose poking through the open gate.

Kassani had desperately wanted to have the

honor of being part of this attack. But Bourgua had told him the night before that he was too important to die.

"What about you, Raouf?"

"I only give orders. You're a scientist."

"Anyone can do what I did."

"It seems not. They've barely made any of the stuff since you left. Back to Raqqa for you."

"But—"

"These orders, they come from the caliph."

"If you say so."

"**He** says so."

"Let me do something tomorrow, at least."

"Like what?"

"Bring in the AKs from the garage." Bourgua's jihadis could hardly ride the RER and Paris Métro toting assault rifles. The weapons were being transported separately in cars that would be parked close to the perimeter and serve as rendezvous points.

"Soufiane—"

"You said yourself you're short on drivers."

"Promise to leave by nine. I want the car there by nine forty-five, you on the ten thirty-seven to Marseille." French TGVs ran nonstop from Paris to Marseille, three hours and four hundred miles south, on the Mediterranean coast.

"Of course."

So Kassani was a few minutes late. Even so, he should have the Mazda parked by 10. He'd reach the Gare de Lyon station twenty or thirty minutes later, depending on the Métro connections. He might have to run, but he should make the train.

"Let's go, Soufiane," Firas said now.

"Two minutes." Kassani grabbed another canvas bag.

WELLS DROVE, with Shafer next to him in the Yukon's front seat. This road passed between the two **cités** that Wells had visited Saturday. A half-dozen police cars and vans were parked on the side of the road, with only a dozen or so cops posted around them. Wells had expected more. Probably the police had moved officers to the center of Paris today, trying to make sure nothing happened during the funeral. Wells wondered how long they would need to respond to shots fired a kilometer south. Not very. Though they might have orders to stay near the **banlieue**.

"How's this go?" Coyle said from the back.

"Remember Helmand? The garage, same ROE." Rules of engagement. "Men with weapons, don't need to identify yourself or wait for fire. Assume hostile intent."

"What about taking them alive?"

"Fine if we do, but nobody there is going to tell us anything in time to make a difference. Most important thing is to make sure we get inside quick and clean."

"It's like that."

"**Exactly** like that."

"If we're wrong?"

"Hope you liked that cell."

Left onto the N370. Maybe ninety seconds out. The traffic circle where the N2 met the N370 lay a couple hundred meters to the right. The roadblock that had undone Wells was gone now.

"We'll take one fast pass from the north, I'm not even going to slow down. See if the gate's open, anyone's inside. Then around the block, I'll park one building up, we'll go right in." Wells didn't love making the pass. The Yukon stood out, especially with the diplo plates. But they couldn't come out shooting without knowing if civilians were close by.

"Hope nobody's there," Shafer said.

"Wrong," Wells said.

"If they're present, the gate will be open already," Coyle said. "Probably the door, too. Easier breach."

"Military genius in stereo," Shafer said.

Wells swung left onto Avenue Liégeard, then right onto Allée Richelieu. The garage was fifty meters down, on the east side. He was happy to see they had the street to themselves. The plumbing store was open but empty. The good and not-so-good citizens of Sevran were battening down.

They sped by the garage. The gate and front door were open. A white Mazda sedan was parked at the edge of the driveway. Wells just had time to see its back lid was raised. A man was putting a big duffel bag into the trunk. The bag's canvas was stretched from the inside by—

Rifle barrels—

"You saw," Coyle said.

"I did."

"Saw what?" Shafer said.

"AKs." Wells swung left. These blocks were short, no more than fifty meters. They'd be back in front less than a minute.

"Come on, Soufiane! We're going to be late, this isn't a joke."

Kassani looked around the garage one last

time, pulled the door shut. Firas slammed down the trunk lid.

LEFT, LEFT, LEFT, they were back on Allée Richelieu. The white sedan was edging forward now from the open gate.

Wells jammed the gas. The Yukon was a beast, four tons with the armor, but it had a V-8 engine bored out for 495 horsepower. After the briefest lag, it jumped ahead.

IN THE MAZDA, Kassani was looking left when he heard the Yukon's engine roaring on the other side of the car. He glanced right, saw the big black SUV speeding. Strange. Hadn't it just passed?

"Soufiane—"

Real fear in Firas's voice. A second later, a second too late, Kassani understood.

Firas reached between his legs as Kassani pressed the accelerator.

WELLS SAW the Mazda jump ahead as the man in the passenger seat came up with a pistol.

The shots were surprisingly accurate, two hitting the windshield and flattening into the ballistic glass. The Mazda turned left, into the street, south, away from the Yukon. Wells fought the natural instinct to lay off the gas as the crash came. He kept the pedal pressed to the floor.

Impact. Crunch of steel bending, crinkle of glass breaking. With the sedan turning away, the initial collision came not quite broadside but at an angle to the Mazda's right rear door and trunk. The Yukon weighed three times as much as the Mazda. Its engine block beat through the Mazda's skin like a fist plunging into an apple pie.

The crash didn't end there. The Yukon was so much bigger and heavier than the Mazda, and moving so much faster, that the collision turned the Mazda around. The sedan had been turning counterclockwise. Now it spun the other way, clockwise, bringing its passenger side back toward the Yukon. The SUV still had plenty of forward momentum. It was this second half of the collision that caved in the Mazda's front passenger door and crushed Firas's legs and drove the door frame into his ribs, tearing open his heart, killing him instantly.

The Yukon's crash sensors turned off its engine, but its momentum carried the Mazda another five meters before the two vehicles finally skidded to a stop. A dozen air bags exploded inside the SUV. Wells and Shafer and Coyle were jolted hard against their belts but unhurt otherwise.

Wells extracted himself and pulled the Sig from the center console and looked down at the Mazda that was now grafted to the Yukon's grille.

The man in the passenger seat was dead, his head hanging over the steel bar that had pierced his chest. The driver was very much alive. The body of the Mazda had protected him from the worst of the crash. Because of the way the Mazda had spun, he had wound up on the right side of the Yukon, closer to Coyle than Wells. Wells recognized him, the man with the strange gray skin Wells had seen at the store two days before.

Wells checked over his shoulder, one last look to be sure he wouldn't be ambushed by someone coming out of the garage. The door to the building itself was shut tight now.

In the back seat, Coyle racked his shotgun.

Wells opened the door, stepped out.

KASSANI HAD WANTED his own pistol. He'd wanted to be sure that if everything went wrong the **kaffirs** wouldn't take him alive. But the Puma had absolutely forbidden him to carry any weapons to Marseille. If he ran into a police checkpoint or a metal detector, he could never explain a pistol. And the police would be watching the TGV trains hard.

He shouldn't have listened.

He didn't know what had happened, how these men had found him. He didn't know who they were, though he recognized the driver from the store on Sunday. American, French, Syrian secret police, no matter. All that mattered was that he kill them. And leave at least one bullet for himself.

The attack was barely an hour away, they couldn't stop it.

He reached over Firas's corpse, not just slick but wet with fresh arterial blood. The pistol must have fallen between his feet. It must have.

He couldn't find it in the wreckage. Then he felt the grip square in his hand.

WELLS WAS STEPPING around the front of the Yukon when the driver came up with a pistol. The guy twisted toward him, and he and Coyle fired almost at once, the shotgun's roar and the Sig's pop blending, echoing through the morning. Not a fair fight. The driver's chest exploded. He slumped in his seat, twitching. Wells ran for him as Coyle pulled open the driver's door, dragged him out, laid him on the pavement.

He was alive, but he wouldn't be for more than another minute or two. A mass of shotgun pellets ripened his skin. Blood drooled from the spaces between. All the king's horses and all the king's trauma surgeons couldn't put him together again. His eyes were glassy and unfocused, and he was mumbling in Arabic. Wells got on his hands and knees, put his ear an inch of the man's lips.

"Too late, too late . . ."

"For what—"

"**Allahu akbar**—" He didn't finish the prayer, and never would. His breath went throaty and liquid and dried into a gurgle.

"John—"

Wells looked up. Shafer stood by the garage door.

"Locked."

"Check the car," Wells said to Coyle. The driver wore cargo pants with deep pockets. Wells rifled them, came up with a wallet fat with euros, a key ring.

He tossed it to Shafer, went back to the body, pulled a Belgian passport and identity card that both looked real. Beji Nounes. The name meant nothing. Wells patted down the corpse once more, then went to the car to search the passenger.

SHAFER STEPPED into the garage, flipped on the lights. The shoe boxes were stacked neatly on racks against the walls. Beside the racks, open cardboard boxes whose labels showed they'd once held fans and heaters. Beside them, more open packages, these for short-range radio gear. Shafer didn't see anything fancy or military-grade. Everything was off the shelf. Against the other wall, two whiteboards, both nearly new, both wiped blank. Something planned here. Something **built** here. Bombs? But the dogs would have found those.

At the back of the garage, an area Bourgua seemed to have used as an office, with a desk and a couple of old-school ledgers. Shafer turned for it.

COYLE TUGGED at a little black roller suitcase that lay on the Mazda's back seat that the crash had pinned tight. Wells joined him. Together, they pulled it free, its side ripping open. Coyle looted it, tossing out plain white T-shirts, socks, leather sandals.

Wells climbed into the driver's seat, ignoring

the bits of bone and muscle embedded in its gray cloth, and reached for the dead man beside him.

"John!" Real urgency in Coyle's voice. He held a paper bag. "Look."

SHAFER REACHED the back. The desk was simple, four metal legs and a top, a single drawer underneath. Shafer tugged at it without much hope. It opened.

Inside, a picture frame.

He turned it over.

A black-and-white photograph of Mecca in the 1980s. It wouldn't have meant anything to anyone.

Except Shafer. He'd seen it before. In a conference room at the Islamic Center of Northern Virginia.

IN THE BAG, two glass ampules.

Wells pulled them out. Brown glass with a powder-blue label. **Atropine Sulfate Inj. 1 mg 1 ml.**

Atropine. Nerve gas antidote.

All at once, Wells understood.

He turned, ran for the garage, just as Shafer emerged, arms flapping, holding what looked like a picture frame.

"John."

"Ellis. I know—" Wells held up the ampules.

"I got the mole."

Here Wells thought he had the big news. "What?"

Shafer raised the picture. "Bourgua was in Mecca, thirty years ago, same time as a imam in Virginia that Walter Crompond knows. That's the connection. How the mole feeds Daesh. It's Crompond. It has to be."

"Okay, I get it."

"What's the plan?"

Wells held up the atropine capsules. "Nerve gas."

SHAFER STARED at the ampules, putting everything together. "In the church. They attack. Everyone shelters. I saw empty boxes of short-range radio gear in there. Crompond triggers from inside."

The enormity of what Walter Crompond and the Islamic State were about to do silenced them both.

THEN the first sirens sounded.

"Call down there," Wells said.

"Call who? They're blocking mobiles within a kilometer of Bonne-Nouvelle. No car bombs,

s'il vous plaît. Anyway, no way can Bourgua's men get inside. Crompond's what matters."

"Maybe wait for the local cops?" Coyle said.

"With **this** in the street? At best, they'll take us in until they sort it out, and we don't have time. Crompond's set to land at Le Bourget around nine forty-five, ten minutes from now, he's got an escort, he'll be at the church by ten-fifteen, and, once he's inside, it's too late."

"Ludlow—"

"You think he'll take a call from me? He hates my guts."

Shafer was right about that, too. Wells thought about the geography, realized they had only one play.

It wasn't the church.

"Get the Remington," Wells said to Coyle. "We're going next door."

"What?"

Wells nodded at the van parked in front of the plumbing store, with its cheery faucet logo. "Even if we have to shoot somebody. We need a ride."

30

LE BOURGET was one of the busiest private airports in the world, with eight separate terminals for private jets. But the super-rich were staying away from Paris this morning. With no traffic in its way, the CIA's Gulfstream landed ten minutes early. By 9:40, it had reached the edge of the arrival apron.

One by one, the agency's top officers stepped out, where the Paris chief of station waited with three DGSE officials in somber black suits. Crompond saw an officer he'd known in Iraq, a friend of Martin's. She was crying, not hiding her tears. She put her arms on his shoulders, kissed both cheeks.

"I'm so sorry, Marianne."

"Awful, Walter. I can't believe I'll never see him again. And Damien."

"I know."

"You're coming to **la piscine** after, right?" The DGSE's Paris headquarters was nicknamed **la piscine**, the swimming pool, because the French national swimming team had its training facility directly across the street.

"Of course." A finger of humanity tugged at Crompond. A drowning man in the deep end, trying to take him down. He kicked the feeling away. **At least we won't have to sit through any bilingual meetings this afternoon.**

"This way," the chief of station said. The **douane**, the immigration office, was not even a hundred feet from the jet. "We'll get your passports swiped, five minutes max. The convoy's right outside."

NINE FORTY-THREE, read the little digital clock in the van's dashboard. Shafer drove, since Wells and Coyle couldn't have passed even a cursory look from a cop. They hid in the cargo compartment with the plumbing store owner. They'd kidnapped him, bound his hands and feet with duct tape. No shortage of duct tape in the back of a plumber's van. Wells had told him in Arabic that they wouldn't hurt him. Still, he stared at them with miserable, terrified eyes.

Fine by Wells. Miserable and terrified beat angry and looking to escape.

The cargo compartment didn't have windows, but Wells heard sirens swoop by as Shafer turned onto the N370. After a few seconds, they faded. Lucky. After having seen Shafer on the Dulles highway, Wells didn't like his odds in a chase. Suddenly Shafer laid on the horn, swerved right, then left.

"Ellis—"

"Want to get there?"

"What now?" Coyle said.

Wells liked this kid more by the minute. Blood on his shirt, but he was only thinking about the next move.

"This guy Crompond, he's got to have the trigger."

"Someplace he can reach it easily," Shafer said. "Won't want to be fumbling for it."

"Might be small."

"Yeah, but we'll know it as soon as we see it. Not like they hid it in a smartphone or something. It'll look like what it is."

"So we've just get him to turn out his pockets," Coyle said, his tone arch.

"No problem, right?" Shafer said. Without warning, the van braked hard enough to throw Wells and Coyle into the metal mesh that split the passenger compartment from the front seats. "Stupid traffic circles."

"No accidents, Ellis. **Please**."

UNLIKE CUSTOMHOUSES at regular commercial airports, this immigration area was windowed, a nod to the sensitivities of the super-rich who used Le Bourget. Through the front glass Crompond saw the convoy, police vans and motorcycles surrounding armored Yukons. The French were going all out on security today.

Perfect.

The immigration officer at the diplomatic/VIP desk, a fleshy woman in her forties, barely looked at the photo pages of the CIA officers' passports before swiping them through.

Crompond was second to last in line, only Pushkin behind him. Then they'd be through. To the convoy, the church . . . where the world would hear what he had to say. He gave his passport to the agent. She swiped it, muttered a welcome, handed it back.

Behind him, Pushkin reached into the pocket of his suit. He came up with air, shook his head, patted down his other pockets. His expression was more irritated than panicked.

"Must have taken it out, left it in my seat

back—I do that sometimes on long flights." He smiled at the agent. "Can we just—"

"I'm sorry. This is necessary."

"Go get it, Reg," Ludlow said. "Come **on**."

NINE FORTY-SEVEN. "Here we are, campers. Just about." The van swung around one more traffic circle, and Wells glimpsed a runway fence through the windshield. "Any idea where they'll be?"

Wells had googled a decent map of the airport on Shafer's phone. "Make the first right, the immigration office is there. Let's hope we see a whole bunch of Police Nationale and black SUVs."

"When we get there—" Coyle said.

"Leave the shotgun. And take off your shirt now."

"Because of the blood?"

"So they see we aren't wearing vests."

PUSHKIN JOGGED BACK, passport in hand. "Sorry, Chief." The agent lifted her hand, reached out wordlessly, the gesture somehow communicating her disdain for this American. She swiped. "**Merci**."

THE VAN was on airport grounds now, speeding down the access road that paralleled the D317.

"I see you," Shafer muttered. "Jeez, think there's enough cops?"

Through the mesh and the windshield, Wells saw. Police vans, sirens flashing, armored SUVs, motorcycles.

Shafer slowed, swung onto Avenue de l'Europe, the main access road—

"No."

POLICE OFFICERS stepped into their vehicles, pulled doors shut. The lead van rolled forward, stopped, and the driver leaned out, looked back, yelled to the vehicles behind.

Then turned, looked ahead, to the van. He honked . . . air-horn loud and sounded his siren, his meaning clear: **Move aside.**

"Think they'll light us up?"

"Might," Wells said, thinking, **yes.**

"Sorry about this, boys."

Shafer braked hard and swung the wheel right. The van turned sideways, rocked up on two wheels, rocked back down. The owner's eyes were wide and terrified.

"You two," Coyle said, with real admiration.

Even before the van settled, men outside screamed in French. Then the chaos of sirens and amplified voices began.

Wells clambered back, threw open the doors,

found himself looking at a mostly empty parking lot, the airport's buildings to his left. He jumped down. His hands pressed to his skull. French police in full Kevlar ran toward him with their H&Ks raised high, screaming. He sank to his knees.

"American! CIA!"

In front, Shafer opened his door, stepped out, held his arms high, passport in one hand, his CIA identification in the other. "**Ne tirez pas, ne tirez pas!**"

SITTING next to Ludlow in the lead Yukon, Crompond heard the shouts before he saw the van.

"CIA! CIA!" The voices American, and strangely familiar.

"Come on," Crompond said. "Let's go."

"What's going on?" Ludlow said to the driver.

THE YELLING hadn't stopped, but it had settled. The cops circled around the van, slowly, keeping their distance, keeping the rifles on Wells and Coyle. One of them was more trigger-happy than the others, his rifle shaking notably. He'd be the one to pull the trigger.

Wells looked away from him, locked eyes with the officer beside him, a woman, small even under her armor, but calm. He nodded at the back of the van, empty except for the owner trembling in a corner.

"Nothing dangerous. See?"

"What is this? What is going on?" But she stepped closer. Wells knew they'd be okay.

"**NE TIREZ PAS**." Shafer was on his knees, staring at three assault rifles, though only one would do the trick. Still holding his passport and ID over his head. For whatever reason, he could hear the van's engine ticking to a stop above all the other noise.

"Please. I know the DCI's here. Peter Ludlow. Give these to him. **Please**."

The cops looked at one another and one shrugged—the gesture Gallic, somehow, even under all the armor—and reached down.

"ALL RIGHT," Ludlow said. "Let's move. Sort this out after."

Crompond, not a prayerful man, found himself thanking God.

A French cop trotted over, holding something out. The driver reached for it. "Sir." He handed the stuff back to Ludlow. A passport and identification. Ludlow looked at them, his confusion obvious.

"Walter? What in God's name is **Ellis Shafer** doing here?"

A voice in Crompond's head, Jane's voice, whispering, shouting, **You've lost, you've lost, you've lost . . .**

EPILOGUE

AT EXACTLY 10:04 a.m. Paris time, the pool feeds the networks were using to cover the funeral cut to a bland Interior Ministry pressroom. A spokeswoman announced Antoine Martin's wife had suddenly taken ill and asked for a short delay before the funeral began. "No questions, please."

While the cameras were occupied, the GIGN evacuated the fifty or so mourners already inside Bonne-Nouvelle. Simultaneously, a French military chem/bioweapons response team suited up to scour the church. Its soldiers would find all four sarin ventilators within an hour.

EVEN BEFORE the announcement, the Puma feared something had gone wrong. Kassani hadn't delivered the AKs and wasn't answering his phone. Bourgua hoped Kassani's vanishing act wasn't related to the delay.

Then Agence France-Presse reported a shoot-out on Allée Richelieu in southern Sevran, and he knew.

He wondered if he should go ahead with the attack after the church reopened, knowing the French would be primed and ready, knowing it was doomed to fail. His men wouldn't even breach the outer perimeter before they were cut down, every one.

And decided . . . he would.

Maybe Allah would smile on his men and they'd break through. Maybe the French hadn't found the sarin and the mole could trigger it.

Anyway, what was his choice? If he was wrong, the attack had a chance. If he was right, he was already the most wanted man in all of Europe. No more Air Jordans for him either way.

So when the Interior Ministry thanked the people of Paris for their patience and said the funeral would go ahead at 3:30 that afternoon, Bourgua strapped on his vest. He didn't believe for a moment that seventy-two virgins were in his future, but he was ready to die nonetheless.

TOO BAD FOR him, the French found him first. He'd used his burner phones and email heavily on the morning of the attacks. He didn't have time to coordinate with all his lieutenants face-to-face. He didn't expect anyone was watching him or would figure out his importance in time to matter. He would have been right if Wells hadn't found Kassani and his phone, which had a dozen calls from Bourgua's burners.

Once the NSA and DGSE had these numbers, the Puma was doomed. But even if he'd tossed that phone and all the others he was carrying, he wouldn't have had a chance, not against facial recognition software and thousands of police and soldiers. He and his jihadis had surprise and the willingness to die on their side. Once they'd lost the former, the latter didn't make much difference against the French advantages in manpower and technology.

At 2:35, Bourgua and his top lieutenant walked on Boulevard de Strasbourg, a quarter mile northeast of the church. Strolling, really, trying to stay calm.

A GIGN sniper and DGSE officer lay side by side on the roof of Théâtre de l'Archipel.

"**Je le vois,**" the sniper said. "**Quatre-vingt mètres.**"

The DGSE officer murmured into his radio. Then: "**Comme vous voulez.**"

"Ça va." The sniper drew one more breath, held it, squeezed the trigger.

A PERFECT HEADSHOT. The brain has no nerves, so aside from the briefest spasm of pain as his skull exploded, Bourgua never even felt himself die.

WELLS didn't stay for the funeral.

"Ms. Martin would like to meet you," Ludlow said around 2:45, after the French police passed word of Bourgua's death. "The French president, too."

"I need to get home."

"What about Walter? Don't you want a say?"

Already Duto and Ludlow were hinting they preferred to handle Crompond quietly. A one-car crash, an accident at the gun range, a pulmonary embolism. A tragedy. One that would leave Crompond's family with his pension and insurance and name. And the agency and Duto free from the bad publicity of another crisis in Langley's top ranks. **American Traitor: CIA's Counterterror Head Betrays Agency to the Islamic State . . .**

Everyone would win, even Crompond. The greenest prosecutor couldn't lose this case. Crompond was bound for the execution room or the living death of solitary at the federal Supermax in Colorado. Everyone except the truth and the public, and Duto hardly cared about those two.

"You'd rather not have me here for that conversation, believe me."

"Fine," Ludlow said. "If that's what you want . . ."

So Wells hugged Shafer good-bye, and told Coyle that if he ever decided to stop being a pretty embassy Marine, the Farm would be waiting.

TEN HOURS LATER, a black SUV dropped him outside the farmhouse in North Conway. The lights were on against the gathering dark, and as Wells walked up the flagstone path, he heard Emmie's voice tinkling. Tonka bolted to the window to see this stranger and then barked long and loud in recognition. Wells reached the porch as the door swung open and Emmie darted around her mother and came to him. He scooped her up, kissed her chocolate-smeared chin.

"We're making a **cake**."

"How . . . ?" He hadn't wanted to tell them, to tease them.

"Ellis called." Anne put her arms around him

also, and they stood, three as one, in the cool dusk, as Tonka made mad joyous loops around them.

"A **chocolate** cake," Emmie said.

"I never would have guessed."

"It's good to see you, John."

"It's good to be home." Wells closed his eyes and hoped he spoke true.

ACKNOWLEDGMENTS

Publishing is hard. The Putnam team makes it look easy. Thanks to Neil Nyren for his wise suggestions, Ivan Held for his belief in John Wells, Karen Fink (who was present at the creation!) for her publicity efforts, and the rest of the team for answering my often obscure questions. Bob Barnett and Deneen Howell prove that not everyone in D.C. is untrustworthy. Deirdre Silver and my brother David made invaluable suggestions on the first draft.

As for Jackie, Lucy, and Ezra . . . you make every day the best possible adventure . . . John Wells doesn't know what he's missing (though he's learning).

If you've gotten this far, drop a note to me at alexberensonauthor@gmail.com, or follow me on Facebook or Twitter. I promise I'll write back, though I can't promise you'll want to hear what I say.

Thanks, and see you next year . . .